ENDURING CONNEXIONS

J MARIE CROFT

Quills & Quarto
PUBLISHING

D0904018

Edited by Jan Ashton and Jo Abbott

Cover by CloudCat Design

ISBN 978-1-956613-57-5 (ebook) and 978-1-956613-58-2 (paperback)

To Darcy and Elizabeth
Yes, they're fictional characters, but Jane Austen brought them to life.

Prologue

One day, perhaps on her deathbed, she might feel a whisper of guilt over the decisions she had made and the lies she was about to tell.

On that particular winter morn, though, all she felt was dizziness, nausea, and a sense of urgency. The gravity of her dilemma grew with each passing day, as did her girth. Only her personal maid knew of the morning sickness and of her increase.

She was eighteen, unmarried, of gentle birth but recently motherless, and accustomed to having her own way. Behind her back, former friends called her cunning and said she was ruled by nothing but avarice. She, however, considered 'ambitious' a more fitting representation of her character.

None of the men involved would ever learn the absolute truth of the matter; she would make certain of that. First, the wealthy but married brewer and coaching inn owner. Second, his nephew, a naïve gentleman scholar. Both of them were inconsequential; she had bigger fish to fry. Third, the easily-caught gudgeon—a smitten peer of the realm. And finally, her biddable father, her very own cat's paw. He was, at that very moment, in conference with the nobleman, and she was expected.

"Tighter, Durand, tighter!" Holding her breath while her abigail girded her in the constricting long stay—itself a symbol of a lady's uprightness and virtue—she thanked her lucky stars for the decade's rather spherical female silhouette. "I have changed my mind and shall wear the striped *chemise de la reine,* and the fichu trimmed with scallop-edged lace is to be crossed over my bosom."

"Oui, Mademoiselle."

They both liked to pretend the lady's maid was French, although her real name was Mary Smith, and she hailed from London.

"And fetch my finest white silk stockings and slippers. They will show to advantage beneath my petticoat." The young lady tossed flaxen locks over a shoulder. "Dress my hair to hang in ringlets down my back. My 'intended' prefers it that way...and perhaps the nobleman will, too. He must become besotted."

"You will look *magnifique!*"

"Let us hope so."

Durand dropped her feigned accent. "Do you not feel sorry, though, for your young gentleman? He *is* in love with you."

"His affection is—*was*—returned in some measure. So yes, of course, I pity him. However, the estate he will inherit is much smaller and generates a far lower income. To his even greater misfortune, he has no title."

Half an hour later, she gracefully entered the drawing room and greeted her father and the nobleman who had come to call.

A se'nnight later, her father, at her sobbing behest, rescinded his consent for the young gentleman scholar to marry her.

A fortnight after that, she was wed to the nobleman and whisked north to the Midlands.

Months later, she presented to her husband a healthy daughter, born prematurely.

Years later, that girl, too, would be told a lie.

Chapter 1

August 1807, Derbyshire

It was the twenty-first of August, a Friday, when he met her. The exact date was memorable, for the house party was held in honour of her eighteenth birthday and her coming out.

Unacquainted with the Amesbury family, Fitzwilliam Darcy had baulked at attending but was obliged to do so. Four months had passed since he had been out of mourning for his late father. Resigned to an event during which affability would be expected of him, he entered the crested coach along with his uncle, aunt, their daughter, and their second son for the drive to Riverswood, the Amesburys' Derbyshire country house.

He had been saddled with unwelcome company for both his fortnight's stay at Lord Matlock's country seat and, now, the se'nnight at Riverswood: George Wickham, the godson of his late father, was the unlikely friend of Darcy's eldest cousin. As Darcy watched Viscount Winster drive off in a phaeton towards Darley Dale with the son of Pemberley's former steward, he was filled with disgust. *Wickham and Winster. As handsome and ungodly as the devil's own boots, the pair of them.*

Arriving at Riverswood, Darcy had been pleased to discover the Taylors of Wishinghill Park—Pemberley's nearest neighbours—already in attendance. He had known the family since he and Miss Helen Taylor had been, respectively, five and three years of age. Although comely in every way, his childhood friend could not hold a candle to the vision he met that afternoon.

Lord Darley, his stepmother—the Dowager Baroness Darley—and his sister, Miss Amesbury, greeted the Fitzwilliams and were introduced to the two bachelors in attendance as the earl's guests. Charmingly on her part, maladroitly on his, the young lady and Darcy exchanged salutations. Instantly attracted by her winsomeness and engaging manner, he cursed his innate awkwardness and listened with envy as Wickham effortlessly beguiled the three Amesburys.

In the drawing room after dinner, the girls gravitated round Miss Amesbury in a giggling, fragrant fortress that defied breaching. Miss Taylor, he suspected, had deduced his partiality, for when she caught his eye—with a hint of mischief in her own—she moved even closer to Miss Amesbury but spoke so Darcy might hear. "None of the viscount's relations will separate us, and we want nothing to do with any of them, do we?"

Nor do I want anything to do with a gaggle of giddy girls. Darcy stood at a window overlooking the River Derwent, all the while fixing his eyes on Miss Amesbury's reflection and envying everyone to whom she spoke. Glancing over his shoulder, he was somewhat appeased when her gaze settled upon him. He returned her sweet smile, and a silly grin remained in place until unwelcome company intruded.

Shooting suspicious looks between the two, Wickham sneered, "You will get nowhere by standing here, rooted to the spot. For what are you waiting? With your wealth and connexions, you already have what every girl wants."

"A suitor's integrity ought to be an equally important inducement."

"You are entirely too strait-laced. Faint heart never won fair lady. Make love to her, Darcy. Be a man. Go and get her before another beats you to it."

That night in his guest chamber, Darcy made a jumble of his bedclothes. *I am not strait-laced. I may be fastidious, polite, and respectable, but that is not the same as strait-laced. Is it? Strait-laced sounds so dull. Am I uninteresting? Is that why Father was unduly attentive to his godson?*

Flinging off the tangled sheets, he strode to a window. Moonlight reflected on the river, he on his childhood friend. While Wickham had spent more time carousing than studying or doing anything productive, Darcy had always been expected to act in accordance with his father's rules.

He wondered why Wickham had never received, from either of their fathers, a lecture similar to the one he himself had endured about the possible consequences of engaging in the marital act outside of wedlock. He was sick of the profligate's boasts of his many conquests and his strutting about with an irritating sense of prerogative far beyond his family's circumstances.

Returning to bed, Darcy vowed he would never be like Wickham and reminded himself not to clench his jaw, for it gave him a terrific headache.

Sleep came late. Morning came early.

Miss Amesbury was much admired by Darcy that sunny Saturday. Her gown was of the same softly-hued muslin every other girl there sported, but no other pale pink skirts skimmed against legs in the enticing way that hers did. No other vivid green ribbon hugged an upper body with such an enviable embrace. With grace, she moved. In gentle tones, she spoke. With serenity, she smiled. Like the tinkling of a bell, she laughed. Flaxen hair shimmered in the sunlight, not a strand misplaced. Like the delicate blue of a flame, her eyes captivated. A sunbeam's caress paled in comparison to her warmth as she flitted like a butterfly amongst her guests, stopping here and there, twirling her parasol, and bestowing smiles on everyone.

He envied the grassy ground she floated upon and the pure air she breathed. All was blue, gold, pink, and green that morn, and a gentle breeze carried the sweet scent of flowers. As aromatic as a summer garden herself, Miss Amesbury left fragrant, subtle traces of water lilies in her wake. Darcy's blood surged with desire.

Wickham nudged his side in the drawing room that after-noon, startling him from ungovernable imaginings. "Do us all a favour, and lose that besotted expression." Turning to admire the girl, he smirked. "She is fair, though. Healthy, glowing, and oh so rich and ripe."

"Who?" Darcy's ears had grown red hot.

"Miss Amesbury. You do want her, do you not?"

"Hardly. We have not spoken at length, other than a few words exchanged yesterday upon introduction."

"If you are too faint-hearted to secure the girl, you could, at least, get your hands on one of her likenesses." Gesturing at a large, framed painting on an easel, Wickham explained a portraitist had been commissioned to commemorate Miss Amesbury's come-out and had copied the image upon miniatures. Darcy wandered over to admire the painting, but in a trice, its living, breathing subject appeared beside him.

Miss Amesbury picked up and studied one of the detailed little portraits from the easel. "It seems a tedious task to stipple someone's image upon such small pieces of ivory, does it not?" Placing the miniature in his hand, she traced a dainty finger round its oval frame, grazing his palm. "You may keep it if you like."

Eyes wide and entire body afire from her touch, Darcy knew not what to say. But he knew what to think. Strict rules governed the giving and taking of miniatures. An unrelated gentleman and lady could not exchange such tokens unless they were engaged to marry.

Dash it! I am not about to refuse. She seemed to hold him in fond regard, so he pocketed the precious gift, smiled, and thanked her.

That night, while musicians played in the garden, he watched Miss Amesbury partnering with other young gentlemen. When the time came for his own requested set, he moved towards the pavilion, smoothing his coat, rehearsing what he might say, and silently cursing the dampness inside his gloves while going over in his mind the cotillion's elaborate figures and changes. When the dance brought them together, Darcy leant in as she spoke, agreeing with every wondrous, witty, frivolous word she uttered. Certain her expression softened and her cheeks blushed for him more than any other admirer, his heart swelled with pride.

There was to be an interval in the music after he escorted Miss Amesbury from the set, and he was loath to part from her. Rising on her toes, she whispered near his ear, "Walk with me. My chaperon is apt to lag behind." Giggling and holding his hand in both of hers, she walked backwards a few steps, tugging him towards torch-lit flower beds.

Taking twists and turns along sweet-scented pathways, they soon lost the older woman. While Miss Amesbury's actions thrilled him, Darcy still had some wits about him. "Will your mother not be concerned by your absence?"

"She is too busy flirting to notice my doings. Mother was raised in consequence by marrying a baron, and now a baron's widow, she aims higher." She laughed softly. "Do forgive me. Lord Matlock is, after all, your uncle."

"And a married man!"

According to the Fitzwilliams, Miss Amesbury had loved her father, and the baron had doted on her, although he spent most of his time in London, avoiding his second wife. Then, two years past, Lord Darley had died of an apoplexy. Like Darcy, Miss Amesbury had had a lonely childhood and lost a beloved parent.

For one with such a dismal beginning, Darcy thought she had become a sweet creature. Her delightful pinch of impropriety that night only added to her other perfections. "Have you always been at Riverswood?"

"For a time, I was a parlour boarder at seminary where I was taught with other wealthy gentlemen's daughters, including our mutual friend, Miss Taylor."

"Did you enjoy school? What were you taught there?"

"We learnt to gracefully enter or quit a room and, with equal elegance, to take a seat or rise from it. Such wondrous achievements," said she, catching his eye and smiling, "as can scarcely be imagined. Of course, a young lady also must be proficient in the use of a globe and fluent in French or Italian...at least up until she marries. Then she may as well forget about foreign countries and their languages. But such fashionable accomplishments, without reference to one's character, are compulsory if one wishes to secure a husband."

"And do you? Wish to secure a husband?"

"Marriage must be every girl's fondest wish, must it not?"

Egad. Was that meant seriously or facetiously? Tugging his cravat, Darcy struggled to extract an answer from its depths while Miss Amesbury waited expectantly. When the time for a reply lapsed, she enquired about his charming friend and patrician cousins. With great restraint, he resisted describing them as nothing but a pack of dirty dogs. Instead, he made known three implicit facts. Mr Wickham was born the son of Pemberley's steward. Viscount Winster had once slighted Miss Taylor for being too common. Fitzwilliam would soon be aboard a ship bound for Portugal. *So, you see, one is beneath your touch, one above it, and one soon out of reach.*

Sulky when she made no further enquiries about *him*, he scowled as the musicians resumed playing. Escorting her back to the pavilion, Darcy begrudgingly relinquished Miss Amesbury to her next partner.

Later, he climbed into bed with a tightness in his chest, a burning sensation in his stomach, a headache from gritting his teeth, and a guilty conscience for having wished eunuchism upon his cousins and Wickham.

Chapter 2

After Sunday services, Darcy dutifully joined his uncle, his male cousins, and their host in angling along the river. With sighs and longing looks towards a walled garden where the young crowd—Wickham included—had gathered, his thoughts were of luring Miss Amesbury away from other suitors, not fishing trout from the Derwent. Voice low, he turned to his favourite relation, nudging him from a doze. "I am resolved on a course of action."

Fitzwilliam, who had two years' seniority over Darcy, growled his reply. "If you think to swap places with me, forget it. I am content in this shady spot."

Winster moved close and listened as Darcy announced, "My plan is to make Miss Amesbury mine. An offer will be made this week with our marriage taking place in a year or two."

"Marriage! Are you out of your senses? You are too green to get yoked." Fitzwilliam made no effort to lower his voice. "You are not thinking with your brain, are you?"

"She is everything a young lady ought to be—winsome, complying, polite, convivial, and demure." *Well, perhaps not terribly demure.* "I never before met a young lady with so much facility amongst company."

Unsolicited, Winster opined that a female's compliance in all things was of utmost importance. "I might even consider Miss Amesbury a suitable viscountess for me."

Fitzwilliam scoffed at the two of them. "And thereby, a woman's true character is discerned, is it? One need not discover anything more before joining your lives together. Best remain ignorant of any incompatibility until it is far too late." He lowered his voice. "Darcy, have a care. I have heard—"

"You both are ridiculous." His annoyance piqued, Darcy bowed to his cousins. "Gentlemen—and I use the term loosely."

In search of better company, he strode away. Entering the walled garden, he saw his heart's desire on a swing, surrounded by her tittering friends who, in turn, were surrounded by male admirers. Removing his hat, he bowed, heart pounding, feeling every eye upon him. When Miss Taylor impudently asked where he had been, Darcy replied, "I have been angling."

"I am curious about baiting stratagem, angling, and catching." Miss Amesbury leant forwards, eying his person. "What enticements do you employ, sir?"

"In fly-fishing," said Miss Taylor, who he knew had practical knowledge of the sport, "rather than live bait, an artificial insect is used as a lure."

"Your handsome friend"—Miss Amesbury nudged Miss Taylor—"certainly does have *allure*."

Ears burning and without a witty response to her delightfully pert comment, Darcy bid everyone a most pleasant morning, and, with a confident stride, he returned to the river.

"You are back so soon?" Fitzwilliam drawled, yawning.

Employing superior height, Darcy pushed aside his

drowsy cousin, dislodging him from the sheltered spot beneath an oak. Taking up that favoured position, he cast his line across the rippling, sparkling water. He pondered the implication of Miss Amesbury's sweet words, the memory of her hand taking his, and the significance of the miniature while he listened with half an ear to Fitzwilliam's rant.

"And if your nursery maid had not been so exceedingly attentive to Pemberley's heir, I might suspect you went out without your pudding cap as an infant and fell on your stupid head."

"Leave off," said Darcy. "You know not what it is like. You have never been in love."

"Nor have you. I could replace Miss Amesbury with any other fetching girl who might pay you the slightest attention, and you would be as equally besotted."

Darcy insisted he would never be so fickle.

"Go on, then," said Fitzwilliam. "Be your own worst enemy. Make your bed and lie in it. Dig your own grave. Mark my words: I shall have the last laugh when you eat your words and admit you were not in love."

In Darcy's hot-blooded judgment, Miss Amesbury was everything warm and wonderful. She teased, flirted, and dared him to be less reserved. For two days, he pursued her, going at it hammer and tongs, though he liked to think he performed with more finesse than a blacksmith at his trade. Her aloof mother and half-brother expressed neither consent nor objection. Who would disapprove? He was, after all, Pemberley's master and had his own noble connexions.

One of those relations, Lord Matlock, told Darcy he could do better than Miss Amesbury and, on Tuesday, advised that a more suitable candidate would be found when the time came for him to wed. Having been forewarned by his father about the earl's political machinations, he disregarded his uncle's advice.

At dusk on Wednesday, with the negligent chaperon lagging after them, Darcy and Miss Amesbury enjoyed a cosy tête-à-tête while strolling arm in arm along the river bank. She informed him that her parents' marriage had not been happy and her late father often had lamented his first wife's death. "Whenever he did so in her presence, my mother would say, 'I assure you, Husband, no one regrets her demise more than I'. Poor Papa. It has been said that to live happily in marriage, the man ought to be deaf so he may not hear his wife's impertinence and the woman blind so she may not see her husband's intrigues. I daresay you are too honourable for such a union."

Darcy assured her he was.

"I expected as much, and I...I admire you."

When he assured the lady the feeling was mutual, she daringly kissed his cheek before, less than subtly, encouraging him to press his lips to hers.

Carrying Miss Amesbury's miniature in the pocket next to his heart, Darcy became increasingly engrossed in her and less attentive to other people. Miss Taylor laughingly informed him she had spoken to him twice without receiving an answer. With every moment spent with Miss Amesbury, he became more and more certain. He had fallen in love.

Mutual burgeoning regard was tainted by the knowledge they would part in a matter of hours, never knowing when next they might meet. Desperate for her, Darcy planned to make his proposals on the morrow. Half the night was spent praying her brother would agree and the other half envisioning how proud he would be to have such a winsome wife.

Informed on Thursday morning that Miss Amesbury had

ridden to a folly across the park, he strode off in search of future happiness. It was a perfect summer day—full of promises, sunshine, twittering birds, a gentle breeze, and the fresh smell of scythed grass. Giddy with love, Darcy smiled at the cloudless sky, rehearsing a marriage offer and hoping his sweetheart—after accepting his proposals—might allow the liberty of a more passionate kiss. Quickening his pace, he restrained himself from breaking into a run.

Upon approaching the folly, he spotted her mare tethered beside it. Hearing whimpers from inside the costly but purposeless structure, Darcy bolted up its stone steps, two at a time, towards the distressing sounds. Imagining all sorts of calamities, he dashed through the columns and doorway, praying Miss Amesbury was not the injured party within.

His headlong charge came to a grinding halt. Already palpitating with eagerness and exertion, his heart continued pumping, but he forgot to breathe while struggling to make sense of the scene playing out before him. A convulsive catching of his breath apprised the others of his presence.

From a blanket on the floor, a man cursed and rolled sideways, facing away, fumbling with the fall of his breeches. The young woman scrambled to stand, avoiding Darcy's eyes and smoothing her skirts.

A taunting voice roused Darcy from his stupor. "My apologies, friend." Smirking, Wickham gained his feet.

Swallowing hard, Darcy damped down bile, bitterness, and a base urge to lash out. Tenuous control achieved, he rasped, "How *could* you?"

Red-faced, eyes lowered, Miss Amesbury tried to brush past. Barring her escape with an outstretched arm, he choked out an anguished, "Why?"

She wrenched free and dashed down the steps.

"With an indifferent mother, an unfeeling half-brother,

and no father to shower her with affection, the poor dear seeks love in another manner." Wickham strutted away. "And I was more than happy to—"

From behind, Darcy caught the other man's sleeve, cutting off the sick-making talk and forcing him to turn and look him in the eye. "Say no more," he snarled. "Not…one… word." At Wickham's smirk, he saw red. Grasping his cravat, he twisted it in his fist and might have strangled him had Miss Amesbury not screeched from below.

"Stop! You are killing him!"

He gave Wickham a good shove. "Leave my sight. Go! See to your woman. She cannot gain the saddle alone. Help her. Or, so help me, I shall not be held responsible for my actions."

Miss Amesbury seemed unharmed, unaffected even, by her fall from grace. *So, the injured person inside the folly, it turns out, is me.* A knife had been thrust into Darcy's back. His tender heart had been pierced, his soul cut, and his pride stabbed. But he would do what Wickham had recommended. Be a man.

And, like Father always said, a gentleman shows no emotion.

He swore then to never again place himself in a vulnerable position. Never again would he be made a fool. Never again would he trust. He vowed to spare his heart and his pride from another crippling blow. Never again would he succumb to romantic love.

Love! This was nothing more than infatuation. My heart was only slightly touched. That was what Darcy told himself, and his pride was assuaged by believing it.

As Miss Amesbury on her mare and Wickham, walking alongside, disappeared around a bend, Darcy wondered how little of permanent happiness could belong to a couple brought together only because their passions were more potent than their virtue. Absorbed in his thoughts, he picked up the blanket, crumpled it into a ball, and flung it across the folly. He sat awhile, aimlessly walked awhile, then found himself climbing the steps to the manor without any memory of having crossed the lawns. Wickham and Winster, he discovered, had left Riverswood together.

Subdued, averting her eyes, Miss Amesbury avoided him as much as possible for the remainder of the day. Fitzwilliam pestered him about his foul temper until Darcy said sharply, "You had the right of it, Cousin. I have never been in love. Satisfied? Now, shall we accept that billiards challenge from Lord Darley and his friends? I would enjoy giving some balls a hard good whack."

At dinner, he picked at his food without tasting it. When others laughed, he followed suit, not knowing why. Later, as young ladies exhibited at the harp or pianoforte, he applauded at the appropriate times with no recollection of hearing their performances. Declining invitations to participate in card games, he apologised and retired early. Summoning his valet, he ordered his belongings packed.

The following day—alongside the earl, the countess, their daughter, and Fitzwilliam—Darcy said his thanks and farewells to the three Amesburys. Blushing, Miss Amesbury rose from her curtsey, met his eyes, and whispered, "Forgive me."

He bowed. "It has been a pleasure, Miss Amesbury." Darcy turned his back and walked away.

During the journey from Riverswood to Lord Matlock's estate, Torway Hall, he remembered the miniature he had intended to leave behind. *Blast! Jonesby must have packed the wretched thing in my trunk.* Imagining the portrait tainting everything it touched, he considered flinging it into the deepest depths of the Derwent; but he would not pollute the river.

As Darcy worked the following month in Pemberley's well-ordered library, the only discernible sounds were the fire's low crackle and the comforting tick of a long-case clock. No bustle, no chatter, no laughter shattered his peace. *Just as it should be, for now.*

Despite being satisfied with his privileged bachelor life, and although his estate was not entailed, he would be compelled eventually to choose a wife. Marriage was not an altogether unpleasant prospect, but the daunting selection process was. When he entered the parson's mousetrap, he hoped it would not be while kicking and screaming.

Setting aside a neat stack of answered correspondence and another of pending invitations, he stared into the flames. Grabbing a fire iron, he stirred up both lambent embers and glowing memories of his parents. He assumed they had been content, although no words of love between husband and wife had been spoken within his hearing. Nevertheless, he sensed there had been fondness and fidelity in the union, and he aspired to the same harmony.

His parents and Fitzwilliam relations had been explicit about duty and the importance of choosing an appropriate wife, but they had provided differing qualities for his consideration. He contemplated a list of prerequisites for the position of Mrs Fitzwilliam Darcy. When the time came, he could be scrupulous in choosing a bride. There were far too many ladies in want of desirable husbands, and there was, after all, only one of him. *In my position, a lesser man might become jaded or puffed up by his own importance.*

Dipping pen into sterling silver ink-pot, he wrote, in no particular order of precedence, all the advice, both useful and dubious, he could recall from his elders regarding the qualities he might seek in the future Mrs Darcy.

When the clock struck one, he stashed away the nine-page sheaf and called for his carriage.

Chapter 3

Autumn 1811, Hertfordshire

Closing her eyes, breathing in crisp air with undertones of earthiness, Elizabeth Bennet lifted her face sunwards and basked in its waning warmth. Her pleasure in the day's outing was made complete by her favourite sister's company, the children, and the day's freshness. Disregarding the little ones' laughter for a moment, she listened for other sounds—the hurry-scurry of an industrious squirrel in the undergrowth, the flute-like flourish of a blackcap's warble, and the lazy drone of a bee in search of nectar amongst the last goldilocks asters.

Recollecting herself and determined to enlighten the four tenant children under her and Jane's temporary charge, she handed them an acorn apiece. "Inside those nuts is the seed of an oak tree. Do you know the meaning of 'great oaks from little acorns grow'?" At their blank looks, she explained that something small, from humble beginnings, could become something strong and impressive over time.

"Mith Lithy, can we grow great oakth from our acornth?"

Jane smiled at the gap-toothed girl skipping round Elizabeth's skirts. "It takes many years for a seed to sprout into a stately tree, Miranda. Choose a spot to plant your acorn, and there will be treats for you afterwards."

Elizabeth produced—to a chorus of cheers—a jar of apricot cakes from a basket. While the children enjoyed the dried, chewy sweets, she reflected on autumn and why it was associated with maturity and melancholy. To her, the season represented invigoration. Throughout the countryside, the natural world burst forth as diligently as in spring. Seed pods split asunder and scattered progeny to the four winds. Leaves changed hue and plummeted. In fields and orchards, farmers harvested ripened crops. Animals scurried about the forest. Gentlemen raced horses or took to their parks with guns and dogs. Birds migrated. Even darkness rushed to supplant daylight. Everywhere was industry and bustle.

Watching the children scamper about, Elizabeth longed for a family of her own. But where, amongst the local gentry, was the man who, in disposition and talents, might best suit her temperament? *One in my position should not be so exacting. Should I end up unmarried, it will not be because of my own expectations. A man of sense cannot afford me, and I do want a man of good sense.*

Later, Jane returned home while Elizabeth escorted the children back to their cottages. As she crossed the field closest to Longbourn, Elizabeth was surprised to see Mary, the Bennet sister least likely to venture far from the house. Giving Mary a moment to catch her breath, she asked, "Is something amiss at home?"

"Patience may be a virtue, but I required respite from the weary task of forbearance. Mother is in a pother. Netherfield Park has been taken by a bachelor with deep pockets, and he will be in by Michaelmas. You can well imagine the flutter that piece of news generated."

"I suppose Jane has been engaged to him already," Elizabeth joked.

"Aye, and the rest of us are to be thrown in the path of his rich friends." Mary huffed. "I do not want to be thrown, or even lightly nudged, at any strange man."

"Then adhere to your morals as you see fit." Elizabeth pulled the jar from her basket and thrust it into her sister's hand. "Have the last apricot cake."

Mary popped the confection into her mouth, quickly complaining that it stuck to her teeth.

"Just as you must stand to your guns. If thrown at some wealthy gentleman, be a stickler, as tenaciously sticky as an apricot cake."

A rare smile appeared on Mary's face. "That sounds as though you want me to cling to him."

Linking arms and giggling, they set off across the field. Having made her most solemn sister laugh, Elizabeth was satisfied she had accomplished at least one good deed for the day. "So, do you happen to know the name of Jane's intended?"

"Mr Bingley."

"Mr Bingley?" Elizabeth stopped and tilted her head. "That name sounds familiar." *And I feel a sudden urge to run.*

Mary only shrugged, and the sisters resumed walking at a slower pace. Elizabeth thought about a story her friend, Miss Taylor, had lately told her—to much laughter—of the former suitor who objected to her needlessly walking about. *Was his name Bingley? I remember thinking I would run in the opposite direction if I ever met the dullard. I must ask Miss Taylor about him in my next letter.*

The first and only one of the Bennets to have met Miss Taylor, Elizabeth had been delighted to discover she and her cousin's future wife had much in common, especially in their preference for parks over parlours. While staying with her aunt Browne and cousin on Portman Square, she had accompanied the engaged couple during a stroll through Hyde Park. *Good heavens.* Elizabeth realised the lady they had met there also had a complaint about a Mr Bingley.

⟨◦⟩

Weeks later, with a flock of boys and girls under her wing, Elizabeth produced, to their delight, a bat and ball. Jane was at home, indisposed, and without her sister's sedate guidance, alphabet lessons were abandoned in favour of activity. Casting aside her bonnet, she hitched up the hems of her plainest morning gown—a worn, yellowish-grey wool—and joined in a game involving shouting, laughing, and dashing pell-mell round the lea.

"Look yonder, Miss Lizzy," cried one of the boys, pointing to a party of three men and two ladies riding along the track and halting at the field's edge. "Who are they?"

"Judging by their fashionable attire, they must be Netherfield's new occupants." Snatching up her bonnet, she plunked it upon her head and curtseyed as the mounted men tipped their hats.

⟨◦⟩

"Good heavens, Charles," cried Miss Bingley. "Urchins! And so close to our manor. When you invited us to explore the countryside, I had not expected to encounter ragamuffins or riffraff. Shall we next be set upon by a band of robbers or cutthroats?"

Miss Oliverson asked whether the lea constituted part of the Netherfield lease.

Bingley turned to Darcy. "Should I ride over and investigate?"

"No. I examined the title deed and drawings." Darcy wondered why his friend had not done the same. "The area belongs to a neighbouring estate. They are not trespassing."

"In what activity were they engaged?" Miss Oliverson looked to Bingley for an answer.

"They were playing rounders," said Caulifield. "I assume the young woman is their nursery maid."

Miss Oliverson paid him no mind. "If they are a gentleman's children, they should be at home, unseen, unheard, and better garbed."

"Quite right," agreed Miss Bingley. "And why on earth should a slatternly nursemaid be scampering about, hair untidy, skirts indecently raised six inches above her ankles?" Catching Darcy's eye, she rearranged her skirt's drape to cover an expanse of stocking that had been exposed—for his benefit, he assumed—above her boot top.

"She was running to one of those bases." Caulifield indicated four twigs stuck upright in the ground. "While doing so, her shapely shanks appeared to great advantage."

"You, sir," cried Miss Oliverson, glaring at him, "are a beast!"

Darcy was surprised at the insult, but the Oliversons and Caulifields were distant relations of some sort. *Kentish cousins, as they say.*

"She should exert better control over her filthy, unruly little charges," Miss Bingley said. "When I have a family, I shall employ only those of the finest character to rear them —responsible, decorous servants and the best schools." Noting Darcy's scowl, she held a hand over her heart. "But how I shall despise every minute parted from my little darlings."

Little darlings who will not be sired by me. Darcy could not abide the practice of youngsters remaining unseen and unheard in the nursery, presented only for a daily inspection. Of course, there would be a nanny, nursery maids, a governess, and, perhaps, boarding school. But he rather fancied being surrounded by joyful laughter while running about with his brood on Pemberley's lawns. *And my children will shower their mother and me with sloppy kisses and heartfelt hugs.* The thought of sloppy kisses was unexpected, giving him a moment's pause.

Miss Bingley was still griping, and Darcy pitied Hurst; the man had to endure not only his sister-in-law's residence in his smallish Grosvenor Street house but her complaining about it. In truth, the woman complained about most everything. *Little wonder Hurst refers to her as 'Carowhine', but never to her face. He may be a glutton, a drunkard, and a sluggard, but he is no dullard.*

"...And poor Louisa must be worn out by now from wandering round Meryton, the deadly dull hamlet. Still, I hope the apothecary there might have a tonic to settle your stomach, Dottie. Rest assured, I shall have words with Mrs Nicholls about Netherfield's cook and the inferiority of the viands. Obviously, the locals are unaccustomed to serving those with superior taste and refined palates."

"Miss Bingley, we should return to dine and prepare for tonight's assembly"—Darcy scowled at his friend—"since your brother insists we all attend." Bingley answered with a tip of his hat and a cocky grin.

The Netherfield party totalled only seven, although a larger party had been invited. Through Miss Bingley's machinations, Caulifield's sister had been dissuaded from attending a house party some twenty miles from England's capital...*and, I suspect, in unacceptably close proximity to me.* Miss Oliverson, however, had been allowed to attend, having met Miss Bingley's approval as an appropriate match for her brother. As for Oliverson himself, he had sent his regrets and remained at Brighton. To Darcy, his reason for declining had been an offensive revelation scathingly delivered by Bingley before they left London.

"Have you never wondered why, in five years, you could count on the fingers of one hand how often the two of you have been together in my company? It rarely occurs because of careful planning."

Darcy had replied, "Are you saying Oliverson purposely avoids my company? What offence has the scoundrel committed against me?"

"Quite the contrary, my friend. To be honest, he finds you...Oh, where do I begin? Arrogant is one of the words he has used over the years. Ollie wishes he and you may be better strangers."

Now, recalling that earlier exchange, a mighty surge of umbrage swept through Darcy. Displeased with Bingley and his guests, with the absent Oliverson, with George Wickham, Mrs Younge, and the world at large, he drew himself up in the saddle and spoke forcefully. "Why are we wasting time looking at an unkempt, unattractive milkmaid and her bedraggled charges? Such riffraff, as Miss Bingley so kindly pointed out, is not worth our bother."

Turning his mount round, he took a parting glance at the little ones as their nurse hugged them close. *She appears terribly nurturing.* Breaking away and giving his horse its head, he raced towards Netherfield as though hellhounds nipped at his heels.

In his guest apartments, he plucked from a leather satchel

his lengthy list. At the desk by a window, he put pen to page, adding a mandatory requirement for the companion of his future life. Each dot above the letter 'i' pierced the paper as he wrote: *The woman who will give life to the Darcy heir must love children and prove herself to be nurturing.*

With a heavy sigh and a lighter hand, he tacked on another line. *Never would she refer to inferiors as riffraff.*

Lady Lucas had reported that seven gentlemen and twelve ladies were expected in time for the assembly. Such promising news had filled Mrs Bennet with glee, and in the hour before the assembly, she was nearly dancing round Longbourn's sitting room. "Seven gentlemen of fortune! One each, at least, for my girls."

"No matter what the dozen ladies in the Netherfield party might think," said Elizabeth, "do you assume, sight unseen, the wealthy bachelors are our rightful property, Mama?"

Mr Bennet winked at her while addressing his wife. "I would deem it prudent for my girls to have a glimpse of said goods and chattels before taking possession, so it is providential tonight's event will enable you to appraise their holdings and ascertain whether they have heads and limbs enough for their number."

"Once the young men have met my Jane," said Mrs Bennet, patting her eldest's cheek, "they will lose their heads over her."

"Well, my dear, whichever headless gentleman claims you as his mother-in-law, he will be spared the inconvenience of headaches." Mr Bennet rubbed his temples before rousing himself to kiss his wife's cheek. "Off with you. Enjoy yourselves, but not too much." He reminded her they did not yet know their new neighbours' characters. "While I am indifferent to those young bucks losing their heads, I charge you with assuring our daughters remain intact." Giving her a pointed look, he added, "If you take my meaning."

Settling in his chair, he poured a glass of port and picked up some papers. "I would go to supervise the affair myself, but I have a terrific ache in my head. Fortified wine and this compelling treatise on Sanskrit's common origin with Latin and Greek may prove fitting remedies. In fact, I am confident the pain will be forgot the instant you lot leave. Off with you now."

Inside Meryton's assembly hall, Mrs Bennet insisted her daughters remain by her side, arrayed by descending order of birth, until the much-anticipated entrance of their goods and chattels. *In what manner does Mama plan to match us with the gentlemen? By stature?* Elizabeth and all her sisters were of average height, with Lydia the tallest by a mite. *Hair colour?* Jane was the sole fair-haired one. *Or some other equally critical criteria?*

The Bennets, in company with the Philips and Lucas families, were a merry bunch until the Netherfield party entered. As one, the locals fell silent until a shrill, somewhat foxed voice rang out from their midst. "Lawks! Were I single, I'd fall arsy-varsy over that tall, dark-haired, handsome one."

Praying her uncle Philips might keep a tight rein on his wife's tongue to prevent it from running off again, Elizabeth cast an appraising eye over the remarked-upon gentleman in all his sartorial splendour. She could not fault her aunt's assessment. *A magnificent specimen of refined masculinity, indeed.*

Already acquainted with the visitors, Sir William Lucas made the introductions, starting with the Bennets. With easy, unaffected manners, two of the gentlemen—Mr Bingley and Mr Caulifield—chatted amiably awhile with Elizabeth and her mother and sisters. *Mr Bingley seems so amiable, he cannot be Miss Taylor's petty-minded, former suitor. Can he? I really must write to her.*

When the newcomers moved along to speak to others, Mrs Bennet whispered to her daughters. "Well! I am quite put out. Only four gentlemen. And that dreadful Mr Hurst! Already married."

"Yes," said Lydia. "I would not want such a fat-headed, sluggish lump for a husband. At least there are only three ladies, not twelve. That coquelicot gown would look far better on me than it does on Miss Bingley. But Mrs Dexter told me that colour is permissible only on trimmings for well-brought-up young ladies." Turning to Kitty, she said, "And did you notice the cut of Miss Oliverson's gown? Faith! It concealed none of her horrid bulges."

Aside from tailored elegance, the gentlemen were deemed by Elizabeth to be proper in their civilities, although Mr Caulifield did sweep his eyes up and down her person. *I wonder whether he made the 'unkempt-unattractive-milkmaid-riffraff-not-worth-his-bother' remark.* Not one to wallow in self-pity, she pretended the insult had amused her. *Daft slurs shall wound neither my pride nor my vanity, modest though they both may be.*

Later, passing within arm's reach of Mr Darcy's left shoulder, she overheard him say to Mr Bingley, "The appeal of the two eldest Bennet sisters is widely dissimilar. The ethereally beautiful Miss Bennet seems serene and demure but—like the sky's unworldly perfection—cool, distant, untouchable. Her constant smile is as bland as this wine, and she strikes me as vapid. Miss Elizabeth, though, is quite a different matter."

Elizabeth immediately recognised that it was his deep

voice which had described her to his friends as an unkempt, unattractive milkmaid. She turned to Charlotte Lucas. "Did you hear that? According to his appraisal, my defects are many, indeed. In his opinion, as Jane's diametrical opposite, I am ill-favoured, overwrought, brazen, earthy, forever frowning, and agitated. Shall I confirm to him I am, at least, brazen?"

"Do not—" Charlotte's restraining hand was too late.

Elizabeth turned, intent on catching Mr Darcy's condemnatory eye and bestowing upon him a malevolent scowl. Confused by his eyebrows' quick motion and tender smile as he spotted her, she faltered and looked away, frowning.

"Oh, well done, Eliza. Your frown does much to lessen any unfavourable impression he might have had."

"Your parents will not thank me should you develop a sarcastic bent." Elizabeth linked arms with her dear friend as they crossed the room. "Mr Darcy shall vex me no further, I am determined. We care nothing for his injudicious views, do we?"

"Nothing disparaging was said about you. As is your wont, you jumped to a conclusion. Do not give me that scowl," her friend cried. "You are, at times, too quick to judge. I suspect you might have overheard a compliment had he continued. Besides"—Charlotte bumped Elizabeth's hip—"if he thinks Jane bland and vapid, you must be just the opposite...interesting and stimulating."

Elizabeth felt her cheeks redden, though more with indignation than embarrassment. "Nay! If the gentleman finds Jane lacking, he cannot be pleased by anyone. How dare he proclaim she smiles too much?" She looked at Charlotte, who agreed it was an odd thing to say. "I hereby vow to vex Mr Darcy by being all smiles in his company."

Chapter 4

Attending an assembly seemed a less painful way to spend an evening than remaining at Netherfield, where his hostess would insist on staying and seeing to his every comfort and then some. Yet Darcy's arrival at Meryton's assembly room was not without disquiet. Within five minutes of his entrance, a susurration of his having ten thousand a year winged its way amongst the crush.

His eye was caught by a young woman seemingly unaffected by the rumour as she chatted and laughed amidst a merry band of friends. Her smile unaccountably eased his anxiety and her esprit intrigued him. He anticipated an introduction to her by Sir William Lucas, but that was before the surprise of coming face to face with her elder sister. Bad memories punched him in the stomach, and the resulting nausea was reminiscent of how he had felt upon discovering Miss Amesbury's true nature. Dumbstruck and shaken, he had spoken a few curt words to the Bennet family before fleeing their presence. Seeing Miss Amesbury's image everywhere was nothing new, even four years after the awful events at Riverswood. *But this resemblance is downright eerie... unless my memory is faulty. Would that I had the miniature with me for comparison!*

He stood off to one side of the room, where he eventually was joined by Bingley, Hurst, and Caulifield. "Who knew," said the latter, "that such an impressive array of femininity awaited us in Hertfordshire? Why, even the mother is attractive for her age."

Darcy thought Mrs Bennet had the same general appearance as Miss Amesbury's mother, which was amazing considering the evening's earlier shock.

"Her daughters were lauded as local beauties, and seeing is believing." Bingley craned his neck. "The eldest is an exquisite creature."

Caulifield elbowed Darcy. "As a man of the world and our resident connoisseur of beauty, what is your opinion?" Darcy made no reply, prompting Caulifield to peer at him closely. "You are as pale as a ghost. Are you unwell?"

"She...Miss Jane Bennet, that is...She is the—" *The very image of the former Miss Amesbury,* he thought, before managing a reply. "She is the only handsome woman present." *And I cannot abide the sight of her.*

"Do not let the ladies of our party hear you say so," Bingley muttered.

"I stand corrected. Miss Bennet is the only handsome *local* girl in the room."

"Will wonders never cease? Darcy has finally fallen." Caulifield chuckled. "Bingley, if you wish to stand up with Hertfordshire's Aphrodite, you had best get in line behind your friend. He is about to acquire another fine work of art."

"Hardly," said Darcy. "I grant you Miss Bennet is well-favoured, but she cannot be wealthy enough or have valuable connexions enough to tempt me." *I shall avoid her like the plague.* "In any case, she smiles too much. She brings to mind the enigmatic *Mona Lisa* I viewed with my father at the Louvre in the year two."

Caulifield looked at him with interest. "You were one of the countless English tourists carousing round France that summer? I suppose you are too tight-lipped, though, to tell us of your escapades." Darcy glared at Caulifield, who took no notice of him. "Speaking of tight-lipped, refined ladies—similar to the *Mona Lisa*, they do not show their teeth while smiling."

When Bingley remarked that Miss Bennet's smiles were sublime, Darcy said, "You do understand that smiling is not an accomplishment, do you not?"

"Of course. Fortunate, too, lest one of us be found wanting." Bingley stared across the room, heaving a sigh. "She is the most beautiful woman I ever beheld."

"What of Miss Oliverson?" Exasperated, Darcy added, "You are as fickle as the wind."

"If you ask me," drawled Caulifield, "the second daughter, the one with beautiful eyes, dazzling smile, and light, pleasing figure, is the most engaging of the five. "She is a tempting armful, and her clever mouth is uncommonly alluring."

"Clever, to be sure," said Bingley. "Too quick-witted for me, too vivacious for Darcy. Besides, I cannot tolerate her lavender perfume. It irritates my eyes and nasal passages." He nudged Caulifield's side with his elbow. "Too bad you are a confirmed bachelor. Miss Elizabeth seems your sort."

Darcy watched Caulifield gaze with evident approval as Miss Elizabeth held court amidst a cluster of laughing locals. "Someone once wrote that a cheerful temper joined with innocence will make beauty attractive, knowledge delightful, and wit good-natured. Or something like that," said Caulifield.

"It was Joseph Addison," said Darcy, somewhat surprised the man had recalled the quote.

"I suspect Miss Elizabeth is that saying's very embodiment." Chin high, Caulifield adjusted his cravat. "I shall ask her to stand up with me directly."

Having promised to dance first with Miss Oliverson, Bingley beckoned. "Come along, then. Let us enjoy the ladies' company until you utter something inappropriate and scare them off." Looking back at Darcy, he whispered, "I expect we shall return in a trice."

Darcy remained where he was, watching the dancers until Bingley returned in a miff. "Blast! Caulie secured Miss Bennet for the next set before I had a chance. Perhaps I should dance with Miss Lucas."

"Or ask a different Bennet sister." Darcy observed the youngest three. "On second thought, I would advise against it. The middle one seems dour and unwelcoming. Conversely, the other two appear immoderately eager to entertain gentlemen. I would not trust them and shall not dance with any of the locals."

"Why ever not? I never before met so many pleasant girls in one place."

Darcy rolled his eyes. "You, my friend, have been violently in love with more girls than are here tonight."

"I love the ladies, old man, and never could be as notoriously fastidious as you." With a smile, Bingley accepted another proffered glass of wine while his friend declined. "I have been wondering..." Taking a sip, he avoided Darcy's eye. "Do you begrudge my easy manner round the fairer sex?"

"Do you expect me to dignify that with an answer? I thought to ask whether you might care to join me when I soon leave, but I expect you and your 'easy manner' prefer to remain here amongst inferiors and their insipid smiles."

Bingley set down his glass and, taking hold of Darcy's

sleeve, yanked him into a corner. Darcy listened as his friend told him he dare not leave so soon. "The Bennets, as landed gentry, are not my inferiors. As you have repeatedly reminded me, my ambition is to marry into their sphere. Yours is to wed an heiress, a peeress, or a goddess. But do you know what I think? I think you might never marry. You are entirely too difficult to please."

Scarcely had he recovered from being detained and insulted before Bingley asked how many items were on his list of wifely essentials. There were, in fact, more than Darcy would care to admit to his friend.

"Whoever could be good enough for you?" Bingley concluded with a laugh.

In mingled disbelief and affront, Darcy smoothed the wrinkles on his sleeve, frowning just enough to make his displeasure known. Comprehending him, Bingley offered an apology. Although utterly offended, Darcy told him to think nothing of it.

"I need to establish myself in the neighbourhood," said Bingley. "Meryton's populace might not be as elegant as you are accustomed to, but nevertheless, I had hoped you might help me. Do I ask too much?"

Observing the assemblage, Darcy agreed to assist his friend.

"Splendid!" Bingley prodded him forwards. "Now, go. Stand up with one of the local girls."

"I agree to engage in a bit of conversation with a few gentlemen," said Darcy, digging in his heels, "but I shall dance with none other than your sisters and Miss Oliverson."

"Fie, Darcy! There is a scarcity of gentlemen here. Many young ladies are not dancing, and your aloofness could be perceived as an insult." Bingley gestured at the dancers.

"Follow Caulie's example. Acquaint yourself with the lovely Longbourn ladies."

Darcy lost patience with his undiscerning friend. "Miss Jane Bennet could be Miss Amesbury's—rather, Mrs Maguire's—identical twin."

"You mistakenly see that woman everywhere you go." Bingley shook his head. "As for the Bennet girls, although different at first glance, they definitely are sisters. Similar heart-shaped faces, the same noses, those kissable lips, and—"

"Have a care, Bingley. I warn you."

"No need. I am quite attached to Miss Oliverson."

When the set ended, Darcy and Bingley watched Caulifield lead Miss Bennet to a refreshment table where the Lucas family stood chatting with some local ladies, Miss Elizabeth included. After observing the two eldest Bennet sisters, Darcy turned his back to the room and made a few remarks about the elder sister and her vapidity to Bingley. When he glanced over his right shoulder, the ladies had dispersed, no longer within his line of sight. "Miss Elizabeth, though, is quite a different matter." *Egad. She is right here!* His eyebrows and the corners of his mouth rose without his permission.

In strikingly different ways, the two eldest Bennet sisters had flustered him. One lady brought Miss Amesbury's betrayal to mind, while the younger, livelier one aroused his interest. *Balderdash!* What did he care for dazzle? To beam and banter in such an open, cheerful manner was almost unheard of amongst the *ton*. Miss Elizabeth did not belong in his world. *And I hereby vow to pay her no mind.*

Although experienced in the ways of elegant company, he was, in certain instances, equal parts confidence and insecurity. In truth, he envied Bingley's ease with members of the opposite sex. Fortunately for him, Darcy would never need to woo and try to win a woman. When the time came, he would crook his forefinger, and the chosen one would come running. *Let the poets and romantics seek female favour through flowery words and…um…flowers and whatnot. I am not so pathetic.*

He, however, acknowledged it would be advantageous to have some of the charming manner he envied in Bingley, Caulifield, and Fitzwilliam. *Ah, well, one man cannot have it all.* Cursing his ingrained, stiff formality, he feigned disinterest in watching Miss Elizabeth being escorted to the dance.

Circling the room, he came upon Miss Oliverson and the middle Bennet girl engrossed in a moralistic discussion of *A Father's Legacy to his Daughters.* Veering off in search of a less righteous woman with whom to stand up, he applied to Miss Bingley, who agreed with alacrity. He suspected she found little pleasure in his distraction during their set, for his gaze more often than not strayed from his partner towards wherever either Miss Bennet or Miss Elizabeth happened to be in the formation.

"…And I cannot think of her as Miss *Elizabeth,*" said Miss Bingley. "She is far too ebullient, too uncouth for such a regal name. Miss Eliza suits her better. And, if I were you, I would pay no further notice to any of those Bennets."

That he might look at a country maiden rather than at Miss Bingley's cultivated fashion and carriage was inconceivable to him. Still, Darcy watched as Miss Elizabeth skipped nearer. *Barely handsome. Lacks symmetry. Are those freckles?* Palms damp inside his gloves, he anticipated the touch of her hand in his. *Certainly not comely enough for me.* Then, within arm's reach, he caught a whiff of lavender and citrus.

Clasping her gloved hand, he searched Miss Elizabeth's countenance, hoping to solve the puzzle of her appeal. Smiling, she met his gaze with a mysterious gleam in her eye. *Ah, there! You look into those unique eyes, and an uncommon intelligence suffuses her sweet face. Of what, I wonder, is she thinking?* Her fingers slid from his. Darcy stumbled as he heard his father's voice. 'Look not upon a woman's figure, but into her eyes. Character is to be found there.'

She moved away, leaving him shaken. Merrily then, she chatted with her partner, and the mellifluous sound of her laughter drifted Darcy's way, swirling round him, enveloping him in unaccountable joy. The outer corners of his eyes crinkled as he smiled. *Egad, why am I smiling at nothing? Have I gone mad?*

Later, with Miss Elizabeth still prominent in his mind's eye, he passed behind the Bingley sisters and heard one triumphantly speaking his name. "Mr Darcy finally has shown me some marked interest. As we danced, Louisa, I elicited from him the most favourable response. You know how rarely our staid friend shows off that divine dimple. His smile demonstrated how well-pleased he is with me, and I have every reason to expect his addresses."

"Indeed, Sister, I saw it. A man dare not unleash such a devastating smile upon any woman, save his wife or his intended."

Aargh! This is why I rarely ask a woman to stand up with me.

At Netherfield that moonlit midnight, Bingley, pleased with every aspect of the assembly, could not praise enough his new neighbours and their hearty welcome. "My only irritant was Miss Elizabeth's fragrance. Some of you will remember my sneezing fits the summer Miss Darcy's lavender-soused friend joined us at Pemberley. I am resolved to henceforth keep my distance from the second-eldest Bennet sister."

"Delighted to hear it. I am keen to further my acquaintance with Miss Elizabeth's sweet scent, comeliness, and cheerful wit." Caulifield sank into a chair, stretching out his legs and crossing them at the ankles. "Why does such a gem of a girl not have a bevy of suitors? Come to think of it, why does her elder sister remain unwed? What the dickens is wrong with the men hereabouts?"

Miss Bingley unintentionally defended the local male populace by collectively and individually flaying the Longbourn ladies.

After making his own disparaging comments about the vulgarity of Mrs Bennet and Mrs Philips, Darcy fell silent, still reeling from Miss Bennet's resemblance to Miss Amesbury and from Miss Elizabeth's appeal—her cheerful manner, her laughter, her charming wit, and the gleam in those unique eyes that spoke of an uncommon intelligence. Why had he gazed into her eyes? And why did she have to smile so sweetly? Then there had been his own resulting smile. *Fool!*

Having learnt his lesson at twenty-three, he dismissed any notion of instant attraction. *No matter how fresh, how fetching she may be. No matter she has wit enough for Caulifield. No matter how captivating her eyes, how dazzling her smile, how…* Rubbing his brow, dispelling hot-blooded thoughts, he noticed Miss Bingley making sheep's eyes at him as she continued to bleat on about the Bennet family's faults.

"At least Dottie and I have respectable dowries. At the assembly, Mrs Long and her nieces told me the Bennet girls' portions are not worth mentioning. They would bring nothing to a marriage."

Caulifield gave a bark of laughter. "No seeing, feeling man

could ever repine what Miss Elizabeth would bring to a husband."

Darcy shot him a black look. *Neither you nor I can be interested. She may be desirable, but her situation is not, and one must only raise expectations where they can be met.* A soft cough prompted his gaze to shift to Miss Oliverson. *Do I detect fear or anger in her countenance?* Whichever, it seemed to be aimed at Caulifield.

"Really, sir," said Miss Bingley, looking at Darcy, not Caulifield. "No right-minded gentleman would consider leading a penniless bride to the altar."

Considering himself a gentleman with sound views and principles, Darcy rubbed the ring on his little finger. The family seal, set in his signet ring and firmly in his grip, was a mighty amulet against Miss Elizabeth's allure. The intaglio would safeguard him from her feeble charms. *A battle not even worth fighting.*

Later, though, in bed, as restless body and mind tossed and turned, he questioned whether he could resist such an engagement.

Chapter 5

After exhibiting little curiosity about an event that had raised such grand expectations, Mr Bennet listened with obvious impatience as his womenfolk, half with exuberant frivolity, half with a bit more sense, rattled on about the assembly. Her father's growing exasperation amused Elizabeth, who thought it only recompense for not attending the event with them. It was well after midnight when the others retired and he asked her to remain behind.

He looked at her with a grave expression. "I hope, Lizzy, that you, at least, disregarded what I earlier said about the newcomers being your 'property'. Despite what your mother thinks, men of such standing do not look for wives hereabouts."

"You did."

He shook his head. "I was—*am*—not of their station."

"That is untrue," she insisted. "As I understand it, their fortunes, save those of Mr Hurst and Mr Darcy, were acquired through trade. None of them is titled, and you, Papa, are no pauper. As landed gentry, you are their equal or higher."

"Such flattery to my importance, while mistaken, is not unwelcome." Her father gave her a fond smile. "But beware, my child. Men are not always gentlemen." Heaving himself from the chair, he kissed her forehead, bid her a good night, and admonished her not to talk with Jane till dawn.

Already exhausted, Elizabeth chatted with her sister for only half an hour, offering a few final observations on their new neighbours before succumbing to sleep. "Jane, how common a name is Bingley?"

"Quite prevalent in Yorkshire, I believe. Why?"

Elizabeth worried her bottom lip. "Something niggles me about Mr Bingley. The name, that is, not the person. And his friend, Mr Darcy, irritates me. Heed my advice: if you wish to avoid Mr Darcy's censure, do not smile. For some reason, he frowns upon it."

She felt Jane shift beside her on the mattress. "To be honest, the way he stared at me was so unsettling it made me blush."

"If Mr Darcy glares at me again, my sarcastic tongue will tell him what I think of his sardonic eye." Elizabeth thumped her pillow several times before settling and closing her eyes. Without meaning to, she remembered how the outer corners of his eyes crinkled when he smiled.

The following morning, the arrival of Charlotte Lucas instigated another review of the assembly.

"...And such elegant dancers the Netherfield ladies were," cried Mrs Bennet.

"Did you notice," said Charlotte, "that Eliza was of particular interest to two of the Netherfield gentlemen?" Having taken a larger mouthful than she ought, Mrs Bennet could not chew quickly enough to protest such a likelihood, so her guest continued. "Mr Caulifield blatantly admired her. And although Mr Darcy displayed a disquieting interest in Jane early on, he could not take his eyes off Eliza for the rest of the night."

"For pity's sake," said Mrs Bennet. "What good does watching do? He should have asked my girls to stand up with him rather than skulking and spying on them from dimly-lit corners."

Elizabeth frowned. "Being the proud, critical sort, if Mr Darcy did watch me, he was, no doubt, wary of my doing something graceless and wild. Flinging off my shoes, perhaps, or letting down my hair and skipping madly about the room."

"When you say Mr Darcy is proud, do you mean a selfish vanity or a confident opinion of himself and his position in society?" Mary asked.

"A good question." Giving her sister's arm a pat, Elizabeth told her the matter was of little consequence. "We were introduced but did not speak directly thereafter."

"So, does your prejudice stem from his being too handsome, too wealthy, or too powerful?"

"*My* prejudice?" Elizabeth gave a surprised laugh. "Good heavens, Mary. We are speaking of his defects, not mine. My impression of Mr Darcy is not unfounded. Simply put, I am an excellent judge of character and find his lacking."

"But you said you did not speak at length," Mary pressed on. "How could you—"

Such persistence! "His voice carries. I heard, on two separate occasions, a profusion of derogatory remarks. Now may we please change the subject to something more pleasant?"

"Lizzy," cried her mother. "Do not discourage a potential suitor, even a disrespectful one. Mr Darcy has ten thousand a year, you know. According to Sir William, Mr Caulifield's situation is less agreeable. He lives with his father and sister at some paltry property somewhere."

Pushing back her chair, Elizabeth flung her serviette upon the table. "Pray, excuse me. I promised some tenant children an airing this morning."

"But look at his face," said Bingley. "He is heartbroken, poor boy."

Swinging himself into the saddle, Darcy muttered, "Better disappointed than eviscerated, I should think." Reins and hunting whip in a loose grip, he studied the countryside through a veil of brume. "Trust me, the males can be brutally aggressive this time of year."

Crouching, Bingley scratched behind his dog's ears before gesturing to a groom. "I would be gutted if harm befell you, Gaius." Tail between its legs, the Italian greyhound was led away. The dog, acquired prematurely in anticipation of one day gracing his master's estate, had been banned from the Albany for a number of infractions and subsequently boarded with the Hursts. Reunited at Netherfield, Gaius rarely left Bingley's side.

Trotting off into the misty morning, the riders were greeted by the sun's upper edge as it appeared above the horizon. Rays of golden light softly dissipated the fog and touched upon tawny leaves, bathing the park in a hazy, bronzed glow of mellow, pastoral splendour. The air had a nip to it that smelt of wood smoke, hay, and humus. Coppery leaves wafted downwards. To their right, a woodpecker drummed and drilled on dead wood. Off in the distance, geese honked, heralding their southerly migration.

Side by side the two men rode, unwilling to shatter the peacefulness of the setting with other than hushed tones. Even their horses' hoofbeats were muted by a carpet of bestrewn leaves. Passing through an open gate in the hawthorn hedgerow, Darcy reined in his mount and pointed. "Now do you understand why I suggested a dawn inspection and that Gaius remain behind?"

From its rutting stand beneath the oaks, a mighty stag emerged into the clearing. A rival stamped and bellowed, pacing a parallel track, judging his opponent's size and strength, willing to fight for access to the harem. The first deer thrashed the ground, hooking vegetation in his antlers.

"He is a red deer, is he not?" At Darcy's confirmation, Bingley frowned. "Why, then, is he so darkly coloured?"

"During the autumn rut, he will do all he can to defend the right to mate with the females hereabouts, including wallowing in his own urine."

Bingley wrinkled his nose. "Thank God human males do not engage in such bizarre rituals."

The stags locked antlers in a shoving match, each trying to gain advantage.

"I expect human courting—all that smiling, sighing, blushing, kissing, and such—seems deuced odd to our counterparts in the animal kingdom," Darcy observed.

Bingley chuckled. "Well, old man, you occasionally smile, rarely sigh, never blush. But I look forward to the day you meet your efficient, symmetrical, peaceable goddess and engage in such deviant behaviour."

They observed the deer in silence until the challenger yielded. Fired with energy, Darcy issued his own challenge, and the race was on—across fields, over fences, along hedgerows—their mounts eager and evenly matched. When hunger set in, they retraced their route towards the stables.

"Splendid excursion," cried Bingley as he dismounted. "My slugabed houseguests missed a perfect daybreak. Such idyllic surroundings are quite to my liking."

The horses were handed over to grooms for a respite while the two friends broke their fast. Bingley's lease included liberty of the manor, so he asked Darcy to help him understand his rights.

They rode out later in a more leisurely fashion. Attention was paid to areas where shooting would be best and, if Bingley decided to purchase the estate, where timber might be culled and sheep might graze.

"After this morning's exploration, I am tempted to make a purchase offer." Crossing into a large field bisected by a stone wall, they stopped to inspect the sunlit view. "What is your opinion?"

"Netherfield Park has a natural appeal, without artifice or contrivance. The manor is large enough to place you in a higher station and close enough to London to appease even Miss Bingley. However, I caution against haste in making any decision about— *Her* again!"

"Who? Where?" Bingley surveyed the countryside as Darcy stared at a lithe, young woman—followed by a gaggle of children—walking, arms extended for balance, atop the wall at the estate's boundary before jumping down a stile on the far side.

Darcy's gaze remained so intent on the merry little group he hardly heard Bingley's next words.

"Let us ride over there directly, shall we? I look forward to your thoughts."

Disregarding Darcy's protestations that introduction to an unkempt nursemaid was hardly necessary, Bingley trotted away.

Before Darcy could decide whether to follow, pounding

hoofs off to the left alerted him to another horseman's approach. Shading his eyes, he watched the skilled rider streak towards a coppice, seat bones barely touching the saddle. The nursemaid and her charges watched them clear the wall. The rider dismounted, tipped his hat, pitch-black hair shining in the sun, and made a deep, courtly obeisance before the woman.

"Caulifield," growled Darcy, urging his horse to a canter. After securing his gelding near the others, he followed the sweet sound of children's laughter. Ducking beneath branches of a stately beech, he entered a coppiced woodland of hazel and hornbeam amongst ash and oak standards. There he espied five children and two gentlemen, heads bent, eyes searching the ground for he knew not what. Then *she* came into sight, and the rhythm of his heart went awry upon recognising the face below the bonnet.

"Do it again, Mith Lithy," cried a little girl. "Do it again!"

As she stepped carefully through grass and undergrowth, gaze intent upon the ground, Miss Elizabeth laughed without inhibition. "We first have to find another one, Miranda."

Regular heartbeat restored, Darcy was pleased to discover the woman was none other than she of bright eyes and brilliant smile. The realisation he had not been beguiled by a nursery maid came as a relief, but with it came the unsettling intensification of attraction and the knowledge that he was, after all, intrigued by a lady beneath his touch. Was it his imagination, or had his ring's intaglio become heated? *I have gone mad as a hatter!* "May I be of assistance, Miss Elizabeth?"

Smiling brightly, she curtseyed to his bow and instructed the children to greet him properly. All he wanted was to hear her sweet laughter again.

"So, Darcy." Bingley stood upwind from the lady,

shooting his friend a pointed look. "I daresay you are surprised by our present company."

Tugging shirt cuffs below the sleeves of his rifle-green coat, Darcy forced himself from staring at the strangely alluring country miss. "Has something been lost?" *Other than my equanimity?*

"No, sir." She offered another smile. "We are on a hunt for ripened fungi. Puffballs, specifically. Your friends have kindly volunteered their services."

"Mith Lithy poked one with a thtick." The gap-toothed girl danced in place. "It burthted open and belched brown thmoke. Will you help me find one?" At Miss Elizabeth's prod, she sweetly added, "Pleath?"

"I would be delighted, and I happen to be a dab hand at finding puffballs."

Caulifield made another sweeping, chivalric bow. "Nay, allow me to be your knight in this quest, milady."

While Bingley leant idly against a tree, Darcy and Caulifield set about outdoing one another, bent on finding the plumpest, ripest puffballs for the children. When, at the same instant, both men came upon a particularly fat, brittle one, Caulifield elbowed Darcy out of the way. Chin lifted, shoulders back, he beckoned. "Here you are, Miss Elizabeth. I daresay a more perfect specimen of mature fungi could not be found."

Darcy's first instinct had been to shove back, to stake his claim. *Claim?* There was nothing to claim, and there was too much at stake even to consider it. And unlike Caulifield, he was too much the worldly-wise, cultured gentleman to stoop to such pushy behaviour.

Reaping the benefits of competition between their elders, the children took turns popping puffballs and exclaiming delight over each explosive release of spores. To Darcy, the eruption of the puffballs was nothing to the gratification of observing Miss Elizabeth's shape whenever she bent forwards. Cursing beneath his breath, he turned away, only to notice Caulifield, with a flourish, presenting her with a weedy bouquet of late-flowering autumn gentians. She seemed delighted, but Darcy was unimpressed. Were he wooing a lady, she would receive an expensive tussie-mussie from a florist rather than being handed some hastily plucked, uncultivated, spindly vegetation.

He tipped his hat to her, then, thrashing his riding whip at plant life in his path, strode towards the tree where his horse was tethered. At a tug on his coat-tails, he whirled round.

A wide-eyed boy yelped and stumbled backwards until Darcy caught him by the arm. "Beggin' yer pardon, sir!" Glancing at the whip in the gentleman's other hand, he struggled to break free.

"Steady, lad." Crouching to the youngster's level, Darcy spoke gently. "I was unaware I was being followed, and you gave me a start." Patting the child's shoulder, he released him and stood tall. "What is your name?"

"Ben, sir." Peering round Darcy's long legs, he pointed. "Is him yer horse?"

From the coppice, more frantic by the moment, Miss Elizabeth repeatedly called the boy's name. "He is here," shouted Darcy. "Ben is here by the big beech." He beckoned the child to approach the horses. "This beautiful-stepper is mine. His name is Aether, personification of the pure, upper air the gods breathe. The impressive black is Imperious, but Mr Bingley calls him Imp. Mr Caulifield owns Hengist, the dark bay roan over there." Watching the others draw near, he asked which horse Ben preferred.

"I like yers best."

"Smart lad. Would you like to ride him?" Nodding, Ben gaped at the tall horse. "Up you go, then." Darcy hoisted the beaming youngster upon Aether's back. "Hold tight to the pommel, the frontmost part, with both hands. Do not let go. Understand?"

"Aye, sir." The boy bounced in the saddle. "Gee! Gee!"

"Ben!" Miss Elizabeth stopped short of Aether.

Darcy assured her the boy was safe and the horse well-trained. After untying the lead rope, he led Aether to the field. Passing Caulifield, he said, "The lad likes Aether best." *How old am I, ten?* After a few short circuits, he halted the animal and, foot in the stirrup, thrust himself upwards. Swinging his right leg over Aether's back, he landed lightly behind Ben. The manoeuvre, if he did say so himself, was accomplished smoothly. Miss Elizabeth watched as they trotted past, and he hoped her scrutiny was in appreciation of his excellent seat rather than any unnecessary concern for the boy's welfare.

Abed that night, disgusted and berating himself for succumbing to puerile competitiveness, he settled into the mattress and into musings quite the opposite of childish.

Ben's cottage was the last stop on her way home to Longbourn. All the while, Elizabeth held his hand and listened with ill humour to the boy's endless gushing about the great Mr Darcy and the equally great Aether. Both man and beast were, she conceded, magnificent physical specimens. Too great for her liking—she had no use for such a majestic mount or such massive vainglory. *The man's swelled head would hardly fit through any regular-sized portal.* Overcome by a fit of laughter, she told her companion to pay her no mind. "I was imagining Mr Darcy's head stuck fast in one of Lucas Lodge's smallish doorways."

After giving Elizabeth an odd look, Ben freed his hand from hers, and they walked in silence the rest of the way to his father's cottage, where they parted.

Stooping to collect a few scattered pheasant feathers to add to her bouquet, Elizabeth pondered the three men with whom she and the children had shared the morning. *Such varied attentions!* She understood why Mr Darcy barely spared her a glance, but why he put on such a display for a handful of tenant children was beyond comprehension. Surprisingly, he might be a good father one day, but she pitied his poor wife.

Chapter 6

On the twenty-seventh of October, the Netherfield party attended what Sir William and his wife called a soirée. The gathering did qualify as such, Darcy supposed, for it was held at a private residence in the evening and included conversation and music. For him, however, the occasion was not so much a soirée as an ordeal. The lintels at Lucas Lodge were low, forcing him to duck through narrow doorways. Even more detrimental to his peace of mind, there was in attendance that most bewitching of creatures, Miss Elizabeth Bennet. She filled his vision and his thoughts in a highly compelling manner, distracting him from his host's scintillating babble.

Because country folk mingled in a confined, unvarying society, Darcy often had found himself in Miss Elizabeth's resplendent company. When she was not there, even a crowded room seemed empty. Radiant, witty, and fascinating, she held strong opinions and defended them with passion. Her physicality—twinkling eyes, irresistible smile, swaying hips, *and that blasted 'follow-me-lads' curl on her lovely nape*—aroused his senses, teasing him with promises of the unobtainable.

Of their own volition, his feet were drawn towards her. Skirting the young lady's periphery, he stole admiring glances, eavesdropped on her intelligent discourses, and admired her grace and liveliness.

Closing in on her once more, he stood in silent appreciation as she spoke to the commanding officer of the militia. Forcing his gaze upwards, away from the temptation of full lips uttering impertinence tempered by wit, Darcy was drawn in again, undone, by her dancing eyes. Lowering his gaze—and lingering a moment too long on her bodice—he knew not where next to fix his regard. *That freckled nose perhaps or—damn!—that amused, raised eyebrow aimed directly at me.*

"What say you, Mr Darcy?" Miss Elizabeth smiled as he flinched. "You must have heard me teasing Colonel Forster about his command of a scarlet tide spilling into Meryton, contrasting it to Napoleon's failure to take control of another Red Sea."

"Indeed, I did, madam." For the first time in years, the tips of Darcy's ears grew uncomfortably hot. Wanting to say more, he instead bowed and turned away, liking her but despising himself for it. Such a singular young woman might not outshine those of the *ton*, which had its share of handsome, intelligent, witty ladies, but she would sparkle amongst them.

His mind was full of improper thoughts—thoughts of her by his side as the next mistress of Pemberley, as his future children's mother. Improper, impossible thoughts.

Emulating a certain flower's propensity to vegetate against stone walls, Darcy leant an elbow on Sir William's chimneypiece. From that vantage point, he watched Miss Elizabeth flit like a butterfly from Colonel Forster to Caulifield. *By the look in his eye, I am not the only one thinking inappropriate thoughts of her.* Bingley, however, kept his distance from her and her sweet fragrance. Good friend that he was, he also tried to separate Darcy from her.

"See here, old man," he said, pulling Darcy into a corner. "You advised me against Miss Taylor, Miss Whitham, Miss Barker, and Miss Rimmer, claiming they were too lively, too light-hearted, too sharp-witted, or too erudite. Now you stand here admiring Miss Elizabeth Bennet for those very same qualities. Since when are exuberance, blitheness, or nimble-mindedness desirable traits in a lady?"

Darcy crossed his arms. "I find the combination refreshing."

"Refreshing? You want refreshing? Perhaps I should shove you into the Derwent's equivalent hereabouts. How would that be for refreshing? The cold water might bring you to your senses or at least allay your ardour."

Forehead wrinkling, Bingley gazed into the distance. "How deep do you suppose Longbourn's bourn is?"

"About as deep as your thoughts, I expect," muttered Darcy. His friend's attempts at dissuasion were, at best, half-hearted that night. Miss Oliverson had remained at Netherfield, indisposed, leaving Bingley susceptible to bewitchment by the eldest Bennet sister. One shy smile from her, and he was drawn to the siren's call, lured like an unwary sailor to the rocks. What else could come of an alliance with the Bennets but a shipwreck?

Swept along in Miss Elizabeth's wake as she moved towards her attention-seeking youngest sister, Darcy was accosted by Sir William, who spoke of a fondness for London's superior society. "If not for the odious air, I would have fixed my family there. Ah! My dear Miss Eliza," he called out, "why are not you dancing?" Nudging Darcy's arm, he suggested asking the young lady to dance. Darcy could not help but reach for the dainty hand being presented to him and make the request, but Miss Elizabeth drew back her hand and politely declined his offer.

For what perverse reason had the confounding creature denied herself the pleasure of standing up with him? *Any sensible man would now give her the go-by—as would I if I were not so intrigued by her pertness.* Undeniably nimble in body and mind, why did Miss Elizabeth not give a gentleman like him his due respect? Darcy walked away, thinking deep, deep thoughts of her until he was once again accosted by Bingley.

"The entire neighbourhood is crowded round Miss Bennet in an impregnable ring, which I liken to medieval walls encircling a town," he grumbled.

Darcy glanced over. There were but four people chatting with Miss Amesbury's twin.

"I should not be surprised if birds and woodland creatures start gathering round the angel to bask in her glow," Bingley continued. "And did I not hear a heavenly choir a while ago?"

"What you heard was Miss Elizabeth performing *Lavender's Blue* with inimitable sweetness, expression, and taste... adding to her appeal." She thereby met his father's prerequisite that Mrs Darcy be a skilful performer on the pianoforte as well as a polished songstress. It was a satisfying thought and far more gratifying than watching her exchange smiles and nods with Caulifield, who was at the punch bowl raising eyebrows and a glass at her. Darcy was pleased Miss Elizabeth returned quickly to her conversation with Miss Lucas, and he strode away from Bingley towards the two ladies.

"If intrusion upon your little tête-à-tête is not unwelcome, ladies, might I join you?"

"You are not intruding," Miss Lucas assured him.

Miss Elizabeth smiled sweetly. "We were speaking of the negus, sir."

"Ah. Well, did you know," said Darcy, thinking to impress her, "that in the last century, a Colonel Negus recommended adding water to the port during a heated debate between some Whigs and Tories? Apparently, the politicians were about to land themselves in, um, hot water." Miss Elizabeth's cool reception of his information prompted him to ask if he might fetch some of the warming drink for her and Miss Lucas.

"No need, Darcy." Caulifield appeared from behind, two cups of negus in hand. "The ladies' needs have been anticipated." While accepting their thanks, his eyes were fixed on the younger of the two. "Sugar and spice in tonight's wine are nothing to your own sweetness and zest, Miss Elizabeth."

Darcy's lip curled at the blandishment, a look that Caulifield did not miss. "What a peevish expression, old man, sourer than the lemons in the negus. One might think you ready to beat the pulp out of someone."

"Not at all, I assure you." Excusing himself, Darcy walked away. Espying an interesting arrangement on the far wall, he stopped to admire the grouping, finding it uncommonly pleasing amongst Lucas Lodge's humdrum trappings.

"Ah, Mr Darcy." Sir William stepped up beside him. "I see you appreciate the newest additions to our drawing room. Capital, are they not?"

The Chinese panels on either side of a gilt-framed mirror were agreeable, and Darcy said as much. However, what had captured his fancy was the reflection of Miss Elizabeth's pretty smile as she chatted with some local buffoon. As tempting as her lips were, such a dazzling display was as improper as his spying upon her. He snapped to attention as Sir William spoke the woman's name.

"Miss Elizabeth salvaged those lovely paper remnants from her relations' warehouse several months ago, had them framed, and presented the pair to my wife, knowing how well they would complement this room. She may deny having an artistic bent, but that girl does have an eye for such things."

Breaking into a cold sweat, Darcy heard his father's voice. 'The future Mrs Darcy should have a discerning eye and an ability to furnish and decorate with refinement.' *Blast it all! Why could the clever girl not have painted a hideosity upon Sir William's table as Miss Bingley did to Hurst's?*

Nearby, Miss Bingley whispered in Mrs Hurst's ear while aiming her fan at Miss Elizabeth. Darcy watched the object of his desire as she walked towards the sisters. "Miss Eliza," Miss Bingley called out. "I rather enjoyed hearing you sing *Lavender's Blue*. It is such a simple song, and your performance was reminiscent of my lessons with a London vocal master."

"Am I to understand, Miss Bingley, that your sojourn here has interrupted an ongoing schedule of rudimentary instruction?"

Darcy fought back a laugh at Miss Bingley's astonished expression. Miss Elizabeth had delivered her rejoinder with what seemed to be sweet commiseration, proving she could defend herself. *She is a mighty force of wit and intelligence and deserving of respect.* But much as he admired her, he could not afford to trust her with his heart—the price was too high. Long ago, he had vowed never again to place himself in a vulnerable position, and he feared she, with her charming smiles and tempting manner, might be seeking his favour for unscrupulous reasons.

The room became cramped, airless. Walls closed in. Breathing became a chore. He needed to get away from the noise and find a quiet place. To all appearances calm, Darcy strode across the room, down a narrow passage, and out of a back door. Pacing in a withered garden, he admitted to himself he was afraid of a young lady, some years his junior, without powerful connexions or influential fortune. His noble Fitzwilliam relations had considerable clout, but never had he feared them.

With the power to beckon him to degradation with one crook of her dainty finger, Miss Elizabeth was a real danger. Was she aware of her power? Did she use her appeal to trap him? Taking great gulps of the night air, he called himself every sort of fool. He was not unprincipled. Desire would be kept under regulation, and she would be kept at arm's length. He was in no peril.

Clutching his ring and ducking his head, he re-entered the drawing room, immediately forgetting any foolish resolution made under the stars. Engaged in a cosy tête-à-tête, Miss Elizabeth and Caulifield sat across from one another, close enough that their foreheads might touch if they each leant slightly forwards. Darcy looked upon her with a proprietary air, a primitive part of his brain screaming, *Mine!*

Two pairs of eyes widened at his approach.

"Good heavens, Darcy. Do you mean to frighten us with those flaring nostrils? Are you next to snort and paw the ground?"

No, but I shall take the bull by the horns. Darcy jerked his head sideways towards a vacant corner. "A word, Caulifield." He waited while Miss Elizabeth's unworthy admirer excused himself with a kiss of her hand. Once in relative privacy, Darcy rounded on him. "You, a confirmed bachelor in near penury, can have no honourable intentions concerning that young lady. She has no brother to protect her, only an indolent father. Desist."

"What concern is it of yours? You can have no honourable intentions in that quarter, either. You would never stoop so low. Now, let me be." Caulifield rammed his shoulder against Darcy's as he passed.

Fretting over who would keep Miss Elizabeth from harm, Darcy's heart whispered, *Me. I shall protect her.* Unable to act freely, he cursed the bounds holding him so tightly to duty and honour.

A moment later, he heard the youngest Bennet say, "Mary, what does the word indolent mean?"

Chapter 7

A lthough Darcy had experienced difficulty sleeping at Netherfield since the assembly, his valet had been ordered to wake him at daybreak. Following a hurried toilette, he put on the fresh clothing set out the night before. At his master's urging, Jonesby tied a simple cravat, helped him into boots and coats, and, at the door, handed him his hat, gloves, and whip as he eyed Darcy's unshaven jaw. "I bid you a good morning, sir, and hope, for your sake and my reputation, you are not met by anyone of consequence during your ride."

"Chance upon someone of consequence hereabouts and at this hour? And offended, are you, because I refused a more elaborate ablution and fancier knot? Jonesby, your pride, at times, can be insufferable."

Darcy told himself there was no ulterior motive for the early morning outing. He simply craved physical activity of one sort or another. After riding to an advantageous position near a stream, he sat atop Aether and waited. And waited. He glanced at his watch for the seventh time and was on the brink of resignation when he heard her sweet voice.

"Call up my maids, diddle, diddle, at four o'clock,
some to the wheel, diddle, diddle, some to the rock;

some to make hay, diddle, diddle, some to shear
corn..."

Holding his breath, he leant forwards in the saddle and anticipated the song's next line, something about the two of them keeping a bed warm. Instead of the desired lyrics, there came from behind him a yelp.

"Mr Darcy!"

Startled, he twisted his upper body round to meet Miss Elizabeth's wide eyes.

Previously Darcy had noticed the dominant colour of her irises changing to either green or brown depending on her clothing, surroundings, temperament, or the ambient light. Now, gazing at the flecks of warm honey in her eyes, he was transported to a mossy forest with sunlight flickering through leafy trees and evergreens. Bundled in a yellowish-brown pelisse and golden-hued bonnet, she curtseyed and smiled sweetly. Against the morning sun, she glowed like amber or...

"Honey. You look like—"

"I beg your pardon?" Miss Elizabeth stared at him in shock.

Searching his brain, Darcy wheeled his mount round. "Um...Hunting. You look as if you are hunting. That is, *I* was hunting...for...um..." *Words, apparently.* "Water?" The word came out as a croak.

Drawing himself up, he cleared his throat. "Pray, can you tell me where one might water a horse nearby? Aether, you see, has been worked into quite a lather this morning. The poor fellow is thirsty, I fear."

Clearly sceptical, Miss Elizabeth hesitated, tilting her head before she made her reply. "You have crossed the boundary onto Long*bourn* land, sir. Bourn, as in an insignificant stream. Did you not notice our winterbourne on your immediate left as you rode in this direction?"

"Ah, no. Um...Did the bourn dry up, perhaps, during the summer?" *Oh, for pity's sake, fool, dry up yourself!* Trickling water off to the side rushed and roared in Darcy's ears like the raging torrent of a cataract. He politely took leave and, for the sake of appearance, led Aether to the chalky bourn. The stubborn creature refused to drink.

A militia regiment, having made the nearby market town its winter headquarters, was responsible the next day for the absence from Longbourn of Elizabeth's mother and two silliest sisters. She wondered why Kitty and Lydia, for their own convenience, did not encamp in Meryton themselves for such was the frequency of their visits there in attempts to catch—at least sight of—red-coated officers. As her excuse for not joining them on their manoeuvres, Elizabeth had chosen to write overdue letters to her two aunts in London and to Miss Taylor.

Miss Helen Taylor, the young lady engaged to marry Michael Browne—the son of Mr Bennet's sister—had become a true friend while Elizabeth visited her aunt Browne in London, and they now kept up a steady correspondence. Dear Miss Taylor, she recalled, hailed from Derbyshire. *Does she know Mr Darcy and his friends? Perhaps she will know why the name Bingley had sounded so familiar to me. Dare I ask?*

At a quarter to one, the sound of a deep male voice in the hall roused her from pleasant employment and relative quiet. Her father was out on the estate somewhere with his bailiff. Jane had gone to Lucas Lodge to see Charlotte, and Mary was at the pianoforte in the sitting room, ponderously plunking its keys. Elizabeth's spirits fluttered at the idea of the caller being Mr Caulifield. That happy notion was somewhat granted when, at the drawing room's threshold, Mrs Hill announced, "Mrs Hurst, Miss Bingley, Mr Darcy, and Mr Caulifield to see you, miss."

The Bennets had met often with the Netherfield party, but never had Elizabeth, alone, played hostess to them. *Botheration!* One charming caller could not offset a quarter of an hour in company with a bad-mannered man and two supercilious silk stockings.

Once Mr Caulifield had kissed her hand and all were properly greeted and seated, Elizabeth noticed Mrs Hill lurking beyond the door, awaiting her orders. "We shall have tea, please, with the usual accompaniments." Forcing a smile as she assured herself the visit would last no longer than fifteen minutes, she turned to her guests, asking after the rest of the Netherfield party.

"Miss Oliverson remains at Netherfield." Rather than looking at Elizabeth, Miss Bingley seemingly spoke to the rather large spider making its way across the ceiling.

Mrs Hurst added, "Charles and my husband set out this morning to visit our second-cousin-once-removed at a local college...something to do with the East India Company."

"Oh, Hertford Heath," said Elizabeth. "Dubbed Haileybury, the college is where young gentlemen are trained to become overseas clerks in the John Company. Some of Cambridge and Oxford's most brilliant minds are employed there. My father met and became fast friends with its principal, Mr Henley, who shares his interest in philology and, particularly, Sanskrit." She would not look his way, but from the left, she sensed Mr Darcy's eyes upon her.

"And you, Eliza—do you speak foreign languages?" Miss Bingley stifled a yawn.

Such blatant ennui! Elizabeth watched as Miss Bingley turned, what seemed, a critical eye on a vase in which edges of autumn gentians had turned a seasonal brown. The room was otherwise clean and neat and not lacking showy but useless items. Nothing was out of place—save for the spider, dangling from a silk dragline above the plume on Miss Bingley's turban.

Climb back up! Climb back up! No, on second thought, do drop down. About three feet should suffice. Biting her lip and looking away, Elizabeth spotted a volume of Byron's works where she had left it the previous night. She cared little if her visitors took notice of it as she refused to be intimidated by anyone who might judge her by the authors she dared read. That observance was followed by the remembrance of her aunt Browne telling her of a Miss Rimmer in town whose unworthy suitor rejected her for reading too much. *Was his name Mr Bingley?*

She turned her gaze back to Miss Bingley. "I claim fluency in none but English and know only a smattering of French. *Et vous, Mademoiselle Bingley? Parlez-vous français?*" Just as Elizabeth's perfectly pronounced smattering of French had reached its rudimentary limit, a footman carried in a large tray with the tea service, seed cake, and sliced fruit. *Bless Mrs Hill's soul!*

Elizabeth thanked the servant and poured steaming cups of tea for her guests. Mr Caulifield preferred coffee, and with pride, she watched his eyes widen upon his first sip. "By George, this is, by far, the most flavourful, most aromatic coffee I ever have sampled. Miss Bennet, I must know the source from whence your family acquired such excellence."

"The beans arrived via the Thames from Africa, their

destination being the Gardiner-Browne Importorium in Cheapside, owned by my uncle Gardiner and my cousin, Mr Michael Browne."

Mr Darcy sputtered into his tea, then exclaimed, "Of course! You are related to Browne and are one of Mr Gardiner's famous nieces. I am sure Browne spoke of you several times, and my cousin Colonel Fitzwilliam mentioned…um…something…about you."

"Your cousin, a colonel whom I have never met, spoke to you about me?" Such information caused no small amount of alarmed curiosity.

"Um." Mr Darcy sat forwards. "Colonel Fitzwilliam and I saw you in company with your elder sister at the Importorium this past summer. Browne told us who you were."

Was she so noteworthy in her unworthiness that Mr Darcy found such a meeting memorable? Elizabeth's cup rattled against its saucer, in time with her quickened pulse.

"Really, man." Mr Caulifield glanced between them, evidently noting the heightened colour on her cheeks. "You have quite unsettled our hostess."

Another apology was offered, and Mr Darcy assured Elizabeth nothing uncomplimentary had been bandied about. Thereafter, his forehead alternately furrowed and relaxed as he stared at her, then gazed into space. "Pray tell," he said at length. "Does your family have any relations by the name Amesbury?"

Elizabeth informed him they did not. He looked away, retrieved a watch from his waistcoat's fob pocket, and fiddled with the chain. Gratified by his awkwardness, she made no protest when the punctilious gentleman flipped open the timepiece and announced it was time to take leave.

As they all stood, Mrs Hurst handed Elizabeth a note. "Please be so kind as to give this to your elder sister."

Catching the displeased look on Miss Bingley's face, Elizabeth silently snickered as the spider crept down the woman's jaunty ostrich plume. She rang the bell to have her guests shown out and, as the front door closed behind them, blew out her cheeks in a gusty exhale. Finally, she heard the anticipated scream. Dashing to the window, she espied Miss Bingley holding up her hems, stamping her foot, and peering at the ground. *Poor, poor spider!*

The next day, halfway along the beaten path between Lucas Lodge and Longbourn, Elizabeth continued her rant while Charlotte listened with increasing amusement.

"If disturbing my early morning constitutional the other day"—*with his oddly appealing stubble*—"was not bad enough, Mr Darcy came to Longbourn yesterday. Apparently, we were in the same place at the same time months ago in London, but I do not remember seeing him. By the by," she said, scarcely noticing Charlotte's confused expression, "he says he knows Mr Browne."

Wincing, Elizabeth squeezed her friend's hand, and they spoke of Charlotte's disappointed hopes in that quarter. "I cannot believe my cousin would befriend such a curmudgeon. And, if Mr Darcy despises our society so much, why does he keep turning up like the proverbial bad penny? He should stay away instead of spoiling things for others and discomposing me."

"So his rapt regard and long, lustful gazes unsettle you, do they?" Charlotte smirked at her.

Elizabeth replied quickly. "Did it ever occur to you his mind might simply be vacant while he stares?" She shook her head as her friend insisted the gentleman seemed intelligent if somewhat inept in company.

Finally, she had had enough of Charlotte's attempts to rationalise Mr Darcy's behaviour. "Tell me, how can a man of sense and education, who has lived in the world, be so inexperienced, so awkward?" Before her companion could reply, Elizabeth continued. "At any rate, he of the decrying eye thinks of me scornfully, a contempt comparable to mine for horrible garden slugs and their slimy trails."

"Mr Darcy seems neither slow nor slimy, though I would never describe him as lively."

"Does he not know staring is rude?" Drawing herself up, Elizabeth deepened her voice. "I was not *staring* at you, Miss Bennet, but looking *through* you. In truth, madam, you might as well be invisible. You are decent enough to be seen in public, I suppose, but you do not measure up to my standards of acceptability."

Her antics did not amuse Charlotte, who asserted, "A gentleman would never utter such disrespect or abuse. I stand by my opinion. He looks at you in admiration. You are both, I think, attracted to the other but will not admit it."

Could he be? Surely not! Elizabeth laughed in disbelief. "Mr Darcy beholds me with disgust. I am an odious aberration."

"Nay, a person turns away from repulsiveness. Fixed regard is reserved for agreeable aspects such as kittens, a sleeping babe, a painting, or awe-inspiring sunset." Charlotte gave Elizabeth a knowing look. "I liken the way Mr Darcy stares at you to the way Lydia gazes at the officers...or Mr Hurst a ragout. You look with wonder upon summer verdure or autumn foliage from Oakham Mount yet cannot abide the sight of the lacy, green eyesore your mother expects you to wear at the next assembly."

"Ah yes, the horror that oozed from the depths of her

closet." Elizabeth feigned a shudder. "She had it altered to fit me and bedizened it with even more frills and flounces until the ghastly creation foamed and frothed at the mouth. My father offered to fetch his gun and put the monstrosity out of its misery, but my mother made such a fuss that he let it be. But I shall not wear it. Can you imagine Mr Darcy's response should he see me in such a horror?"

"One patrician eyebrow might lift, I suppose, but his eyes would burn with rabid admiration."

"You are mad, my friend." Arm extended, palm upward, Elizabeth confirmed the onset of rain.

"Oh? I am not the one fretting about Mr Darcy's response to my apparel," Charlotte said as she adjusted her bonnet. "And you did not deny my earlier claim that you are attracted to him." Giving a shriek as the rain set upon them, she bid Elizabeth a hasty farewell before turning back towards Lucas Lodge.

Chapter 8

A fter dining with the militia officers in Meryton, Darcy thought the giggling, immature Mrs Forster was not only much like the youngest, silliest Bennet sister but an appallingly poor hostess. *Unlike Miss Elizabeth, who, at Longbourn, was perfection itself in that role.* One of the requirements on his list of wifely essentials had been insisted upon by his father. 'As mistress of Pemberley and of our leasehold in town, Mrs Darcy must plan discerning menus, be a consummate hostess, and entertain with panache'.

In a downpour, he, Bingley, Hurst, and Caulifield returned to Netherfield and learnt that in their absence, the eldest Bennet sister—having ridden three miles to dine with the ladies—had been caught in an earlier rainstorm, had taken ill, and was bedridden above stairs. He nearly groaned his discontent. Just what he needed—Miss Amesbury's twin there in the house. *What can she mean by venturing out in foul weather?*

The next morning, those at the breakfast table were entertained by Miss Bingley ranting about Netherfield's kitchen servants—her wrath brought on by one guest's inability to keep down her food and another's poor appetite.

"I am not hungry. No one below stairs is to blame," Darcy

assured them all. *The fault for my upset lies with someone three miles distant by the name of—*

"Miss Elizabeth Bennet," announced a footman.

Sporting dirty hems and stockings and with a complexion glowing from exercise, she appeared in the breakfast-parlour doorway, having come—*on foot, by God, and alone!*—to tend her sister. *Why, of all women in England, is this one bent on driving me to Bedlam?*

Miss Bingley greeted the visitor with a "Good heavens!" That warm welcome was seconded by Mrs Hurst's titter, Miss Oliverson's unladylike gasp of derision, and the scraping of chair legs as the men gained their feet. Only Bingley addressed the new arrival with good cheer, inviting her to join them at the table. Caulifield offered her the seat next to his, looking upon Miss Elizabeth in a way offensive to Darcy's sensibilities. She, however, declined and asked to be taken to her sister's bedside.

The gentlemen spent the day shooting. Although he and Caulifield shot nothing more than black looks and barbs at one another, Darcy joined the rest of the party in thanking the beaters, loaders, and dog handlers, and in paying the gamekeeper a gratuity.

Walking towards the manor and arranging for the two braces of pheasants he had bagged to be taken to the kitchens, Bingley—with Gaius trotting at his side—hastened to catch up with Darcy. "You aimed quite a taunt at poor Caulie earlier when you said he might as well have worn a blindfold."

"I spoke in jest. Had Caulifield worn a blindfold, he would not have known what he was missing." Darcy slowed his pace. "Speaking of misses, do you suppose the Bennet sisters have left by now?"

"I hope not. Miss Elizabeth might return to Longbourn, but Miss Bennet must remain."

Upon arrival at the house, the gentlemen learnt Miss Bennet, having taken a turn for the worse, had begged her sister to remain and that Miss Bingley, after some prodding from Mrs Hurst, had made the invitation. Two small trunks with the Bennet sisters' clothing and necessities had been requested and delivered from Longbourn, and Miss Elizabeth had been installed in the room next to her sister.

Splendid.

In his own guest chambers later that night, Darcy was plagued by wild imaginings. He dreamt of floundering about in unknown waters. Miss Elizabeth was a siren, drawing him to the rocks. Awakening with a start, he spent hours tossing and turning, half asleep, thoughts muddled. He lay in the tangled sheets, staring at the ceiling, lost in his musings. If she lured him astray, dragging him beneath the waves, he never again would be able to lift his head in the *ton*. But what if he wanted to drown under her power? At least he would die a happy man. *Take me down, Elizabeth.*

Upon entering the drawing room—much against her own inclinations—the following afternoon, Elizabeth found only the ladies present and was invited by Miss Bingley to join them in a card game and gossip, which she refused. "I shall content myself with a book."

"You may fetch something from the library, if you wish." Mrs Hurst pointed towards the next room.

Some books were stacked on a nearby table. "One of

these will suffice." Although she had read it before, Elizabeth selected *Love in Excess; or the Fatal Enquiry*.

"Oh, that is mine," said Mrs Hurst. "I have yet to make a start, so you are welcome to borrow it. Do you suppose the story is a good one?"

Elizabeth said she applauded Eliza Haywood's diverting plot.

Cards, idle gossip, and *Love in Excess*—all were forgotten once the gentlemen entered. Occupation became the pouring of tea and coffee and the serving of cake, flattery, and uniformly flawless accomplishments. Mrs Hurst played the harp while Miss Bingley and Miss Oliverson did their utmost, without open expression of affection, to win the esteem of their preferred gentleman. Such excessive fawning might have amused Elizabeth had she not become unsettled during Miss Bingley's performance of an Italian love song directed squarely at Mr Darcy. *Why does he look at me instead of at her?*

Mr Caulifield requested a lively song from the performer and asked Elizabeth, beside him on the sofa, to stand up for a reel. She declined. "Then, will you not grace us with a song? Your performance at Lucas Lodge was delightful."

"Thank you, but I would rather not do so in front of those in the habit of hearing only the best performers. The three ladies in your party are prodigiously talented. I recommend their performances over mine, lest some dissonant notes bombard your ears."

"How singular! Not only do you perform delightfully, but you are a paragon of charity and humility." Mr Caulifield leant forwards, shifting closer, uncomfortably so. "While your sister's illness is regrettable, I am grateful for your presence. In nursing her, you add patience, compassion, loyalty, and diligence to your other virtues."

When Elizabeth looked away, he asked whether compliments made her uneasy. *Your proximity makes me uneasy,* she thought, but gave no reply.

Sitting back, he let his hand brush hers. "Very well. For the time being, I shall leave your praises unsung."

"Mr Caulifield," cried Miss Bingley, "what did you say to cause such a bloom upon Eliza's face?"

"I spoke of her virtues."

"Virtue," said Mrs Hurst, "is a quality every young lady holds dear."

Eager to avoid further notice of her 'bloom', Elizabeth sat quietly, watching and listening.

Miss Oliverson glanced from Mr Caulifield to Mr Bingley, then lowered her lashes. "He meant good qualities when he spoke of virtues, Louisa. As for purity, though, you speak the truth." The lady reached within the folds of her gown, withdrew a handkerchief, and dabbed her nose. Crumpling the cloth into a ball, she spoke in hushed tones. "As Miss Mary Bennet and I discussed at the assembly, our reputations are no less brittle than they are beautiful. Loss of virtue is irretrievable, and a woman may suffer endless ruin." On the brink of tears, she stood. "You will excuse me, please. A sudden indisposition."

As Miss Oliverson crossed the room, the gentlemen scrambled to their feet. Once seated again, a tangible awkwardness overcame them all. The room went quiet, save for the fire's hissing and crackling. Elizabeth looked longingly at her book, sitting just beyond her reach, and wished to follow the lady.

It was the most taciturn person in the room who broke the silence. "Young ladies cannot be too much guarded in their behaviour. Unscrupulous men lurk in the shadows, waiting to swoop in and wreak havoc upon the unprotected, the innocent, the—" Mr Darcy stood. "You will excuse me. I am a letter in arrears to my sister." He bowed and, in passing the sofa, delivered a withering glare.

Turning to Elizabeth, Mr Caulifield asked what on earth had he done to deserve such a fierce look.

"That, no doubt, was meant for me, sir. I have been the recipient of Mr Darcy's mysterious stares these several weeks now."

"Fret not. Darcy is one of those brooding sorts, you know. It is, at times, difficult to interpret his stony visage." Mr Caulifield's palm came to rest over her fingers as he whispered, "Hopefully, my intentions are not as ambiguous. I would not have you misinterpret them."

A quarter of an hour later, reunited with her sister and speaking in undertones while a maid bustled about the room, Elizabeth related details of Mr Darcy's puzzling speech and Mr Caulifield's inappropriate behaviour. "Covering my bare fingers was bold, but my hands were folded on my lap at the time. He grazed my thigh, intentionally, I believe."

Jane made excuses for everyone's lapses, but Elizabeth was not so forgiving. "Mr Caulifield did not show proper respect, particularly in a room already filled with contempt for my presence. I was mortified. I do not usually blush, but I thought my face might burst into flames."

Remembering her sister's fever, Elizabeth put a hand to Jane's forehead, which was still warm but less worrisome. "It is evident Mr Bingley and Miss Oliverson have some sort of understanding, but I fear his attachment may not be constant. Clearly, he also admires you."

"I like him, Lizzy, but only as an amiable acquaintance, nothing more."

After administering a draught and stroking damp hair from Jane's brow, she helped settle her snugly beneath the bedclothes. Praying her sister might have a restful night, Elizabeth left her in the maid's care and slipped into her own room. Abed and in turmoil, she contemplated Mr Darcy's emotional speech. Could it be guilt over the loss of some young woman's virtue? *Poor Miss Bingley. Does she not at all understand his character?*

Chapter 9

On Friday evening, Caulifield again claimed a seat on the same sofa as Miss Elizabeth and said to her, "Shall we dance? You deserve some jollity after caring all day for your sister. Miss Bingley, will you not play a Scottish or Irish air? You there," he called to a footman, "move away these chairs and tables. Roll back the carpet so this lovely lady and I may dance a reel." Standing, chest thrust out, he extended an elbow to her.

"I shall not be staying long enough to go to such bother," Miss Elizabeth replied.

Pouring himself a drink, Darcy silently scoffed. Caulifield's actions reminded him of a vociferous rooster at the home farm—puffing out its feathers, strutting in a half circle, one wing extended, signifying his dominance to the hens in the yard. He was pleased by Miss Elizabeth's rebuff of the coxcomb.

Taking a chair near her, Darcy enquired, with genuine concern, after her sister's health.

Within moments, Miss Bingley interrupted with enquiries about Georgiana, which initiated a discussion of ladies' accomplishments.

When that topic was thoroughly covered, Darcy was gratified by Miss Elizabeth's unmistakable agreement with his expressed opinions.

"Now, sir," she said, "turnabout is fair play. What of a gentleman's accomplishments?"

Darcy basked overlong in her arch smile, and before he could reply, the loathsome Lothario beside her intruded upon the conversation.

"Do enlighten us, Miss Elizabeth," said Caulifield, "as to those abilities and qualities a lady expects."

Darcy scowled at him. "Yes, define a *true* gentleman for us, madam."

"Gladly, sirs. A gentleman is well-educated, well-dressed, and has impeccable manners."

Disappointed in that answer, Darcy leant forwards and noticed Miss Elizabeth's eyes were framed by dense lashes, the irises surrounded by pronounced black rings adding to her youthful beauty. "Surely you perceive more than the superficial."

"Indeed! A true gentleman must be honourable, striving always to do what is right. As a moral man, but not necessarily a pious one, he adheres to a high standard of proper behaviour. He is dependable and loyal. He protects not only his integrity but that of loved ones under his care. He respects tradition while being open-minded. A gentleman is amiable, charitable, attentive, and considerate. Confident without arrogance. He listens and learns and always tells the absolute truth."

"Faith!" Caulifield's eyes widened. "You expect a great deal."

"Are you so severe upon your own sex, sir," said Miss Elizabeth, "as to doubt the possibility of such a man?"

Across the room, Bingley scratched behind his greyhound's ears. "I never have met such a paragon as you describe. Even Darcy falls short."

Miss Bingley protested, "As the very definition of a gentleman, Mr Darcy personifies perfection and..."

"And so her fulsome praise goes on and on, *ad nauseam*," Darcy muttered under his breath. When Miss Elizabeth's eyebrows climbed towards her hairline, he added quietly, to her alone, "There goes any chance of my meeting your 'impeccable manners' criterion, but I do always tell the truth."

"Miss Elizabeth, I am afraid to ask," said Caulifield, "but, pray tell, have you anything else to add to your list of requisites?"

Giving Darcy a stern look, she replied, "A true gentleman gives women respect rather than insults. He asks ladies, particularly overlooked ones, to stand up with him. He is neither libertine nor laggard, and he never judges a book by its cover nor a person by appearance alone."

"And this exemplar of yours..." Darcy leant forwards. "Is he someone of your acquaintance?" *To our mutual regret, I cannot offer for you.*

"Alas, I have yet to meet an eligible exemplar. As far as I am concerned, he may be barrister, vicar, military officer, physician, or tradesman."

Darcy sat back, dissatisfied with any man in such a career as her husband.

Bingley cried, "Darcy, if you and Miss Elizabeth will desist in making me feel frightfully deficient, I shall be thankful. If you please, I should like to tackle that hunting rights enquiry letter once more."

Darcy complied but, by then, had become frustrated with his friend's needing so much of his time and advice. For two mornings in a row, Bingley had requested his assistance, thereby thwarting his plans for chancing upon one of Miss Elizabeth's walks. Bingley swore he was doing him a favour in trying to separate them, and Darcy knew he had his best interests in mind. *But how many times must he request my assistance with loathsome letters or infernal investments?*

Although he could not offer for her, Darcy would not idly sit by while Miss Elizabeth succumbed to another's seduction. Were he in a position to defend her honour, he would wave a velvet-lined mahogany chest beneath Caulifield's nose, demanding he choose a pistol. Accustomed to defeating all challengers, be it in business matters or at Tattersall's, Angelo's, or Jackson's, Darcy, as a gentleman ought, kept ignoble urges under control. But—even though Miss Elizabeth was not his to protect—some primordial part of his brain goaded him into chivalrous behaviour where she was concerned. Confronting Caulifield later that night, he again asked his intentions concerning her.

"My intentions are none of your concern, but I intend to proceed in a manner that will constitute my happiness. You and your moral righteousness can go to blazes."

Upon entering Miss Oliverson's bedchamber on Saturday, Elizabeth was met with a sour expression and sharp tone.

"Someone finally has come to determine whether or not I am still amongst the living. I had not expected to see you this morning, Miss Eliza. I suppose you feel some responsibility for my malady. After all, your sister brought illness into this house."

As Elizabeth understood it, Miss Oliverson had been ill off and on for a month complete. Smiling brightly whilst biting her tongue, she set a tray on the nearest table. "Having suffered no adverse effects while nursing Jane back to health, I am the logical candidate to do the same for you. It seems neither our hostess nor your particular friend, Mrs Hurst, are up to the task."

The patient feebly waved away the comment. "Louisa's maid has been attending me, but I have been desolate, suffering in isolation and silence. Be sure to tell Mr Bingley how poorly I am, how stoically I endure ill health. Tell him I do not complain even though I have the worst headache imaginable, on top of recurring nausea, exhaustion, and dizziness."

"Mr Bingley bade me to convey his best wishes for your speedy recovery." Bustling about, Elizabeth straightened the counterpane, adjusted the bolster, and plumped pillows. "Is your throat sore? That was Jane's primary complaint, along with fever and shivering fits."

"My throat is not sore. But I am so fatigued, I scarcely have the strength to speak of it."

"After my ministering, you must rest." Elizabeth poured soothing lavender water upon a soft cloth and dabbed the woman's brow. "If you had a fever, it has broken. I am happy to report your skin is cool to the touch." Setting aside the cloth, she gestured towards the tray. "Might I encourage you to drink some tea with honey and willow bark?" When Miss Oliverson nodded, Elizabeth helped her sit up. After one sip, the cup was pushed away, a portion of the brew splashing the eiderdown coverlet.

"Foul, nauseating concoction! I am queasy again. Fetch the maid. Quickly!"

Summoned by the bell-pull, Mrs Hurst's maid arrived in time to get a clean chamber-pot in place. Elizabeth held away Miss Oliverson's hair until the heaving subsided. Settling her against the pillows, she wiped her ashen face with the damp, scented cloth. "I shall have the maid fetch you some arrowroot and a cup of camomile tea with tansy. Or barley water?"

"I thank you, no." Improving by the minute, Miss Oliverson added, "But I fancy a plate of pickled anchovies on buttered rusks, if you please."

After dinner, while Mr Bingley's sisters retired to the drawing room, Elizabeth dashed upstairs to ascertain whether the two patients were well enough to join the others. They were, and she attended them downstairs to ensure they were protected from cold.

The gentlemen had returned to the ladies, and the entire party welcomed Miss Oliverson and Jane with professions of delight. With amusement, Elizabeth observed the room's occupants.

Inattentive to all but his recuperating guests, Mr Bingley ordered logs be piled on the grate. The two blonde convalescents were moved to chairs on one side of the hearth, then the other, then back again. After fussing with the fire, he sat with one knee bouncing while the other was held in place by Gaius's chin. Rubbing a palm down his thigh, he stilled his jerky leg and addressed the room in a carrying tone. "I am glad everyone is in good health at present, for I have been contemplating a grand notion. It is my understanding that while Mr Standish was in residence, an annual ball was held at Netherfield every November. What do you think of my giving one?"

Divided in their eagerness for such an event, all sat in momentary silence. Speechless, Miss Oliverson had, in fact, nodded off. Likewise in a drowse, Mr Hurst voiced neither aye nor nay. His wife's vote was delayed until her sister's was given, but, as Elizabeth observed, Miss Bingley postponed her opinion in anticipation of Mr Darcy's. She waited in vain; the man remained silent. Jane, fatigued from illness and from being shifted about, had little energy for any thought of dancing as she drooped by the stifling fire. Elizabeth and Mr Caulifield alone were agreeable enough for Mr Bingley to proceed with his scheme. He quickly excused himself to speak of it to his housekeeper.

The three healthy ladies provided musical entertainment while cards were played, books read, needlework attempted, and letters written. While Mr Caulifield and Mr Darcy attended to the latter activity at separate ends of a large table, their scribbling aroused Miss Bingley's interest. Wandering over, she asked to whom they secretly wrote.

Mr Darcy replied, "My correspondence is confidential, madam."

"As is mine." Hunched over his own page, Mr Caulifield covered it with a blank sheet.

Elizabeth smirked behind the pages of her book.

On Sunday morning after church, not inclined to follow in the footsteps of Mrs Hurst and Miss Bingley as they strolled along the shrubbery arm in arm with Mr Darcy, Elizabeth rejoiced that she and Jane might soon be at Longbourn. Mr Caulifield's appeal had waned. Mr Darcy had never had any— apart from handsome features…and athleticism…and intelligence…and a way with children…and concern about Jane. *Good heavens! The man does have some redeeming qualities.*

In the drawing room, she settled at the large table to answer her aunt Browne's last letter. Rummaging about, she snatched a few sheets of paper from the drawer and jabbed a pen into the ink pot. Having soon filled an entire page, she turned it over and discovered the sheet beneath had already been written upon in a masculine hand. Without the conscious intention of doing so, she read the unfinished note.

Dear lady,

As I write this, in the clutches of ardour, desiring you most fervently, another, far less desirable, hovers over my shoulder. I wish you were so near that I might cover you with passionate kisses. Knowing you again sleep under the same roof is sweet temptation, and

Elizabeth gasped. Was it meant for her? Was that what Mr Caulifield so secretly wrote last night? Outraged, she tossed the atrocity back into the drawer from whence it came. Wild to escape the *billet-doux*'s author, she sent a note to Longbourn pleading the carriage be sent over directly. Mrs Bennet replied she was not in favour of Jane's quitting Netherfield before securing her place as its mistress. Exasperated by her mother's scheming, Elizabeth fled to Jane's room and urged her sister to beg the use of Mr Bingley's carriage. The request elicited professions of concern and the gentleman's insistence that their departure be deferred until Monday morning.

At dinner, Elizabeth sat far removed from Mr Caulifield, refusing to meet his questioning eyes. Excusing herself soon afterwards, she retired early, turned the key in her bedchamber's lock, shoved her trunk against the door, and slept fitfully until dawn.

Chapter 10

Other than an indifferent greeting of 'Good morning', Darcy, for his own sanity, treated Miss Elizabeth with studied neglect. While the others were engaged elsewhere, he fetched from his room a satchel of correspondence and the book he had started. Slipping into the library, hoping to read in peace or attend to business, he found no patience for *Madoc*. Tossing the tedious poem upon a table, he extracted the sealed letters and an unidentified sheaf of papers from his bag. Glancing through the pages, he found his catalogue of wifely essentials.

Skipping over his own stringent specifications, he read through his parents' advice before chuckling at the late Sir Lewis de Bourgh's recommendation to 'marry a modest, amiable, malleable woman who in no way resembles Lady Catherine'. *The eldest Miss Bennet might have met Sir Lewis's approval but not mine.* Through no fault of her own but because of her strong resemblance to the woman who had so grievously disappointed him, Miss Jane Bennet was Darcy's personal bugbear.

She is nothing compared to her younger sister. But it mattered not, for he could never endure a connexion to such a family.

He wondered whether Miss Elizabeth might consider severing her Bennet bonds but thought it unlikely. She seemed rather attached to them. Of course, that was one of the reasons he so admired her: she had a generous, forgiving nature. But his superior sagacity would prevail, and he would choose the future Mrs Darcy with calm rationality, not rash stupidity.

His great uncle, the judge, had recommended his nephew choose a bride who enjoyed a bit of banter. *Banter? No, no, no! Such a misalliance would be sheer madness on my part.*

The crumpled pages in his hand were cursed and glared at for spelling out his duty to Georgiana as well as the Darcy name. Smoothing the papers, he wondered why one woman, one worthy of his regard, could not embody all his ideals.

Then *she* walked in.

Stupefied into an uncharacteristic fluster, he stashed the list behind the cushion on his chair. Scrambling to his feet, he bowed and waited while Miss Elizabeth picked up a book, smiled at him, and perched on the armchair across from him.

Sitting and opening his own dull book, Darcy studiously paid her no attention until his gaze, of its own volition, drifted across the divide. *Why must you sit there, directly in my line of sight? Take your blasted book closer to the window. The light is better over there. Leave me in peace, woman.* She was, at once, too close for comfort yet much too distant.

Bending his head towards the page, he recoiled. Nothing there made sense. *Gadzooks. This rubbish is not Robert Southey's poem. What is this rot?* Peering at the title—*Love in Excess; or the Fatal Enquiry*—Darcy sucked in a breath. An unwelcome flush spread over his ears. A taint of disgust prickled his fingers. A furtive glance around the room provided no insight into the location of volume one of the prolix poem through which he had been labouring. *Blast! I cannot be caught with this...this... romantic twaddle.*

Miss Elizabeth looked his way, smiling, but he could not

return the gesture. Nestling into the comfortable armchair, she resumed reading.

Never before had Darcy envied a piece of furniture. While she settled into the thick cushions, he imagined her snuggled on his lap, enfolded in his arms. Taking a deep breath, he inhaled her sweet scent, wondering where on her body she had applied it. But what were her arts and allurements to— skimming through the book, he mentally groaned—the amorous escapades of the rakish Count D'Elmont?

How could she sit there so peaceably while he was in torment? Did her heart not race? Were her palms not clammy? Did her lips, fingers, and other body parts not itch to perform illicit acts? Chancing another look, he gaped as she wetted a finger, dragged it over her bottom lip, across the page, and, magically, down his spine. *Sorceress!*

Slipping a finger between his Adam's apple and his cravat's intricate knot, he tugged ineffectively. *Stupid anfractuous garrotte! And these close-fitting breeches…Well, never you mind my inexpressibles, Miss Elizabeth Bennet.* Forcing himself to not squirm, he glanced at her progress. How did she manage to read in his presence with no apparent difficulty in focusing?

She turned another leaf, eyes glued to the page. What did she mean by taking no notice of him? Or was she pretending? As she feigned being unaffected by his presence, Darcy vowed he would retaliate. Turning a bunch of pages together so it appeared some advancement had been made through the story, Darcy skimmed a few random paragraphs. *Good Lord, Georgiana never, ever, will be allowed access to such a novel.*

Miss Elizabeth emitted a long, deep, audible sigh. He looked up to see her twiddling the pendant suspended from a delicate chain round her neck. *Cease drawing attention to yourself in that provocative manner!* Heart thumping, he averted his eyes. Turning a few more pages together, he came across the section where the count decides to marry not only for wealth and standing but love. *Love!*

Miss Elizabeth looked at him, closed her book, and placed it on the table next to her chair.

Why was she closing her book? Darcy took a sharp breath. *That is my book!* She had been sitting there, all that time, contentedly reading *Madoc* while *he* pretended to read romantic rot. *Wait! You are not leaving, are you? Now I must stand, exposing myself to ridicule.* Gaining his feet, Darcy offered a slight bow, using the book as a shield.

Glancing at the title, she quirked an eyebrow. "I would not have thought you a devotee of amatory fiction, sir. Do you champion the declaration of female affection? Or do you believe ladies should remain forever silent on the subject?"

Dear Lord, how does one answer such a fatal enquiry? Feigning a cool hauteur he did not feel, Darcy blurted the truth. "This, madam, is not my book."

"Yes, I know," said she, smirking. "It belongs to Mrs Hurst. Nevertheless, you have conscientiously adhered to it for half an hour, so I shall leave you to continue in peace. Good day, Mr Darcy."

He fell heavily into his chair, devouring the fragrant traces left in her wake. Tossing the mawkish novel aside, he snatched up *Madoc* and strode with great dignity out of the library, congratulating himself on having given a convincing portrayal of a sentimental noddy devoted to romantic rot. *Splendid performance. Bravo!*

Stopping short in the hall, he frowned at the niggling notion he had forgotten something important. Ah, yes. He should summon a footman to open the library windows. He doubted Bingley would set foot in there, but, if it could be helped, the poor fellow should not be exposed to lavender's aroma. *That sweet scent wreaks havoc on more than a man's nasal passages.*

Half an hour later, Elizabeth returned to the library, which, she discovered, was being aired. Window sashes had been lifted, floor-length dimity curtains billowed inwards, and there was an uncomfortable chill in the room. She fetched *Love in Excess; or the Fatal Enquiry* to return to Mrs Hurst. As she turned to leave, her eye caught a stash of papers protruding above a cushion, edges fluttering in a current of air.

Intending only to prevent the documents from taking flight like autumn leaves in an eddy, she gathered them up and glanced at the first page. Curiosity aroused, she sat and skimmed through the entirety. Her hand clamped over her mouth, Elizabeth stifled a series of laughs and expressions of outrage. Thinking the list's absurdity begged to be shared, she rushed to her sister's room.

"Please, stop!" Jane's laughter triggered a coughing fit.

Undeterred, Elizabeth imitated Mr Darcy's deep, cultured articulation as she read his handwriting. "'Neither gaunt nor excessively plump but of an alluringly rounded, symmetrical form.'"

Her sister's laughing and coughing put a stop to the parody. "Oh, Jane, forgive me. Far be it from me to cause your throat further discomfort by such an atrocious impersonation." She lowered her voice and puckishly continued. "Gaunt, however, aptly describes the elegantly angular Miss Bingley. At the dinner table last night, instead of devouring Mr Darcy with her sheep's eyes, she should have been attentive to the mutton in front of her. She could use a bit of meat on her bones."

"For shame, Lizzy, and you should be ashamed for absconding with that ridiculous list." Looking round the room for the last of her possessions, Jane stopped in front of her sister, snatching at the crumpled pages. "We must return it before we leave."

"No." Backing away, giggling, Elizabeth held the papers aloft. "This is a valuable document. Fortune-hunting women intent on discovering the mysterious qualities Mr Darcy seeks in a spouse would pay dearly for such intelligence. That a preference for Constable over Turner earns a mark against them is vital information, is it not?"

"Lizzy, you must know the maids have been whispering about Mr Darcy's evident admiration of you and Miss Bingley's jealousy."

"Were you delirious with fever when you heard them?" Elizabeth rolled her eyes. "Even if he desired my company, the notion of Mr Darcy paying addresses to anyone hereabouts is beyond belief. He is too fastidious. Too haughty for Hertfordshire. Such a man could have any woman of the fashionable world, and he knows it." *And I never told you, but he called me an unkempt, unattractive milkmaid not worth his bother.*

Jane shook her head. "He is just a gentleman, and you are a gentleman's daughter. You are equals."

"Hardly equals. His grandfather was an earl."

"Lizzy—"

"I did not read to you the most horrid criteria on Mr Darcy's list, but, according to a Viscount Winster, wives must look the other way while their husbands conduct adulterous affairs."

At Jane's gasp, Elizabeth went on. "At any rate, Mr Darcy's unfortunate wife will not be me. I hold myself to higher standards. According to this"—she shook the papers —"he must marry a peeress or an heiress. The lowly Bennets have neither titles nor wealthy relations, other than the well-to-do Brownes and prosperous Gardiners, so there can be no largesse expected to come my way."

"Return the list."

"I shall, but for now I am protecting it"—Elizabeth reached for the door handle—"from shameless, unscrupulous eyes." Yanking open the door, she yelped as their red-faced hostess rose from the sort of crouch one might assume while putting one's ear against a keyhole.

Involved in a methodical search, Darcy probed the library's every surface.

That the Bennet sisters had vacated the premises was welcome intelligence. He had lived under the same roof as Miss Elizabeth longer than was healthy, and his admiration had only deepened. While the so-called ladies there had treated her with incivility, she had handled them with grace, sweetness, and tact. She even cared for Miss Oliverson when no one else could be bothered. *And—hurrah!—she now seems wary of Caulifield's advances. Miss Elizabeth Bennet might not be perfect, but she is perfect for me...and so utterly, utterly unsuitable.*

His hunt became more frantic. No nook nor cranny was neglected in his search, including looking thrice behind a particular cushion. *Blast! I must be mistaken about the last place I had the deuced document.* It was Miss Elizabeth's fault. The confounding woman put him in a dither.

At dinner, he asked whether anyone had come across a sheaf of handwritten papers belonging to him, half dreading, half hoping someone had. When Bingley asked when last he had seen it, Darcy replied, "This morning."

"What a coincidence, sir," said Miss Bingley. "Your list's disappearance coincides with the Bennet sisters' departure."

"I did not say it was a list, Miss Bingley." *Does she have it herself?* Having lost his appetite, Darcy excused himself from the table.

Chapter 11

Almost immediately upon arriving at Longbourn, Elizabeth questioned why she had been so keen on returning there. Even before entering the house, they had been assailed by her mother crying, "Jane! Jane! How could you have caught a cold instead of a husband? And you, Miss Lizzy, what good came of your traipsing over there?"

"Mama," said Jane, "I could not have coped at Netherfield without Lizzy's loving care."

Mary stepped up, gave Elizabeth a perfunctory hug, and recited, "For I was hungry, and you gave me food. I was thirsty, and you gave me drink. I was sick, and you visited me—"

"Speaking, as you were, Mary, of providing sustenance and being visited," said Mr Bennet, tapping a thick missive against his thigh as he stood in front of the fireplace. "Our own houseguest arrives tomorrow at about four o'clock and will remain, uninvited, for a week complete. He is a clergy-man, Longbourn's heir presumptive, the distant cousin who may oust you from here the moment I am put to bed with a shovel." He held up the letter. "However, Mr Collins makes mention of—amongst many, many other words—an olive branch."

Eager to escape the cacophony of complaints, prognostications, and flutterings that followed such an announcement, Elizabeth slipped upstairs to her chambers.

When Mr Collins arrived the following day, he was found to be in his mid-twenties, heavy, sycophantic, and—with nary a word of sense—able to talk the hind legs off a donkey. One might think his praise, as a clergyman, should have been for one even higher than his patroness, the exalted Lady Catherine de Bourgh of Rosings Park. But it was upon that grand lady's recommendation he had come to Longbourn seeking a wife.

In Mr Collins's favour was a pliability in dissuasion from the lofty goal of attaining Mrs Bennet's eldest, most beautiful daughter as his helpmate. As equally effortless was the subsequent task of persuading him to lower his sights and settle for her next daughter in birth and beauty. Then, most unfortunately for Elizabeth, all the cloying attention expected from an inept suitor was duly paid to her.

Hoping for sanctuary in her father's book-room, she instead found sarcasm. "Reluctant as I am to see you espoused to a fool, who else of your sisters could so ably manage both Longbourn and Mr Collins? Clever girl that you are, you may spend an entire lifetime making sport of your spouse without his ever knowing it. Think of it, Lizzy," Mr Bennet said in a mocking tone. "Every day, filled with diversion. Every day, bound to a mate with whom you have nothing in common except a surname, a place of residence, and offspring."

Elizabeth bit down hard on her lip and her anger, stifling what she truly wanted to say. "I could not accept your cousin. I am a selfish creature and"—*like you*—"think only of my own comfort and happiness. I want a husband I can love and respect and have his love and respect in return."

Mr Bennet's eyes lost their twinkle. "I have more on my mind than silly, romantic dreams, child." Picking up Thomas Paine's *The Rights of Man*, he dismissed her with a jerk of his head.

Elizabeth turned on her heel, silently closing the door but wanting to hear a satisfying slam and a rattling window or two.

The next day after breakfast, insensible of Elizabeth's thoughts and her father's thinly-veiled set downs, Mr Collins accepted Mr Bennet's recommendation that he accompany his cousins to Meryton.

Along with Jane, Kitty, and Lydia, Elizabeth set out with her unctuous relation, gratified the better part of his attention and censure was directed at her younger sisters. Overly preoccupied with militia officers, the two girls progressed from discussing the men's comings and goings to the admiration of their red coats and how they might look in shirt-sleeves. When they began talking about their calves, Mr Collins put his foot down. His admonishment to cease the wickedness came a second before Elizabeth opened her mouth to state her preference for long, muscular thighs encased in buff breeches above tall boots. Unable to help herself, she glanced at the cleric's black-clad, spindly legs and grimaced. Mr Darcy's, on the other hand, could not be criticised. Mortified by such thoughts, she feared Lydia was not the only Bennet girl with high animal spirits. In some ways, she was more like her mother and youngest sister than she cared to admit.

Giggling and disregarding all tut-tuts of disapproval, Kitty and Lydia hied off at Meryton's thoroughfare in quest of, they claimed, smart bonnets or new muslin. Elizabeth suspected they were browsing for good-looking members of the opposite sex. *And one need not look far!* For there, on the other side of the street, standing beside Mr Denny and chatting with her coquettish sisters, was a magnificent specimen of male beauty.

When Elizabeth, Jane, and Mr Collins joined them, whatever the attractive stranger had been saying to Lydia was cut off mid-sentence. Ashen-faced and wide-eyed, he stared at Jane as though seeing a ghost and whispered a feminine name. Mr Denny made the necessary correction and introductions, and his friend appeared relieved to have not encountered someone named 'Miss Amesbury'.

Some memory of hearing that surname caught Elizabeth's attention, but her ear was soon turned to learning more about her new acquaintance.

Having recently accepted a lieutenancy in the corps, Mr Wickham had yet to wear regimentals, a deficiency mitigated by his having not only a matchless appearance but a cheerful readiness for conversation. Elizabeth could not tear her eyes from him until his countenance again lost colour. Following his startled gaze, she saw two riders approaching: Mr Bingley and Mr Darcy.

While Mr Bingley enquired after Jane's health, Mr Darcy sat upon his horse, glaring at Mr Wickham. The latter touched his hat, but the other refused to return the gesture. It was impossible for Elizabeth to imagine the meaning of it all and impossible not to be intrigued.

The two Netherfield gentlemen rode away, and the others chatted awhile. Then, with a panting, wheezing cleric trailing behind, Mr Denny and Mr Wickham accompanied the Bennet sisters as far as their aunt and uncle's door. Mrs Philips opened the parlour window and, to Jane and Elizabeth's mortification, leant out and invited everyone inside, including the deceased in St Mary's graveyard, a half mile distant. The handsome men—a collective that did not include Mr Collins—had to decline, and so took their leave. Waving her handkerchief after the young men, Mrs Philips informed her nieces that the militia officers were to dine with her husband the next evening. The Bennets and their house-guest were to join the party later for cards and supper.

⌒

For the third time in his life, Darcy had come close to slaying someone—albeit, in each instance, it had been the same low-life ne'er-do-well. The surprise of seeing Wickham so soon after Ramsgate had thrown him into a fury. Initially, he thought he was seeing Miss Amesbury and the debaucher together again, but, on closer inspection, the woman had been Miss Jane Bennet. What had further infuriated him was the sight of Wickham with Miss Elizabeth; it immediately made him fear a repeat of the betrayal at Riverswood.

All that worthless, currish, sneaking scoundrel ever does is take from me. Well, not this time! Feet out of stirrups in a trice, gripped by violent revulsion to an immediate threat, he had been set to attack and wrap his hands round Wickham's worthless neck. Then, within a maniacal tempest of hatred and jealousy, time had slowed, and clearer thought prevailed, reminding him that should he throttle the rat and be sentenced himself to capital punishment, Georgiana would be left under the guardianship of an unmarried army officer. *So, once again, the louse escapes retribution.* Remaining in Wick-ham's presence, though, had been beyond endurance. He turned away before rage changed his mind.

There had been no opportunity for him to privately confront Miss Amesbury or Wickham after leaving the folly at Riverswood, and for four years, Darcy had subdued his anger over their betrayal. As his father had told him, he could not be ruled by emotion. But what was he to do with those emotions if he could not seek satisfactory retribution? *I may not allow such feelings to rule me, but—Blast!—I cannot help having them.*

At Netherfield, his entire body still shook, his jaws and head ached from grinding his molars, and he kept reminding himself to unclench his fists. Like a caged animal, he paced the bedchamber.

What business has Wickham in Meryton? Maligning the Darcy name? Extortion? Georgiana must be protected and her reputation preserved, but that scheming pustule shall receive no further funding from our coffers. How dare he come here and endanger another I hold dear.

Stopped in his tracks, Darcy bowed his head. He did hold her dear. Miss Elizabeth was no passing fancy or trifling desire of the flesh; he cared deeply about her welfare. He prayed Wickham's good looks and glib words would not turn her head. Unlike Georgiana, she possessed a maturity beyond her years. He did not know Miss Elizabeth's actual age, but everything about her, save an atrocious family and a dearth of prerequisites, enticed him. She radiated an exuberant enjoyment of life, and he wanted her in his.

If he offered for her, in variance with his family's strictures, could he endure gaining Mrs Maguire's near twin as his sister? Most importantly, could he trust Miss Elizabeth with his heart? It was with ease that he realised he could do so. *I finally can trust a member of the fairer sex, and I need not fear loving again. Never would she disappoint me.* His heart felt lighter. All would be well.

Chapter 12

At the Philipses' home, while Mr Collins entertained his hostess with comparisons of her humble abode to the grandeur of Rosings Park, others enjoyed a noisy game of lottery tickets and a bit of hot supper with the officers.

Mr Wickham spoke eloquently and at length to Elizabeth about his pleasure in being encamped in Meryton, his accord with the local populace, and his occupation.

"We are here for training, but we also would be your defence against a threat of civil disturbance." Sliding closer on the sofa, he leant in, lowering his voice. "To that end, it is my duty to warn you of a menace lurking within your populace."

"A menace, sir?" She accepted a warm cup of negus from her aunt's maid, inhaling the spicy aroma before taking a sip.

Lydia's raucous laughter rang out above the hubbub, diverting Mr Wickham until he schooled his expression into one more appropriate for the subject. "There is a person, recently arrived hereabouts, who is not as he seems. I know him well, for we both hail from the same estate in the north, Pemberley."

"I know of whom you speak. Although not liked hereabouts, he seems harmless enough…unless arrogance can be regarded as menace rather than folly."

"I am too much a gentleman to divulge private information or defame a well-respected Derbyshire name," he assured her before lowering his voice as if to exchange a confidence. "But you must be wary round him. He preys upon comely young ladies…like yourself, if I may be so bold. He has left behind more than one broken heart and worse. Innocent, naïve maidens have thrown themselves into his power, only to be abandoned, disgraced, and forced to leave their families."

"A rake in our midst!" While her eyes sought out the location of each of her sisters, Elizabeth weighed his words. Turning back, she caught a smirk on Mr Wickham's face, a leer almost, before a blank, inscrutable expression replaced it.

"It is a delicious, devious game to him, acting the proper gentleman, all the while scheming wicked seductions. Everything he does is for personal indulgence or gain, even for his future wife. I know for a certainty he will wed only a wealthy woman." Sitting back, he crossed one leg over the other. "Did you know Darcy is destined for a union with his cousin, Miss Anne de Bourgh of Rosings Park? 'Tis true. Your cousin can confirm it. Their two great estates must stay in the family, you see. But to a debaucher, marriage is no detriment. In Darcy's circle, it is common practice for married men to take mistresses."

"Such behaviour, such unfaithfulness is reprehensible to me," Elizabeth managed to reply. *As is your speaking of it.* The unseemly subject matter made her skin crawl. How could he speak of such sordidness without showing disgust, anger, or embarrassment? *Your expression, sir, seems practised.*

"Of course, loose morals are often inherent in such families." Mr Wickham leant in again, whispering. "Just this past summer, Darcy's own sister, then but fifteen, consented to an elopement."

Elizabeth gasped. "She and her young man must have been deeply in love."

"Even in your innocence, Miss Elizabeth, you must realise one's actions may be fuelled by an appetite for pleasures of the flesh, for power, money, or revenge. If you doubt my judgment of the man's character, ask him whether he knows a Mrs Younge—an unprincipled woman from his past who runs a certain sort of house in London. The look on his face, I assure you, will be priceless." Mr Wickham bent his head closer to hers. "Then there are the unfortunate Derbyshire girls cast off by their parents when discovered with child. Ask Darcy whether he spent a se'nnight at Miss Amesbury's country house years ago and whether she was sent away months later, never to return. Fallen women are often set up with lonely tenant farmers or military men willing to accept another man's—" He rubbed a hand across his mouth. "I beg your pardon. For some reason, I feel I could tell you *anything*." And he went on to tell an abominable story of his ill treatment at the hands of Fitzwilliam Darcy.

"I had not thought him so bad as all that," Elizabeth said when he finished the overlong tale. "To descend to such malicious revenge, such injustice, such inhumanity! I am appalled." She was exceedingly appalled. It had been beyond the pale for Mr Wickham to speak such grievances to her. They had met just the day prior, for heaven's sake. She may have sketched a rosy portrait of his character then, but that night's offensive words painted an entirely different picture. Granted, there might have been some truth to his tale, but she suspected he had concealed far more than he revealed.

Were she less intuitive, she might have heard only what he wanted her to hear.

Elizabeth remembered telling Mr Darcy a person should never be judged by appearance alone. So, what had she done? She had deemed Mr Wickham the most handsome, the most open and appealing man she had ever met. His countenance, she had assumed, vouched for his honesty. *Stupid, green girl!* Studying his face, she perceived a trace of duplicity lurking behind his flawless outward appearance, and her breath caught.

"Never fear, Miss Elizabeth," said he. "I pledge myself as protector should you or your sisters ever find yourself in need. Think of me as an honourable knight, come to defend your family and friends."

After thanking him for his gallantry, Elizabeth went away with her head full of him. So full, she might be sick. He had played her as skilfully as Mrs Hurst played the harp, stroking her vanity, plucking her heartstrings, and she had allowed him to harp on one string all evening.

Abed later, she contemplated the conundrum of Mr Wickham and Mr Darcy. Could both men be bad? *Not according to dear Jane, of course.* Before succumbing to sleep, Elizabeth decided they would remain guilty until proved innocent.

At Longbourn on Thursday, Mrs Bennet, Kitty, and Lydia were carried away by transports of delight when a personal invitation to Tuesday night's ball at Netherfield was revealed as the reason for a visit from Miss Bingley and her brother.

"I hope such an imminent date is not terribly inconvenient," said Mr Bingley.

"Of course it is, Brother. Five days cannot allow for the creation of six appropriate gowns. Besides, I doubt Meryton's seamstress is capable of creating full-dress gowns at the best of times." Next to Jane, seated beside Elizabeth on the sofa, Miss Bingley leant in, lowering her voice while her brother spoke to the others. "Charles is so unthinking. Terribly flighty and frivolous. But Miss Oliverson, in all likelihood, will be the one to contend with such impetuousness. You, dear Jane, need not concern yourself. After all, as I understand them, your circumstances do not allow consideration from men in my brother's sphere."

Feigning a puzzled look, Elizabeth asked, "What circumstances and what sphere, Miss Bingley?" She grasped Jane's hand and squeezed it. "Oh, of course! But allow me to assure you, although we are daughters of a gentleman, we would never spurn a man simply because his roots are in trade. I beg you not to think so poorly of us."

Miss Bingley's eyes narrowed.

"Indeed," said Jane, gripping Elizabeth's fingers. "Our uncle Gardiner and our cousin, Mr Browne, tradesmen both, are commendable people, deserving of all the acclaim and riches they have earned. They personify the qualities I seek in a husband—dedication, integrity, and decisiveness. But I do," she added with a smile, "wish every felicity for Miss Oliverson and your brother."

Hurrah, Jane! You see how Mr Bingley submits to his sisters and depends on Mr Darcy. Elizabeth spoke as sweetly as Jane, though not as sincerely. "I was hoping, Miss Bingley, you might have advice to offer." The woman, her pique still apparent, nodded her head. "Our youngest sister, Lydia, dominates Kitty who is, in fact, her elder. Can you imagine such temerity? The girl has an exaggerated sense of her own importance...perhaps because she was over-indulged, spoilt, as a child." Elizabeth gave an exaggerated sigh. "She fritters away her allowance and spends more money than she ought. She is selfish, vain, and outspoken. Often downright rude and insulting, she can be insufferable. Do you suppose the denigration of others is an attempt to elevate herself and to assert a position of imagined superiority?" With a wide-eyed look, she added, "I know no other lady in such a knowledgeable position to offer advice as you."

Basking in the warmth of Miss Bingley's ruddy glow and glowering silence, Elizabeth felt not a tinge of remorse, and she turned her ear to what the woman's brother was saying.

"I apologise for my spur-of-the-moment decision, but I had to decide upon a date when everyone could attend. Miss Oliverson will be off to Brighton for Christmas, you see, and Darcy will travel to Derbyshire with his sister."

"Lizzy, also," said Mrs Bennet, "will soon be Derbyshire-bound. She is to attend her cousin's wedding at an estate near Ash-something." Aimed first at Elizabeth, a bitter smile was then directed towards her husband as he entered the room. "We *all* were invited, of course, and might have enjoyed such gaiety, but Mr Bennet would not have it."

"You might have relished the gaiety of an arduous journey, my dear," said Mr Bennet, "but not I."

"Speaking of arduousness, we do have other calls to make hereabouts." Rising, Miss Bingley clapped her hands. "Come, Charles." She hurried off, eager, it seemed, to depart, leaving her brother to scramble after her.

"Girls, girls!" cried Mrs Bennet once the visitors had gone. "Miss Bingley was right. There is scarce time to prepare. Get to your rooms and start reworking your best gowns. Lace! Ribbon! Embroidery and embellishment! Make haste!" All but Elizabeth hied upstairs. "Lizzy, you will, of course, wear the gorgeous green gown that once was mine."

Intent on finishing letters to her aunt Browne and Miss Taylor, Elizabeth kept her head down. "Yes, Mama. And where is it?"

Mrs Bennet shrieked, "What do you mean, where is it? I gave it to you ages ago. Is it not in your wardrobe?"

Elizabeth spoke with complete honesty when she said she had not seen it in the past three weeks. In truth, she had not looked in the gown's hiding place since concealing it there. Her mother called for Mrs Hill and the maids to tear apart the house in search of her precious garment. Mrs Bennet's other daughters were summoned but truthfully avowed they knew not its whereabouts. Elizabeth prayed no one would look in the still-room's rag drawer…at least not until she was as dead as a doornail, for that surely was the only occasion when she would not refuse to wear such a monstrosity.

Later, when Jane entered their bedchamber, finding it in disarray with gowns strewn across bed and chair, Elizabeth was sagging against a wall. "I offered my best muslin to Kitty and my sarsenet to Mary. Now I have nothing to wear on Tuesday night."

"As Miss Bingley mentioned, with such short notice, even Mrs Dexter could not create gowns for all of us. But," said Jane, "if we take in the seams, my layered gown might suit you."

Elizabeth pushed away from the wall to stow her day dresses back in the wardrobe. "I cannot help but suffer a twinge of envy that Miss King inherited ten thousand pounds and suddenly needs an equal number of bespoke garments."

"She ordered only ten new gowns, Lizzy."

"Ten! Can you imagine ever being in a position to order so many at once?" Elizabeth closed the wardrobe doors and smiled. "Nothing shall dissuade me, though, from attending Mr Bingley's ball," she cried, grasping her sister's hands. "A ball, Jane!"

Working together with their diligent maids-of-all-work, the five sisters managed to alter and adorn four gowns in as many days.

"Poor, dear Patty. Off to Meryton in a downpour." Jane sighed, turning from the window. "Just how vital are shoe roses?"

"Bite your tongue, Sister, for I should die without them." Twirling, Lydia admired herself in the mirror before surrendering it to Elizabeth, who wore Jane's gown and examined herself with a critical eye.

"This will never do. The bodice is still too— Enter," she called, to a sound at the door.

"Beggin' yer pardon, Miss Lizzy," said Rose, "but this here delivery just come fer ya all the way from town." The young maid's eyes widened as she handed over the large leather satchel.

"For me? From whom?" As her sisters gathered round, Elizabeth opened the bag and withdrew a package wrapped in brown paper. "Here is a letter...from Aunt Browne." Breaking the seal, she read aloud:

My Dear Lizzy,

As your godmother, I could not, in good conscience, allow you to fret over what to wear to your neighbour's ball, not when I had in my possession such sumptuous raiment as is now in your hands. The items arrived at the Gardiner-Browne warehouse amongst the latest shipment of imported cashmere shawls. Michael placed them in my care and enlisted my help in locating their rightful owner. Until the mystery has been solved, you are welcome to array yourself in splendour. Both gown and slippers appear to be your size, so I hope they fit without alteration. Any adjustments must be temporary in case the owner comes forwards. Oh, I wish I could see you, my dear niece, so beautifully attired. As we sally forth to Derbyshire, I shall expect no less than a detailed account of the event with no minutiae left unsaid.

Yours &c.,

Eliza Browne

PS: The Taylors have departed for Wishinghill Park, but Miss Taylor left the enclosed letter to be sent along with mine. Also, Michael asks you be ready for departure by ten-thirty on the morning of the twenty-seventh.

Elizabeth set aside Miss Taylor's correspondence for later reading. Unfolding the parcel's delicate tissue-paper, she revealed a full-dress gown of immeasurable beauty in both design and workmanship. As she held it aloft, light danced upon metallic threads and spangles, making the exquisite creation shimmer and sparkle. Tiny leaves of pierced metal were sewn upon embroidered sprigs, and the floral pattern was repeated in a vine along the hem.

"Imagine," said Kitty, tracing a finger over a dainty leaf, "how magnificent this gown will look in candlelight's golden glow. You will look like a princess, Lizzy." Mary insisted princesses were not necessarily beautiful, and Kitty argued their gowns made them, at least, appear so.

Rooting round in the parcel, Lydia discovered more items. "Faith, Lizzy! You must not keep all these riches to yourself. We each must have our share. I want the shawl and reticule. Jane may have the satin slippers, and Kitty the fan. La! There is nothing left for you, Mary, save a bandeau."

"We already have everything we need, Lydia. Aunt Browne sent those items for her goddaughter to wear." Giving Elizabeth a hug, Mary whispered, "I am happy for you, Sister. You deserve special treatment."

"Thank you. I am overwhelmed. Never have I seen the likes, not even in *La Belle Assemblée*."

"I wish Aunt Browne was my godmother." Kitty crossed her arms and pouted. "Aunt Philips never visited faraway lands, and her house is not filled with exotic treasures. If Uncle Browne were still alive, he might have invited us to travel with him. We could have found suitors and—"

"We hardly need go to distant places to find husbands." Lydia held the gown against herself, admiring her reflection in the mirror. "Not with an entire militia regiment encamped nearby."

Rescuing the gossamer gown from her sister's clutches, Elizabeth placed it over a chair. "The way you are going about it, chasing after officers, will earn you a reputation and ruin, not a husband."

This prompted Mary to recite what she could remember from conduct books about guarding one's purity from the dishonourable intentions of the opposite sex. "You and your beliefs are to be commended," said Elizabeth gently, "but do not tar all men with the same brush. There are honourable, single gentlemen out there...somewhere. But, please, my dear sisters, do not throw yourselves into the power of the Netherfield gentlemen or Mr Wickham. I have reason to doubt their honour."

"Lawks, Lizzy!" cried Lydia. "You liked them well enough when Mr Caulifield and Mr Wickham first favoured your company."

"It was not only Lizzy whom Mr Wickham favoured. Twice, I saw the two of you behind the— Oh! Get off my foot, Lydia, you big oaf!" Kitty sank to the bed, clutching her left foot.

"We were only talking, you jealous thing." Lydia shrugged. "I plan on standing up with Mr Wickham at the ball and making him fall madly in love with me. Then I shall marry before all of you."

Stepping into the satin shoes, Elizabeth frowned. *Not a perfect fit, but they will do.* "Dance with him, if you must, Lydia. But, *please,* do not trust him beyond the ballroom. I fear his charm is deceptive, his words insincere. Besides, you have no money, no connexions, nothing to tempt him into matrimony."

"La, Lizzy! You are so dull."

Chapter 13

Preying upon Elizabeth's mind before the ball was the suspicion that Messrs Caulifield, Darcy, Wickham, and Bingley were rakes and that the latter was Miss Taylor's former suitor. *Oh, for pity's sake! Her letter!* She fetched the missive from her room and lit a candle. Clad in her finery, she chose the cosy window-seat in an alcove along the passage and read:

Dear Miss Bennet,

I trust you and your family are well. Although I am disappointed neither they nor the Gardiners can attend the wedding, please let your parents and sisters know I understand and shall look forward to meeting the rest of the Bennets at such time as I may be intro-duced, to my great joy, as Mrs Michael Browne.

Full vindication must be granted for my tardy reply to your last letter and the crime more rightly laid to my mother's charge. The thief of time has had me run ragged in search of apparel, linens, and all the frippery necessary before one can be considered prepared for matrimonial bliss. I had not thought my wardrobe deficient until your dear cousin proposed. Since then, Mother has been in—if you can imagine such a condition—a state of nervous exhilaration. Should not such a disposition be reserved for the bride?

After trudging through dreaded shop aisles, I long to ramble along a picturesque country lane or winding footpath. But I should not complain. Soon I shall be home awhile, awaiting the chance to show you Wishinghill Park and its fauna and flora, though the latter —even the blooming gorse and heather—will be sparse. Walking is akin to reading, is it not? When I first pick up a book, I rush through it, eager to reach the denouement. Upon re-reading the story, I take time to savour the writer's words, finding nuances initially missed. Likewise, I may walk the same path countless times, but there always is something new to discover along the way.

Gracious! Upon re-reading what I have written, I must beg forgiveness. Lately my thoughts have been as scattered as chaff in the wind. You enquired about Mr Bingley. I shall say that as a suitor, he was found wanting...as in wanting to please a mutual friend more than he wanted to please me. I suspect that particular friend informed him I walk too much instead of riding or taking a carriage. He always teased me about my love of countryside rambles.

Looking up from the missive, Elizabeth remembered Mr Darcy's list. One of his standards for a wife was being a skilled horsewoman and not so daft as to scamper about the countryside when conditions were sloppy underfoot. Miss Taylor was from Derbyshire, as was Mr Darcy. Could it be? Finding her place, she continued reading.

Also, you must remember the day at Hyde Park when you, Michael, and I encountered Miss Lavinia Jardine. She met Mr Bingley at Pemberley, our mutual friend's estate. It soon ended badly. Mr Bingley blamed her, or rather her lavender fragrance, for causing his dreadful cold. I have heard of other young ladies and their mothers who disapprove of his inconstancy. My dear friend, Mr Fitzwilliam Darcy, means well, but Mr Bingley needs to stop relying on him and

start standing on his own two feet. At any rate, I pity the poor ladies
he has unfairly treated.

On the other hand, I am the most fortunate woman in the world.
Oh, if I could but see you as happy! If there were such another man
as Michael for you!

Father is calling. We are to depart for Wishinghill this morning,
so I must sign off now. May God bless you and your loved ones. Until
we meet again anon, I remain your friend and soon-to-be cousin,

Helen Taylor

Elizabeth blew out her cheeks. That Mr Bingley was an immature scoundrel was no surprise to her. *But that Mr Darcy is friends with not only Mr Browne but Miss Taylor, too!*

"That will be all, Simon." Elizabeth heard her father's voice as he left his bedchamber. "Inform my wife I shall be in the library. Fortification seems advisable."

A few moments later, entering the room where all her sisters had congregated, Elizabeth glanced at the clock and told the others to make haste. Fans and long gloves were fetched, as was their mother, and they all padded down the stairs in various degrees of exhilaration.

One of Elizabeth's slippers slid down the steps before her, and she exclaimed with dismay.

"See?" Following behind, Mrs Bennet poked her fan between Elizabeth's shoulder blades. "You should have given those slippers to one of your sisters, selfish girl!"

Lydia, bounding down the stairs before them all, called over her shoulder, "Although I am the youngest, my feet are the biggest."

"You should have worn your own slippers, Lizzy."

"But these are so pretty, Jane. And I am a stubborn, vain creature who shall make do, even though one of these shoes is not right."

Cloaks were put round shoulders, and Mr Bennet was collected. Slightly foxed, he settled on the seat beside their coachman, allowing his womenfolk more room inside the carriage and, Elizabeth suspected, himself some peace in the cool, night air.

Mr Collins, however, had no qualms about elbowing his way inside, precariously perching his large frame on the pull-down side seat. "I compliment all my fair cousins on their choice of apparel for the occasion. You have managed most admirably...considering you have not the means to bedeck yourselves in the most select fabrics, most fashionable designs, most precious of gems. I speak, of course, of the sort of stately finery only one so elevated as my esteemed patroness, *Lady* Catherine de Bourgh, may claim. And now, may I also take this opportunity, Cousin Elizabeth, to request the honour of your first set?"

Without awaiting an answer, he continued, in vain, to elicit her favour. "I am obliged to counsel you, dear cousin, on the subject of female converse. Yours is to be good-natured and delicate, tempered by courteousness and modesty, seasoned not with wit but with wisdom and discretion. Be not tempted by a thirst for *éclat*. Feminine charm is found in meekness. Wit is dreaded in the fairer sex. Men of the best sense are averse to the mere thought of a witty wife, the company of a critic, so to speak. What misery it must be to find oneself shackled to a perpetual satirist, a flippant, impertinent, self-conceited woman seeking to dazzle with her supposed superiority of wit."

"Then let me assure you, Mr Collins," said Elizabeth, "I *am* at my wit's end."

He seemed smugly satisfied with that success and set about to further endear himself to her. "In addition—while others may congratulate you on such a questionable quality

—that liveliness and verve you frequently exhibit also must be regulated when amongst your betters...in which category I include myself, of course, not only as a cleric but as a man."

Stupid man! Stupid slipper! The errant shoe had fallen off again, and Elizabeth coerced it back upon her foot. Through the glass, she gazed at the waxing gibbous moon that guided them to the brightly-lit sweep leading to Netherfield's front doors.

Inside was warmth, a ballroom redolent of perfume, pomade, and perspiration. Hubbub, laughter, and music filled the manor. Smiles and silly grins of intoxication spread across faces, save those of handsome, expressionless footmen. There were soft hues and jewel tones, red coats and black coats. Flowers, greenery, a wall of mirrors reflecting flickering candlelight. All the finery, all the luxury, all the enchantment of a private ball. All the ingredients of a night to remember.

Elizabeth greeted neighbours, old and new. But, to her disappointment, none of the recently arrived bachelors, neither militia officers nor the three single gentlemen at Netherfield, were best suited to her disposition and talents. The more she learnt of the opposite sex, the more she was convinced she would never find one whom she could respect and love. *I shall end up a bitter old spinster thinking all men iniquitous creatures.*

Finally! The Bennet family, the last guests to arrive, had entered the crowded ballroom, simultaneously preserving Darcy's sanity and plunging him into an absence of all reason. He took a step in Miss Elizabeth's direction, only to be halted by a restraining grip on his arm.

"A moment, if you please, Darcy. Did you not hear me say I need to speak to you on an urgent matter?"

Try as he might, Darcy could not shake Bingley's hold. "Leave me be." His heart's desire, resplendent in an exquisite gown, was on the verge of being engulfed by the crush. Doubling his efforts to wrench free, he snarled, "What are you about?"

"I am about to save your stupid hide by returning years of guidance whenever I was infatuated by an unsuitable woman. You cannot possibly be considering Miss Elizabeth."

Grappling with the fist holding him in place, Darcy spoke with calm restraint. "No, I am not considering her. The decision was made days ago, before I left for town on important business. Tonight, I shall ask for her hand—once I rid myself of yours." Bingley held fast; Darcy rounded on him. "I abhor making a scene but shall wrestle you to the ground if you do not release me at once."

Bingley's grip relaxed, and he held up both hands. "Do what you wish, but your fascination with her must end. Think, man. She has no fortune and comes from a family with no connexions. According to my sisters, she reads extensively and expresses pert opinions for one so young. She muddies her hems during long walks and exposes her ankles while running. Forget her, Darcy, just as I must think no more of her elder sister."

"Never could I forget her." Feasting his eyes, Darcy watched Miss Elizabeth emerge from the throng and join Colonel Forster, his wife, and his officers. "She is meant for me, I for her."

Rubbing his temples, Bingley muttered, "I do not understand."

"Nor do I. But there you have it. As my father recommended, I looked into her eyes and was undone." Darcy took a breath, uncaring that he was blabbering like a fool. "She is the one. I cannot explain it. I just know it. And the knowing is powerful and liberating...and absolutely terrifying."

He started walking in Miss Elizabeth's direction, but Bingley claimed his attention and an officer hers. "Wait," his friend pleaded. "I desperately need counsel. I find myself in an awful—"

"This ball is missing its host. What seems to be the problem, gentlemen?" Clapping their shoulders from behind, Caulifield moved between Darcy and Bingley. "I am facing my own dilemma. A remarkable lady with gorgeous eyes and glorious gown needs rescuing from red-coated admirers and, perhaps, from me. But, to my dismay, Miss Elizabeth seems to avoid me of late. Would either of you know anything about that astonishing development? It is a mystery." Met by silence, he chuckled. "At any rate, what is so important to keep both of you from such delightful duties?"

Darcy shrugged off Caulifield's hand and strode towards Miss Elizabeth, stopping short as she was accosted by the strange man he had seen with her in Meryton. While she and the oddity danced the opening set, Darcy's eyes followed her with admiration and her partner with horrified amusement. *Was there ever a more stumbling, bumbling clodpole?*

While embarrassed on her behalf, Darcy congratulated himself on being a superb dancer, amongst his other areas of mastery. Any shame, any misery the oaf had caused her would be forgot once *he* put himself forwards as her next partner. Such was his intention when the set ended. But, instead of escorting the lady off the dance floor as was proper, the lout gave Miss Elizabeth a hasty obeisance and moved directly towards him.

A solemn, low bow prefaced the man's speech, which was of great length and extraordinary monotony save for weighted emphasis on certain venerations regarding his esteemed patroness, Darcy's aunt. Then, bestowing another deep bow, he added, "William Collins of Hunsford Parsonage at your service, sir."

Darcy eyed the absurd man with disdain at being so addressed and intruded upon without a proper introduction. "I must say it is a pleasure to meet you, Mr Collins." *After all, that is the gentlemanly thing to do.*

Undeterred by Darcy's frosty tone, his aunt's sycophant offered up an unctuous smile in addition to a steady stream of tedious twaddle.

"...And so, in seeking reconciliation with the Bennet family—an olive branch, if you will—I benevolently have chosen one of my fair cousins as the companion of my future life."

Stifling a yawn, Darcy snapped to attention upon hearing his own choice's name.

"I have deemed Cousin Elizabeth worthy. With your aunt's munificent and extensive instruction, my wife will acquire all the necessary knowledge to become a proficient mistress of Hunsford Parsonage and, eventually, of Longbourn itself. I intend to solicit for the honour of a private audience with her on the morrow."

Over my dead body! Or preferably yours! She is far too good for you. "Nay, Mr Collins. As intimate as you are with my aunt, you must comprehend Lady Catherine would disapprove of Miss Elizabeth for such a role. Even with guidance and discipline, she would be far too sharp-tongued, too opinionated for a clergyman's wife. She is utterly unsuitable. Now, the middle daughter? She would be a far better candidate." Darcy sought Miss Mary's location and espied her on the dance floor looking lovelier than he remembered. *My sincerest apologies, madam. Somehow, I shall make amends once I am your brother. A new pianoforte, perhaps, and a music master? Name your price.*

"But I..."

Darcy's contempt increased proportionally to the length of the cleric's complaint. Unable to endure more of the same, he sketched a slight bow and walked away with short temper and long strides. Despite his confident gait, he was brought up short. Miss Elizabeth was partnered with Caulifield for the next set. Scowling, Darcy walked the room's perimeter, every thought pervaded with the wrongness of the situation.

A commotion arose between the two lines of dancers where a delicate satin slipper appeared without its owner. Miss Elizabeth gaped at the errant object, Darcy cringed, and Caulifield bent to rescue the wayward shoe before placing it within easy reach of a dainty, stockinged foot. Jealous ire flared red hot behind Darcy's eyes and under his collar.

Caulifield delivered his embarrassed partner to Miss Bennet's side near the punch bowl. Then he strolled away, smirking at Darcy, whose fist itched to wipe—with one well-aimed blow—the smug, ugly grin from the degenerate's face. Instead, he approached the sisters and bowed. "Good evening, ladies." He forced a smile. "Miss Bennet, may I borrow your sister for a moment?" Turning to Miss Elizabeth, he lowered his voice. "Madam, I must speak to you. In private."

"In private? Certainly not."

Her icy tone set Darcy's blood boiling in another cauldron of jealousy, anger, and desire. "The information I must impart regards mutual acquaintances of ours and is of a personal nature, not to be spoken of publicly." Nor was a proposal of marriage to be spoken publicly. Rather than entering a heated discussion amidst others gathered round the potent Regent's punch, he petitioned for and was granted Miss Elizabeth's next set.

Chapter 14

Having endured one set with an oaf and another with a scoundrel, Elizabeth had no fond expectations for half an hour with Mr Darcy. Nudging Jane's arm, she watched, wide-eyed, as her mother came bustling over, waving a handkerchief with one hand while holding her heaving bosom with the other.

"Oh, girls! Who would have thought? Mr Collins has turned his intentions to Mary!" Panting, she gratefully accepted a cup of punch.

"Yes, Mama, I know." Elizabeth huffed. "I just wish he would turn his attention away from me."

"He has! I just said so!"

"Lizzy," said Jane. "Mr Collins has turned his intentions to our sister Mary."

"Yes, yes! Lord bless me!" crowed their mother. "He asked for a private audience tomorrow with my darling Mary. We are saved, girls, saved!" Gulping her punch, Mrs Bennet surveyed the ballroom. "Have you seen Lady Lucas?"

As the woman tottered away, Elizabeth looked aghast at Jane. "As little as I desired our cousin's attentions, how could he so suddenly turn them to another? Men are such strange creatures. We must put Mary on her guard and discourage our dear little dove from accepting that dull-witted simpleton."

"Hush, Lizzy! Mr—"

"No, Jane, do not defend Mr Collins. I shall not stand by while a sacrificial lamb is led to the slaughter—not unless Mary desires such a fate. Why must the opposite sex, with few exceptions, be so vile?" Her sister was still sending silent signals for her to stop talking. "What?" Glancing over her shoulder, Elizabeth groaned.

Darcy held out his hand. "Miss Elizabeth, this is our set." How was it that she grew more handsome each time he saw her? As they took their places, he talked of having heard her mother speaking of an engagement between Mr Collins and her younger sister. "You must be pleased." *And you may thank me later.*

"Pleased? Firstly, it cannot be considered an engagement until Mary accepts and my father consents. Secondly, how could one not be pleased when a man takes such a casual air about matrimony? To be so easily swayed over the course of a se'nnight from one sister to another and then another is commendable, is it not? I was not aware male affection could be so long lived." As the music began, she smiled, looking him in the eye. "A gentleman's view of constancy might be enlightening. However, since I am partnered with you for half an hour, might I ask something else?"

Darcy nodded, wondering whether Miss Elizabeth realised she had unintentionally insulted him. The evening was not proceeding as planned. He was supposed to escort her to the balcony, warn her about Caulifield and Wickham, console her, then make his offer under the moonlight. Then she, flattered beyond belief, happier than ever before, would express herself as warmly as imagined in his dreams. *Such visions! Who knew I could be such a romantic lover?*

"Do you know a Miss Amesbury and a Mrs Younge?"

What? Wickham, you cur! Schooling his indignant countenance into a gentler mien, Darcy felt a prickle of foreboding creep up his spine. "I did. Those acquaintances, however, have been severed."

"I suspected as much. Such associations rarely last, I expect." Reunited after the dance had taken them apart, Miss Elizabeth said, "Soon I shall gain a new cousin. I believe Miss Taylor is well known to you and Mr Bingley."

"She and I grew up together. I later introduced her to Browne—"

"What do you have to say about the characters of Mr Wickham and Mr Caulifield?"

Had you permitted that private conversation I requested—obstinate, headstrong girl!—I might have had a chance to tell you all about certain people's honour and rectitude, and had a chance to make you an irresistible offer. "May I ask, madam, to what your questions tend?"

"I am attempting to sketch their characters." Distracted, she seemed to search for someone whom Darcy hoped was not Caulifield. Curtseying as soon as the first half-set ended, she said, "I beg your pardon, Mr Darcy. I cannot remain for the second dance."

Confused and disappointed, he watched her hurry away.

Miss Oliverson and Mr Bingley had been in what seemed—if their flushed faces were any indication—a heated conversation until Elizabeth drew near, at which instant they fell silent. "Pardon the intrusion, but do either of you know where I might find Jane?"

"I believe," said Miss Oliverson, without lifting her eyes, "she and Miss Lucas are out on the balcony."

It was apparent the young lady had been crying, and Elizabeth cast a suspicious eye towards Mr Bingley. Taking a deep breath, she reined in self-righteous ire. It was not her place to confront the stony-hearted scoundrel. Furthermore, unlike the rest of her family, she would not embarrass others that night. She would remain polite, even if it killed her.

"Shall I fetch your sister for you?" Mr Bingley sneezed twice. "I would welcome a chance to take the air."

"I thank you, no. I shall find her myself." Extending her hand, Elizabeth spoke in a gentler tone. "Miss Oliverson, would you care to join me? It is uncomfortably warm at present. Do come." The lady demurred, and Elizabeth left her to her misery.

On the balcony, she found not Jane but a man in scarlet regimentals leaning on the balustrade, gazing across the lawn. Turning, he hissed. "Lydia! About time you—"

Although the moon had disappeared behind a cloud and Mr Wickham had mistaken her for another, there was enough light for Elizabeth to witness his surprise upon recognising her. "Colonel Forster said you had not come." Warily she asked, "Why were you expecting my youngest sister out here?"

"I had promised her a set," he said with a small smile, "but when I found myself *uninvited*, we planned to meet here and have our dance. I thought she had come looking for me." He pushed away from the railing. "Instead, the vivacious

Miss Elizabeth has come to chase away my self-imposed gloom."

"My apologies for intruding upon your solitude. I was told Jane was hereabouts." Alarmed when she saw him pocketing a flask, Elizabeth turned towards the doorway.

"Your interruption is not at all unwelcome. Perhaps we might continue our conversation about that certain fellow from Derbyshire." Elizabeth assured him there was no need, but he pressed on. "You should be on your guard. The man cannot be trusted. It is just as well that I am out here alone."

She felt his hand on her shoulder, and he turned her to face him. "Being in the same room as Darcy for so many hours together would be more than I could bear. I often have sacrificed my own enjoyment by staying out of his way. I think of others, you see, not myself. Scenes unpleasant to more than me might arise were I to be in his company...and I would much rather be in yours."

He had been drinking. His breath smelt of spirits, and the heated look in his eyes spelt danger. Glancing over her shoulder towards the ballroom, Elizabeth longed for its welcoming warmth and safety. "I must go." She backed up as Mr Wickham closed in on her.

"Perhaps you should." He touched her cheek. "A winsome woman like you should not be wandering about unchaperoned. I meant it when I said the man cannot be trusted. Such a respectable lady as you can be no match for the devious creature's schemes. He is well-versed in the art of seduction. You or one of your sisters may be singled out as his next conquest and would be neither his first nor his last." Bending, he whispered near her ear. "Ardent admiration might be declared and an offer made, but it will not be honourable."

From the doorway, another male voice called out. "Miss

Elizabeth?" Then it roared, "Wickham! Move away from her!"

Muttering oaths, Mr Wickham bolted down the steps, across the lawn, towards the shrubbery.

"Did he harm you? Are you in any way injured?" Assured of Elizabeth's well-being, her rescuer appeared torn between staying and giving pursuit, but Mr Wickham already had disappeared into the night. Turning back, Mr Darcy scowled. "What were you doing out here, alone, with that degenerate? He was not invited to the ball."

Elizabeth resisted the urge to poke his chest. "I was not *intentionally* alone with him." Less confidently, she said, "He truly is a degenerate, is he? I thought—"

Huffing, Mr Darcy ran both hands through his hair. "Wickham is—"

From the doorway, a footman cleared his throat. "Pardon me, Miss Bennet. Mr Darcy, might you know Mr Bingley's whereabouts? A gentleman is asking for him, and Miss Bingley has requested your assistance."

Following the footman inside, Darcy was met by an exasperated Miss Bingley, who cast him a suspicious look and Miss Elizabeth a murderous one.

"Please be so kind as to pardon us, Eliza." Miss Bingley watched her walk away before beckoning Darcy to a relatively quiet corner. Wringing her hands, she whispered, "Miss Oliverson has taken ill again, and Charles escorted her to her room. Now he cannot be found, and her parents have arrived. Mrs Nicholls has been summoned to arrange rooms for our unexpected guests. Mrs Oliverson was taken to her daughter and Mr Oliverson to the library. He is livid, refusing to keep his voice down until Charles is found. What has my brother done now? What are we to do, Mr Darcy?"

"If you will introduce us, I shall speak to Mr Oliverson, then attempt to find Bingley." For that, he was profusely thanked, and Miss Bingley went with him to the library.

A middle-aged, ruddy-faced gentleman wielding a walking stick stopped pacing to accost Darcy. "You are not Bingley! Where is that lecherous chicken-heart?" The implement was pointed at a nearby footman. "Where is your employer?"

Without awaiting an introduction, Darcy stepped forwards. "I am Fitzwilliam Darcy, Mr Bingley's friend and houseguest. I have, I understand, the pleasure of addressing Miss Oliverson's father."

"My business is not with you, sir. We came from Brighton as soon as we received word our daughter is unwell. Now all I need is to talk to that friend of yours—the fiend!"

Darcy kept his voice low and even. "Mr Oliverson, kindly cease making a scene. We have close to a hundred guests here, and you cannot wish them to know your business. Please wait quietly while Bingley is found. I promise he will meet with you soon. In the meantime, may I offer you some of my fine brandy?" The footman was beckoned. "Have Jonesby give you the decanter from my room and bring it here. Then have this place searched from top to bottom for Bingley."

Nearing the library in search of Jane, Elizabeth could not help but hear an angry male voice.

"My son invited you into our home, you scoundrel! And

this is how you repay our hospitality! You will be made to pay! A few pounds should do it...for a common licence! Either that or I shall have a pound of your flesh. Your choice."

Not caring to overhear more, she hurried past and, farther down the hall, spotted Jane looking frantic and wearing her cloak.

"Lizzy!" Her sister rushed forwards. "Papa sent me to find you. Gather your belongings, and make haste. We must leave immediately. The carriage is waiting."

What on earth? "Are you well, dearest? Has someone taken ill? Did you hear the shouting?"

"Yes. Oh, Lizzy, it was so distressing!"

"Do not give Mr Bingley another thought. I am sick of him, his cohorts, and the militia. They are men of the town, rakes, all of them. I wish they had never come to our respectable neighbourhood." Elizabeth's eye was caught by a male figure, lugging a valise in one hand and a portmanteau in the other, slipping out of the front door. *Good heavens. Why does Mr Caulifield not take leave of us if he is departing? Does he not see us standing here?*

"You are right about the militia, but why did you mention Mr Bingley?" asked Jane. "What has he to do with it, other than finding them?" She tugged Elizabeth's hand. "Please, come away now. My father is in a terrible temper, shaken and horrified by what might have happened. He sits again with James Coachman. Everyone else is in the carriage already, and I must see to my mother."

Elizabeth hied to the cloakroom, snatched her cape from a hook, threw it about her shoulders, turned, and ran straight into a solid male chest clad in a white marcella waistcoat.

Chapter 15

Miss Elizabeth backed away, mumbled an apology, and turned as if to flee.

In Darcy's head, a voice resounded. 'Your future wife will be from the upper orders and in possession of a princely dowry. Choose wisely, son, with your head not your heart.' He regretted going against his father's counsel. *But he told me to look into a woman's eyes.* Try as he might to follow his head, his heart would not be denied. Laying a hand gently upon Miss Elizabeth's arm, he said, "I beg for that private moment of your time previously denied me."

"I cannot. My family awaits."

"You are leaving?"

She looked pointedly at her arm, then at him. "Kindly remove your hand from my person." He complied but insisted she remain and listen to him. "No, Mr Darcy, you listen to me. Recently acquired knowledge tells me everything I need to know. For one thing, either you or one of your bachelor friends wrote a shameful *billet-doux*, leaving it for me, or anyone, to find."

"Never, in my entire life, have I written a love letter," he replied quickly. "If the penmanship was large and loopy, it was Caulifield. Barely legible, Bingley."

"Mr Caulifield then. But all of you, including Mr Wickham, are men of cruel, immoral habits. Mr Bingley is infamous for raising a lady's expectations, only to dash her hopes by objecting to a favourite pastime, her perfume, or some other triviality. A true gentleman would neither toy with a woman's affections nor cause the sort of distress Miss Oliverson now suffers. Behaving in a gentlemanly manner seems foreign to you and the company you keep."

"You are wrong, madam, at least about me." Darcy begged her to sit upon the cloakroom's bench for just a moment while he fetched a footman to stand guard by the door. Although time and place were anything but ideal, he was determined then to carry the day and to do it quickly. "You cannot know, Miss Elizabeth," he said softly, "the struggles I have had to overcome or the conflicts and wars I fought for you. Passionate regard battled against duty and moral obligation. Desire feuded with the disadvantages of your connexions and paltry dowry. This heart combatted the degradation of uniting my esteemed family with yours. The most formidable contention was trusting you are as you seem and not a fortune hunter. Contrary to my better judgment, the advantages of having you in my life far outweigh the drawbacks." *Blast! Add something a bit more romantic.* "I ardently admire you. Please, say you will be mine. Say you want me as I want you. Say—"

"Say not another word, sir!" She gained her feet and glared. "Particularly about degradation or drawbacks relating to my beloved family!"

At such a momentous moment, hers was not the sort of response he had expected. Devoid of joy, her mien was a complete mystery. "Be assured whatever my relations or others in my sphere say about this misalliance, I give not a fig," Darcy said with some urgency. To his astonishment, although the world was being handed to her, she turned away. "Wait, please! I once overheard you express a desire to broaden your horizons, to leave this place and—"

"Leave this place? Indeed, I cannot wait to do so!"

He smiled. "If you like, when it is deemed safe again, we may travel abroad. To Italy, perhaps, or—"

Out of the cloakroom, she flounced.

Darcy trailed along behind her. Others hung on his every word. What was wrong with her? One did not walk away in the middle of a marriage proposal. "I understand your desire to distance yourself from this place, from your family and relations. The world will be your oyster. Think of it." *What more can I say? Have I forgotten anything? Ah.*

Outpacing her, he turned, blocking her progress towards the front doors. "I am, of course, in a position to be the best sort of provider and protector for you and any children resulting from our union. You know how comfortable a life I can bestow. You would want for nothing. We shall be happy togeth—" She darted round him. "Stop walking away from me!" Gentling his tone, he reached for her hand. "Please, say you will accept my offer." He waited in full anticipation of the expected favourable response.

Eyes ablaze, Miss Elizabeth turned on him. "Lay a hand on me again, and I shall scream. As for your offer…What are you offering? You spoke of moral obligation, but I doubt you know the meaning of the word 'moral'. As for my family, we are not mercenary. *You* are the fortune hunter who will marry only an heiress or a peeress. Furthermore, when I said I could not wait to leave this place, I meant *Netherfield*. I meant *you* with your selfish disdain and your unprincipled friends. You are all of an ilk, toying with women for your own cruel amusement. I want nothing more to do with you. Any of you! And I certainly shall not accept an indecent proposition."

"Indecent?"

"Tell me, sir, would you make the same sort of offer to Miss Bingley?"

"Of course not."

"Precisely."

"What, may I ask, is indecent about a man offering marriage to the woman he holds in such passionate regard?" He stared at her in disbelief.

Miss Elizabeth rubbed her brow, taking a few deep breaths. "But you are to marry your cousin, Miss de Bourgh. Both Mr Wickham and Mr Collins said so."

What? "They spoke in error. I am not to marry her." Anne was the complete opposite of the woman who had become the touchstone all others were measured against and found wanting. *Blast! Now what is she saying?*

"...And, furthermore, you have been heard disparaging people within their hearing."

"Who? When?"

"There are several instances of which I am aware. For instance, at Lucas Lodge, one of my sisters heard you refer to my father as indolent."

Darcy nodded. "I believe he is. Slack and, perhaps, callous."

Her beautiful eyes narrowed. "How dare you! Having an insensitive and cruel disposition yourself, you easily recognise apathetic behaviour in others, do you? Tell me, what kind of man permits those close to him—friends, male or female, from childhood or adulthood—to behave in a disreputable manner? Should he not, at least, try to check them?"

"First, you accost me for speaking out when I find fault with someone. The next minute you take me to task for not doing so." He crossed his arms. "Which is it? You cannot have it both ways."

"My point is..." With a small shake of her head, as if searching for words, Miss Elizabeth continued in a measured voice. "If you have a problem with someone, it would be a kindness to speak to them about it, as I presently am doing with you. In Charlotte Lucas, I have the best sort of friend because she confronts me with home truths. Granted, I might not always correct my behaviour, but I am made aware of a need for improvement."

"And what would you think if I told you, here and now, what I think of you?"

"Go ahead, sir. Do your worst."

"You are an ember amongst ashes."

"A cinder? You compare me to a piece of partially burnt wood or coal?"

"It was meant as a compliment!" They were toe-to-toe, chests heaving, eyes shooting flames.

"Mr Darcy, I do not understand this sudden interest, these addresses, so out of the blue. Am I not the unkempt, unattractive milkmaid not worth your bother?"

He tore his gaze from hers and noticed the footman, still in the hall, watching with curious alarm. *Egad, what a public display!* At least a reel was being performed, and the guests were in high revel, laughing while clapping and stamping their feet to the music. He lowered his voice. "I have been fighting this attraction for the best part of two months now. And all the while, you have been smiling sweetly and—"

"I smiled to vex you because you said Jane smiles too much. Did I not smile enough? I most certainly am not smiling now. Nevertheless, I do appreciate the compliment of your offer, which was open to more than one interpretation. I thank you for it, but I cannot accept." Her voice wavered a moment before striking the final blow to his pride. "I am not of a disposition to place myself under the thumb of a man with your inclinations. I could not stomach visiting tenant families, forever wondering whether one of their children might be my husband's natural son or daughter. Looking the other way is not for me. As Milton said, 'better to reign in hell than serve in heaven'."

"Are...Are you *rejecting* me?"

"Yes! Just as you rejected me at first sight, across a lea." She turned then, running faster than Darcy thought a woman could.

Shocked, he stood there a moment before bolting after her, out of the front door. Gripping the landing's railing, he spotted the Bennet coach below. "Halt!" Continuing to move swiftly away from him, Miss Elizabeth turned a deaf ear to his plea, and neither the footman opening the carriage door nor the coachman readying for departure heeded his command.

Hems hitched up, she lightly tripped down the stairs, losing a satin slipper along the way. Without a backwards glance, she greeted her father seated beside the coachman and stepped inside.

Dashing down to the sweep, Darcy shouted after the driver to no avail. In a trice, Miss Elizabeth was whisked away. Snatching up her dainty shoe, he turned, taking the steps two at a time. Tucking the slipper in his breast pocket, he settled upon the nearest seat in the vestibule and dragged both hands down his face. *She is out there, thinking ill of me. I have lost her.*

Anger soon trumped disappointment. *Accusing me of indecency and of being mercenary. Me!* Granted, the words 'heiress' and 'peeress' did appear on his catalogue of prerequisites for a wife. But how the devil did she know that? Had she seen the list? Or—*Oh no!*—did she have it?

His father's voice reminded him of another prerequisite. 'Before making an offer of marriage, son, be certain you are ready to take on the added responsibility of a wife and children. They will depend on you. In turn, you will rely on your wife to maintain household economy and to tactfully manage domestic help. When needed and without being a termagant, a wife must be able to put household servants in their place. However, she must know her place and always be respectful of you.'

Darcy gave a laugh bordering on, he feared, hysteria. *Judging by the looks I am receiving from that footman, I had best confine fits of madness to my apartments.*

Storming into his chambers, he learnt from Jonesby that Bingley, finally, had been located. The valet, obeying his employer's command, helped exchange dancing pumps for Hessians whilst questioning the practicality of doing so while still wearing one's evening attire.

Darcy made, then, for the stable where he declined a groom's assistance and saddled and bridled Aether himself.

At full tilt, horse and rider sped beyond Netherfield to Longbourn's lea. There under the moonlight, still in his finest breeches and tailcoat, Darcy dismounted and walked the field's perimeter, kicking fallen acorns and muttering oaths into the night air. The wind picked up, and clouds scudded across the moon.

The ball ended during his reckless ride, and Netherfield manor was eerily quiet upon his return. Since Bingley had last tried to dissuade him from offering for Miss Elizabeth, Darcy had neither spoken to nor seen his friend. The three Oliversons, he learnt, had departed, bound for Meryton's inn, and Caulifield had mysteriously disappeared. So, besides himself, only the Bingleys, Hursts, and household servants remained. As hirelings tidied up in the dining room, he wondered how to clear up his own untidy state of things and put his life back to rights.

Curious to know what had transpired, he was directed to the library. There he found Bingley, tailcoat off, cravat loosened, the chair turned sideways, slumped behind the desk, staring vacantly at a dying fire.

After pouring two clarets and passing one to Bingley, he set his glass on the desk, slackened his neckcloth, shrugged out of his coat, and was hit with the smell of horse. Dropping onto a chair, Darcy closed his eyes. "I regret not listening earlier when you needed my ear, but I am here now." No response forthcoming, he looked at his friend.

The apology was waved off while Bingley drained his glass. "I take it you are to be married as well."

Downing his drink in one swig, Darcy choked on both it and his reply. "My offer was…found wanting." He poured another round. They both emptied, then replenished, their glasses. "Who is getting married?"

"Me. As I tried to tell you earlier, Miss Oliverson is with child…and it is not mine! Unbeknownst to everyone, save the two of them, Caulifield stole her virtue months ago. Now he has refused to take responsibility. I love her and cannot allow her to experience shame and disgrace. We are to wed at St Nicholas Church in Brighton as soon as a common licence is procured. I had thought to ask you to be my witness, but you will be in Derbyshire by then."

Too much wine, his disgust and anger at Caulifield, and Darcy's own disappointed hopes made clear thinking difficult. "Are you quite certain you wish to go through with this?"

Bingley nodded.

"Your compassion knows no bounds. To raise another man's child as your own..." Darcy raised his glass. "It is an honourable thing you do, my friend, and I wish you a lifetime of happiness."

"You taught me about being honourable, Darcy."

"'Tis hardly honourable that I am envious you soon will be wed, and I shall not."

"Speaking of not marrying, you must be glad the youngest Bennet will not become your sister. Imagine the vexation, the mortification of finding yourself married into the same family as Mr Wickham."

Mind racing, Darcy feared Miss Elizabeth had been seen on the balcony with the reprobate and was being forced to marry him. "What do you mean?"

"Let me tell you about the night I have had. After a few sets, Miss Oliverson became unwell again, so I saw her to her room. Pondering her predicament, I went walking in the shrubbery where I caught Mr Wickham kissing a young woman—Miss Lydia Bennet. I brought her inside, asked her father to accompany us to the blue parlour, and gave him an account of all I had witnessed. Alas, I forgot to send a footman after Mr Wickham, who, by the by, has disappeared. So, of course, has Caulifield, without a word. While I spoke to Mr Bennet, unbeknownst to me, the Oliversons arrived. I appreciate your sorting out that uproar."

"It was the least I could do, but I wish I had done more, particularly regarding Wickham."

Bingley said he pitied the Bennets. "If the youngest daughter is ruined, her sisters will share in the shame. And the eldest is such an angel!" Heaving a sigh, he reached again for the bottle. Too weary to stop his friend or himself, Darcy handed over his own glass for a refill. "Had things turned out differently, had I never met Miss Oliverson, I might have made Miss Bennet an offer. But the Hursts, Caroline, and I shall leave Netherfield anon, and I doubt we shall ever return. I am sorry to curtail your sojourn here."

"No need to apologise. I am eager to be in London myself." Darcy gave Bingley's shoulder a pat and advised him to try and get some sleep.

Wanting nothing more than to fall into bed himself, Darcy ordered his valet to pack and order the carriage for later that morning. Before carrying out his master's instructions, Jonesby handed him a dispatch from Lady Matlock.

Darcy groaned. "Oh, God. What now?"

As a grey dawn broke, and amidst the chaos of an entire household preparing for departure, Darcy considered waiting awhile and going to Longbourn to beg another audience with Miss Elizabeth. But, as desperate as he was to speak to her, he was as equally desirous of getting to town, away from her.

Tortured thoughts sat with him while he journeyed towards London. Why had his father, while turning a blind eye to Wickham's misdeeds, forced his own son to follow the straight and narrow? *How could Georgiana have forgotten that same lesson? How could she have thrown proper comportment to the wind?* Why had his sister, Miss Amesbury, and Miss Lydia Bennet succumbed to a steward's son's seductions? *Because charm oozes out of Wickham like venom from an adder.* Ladies found the snake irresistible, and he was adept at singling out susceptible ones to beguile. Was it their fault they fell victim to a glib-tongued manipulator? Perhaps. But was Darcy himself not somewhat to blame? He could have exposed the profligate's corrupt character to others.

Whatever the result of Miss Lydia's indiscretion, Darcy knew the right thing to do was to step forwards, find the weasel, and remedy his own share in the situation. No doubt

Wickham had debts aplenty, and he would see him thrown in the Marshalsea or, if need be, wed to the Bennet girl. *My fault, my duty.* The beat of the carriage horses' hoofs kept rhythm with the repetitive rise and fall of the chant in his head. *My fault, my duty.*

Chapter 16

As her second eldest climbed into the carriage and sat upon the pull-down side seat, Mrs Bennet pushed away the smelling salts Jane was waving beneath her nose. "Lizzy! Where have you been, child? We feared something had befallen you, too."

"What do you mean?" Within the dim light of torches lining the gravel sweep, Elizabeth observed six unhappy faces. Huddled in a corner, Kitty snivelled while Lydia sprawled against her in a drowse. Mr Collins gazed forlornly at Mary, who cast him puzzled, disgusted looks and moved her skirts away from his knee.

Angry over Mr Wickham's untoward behaviour, fretting about Miss Oliverson, and shaken by Mr Darcy's offer, Elizabeth wanted nothing more than peace and quiet, time for reflection, and, perhaps, a good cry. "Someone please explain what has befallen whom."

"Cousin Elizabeth, I condole with you on this grievous affliction, this transgression of decorum that has befallen us tonight. Your youngest sister was seen behaving wantonly with Mr Wickham. Her conduct will bring infamy to all her poor sisters, shame to her indulgent parents, and heinous offence to me. I hereby rescind my offer of an olive branch to your unfortunate family and shall return, unwed, to my most venerated patroness, at whose feet I shall—"

"Oh, hang Lady Catherine! Lawks! It is not the end of the world, Mr Collins." Yawning, Lydia sat up groggily. "Mr Wickham and I were only kissing. I cannot understand such a fuss over nothing. 'Tis not my fault he kept refilling my cup of punch with something called 'blue ruin'. I was feeling quite merry until Mr Bingley came along, spoiling our fun. No one saw us but him, and he promised Papa his silence. So, there can be no infamy, unless you tell others."

Mrs Bennet sniffled into a handkerchief before saying, in a quavering voice, "That villainous Mr Wickham tricked my dearest Lydia, for she is not the kind of girl to misbehave like that. Colonel Forster and Mr Bingley are entirely to blame— one for not checking his officers, the other for not catching Mr Wickham with Lydia sooner. Miss Bingley is at fault, too. She should not let guests out of her sight. This sort of thing would never happen at Longbourn, for I keep a watchful eye on everyone. And now," she wailed, "now Mr Collins will have none of you."

Mary reached across to hold Lydia's hand. "Although it could have been worse, we may draw from this unfortunate affair a useful lesson..."

Never had Elizabeth felt less like listening to platitudes. Never had she felt such guilt. Mr Darcy had tried to tell her about Mr Wickham, and she should have acted quickly on her suspicions when the lieutenant expected to meet Lydia on the balcony.

"...and guide you to a better understanding of right-eousness." Mary's voice had grown strident.

Elizabeth stopped listening again. The night's gamut of emotions was well beyond her endurance. She was bone-weary, and her foot was freezing. In her haste to get away from Mr Darcy, she had lost a slipper from the pair her godmother had sent.

When she fell into bed, seemingly hours later, Elizabeth had a good cry while her dearest sister rubbed her back. "Hush, Lizzy. Lydia's situation is hardly ruinous, and I trust Mr Bingley to keep his word."

"Do you? I wish I could be as trusting." Elizabeth sat up, dried her eyes, and gave Jane a watery smile. "In hindsight, compared to some others, Mr Collins is not so bad. At least he is not amoral. But is there a man out there I could respect and hold in some regard? That is not too much to ask, is it? I have given up on finding such a man I could love."

Using a snuffer, Jane extinguished the candle. "In a matter of hours, you and the Brownes will be on your way to Derbyshire for a joyful event. You may wear your beautiful gown again and dance with handsome strangers. Perhaps one will be ideally suited to you. Sleep now. All is well."

She was not customarily such a watering pot, but Elizabeth wept because of Lydia's stupidity. *No wonder Mr Darcy had qualms about my family.* She cried because she had rejected a marriage proposal even though she was glad she had rejected it. *And Mama must never learn of it!*

Darcy arrived at Park Lane, intent on seeing his cousin, Colonel Fitzwilliam.

"I begged Mother to not summon you away," the colonel informed him, only a short time later. "But I thank you for coming up so promptly."

Eyes roaming over the form in the bed, Darcy was relieved to find his favourite relation so animated. Perching on a bedside chair, he said, "Your mother's dispatch provided scant detail and quite the fright."

"In a nutshell, I was shot." Fitzwilliam shifted against the pillows, pushing back the bedclothes, pointing at his bandaged side. "Thanks to one of Boney's minions, there was a slug, a French souvenir, jouncing round somewhere inside me. A rib is broken, but the lung is undamaged. I am too hard-bitten to die easily, I suppose."

Springing from the chair, Darcy pushed aside a heavy curtain and gripped the casement frame. A grey pall over Hyde Park mirrored his own gloom. "Thank God for it. I feared you were mortally wounded."

"I was fortunate to have been carried off the field of battle, but my favourite warhorse was lost in the clash. Poor Cadogan."

Darcy turned and looked closely at his cousin. "You seem to be in a great deal of pain. Do you require a physician? Or laudanum? Why is there no one here to see to your needs?"

"Should I want something, the bell-pull is within easy reach. My batman drops by regularly. The parents appear every morning after breakfast and in the evening, if they have no engagements. My chatty sister looks in on me more often than I wish, and my compassionate brother finally deigned to visit half an hour ago."

"How was your voyage home?"

"Excruciatingly endless and endlessly excruciating, if memory serves—which it might not. Forced to swallow a medicament of opium juice, I was not of sound mind." A fleeting smile fell short of the soldier's eyes. "Being my father's son has its advantages, though. While my men remain over there, here I am, on half pay, indulged with every comfort, and stuffed with the finest fare."

"You will fully recover, correct?"

"Despite the ineptitude of our surgeons, I am on the mend." When Darcy told him he might not be as fortunate next time and should sell his commission while he still had life left in him, Fitzwilliam scoffed. "I would go through hellfire to serve king and country and rout the tyrant." Inhaling with a hiss, he cursed, dragging bedclothes over his wounded body. "Enough about me. Judging by those dark circles beneath your eyes, there is something eating at you. Were it not improbable, I might think you had trouble with a woman."

Striding to the wash-stand, Darcy remained silent while fiddling with liniments and jars of foul-smelling physics.

"You have a captive audience, Darcy. I have nowhere to go and am sick of sleeping, reading, and being pampered by those paid to do so. Talk."

"I should not agitate you by speaking of my plight. You must rest, recover."

"If you fetch us something strong to drink, I daresay I shall bear it well enough."

"Are you permitted spirits?"

"Yes, and I expect a bumper, not a thimbleful."

Summoned, the butler appeared, vanished, and reappeared with a tray, two glasses, and a bottle of French brandy. Darcy poured two generous measures of the earl's contraband into the rummers, handing one to Fitzwilliam. Then he poured out his heart. The decanter was down three-quarters by the time he finished.

"Why did you not inform me you had lost your head again over a woman? I could have advised you."

"How might you have presumed to counsel me about

women, especially from a field of battle or in an opium stupor?"

"Good question." Shifting against the pillows, Fitzwilliam grunted in pain. "Love is fraught with more danger than anything I faced in Spain. Heated conflicts of any sort cause injuries, but broken ribs and festering wounds must be nothing to the devastation wrought by losing one's head over a woman."

"It was not my head I lost. This time it was my foolish heart." Darcy's jaw clenched. "Just as I misjudged Miss Amesbury, I underestimated Miss Elizabeth's character...and she misunderstood mine."

"Well, I am no old dog at it, but I think a gentleman should woo a lady a bit before blurting out a proposal. No wonder she rejected you. No, Darcy! Hold your tongue. I am not the noddy who, within the last hour, vehemently asserted his relief that the woman he loves rejected his offer and that duty towards his sister and his future children might now rightfully prevail."

In spite of the generous amount of brandy he had consumed, Fitzwilliam gazed at him soberly. "I know your father instilled in you his sense of morality and duty, and you need not cast off those ideals. But surely happiness can be achieved without forfeiting those principles. Why settle for less than you deserve? If you have found the woman to ease whatever weighs you down, marry her. Do not let your ancestors' voices rule you, and do not let this woman slip through your fingers because of misunderstandings. Miss Elizabeth Bennet sounds like a rum-doxy. I should like to meet the clever girl."

"Yet she is beneath me, and you would not believe the unpardonable conduct of her mother, her younger sisters—"

"You have exemplary relations, do you? They say there is

a black sheep in every family, but you have a whole woolly flock of them." His cousin chuckled. "No matter. Mother undoubtedly has a list of wealthy women willing to marry you and endure both your surliness and deplorable relations. But while I may not have the luxury of following my own advice, I beg you to do anything rather than wed without some affection."

"Affection is, or was, a prerequisite on my list of qualifications for a wife. While some of my other wishes were absurd, those propounded by Lady Catherine, your father, and brother are not at all conducive to a happy marriage." Darcy rubbed his chest. Was it possible for one's heart to shrivel? "She accused me of having selfish disdain for others. But what about me? Is it selfish to want to please myself in this? If I settle for a marriage of convenience, I shall end up living a life I do not want."

His cousin gave him a look that spoke of exasperation. "If she is the one you want, then fight for her. Make her change her mind. Forget duty, and allow yourself some happiness in life. Instead of a marriage of indifference, choose one filled with passion, joy, laughter."

"Hah! A future with her certainly would include laughter because *that* would be her response to a second proposal from me—if I ever succumbed to such a weakness as making another unwanted offer. But I shall not grovel at her, or anyone's, feet. There could be no indignity so abhorrent." Darcy rubbed his face and sighed.

"A little loss of pride might do you good. Go and find Wickham, and toss him in the Marshalsea. Then hie back to Hertfordshire and woo the reluctant damsel." Fitzwilliam yawned. "Faint heart never won fair lady."

"The damsel is more than reluctant. She thinks ill of me. And, let me tell you…That fair lady would eat alive any faint-hearted man." Upon noticing his cousin's flagging energy, Darcy thanked him for his counsel, wished him a speedy recovery, and yanked open the door. "I have a wedding to attend in Derbyshire and shall not return to Hertfordshire cap in hand. I assure you, Elizabeth Bennet will be forgot."

Chapter 17

For the second time in his life, Darcy's heart had been ravaged by a woman. He tried to forget and even achieved some degree of success—not in forgetting Elizabeth Bennet but in forgetting himself and his duty.

Hurling himself into a search for Wickham provided him both the occupation and punishment he sought. After spending long hours in the city's most disreputable districts failing to find the cur, Darcy, accompanied by two of his burliest footmen, stumbled home near dawn. Drunk as an emperor—ten times as drunk as a lord—he fell into bed and awoke in the afternoon, sick, regretful, and disgusted with himself. But oblivion had been preferable to failure, anger, hurt, and bitterness. Bruised and dispirited, he wandered about his chambers, drink in hand, with neither purpose nor direction.

Elizabeth. He considered what she would think of such intemperance. *She would be appalled and offended, even more so than I already appal and offend her.* That thought, as well as his own shame and the image of Georgiana's sad blue eyes, kept him from reaching again for the bottle. Other eyes, darker ones, haunted him noon and night, holding him in thrall. The harder he tried to expunge her, the deeper she became entrenched, ever present within his breast, persistently inside his head, yet painfully absent from his side.

In hindsight, he knew he had gone about it all wrong. What kind of tom-fool tried to win a woman's hand by insulting her and her loved ones? Ingrained duty to the Darcy name had to be upheld, but... *Devil take it!* If he knew its whereabouts, his catalogue of prerequisites for a wife would be tossed to blazes. He had only one requirement, but the heated sting behind his eyelids and the painful lump in his throat reminded him he could not have her.

The next day, despite a roaring fire across the room, he felt cold and dull as he stood looking through the window of his chambers. *Her part of Hertfordshire must be all brightness and warmth this morning simply because she is in it...even in the bone-chilling drizzle of late Nov—*

"What is the date?"

Shaking off his stupor, Darcy consulted the almanack he kept on his escritoire. Immediately he remembered Miss Taylor and Browne's wedding and that he and Georgiana should be on their way to Derbyshire. Staring at the page, he hung his head. *Less than a week ago, I presumed my own wedding would take place before Christmas.* He had been a fool, perhaps he still was a fool, but he was determined to look forwards and remember his obligations to others. Jonesby was summoned and instructed to pack.

"Already completed, sir."

"Good man." Darcy stuffed books and correspondence into a satchel. "The painting in my dressing room is to be carefully wrapped, stored, and kept dry for the journey. Since there is to be a ball, I shall require my best tailcoat. The black one I wore at Netherfield."

"Both already have been packed, sir. Which reminds me..." Jonesby disappeared into the dressing room and returned gingerly holding something between thumb and forefinger. "What would you like me to do with this? It was found in the tailcoat's breast pock—"

Darcy snatched the dainty satin slipper from Jonesby's hand.

The valet tut-tutted and mumbled something about poor, lost souls. At Darcy's puzzled frown he replied, "The shoes, sir. One soul here, missing its mate, its other half left behind in Hertfordshire."

The Bennets, Darcy assumed, would not travel to Ashover for their relation's wedding. It was no easy distance, and he had heard no mention of their going. *I might, though, glean some word of Elizabeth from Browne. At least she and I shall maintain a tenuous connexion once her cousin marries my friend.*

His sister had been on tenterhooks around him since the events at Ramsgate. So the long journey northwards—while it was only Georgiana, Mrs Annesley, and him within the carriage's confines—was a welcome opportunity to re-establish the special bond brother and sister had always shared. Darcy could not help but feel remorse again for having failed her where Wickham was concerned and, more recently, for being the cause of further distress. While her companion slept, he reached across and grasped one of Georgiana's gloved hands and murmured inadequate apologies.

The ensuing tête-à-tête should have taken place long before, but he had avoided it, thinking the acrid smoulder might be smothered by placing a lid over it. By the time the first inn came into sight, Darcy and Georgiana both felt better for having talked.

After dining privately with his sister and Mrs Annesley that night and while writing letters of business, Darcy scrubbed at stubborn stains on his fingers. *Elizabeth is like this blasted ink.* Thanks to her, he had a mark imprinted on his heart. No amount of rubbing his chest removed the memory of fine eyes, lively mind, and indomitable mettle.

Sipping nothing stronger than tea, he stared into the grate. Flames climbed higher, dancing and weaving in varying shades of yellow, orange, and indigo. Green softwood fuelled the fire, and it burnt with startling snaps and pops rather than the sizzle of well-seasoned hardwood used at his homes. Like his hopes had done, glowing bits flew upwards before settling like brilliant gems only to die within grey, powdery residue. *I was wrong.* She was nothing like ink. She was, as he previously thought, an ember amongst ashes. She was fire. Bright, warm, sparkling. Lighting up everything round her, attracting others like moths to flame.

And he was a man of honour, of good substance and credit. A man of the land, of the earth. He was oak. Firewood. The fuel she needed to burn steadily. Artless and unsophisticated, she would have benefited from his judgment, his information, his knowledge of the world. He was exactly the man who, in disposition and talents, would have best suited her. His understanding, his temper, his wealth would have answered all her wishes. They would have been magnificent together. Fire and fuel. Combustible, but magnificent. Incendiary.

Before her refusal, he had been attracted to Elizabeth's form, her wit, her nurturing soul. But, because she rejected him and defended her family, he knew she had integrity and was fiercely loyal. Had she been mercenary, she would have accepted him for the comfort and security his wealth and station could provide.

She is everything I have imagined, the most lovely and admirable woman I have ever known.

Duty to his family name was nothing to the longing in his soul. Forgetting her proved too painful, too heart-rending, too unthinkable. Even images of the Bennets failed to deter him—the father rolling his eyes while his loud, fluttering wife and three youngest daughters engaged in their own peculiar brands of vulgar silliness or pedantic vanity. The depths of Darcy's soul could do nought but silently quote Shakespeare. *'I love you with so much of my heart that none is left to protest'.* With a heavy sigh, he realised, *I must persuade her that I am not the man she thinks she knows.*

He gave not a toss what the *ton* might think, except where his sister's future was concerned. *After all,* he thought, *Georgiana's future will be happier if I can achieve my own felicity.*

When Georgiana entered the small sitting room, she was informed in no uncertain terms that the course he was about to undertake might materially lessen her chances of one day making a brilliant match. She was young still, but he wanted to prepare her for the eventuality. Part way through the talk, she lost control of her emotions, dissolving into blubbering rants about money and connexions being all men ever cared about when considering marriage.

He knew she was thinking of Wickham, but Darcy was impatient with the interruption and the criticism. "Pray do not tar me with that brush. By disregarding wealth and connexions, I shall swim against a powerful current—duty, our Fitzwilliam relations, the *ton*." Settling beside her, he grasped her hands—and a soggy handkerchief—between his palms. Assurance was given of one another's everlasting affection, and Georgiana offered her best wishes for his future felicity.

Her blessing granted and his determination set, Darcy

resolved to head south after Miss Taylor's wedding and win the Bennets' respect. From Elizabeth, though, he wanted much more than mere warm approval. He wanted her love. He would spend the twelve days of Christmas, and many more, if needed, in Hertfordshire wooing her.

But first, Georgiana had to be taken to Pemberley and he to Wishinghill Park.

Chapter 18

On the morning after the ball, the bustle of Elizabeth's leaving Longbourn had been amplified by Mrs Bennet's protests over her second daughter's travelling 'such a great distance at such a dreadful time of year', and by Lydia's indignant complaints over the noise wakening her at such a frightfully early hour. Indeed, the clock had barely struck half past ten when Elizabeth's trunk was loaded and her baggage carried down.

Having seen off a maid, valet, and trunks in another carriage at sunrise from the Browne's home on Portman Square, Elizabeth's cousin was determined to be in and out of Hertfordshire by eleven. "Make haste, Cousin," he urged, as his mother smiled indulgently. "With the sun setting around four, we have only a handful of daylight hours remaining before our first stop, followed by longer days of travel and more nights at inns along the way. But in little more than a se'nnight, Miss Taylor will be my wife." Lifting Elizabeth off the ground, he spun her round, laughing. "I am over the moon, dear girl! Over the moon!"

The door of her aunt's travelling chaise was closed, and the horses set off at a trot. Before Elizabeth, a joyful occasion awaited. There was no room for dismay inside the carriage, only delight in being together with her aunt Browne and cousin, hours of mirthful memories, and moments of serious conference.

The first exchange began with all the minutiae of the previous night's ball, which was a memorable occasion according to Elizabeth, with everything to delight the senses, including sarsenet and lace, at which point Mr Browne grimaced and buried his nose in a book. After remarking on her gown's exquisiteness and that she would wear it again at the Wishinghill ball, Elizabeth thanked her godmother and offered heartfelt regret for having lost one of the satin slippers. "Other than having to leave early, the ball proceeded as most do," she added with false cheer. "It truly was a night to remember."

Although theirs was not a sightseeing tour, Elizabeth soon became engrossed in a road entirely new to her, with every milestone espied sooner than expected. *How wondrous it would be to see such vistas during summer's verdancy!* But it was unlikely she ever again would venture north. Her straying mind, vile thing that it was, sent a reminder she might have been bound for Pemberley before year's end had she accepted Mr Darcy's proposal. She told her mind to hush; but, unbidden, that gentleman occupied her thoughts whenever conversation dwindled.

On the second day of their journey, Mrs Browne suggested her son hire a horse and ride the next leg. He, thinking it a grand idea, put it into early action at the nearest posting house. Alone then with her niece, she asked Elizabeth what troubled her. "Such sighing, such fidgeting as might have done Kitty proud. Although you try to hide it, you are not your usual, vibrant self. Are you homesick already?"

"No, not at all. Forgive me for being dull. I suppose I have not slept well since the regrettable ball, but I assure you I am enjoying myself. How could I not in the excellence of your company and the newness of everything? Do you know the farthest I previously travelled was with my father to see his *alma mater* and his beloved Bodleian Library? Oxford, he often says, was where he spent the happiest days of his life."

"How odd," said her aunt. "Yesterday you told us the ball was not out of the ordinary, other than the loss of an inconsequential slipper and your leaving early. Today you speak of it being regrettable and followed by sleepless nights." She frowned at her goddaughter. "I sent my son off so we might talk privately, but you have prevaricated and digressed. Now, tell me what preys upon your mind."

Gathering her thoughts, Elizabeth gazed at the passing countryside. "I fear my clever first impressions are no longer to be trusted. I now question my study of one gentleman's character in particular."

"Do you mean the illustrious Mr Darcy of Pemberley?" Her aunt laughed when Elizabeth's mouth fell open. "Your recent letters made frequent mention of him." When her niece insisted she had made no such mention, Mrs Browne patted her hand. "Yes, you did, dear heart, and you were quite unstinting on the subject. You often were in his august company, it seems."

"Yes, more often than I liked. Rude and arrogant, he scarcely spoke to my family or neighbours. Mr Darcy was too eaten up with pride, too far above his company to look down from Olympus and see us mere mortals. I care not if he has, as is reported, ten thousand a year. Being amongst common gentry is preferable to the wealthier, loftier, prouder, crueller spheres. Such men are nothing but pleasure seekers…or so I thought."

"Mr Darcy has every right to be proud. Besides, do you suppose *ton* women want him solely for his wealth and standing? If nothing else, have you *looked* at him? Oh, good heavens, Lizzy!" Mrs Browne dissolved into laughter. "I hope you are not blushing on my account. Even an ageing widow may admire a handsome young gentleman."

Elizabeth felt her cheeks burning, as mortified by her aunt's words as by her perception.

"Mr Darcy, though, is not only devilishly attractive but worthy of regard for his respectable character," Mrs Browne continued. "Michael would never have associated with him otherwise. According to your aunt Gardiner, the Darcys of Pemberley have been esteemed for centuries."

Elizabeth was unconvinced and said so.

"Do not be influenced by your father's misplaced prejudice against the peerage and the more opulent gentry—which stations do have their share of honourable souls. Do you know why he refers to the nobility as worthless dregs of society?"

"It has much to do, I think, with the depraved behaviour of the Prince Regent."

"Your father's disdain goes further back than that. His contempt began during his university years. You may not be aware that my uncle Munson—your grandmama Bennet's much younger brother—moved from Essex to Oxfordshire and made his wealth there. Although not a likeable man and a bit of a rake, he did perform one charitable service before his demise. He became your father's patron and was instrumental in obtaining a scholarship for him at Oxford."

Mrs Browne took up the scarf she had been knitting earlier. "I do not have first-hand knowledge, but, as I understand it, my brother was a keen scholar who spent many hours at the Bodleian but also did his fair share of carousing."

Elizabeth's scepticism must have shown on her face for

her aunt added, "Do not scoff. It is often the way of young men." Elizabeth asked how, if he did not tell her, she knew such a thing. "Finding my ear innocently pressed to the keyhole of Father's book-room, I could not help but learn of my brother's pursuit of a young lady, a Miss Hen— Faith! Now what have I said to make you blush?"

"It is awkward to imagine Papa carousing or pursuing someone other than Mama."

"That was before he met your mother, before he inherited. My poor brother was more often than not away from Longbourn—farmed out as an infant, sent to school, then university. Upon leaving Oxford, he seemed to miss more than its wondrous library. He was despondent, and I grew concerned. Inquisitive creature that I was, I learnt from the keyhole my brother had been thrown over by his young lady. She married a nobleman, a wealthy one with a grand estate. Weeks later, still pining for his first love, my brother met the spirited Miss Gardiner, who had it in her head to elope with a redcoat of unsavoury character. He swept in to rescue the silly girl, who apparently resembled his lost love. The rest, as they say, is history. Since it is *his* story, do not breathe a word of it to another soul. I merely wanted you to know why he holds a grudge against the *ton*, and I apologise if I have been too frank or have tainted your respect for your father. At least he does not seek comfort from other women. Men sometimes do, you know, as consolation for regrets caused by their own imprudence."

"Men are not alone in imprudence. Perhaps I am too much like my father." Elizabeth cringed at the thought. "With no compunction about pointing out a few home truths, Charlotte Lucas claims I am too quick to judge. She knows me better than I know myself."

Turning to the window, she fell silent, her thoughts about

the opposite sex confused. While she had not entirely believed everything Mr Wickham told her at the Philipses', his insinuations had influenced her opinion of Mr Darcy.

For the next hours, until they met up with her cousin at the coaching inn, the only sounds inside the carriage were clicking knitting needles, pounding hoofs, turning wheels, jingling harnesses, and a relentless voice in Elizabeth's head telling her she might have been wrong about the gentleman who had made her an honourable offer.

⌒～⌒

Claiming Miss Taylor had provided excellent instructions on how to reach Wishinghill Park, Mr Browne had refused to ask directions until his mother—disliking dizziness and being driven in circles—insisted he do so. In frustration and encroaching darkness, Elizabeth again glanced at her watch. It was nearing four o'clock, and she was wild to escape the carriage's confines, to see Miss Taylor again, to meet Mr and Mrs Taylor, to dine, and to sleep in a comfortable bed.

Dusk and a light rain fell as they came to a stop at the manor's front entrance. From what little Elizabeth could see, the house—with eight bays and a west-range parapet overlooking a good-sized lake—was situated at the base of a hill and flanked on two sides by parkland. A faint glow shone from a second-storey window where a woman holding a child briefly appeared.

A cloaked, hooded figure came flying out to greet them. The footman had yet to put down the steps when Mr Browne leapt from the carriage and did so himself. After assisting his mother and cousin, he swept Miss Taylor, laughing, up into his arms. Head thrown back, she put her arms round his neck while he twirled her. Elizabeth and her aunt grinned at the indecorous but delightful reunion.

Miss Taylor waved and demanded her beloved put her down. "Welcome to Wishinghill Park, everyone," she called. "You are unpardonably late, but I am thrilled you finally are here. Come, Miss Bennet. Meet my parents."

Mr Taylor was the gregarious, garrulous sort, reminding Elizabeth of Sir William Lucas. In being more sedately amiable, Mrs Taylor brought to mind Lady Lucas. With pleasure, the couple welcomed their guests, asked for an account of their journey, and had them comfortably settled in first-floor chambers in the west wing, which was separated by the gallery and upper hall from the east wing's family apartments. Fireplaces had been lit, hot baths poured, and the weary travellers were soon at the dining-room table enjoying chestnut soup, roasted meat, savoury pies, and a warming ginger drink.

Having been so affectionately received and tended, Elizabeth was content with her surroundings and with seeing her cousin and Miss Taylor so happy. She went to bed eager for good company, amusements, and gaieties.

Chapter 19

On Sunday, the first of December, the Wishinghill party attended services at All Saints in Ashover, where Mr Browne and Miss Taylor's banns were read for the third and final time. Afterwards, the men played chess while the two older women went over details for the ball and bride's breakfast.

While conducting a tour of the manor, Miss Taylor pointed out to Elizabeth an immense staircase leading to the second floor. "The picture gallery and state apartments are rarely opened. So, rather than view stodgy old portraits or gilded furnishings up there, let us go for a walk." Elizabeth agreed, although she might have liked a peek inside stately chambers. *How odd.* If it was closed, why had she seen a woman and child up there the previous evening?

While strolling through gardens and orchards, Elizabeth asked for her friend's opinion of Mr Darcy.

"As highly sought after as he is, Darcy is untrusting and suspicious of women's motives. As he is several years my elder, he should start filling his own nursery, but I cannot imagine who might be worthy enough to become his wife. Goodness, Miss Bennet, are you blushing?"

"No! Perhaps your chilly Derbyshire air has put roses into my cheeks."

"We should turn back. It feels like rain again." Miss Taylor linked her arm with Elizabeth's. "I pray Darcy finds a loving lady because he is so kind-hearted himself. I should not speak out of turn, but he became chary round women after a disappointment four summers ago. I believe he thought himself in love with a friend of mine from school, but...A betrayal occurred." Miss Taylor seemed reluctant to go on. "Miss Amesbury's father had died some years previously, and the rest of her family were not the affectionate sort. Her brother arranged her marriage in the autumn of the year seven. While Captain Maguire served in Spain, she stayed with his parents in Ireland, giving birth to a son the following spring. In mid-October of last year, the captain was killed. When the Dowager Baroness of Darley fell ill, Mrs Maguire was summoned to her childhood home, Riverswood. Thankfully, she arrived in time to speak one last time with her mother."

Miss Taylor bent her head closer to Elizabeth's. "It is none of my concern, but it seems the child might have arrived early."

Elizabeth thought she understood the situation. Mr Darcy was the boy's natural father. That was what had distressed him one evening at Netherfield. He had shirked his duty, and the ruined young lady had been forced to marry another. Just when Elizabeth's feelings had begun to soften towards him, she found herself in conflict, not knowing whether she felt sorrier for Mrs Maguire or herself. Thinking Charlotte would be proud of her for not jumping to conclusions, she whispered the burning question. "Is the Maguire boy Mr Darcy's natural son?"

"What? No. Of course not! Good heavens, how could you think that?" Although clearly still shocked by Elizabeth's misapprehension, Miss Taylor softly assured her, "If such had been the case, Darcy certainly would have done the honourable thing and married her."

Oh, when shall I learn to consider all the facts before making hasty judgments? Mr Wickham's allegations at her aunt and uncle's card party had, indeed, taken root in her mind and poisoned her against the gentleman. But never had she witnessed anything that revealed Mr Darcy as unprincipled, irreligious, or immoral. She grew absolutely ashamed of herself. *How despicably have I acted! I, who have prided myself on my discernment! How humiliating is this discovery!*

Rounding the corner, her eye was drawn to a curtain twitching at an upper-storey window. Reminded of the woman and child she had seen the day prior, Elizabeth was about to remark on it when her cousin called from the front lawn, jogging to meet them. "We are to play riddles. Mother and Mr and Mrs Taylor against the three of us. I never can think of one myself, but my clever cousin cannot have much difficulty devising one."

The mystery of the state rooms was yet another conundrum to be set aside for later contemplation. With a three-syllable word already preying upon her mind, Elizabeth remembered an appropriate riddle. "My first has the making of honey to charm. My second brings breakfast to bed on your arm. My third bores a hole in leather so fine. While united, the whole breaks the heart most kind."

"Bee...tray...awl. Betrayal." Miss Taylor's expression grew grim as she whispered to Elizabeth, "It was Darcy who had his trust betrayed."

Further reflection and newly-formed sympathetic thoughts towards Mr Darcy would make her totally unfit for games and conversation, so Elizabeth entered the house determined to appear as her usual cheerful self.

Early the next morning, strolling through the orchards, Miss Taylor had a long talk with Elizabeth. Although her friend would disclose no further details, Elizabeth was assured that young Master Maguire was not related by blood to Mr Darcy. The gentleman's character was then exalted to an almost sickening degree.

"Darcy was great fun when we were children. After his father's death, I saw Pemberley's new master only occasionally. He has no hostess. His sister is only fifteen, so he rarely entertains there. A quiet man, he never rattles on merely to hear the sound of his own voice. He is a listener, speaking up only when he has something worthy to say. Even then, he chooses his words carefully."

Elizabeth's quiet chuckle did not go unnoticed by Miss Taylor. "Why do you scoff? I have seen Darcy converse politely and intelligently with dukes, tradesmen, clergy, cottagers, and servants alike. He even has a wonderful sense of humour, unleashing it only when comfortable with someone. But there are few he trusts enough to reveal his true self. Those making his acquaintance in a ballroom rarely know the real man. In those situations, he is like an actor playing a role, hiding behind a mask. He finds it all rather taxing."

They stopped to watch several deer roaming amongst apple trees. "Darcy is a fastidious gentleman, but he leaves it to his valet to stay current on fashion. You must agree he is in good looks and always impeccably turned out. He is fervent about his duty to his family name...and Pemberley, his legacy. He is chivalrous and fiercely loyal. Woe betide anyone who speaks or acts against those he holds dear, particularly his sister. And I can speak from personal experience. His vile cousin, the Viscount Winster, publicly slighted my parents and me during a musicale at Torway Hall years ago. We all heard it, including Darcy. Although my friend did not take Winster to task immediately, he did privately speak to him later, and his cousin eventually apologised to us."

"By your account, Mr Darcy seems a scrupulous, honourable man."

"Oh, indeed! He can be stubborn, though he is willing to consider new ideas. Abhorring deceit, he is honest to a fault. Imperfect, he has known failure, but he learns from each mistake. First and foremost, he is a gentleman. While not of the peerage—although his mother, Lady Anne, was—Darcy is noble because of fine qualities and high morals. Not only is he a man of principle, he is a man with principles."

Linking her arm with Elizabeth's, Miss Taylor turned towards the house. "Like I said yesterday, I do not know who will be good enough for him to marry, but I do know he would not want a controlling wife—a woman like his aunt, Lady Catherine de Bourgh. Nor a weak one like his cousin, Miss Anne de Bourgh. Or a jealous harpy like Miss Bingley. Darcy admires beauty, but his head will not be turned by it. He needs a true partner to stand by his side, a gentle lady who will be not only a lover but a leader."

Elizabeth's eyes welled up. That she, of all people, had received and rejected an offer from the illustrious and, apparently, honourable Mr Darcy! All Miss Taylor's plaudits, an attractive visage, superior height, and, having proposed to her, excellent taste in women...*Dear God, must You have given so much to one man?*

Chapter 20

Much of Elizabeth's Monday morning was spent in company but also in reflection spoilt by the uncomfortable conclusion that she was guilty of the very crime she had laid at Mr Darcy's door—prejudice against those not of one's own class or gender. Such unjust, deep-rooted bias was unconscionable no matter a person's standing or wealth. Although filled with profound shame, she was determined not to be brought to her knees by it. Disgust soon gave way to a more useful endeavour—the subjugation of her pride, the fixing of the defect in her character, and the restoration of her humour.

Later, while Miss Taylor was occupied with an adjustment to her gown, Elizabeth's cousin suggested she accompany him on a walk. Eager to stretch her legs again and delighted by the scene of a small herd of fallow deer grazing in the fields beyond the lake, Elizabeth agreed. After fetching warmer gloves, she caught sight of Miss Taylor dashing up the staircase towards the state-rooms. *Odd.* But it was none of her concern, so she gave it no further consideration.

The sky was grey, and a damp breeze chilled their bones as the cousins set a steady pace towards a wooded area winding along the right side of the lake. Approaching the field and refusing Mr Browne's offer of assistance, Elizabeth jumped down from a stile, straight into a puddle. Bursting into hearty laughter, she flicked mud from her sloppy skirts and, with a look, challenged him to condemn her for leaping before looking.

"You have not changed, Cousin."

Against the grass, Elizabeth scraped muck from her boots. "I once arrived at Netherfield Park in much the same sorry state as this. The company there, I am convinced, thought me ill-bred and boisterous. Quite the hoyden."

"You and Miss Taylor are much alike. Darcy used to call her 'The Hoyden'."

"I understand he introduced the two of you. Miss Taylor spoke of Mr Darcy, as did your mother while you went on your ride." She gave Mr Browne a sly look. "By the by, it was agreeable to have some peace inside the carriage. I should warn your bride you snore like the dickens." Elizabeth enjoyed her cousin's abashed expression before enquiring about the subject she truly wished to explore. "Now, what can you tell me about Mr Darcy? I imagine he is too dignified a gentleman to snore."

Mr Browne chuckled. "I cannot vouch for him in that regard. We became acquainted at university, played cricket and chess together, and shared an occasional bottle of wine. He made all the necessary connexions but not many close friendships. Like others, I idled away my time at Cambridge while Darcy—who seems to have an insatiable thirst for knowledge—studied the classics, mathematics, and, I believe, moral philosophy. His reputation was, and still is, nearly impeccable, though there was some talk of a woman with whom he…"

The wind picked up, and Elizabeth tied her bonnet tighter. "So there was a woman? Just one?"

"Lud, how would I know? But Darcy is a true gentleman

with strict ideas of right and wrong. Unlike others of his sphere, he treats ladies—young and old alike, highborn or low—with the utmost respect. At least in public. I have, of course, no knowledge of his private life."

Elizabeth's idea of utmost respect included neither insulting a lady within her hearing nor demeaning her family during an ambiguous proposal. "What do you know of his association with a Mrs Maguire...or his dealings with George Wickham?"

"All I know of a Mrs Maguire is that Miss Taylor once had a friend who took on that name. As for Wickham, he was raised at Pemberley and had a falling-out with Darcy. I know none of the particulars. Wickham's depravity was legendary at Cambridge...and still is, hereabouts. Unlike Darcy, he is loose in the haft, devoid of every principle of honour. He received a gentleman's education but never was, or will be, a gentleman."

"Does Mr Darcy always surround himself with feckless men of dissolute habits? Can he truly be so different from Mr Wickham and his ilk?" Elizabeth held her breath, praying it might be so. *Not that it matters a jot to me.*

"He has many acquaintances, but few are allowed close." Mr Browne shrugged. "Like most people, he cannot be without a shade in his character. A bit of devilry inside is what makes us interesting, is it not?"

They walked on, through the field, to the other side of the lake. Elizabeth watched deer scatter into the woods upon their approach. "Do you know Mr Bingley?"

Her cousin's expression dimmed. "The scoundrel paid court to Miss Taylor before I met her. I was introduced to him somewhere, some time ago. He holds the lease on Netherfield Park, does he not?"

"Yes, and hosted a ball there. That same night, Mr Darcy

offered…He requested a set with me. We spoke, and—" Elizabeth looked to the horizon. "I question whether I ever knew him. Or myself."

Sitting on a bench, admiring the view, their backs to the manor, her cousin, with a martyred air, heaved a sigh. "Truly, I cannot claim profound knowledge of the man. Without question, he is an esteemed gentleman. Judging by the number of letters he wrote to Miss Darcy from Cambridge, he is a devoted brother and, now, guardian."

"If he is so decent, so benevolent, why was he haughty and disdainful to the people in Hertfordshire?"

"Away from Pemberley, Darcy feels it is him against the world, and he finds it difficult to trust others." Mr Browne bumped her shoulder with his. "That furrow between your eyebrows signifies scepticism, dear girl, but you have nothing to fear from him."

Fear? She nearly laughed. "True, for never shall I see him again. We do not exactly move in the same circles."

He gave her a strange look. "You *do* realise the Taylors' neighbour will be—"

"There you are!" Startled, the cousins jumped from the bench and turned to see Miss Taylor walking towards them. "Come to the house, you two. Our other guest has arrived."

Elizabeth excused herself to exchange her muddy morning attire and mucky boots for something more refined. Mrs Taylor's lady's maid poured water for washing, helped with her gown, and started on her hair.

"Minett, did you hear that? Laughter from the upper floor, which I understood to be closed." The maid's hands stilled; there was a long pause before she explained the state rooms were regularly cleaned even when not in use.

While the maid finished arranging her hair, Elizabeth reflected on all her cousin had told her. Mr Darcy held the welfare, the contentment of so many, in his charge. A tender feeling towards the gentleman overcame her as she wondered who had custody of his health, his happiness. *For heaven sakes!* He had wanted her to be that person. Tears welled. What had she done?

There was no time for regret. A guest had arrived, and she was expected to join the others. Thanking Minett for her efforts, Elizabeth wended her way to the drawing room, prepared to meet one of Miss Taylor's friends or relations.

Smiling sweetly, she gracefully crossed the threshold... and almost pitched forwards. A sound—something between a yelp and a groan—flew from her throat, alerting the entire room to her ungainly entrance.

He was standing within mere feet of her as he turned. So unexpected was his being there that it was impossible, rooted to the spot as she was, for Elizabeth to avoid his notice. With six pairs of eyes staring at her, she turned ripe-apple red. Mr Darcy's eyes met hers, and she was somewhat gratified to see his countenance also overspread with a flush. *May the ground beneath my feet gape and swallow me alive!*

"Miss Bennet!" He had absolutely started and at first seemed paralysed from astonishment until, recovering, he spoke, if not in terms of perfect composure, at least of civility. "You are here! I mean, what a pleasant surprise to see you...here. You are well, I hope." He looked round. "And your family? Are they also well...and here?"

"I am in perfect health, sir, thank you. My parents and sisters were well the last I saw them. But they are not here. My cousin is here, though. Of course he is." Her embarrassment was impossible to overcome. "His mother, my aunt, is here as well."

Mr Darcy shifted a large, flat parcel wrapped in brown

paper from under one arm to the other. "I had the pleasure of meeting Mrs Browne earlier this year, and…um…"

Miss Taylor gave them an amused look. "Do sit down and have some sherry or Madeira." She looked at her father, standing near the sideboard.

Once Elizabeth was seated, Mr Darcy took the opposite chair. Accepting a drink from Mr Taylor, he set it aside to pass the parcel to Mr Browne, seated next to Miss Taylor on the sofa. "As I was saying, this is given with my best wishes for your future felicity." He glanced at his childhood friend. "As well as a memento of your life here in Derbyshire."

Together, the engaged couple tore away the paper. Smiling, Miss Taylor thanked Mr Darcy. Turning to her betrothed, she asked, "Do you recognise the landscape?"

"Why, yes! The painting includes the historic church, All Saints, where we are to be married." Mr Browne rose to his feet, extending his hand. "I thank you, sir."

Standing and shaking the younger man's hand with enthusiasm, Mr Darcy said he had commissioned the painting upon learning of their engagement. "And may your joy know no bounds." He sat then, gazing at Elizabeth with an unreadable expression.

All those times Elizabeth had watched him watching her, she had never suspected Mr Darcy's admiration. *Now, I would welcome it.* But, once spurned, an intelligent man would never renew interest in a woman who had said horrid things to him.

Dinner was announced, and they repaired to the dining room. Several leaves had been removed from the table, so the seating was intimate. Elizabeth watched and listened while Mr Darcy spoke with his friends. How casual and warm was his conversation. She, too, would speak to him—after apologising for the unkind words she had uttered the night of the ball, and once *he* had apologised to her for his atrocious proposal.

After the separation of the sexes, the three men came into the drawing room still engaged in an ongoing—and, to her, a vexing—discussion of parliamentary issues. Despite her annoyance, Elizabeth admired Mr Darcy's features and athletic build; he was turned out in the finest clothing money could buy. His fingers, so masculine yet graceful, accepted a teacup from his hostess. A lock of hair dangled over his brow, and thick, dark waves brushed his collar. His eyes were like a warm drink of chocolate in the morning. How had she not noticed that before? His cheek sported a dimple, and wrinkles branched out from the outer corners of his eyes as he made a quip that had Mr Browne and Mr Taylor laughing uproariously.

Exuding confidence, intelligence, and good humour, his command of the room was completely different from his aloof behaviour in Hertfordshire. At the time, she had tried to pay no attention to the taciturn man with the arrogant mien and poor opinion of her. Why could he not have been amiable then? Now there he was, all at ease, chatting, smiling, laughing. Everyone hanging on his every word. So relaxed, so amiable. *Well, if he does not speak to me soon, I shall not be sorry.*

A young child's hearty giggle rang out. Mrs Taylor jumped, and her eyes flicked first to her daughter, then to the ceiling. Her guests awaited an explanation. "Miss Bennet, will you perform for us?" The woman's tone was higher pitched than was customary. "Your aunt has spoken highly of your singing voice."

Elizabeth knew her vocals were by no means exemplary. Situating herself at the pianoforte across the room, she expected Mr Darcy to remain with the others. But, moving with his usual deliberation, he drew a chair near the instrument, settling there with one firm shoulder brushing hers. "Do you mean to frighten me, sir, by sitting so close as to witness my every false note?"

While the others listened to *Lavender's Blue*—one of a handful of songs Elizabeth played well—Mr Darcy whispered, "Not at all. I stationed myself here to vocally accompany you. Your song choice intrigues me. Did you know there is an earlier version called *The Kind Country Lovers* with lyrics different from those you use?"

She shook her head and sang.

"Lavender's blue, diddle, diddle, rosemary green."

He joined in.

"When I am king, diddle, diddle, you shall be queen."

The next line, with its alternate lyric, was sung for her ears only.

"You must love me, diddle, diddle, 'cause I love you."

Fingers faltering, she accused him of, indeed, attempting to unsettle her. He inched his chair closer and spoke quietly, "Were it my intention to unnerve you, I would sing the scandalous second part of the verse."

"Upon my word!" Elizabeth's hands wobbled over the keys before playing on. "A *scandalous* version of an otherwise acceptable song? If you intend to corrupt my morals, I should warn you my courage arises apace with roguish intimidation."

Shifting nearer, he sang quietly by her ear.

"I heard one say, diddle, diddle, since I came hither,
that you and I, diddle, diddle, must lie together."

Good heavens! In haste to scramble away from him, she knocked the instrument's lid. It slammed over the keys with a crash. All conversation stopped. Every eye was upon them. A flush rushed upwards from Elizabeth's neck, flooding her face.

Springing to his feet, Mr Darcy apologised to the room. "I have, I fear, offended the lady's delicate ear with my off-key singing." Rushing to her side as she walked away, he whispered, "I beg your forgiveness, Miss Bennet. It is nothing but a well-known alternate lyric. I did not mean to imply you and I should—"

CRACK! An angry clap of thunder drowned out his words. Lightning flashed. Rain pattered against panes. Hailing from southerly climes, Elizabeth and her relations were more accustomed to thunderstorms than the Derbyshire natives who seemed quite concerned by such an unusual occurrence. With every flash, every clap, Mrs Taylor, visibly shaken, exclaimed, "How terrifyingly extraordinary!"

Servants were ordered to keep watch for danger and damage throughout the storm. Everyone else retired earlier than their wont.

Into the night, the storm loomed overhead, thunder occasionally rumbling. Curled up beneath the bedclothes, Elizabeth observed that with each powerful discharge of light, eerie shadows of tree branches were cast upon curtains. She had just drifted off when something other than a rumble jolted her awake. Sitting bolt upright, seized with foreboding, she sought the source of disquieting sounds coming from within the house, not without. She heard muffled voices— one of them a young child's—as well as running footsteps and heavy objects being moved. All seemed to emanate from a room directly above hers. *Unoccupied, my foot!* Fear and curiosity aroused, she flung off the covers. Resolved to determine no one was injured, she slid her feet into mules and pulled on a dressing gown; neither kept her from shivering in the cold. Lit candle in hand, she left her room's safety to venture into the dark passage.

Her clammy palm gripped the hand-rail of the immense north staircase as she gained the first creaky step. Lightning flashed, illuminating her way. Black talons reached out from the left wall. *Just shadows of leafless branches,* she told herself.

Keenly aware of eerie noises from above, Elizabeth crept upwards. A youngster's cry was followed by hushed ones. Halfway up, her skin rose in gooseflesh as a frigid current of air swirled round her. Her candle's flame flickered in the draught, then extinguished. Plunged into complete darkness, her courage sank. Shivering, stumbling, catching her hem, she fell to her knees on the step. *Blast!* Then, from the blackness of the landing above, a glow appeared. A phantasm floated out of the gloom, its white shroud billowing. *Get up! Get up! Run!* Inch by inch, the sinister radiance descended. *Get up! Run! Run!* The wraith's icy fingers latched upon Elizabeth's hand. She dropped the candlestick and screamed.

"Miss Bennet? Is that you?"

Hand over pounding heart, she gave a shaky laugh. "Miss Taylor, what on earth are you doing? You gave me a terrific fright. What is happening? I thought the floor above was closed."

From below, candlesticks in hand and speaking at once, the Brownes and Mr Darcy sought assurance all was well.

"Just a leaky roof, nothing to fret over." Miss Taylor picked up the fallen candlestick, relighting the taper from her own candelabrum. Passing it to Elizabeth, she guided her down the stairs to the three other guests. "I apologise for the noise, and for inadvertently scaring Miss Bennet out of her wits a moment ago. Water is dripping from the attics into a state room, and footmen are placing buckets and shifting things round. 'Tis very late. Please, everyone, return to your warm beds."

"But..." Elizabeth looked over her shoulder. "I heard a child's voice up there."

"Oh, that could have been one of the young maids mopping the floor. My parents are up there directing them. All is well. Back to bed."

In her room, under the covers, Elizabeth tossed and turned and huffed. All was not well. How unsettling to have seen the staid Mr Darcy in his powdering gown...and with his hair all tousled. No man had a right to look so devilishly alluring in dishabille. And sporting provocative, dark stubble on his jaw. *That look could grow on me.* She stifled a giggle into her pillow.

Chapter 21

D arcy could find precious little sleep. As tumultuous
and angry as the storm, his mind raged at him.
Starting in adolescence, Wickham had admonished
him to stop being the proper, respectable boy. *Why the devil
did I decide, last night, of all nights, to heed his advice? What was I
thinking?* He had not been thinking. That was his problem.
Since the surprise of seeing Elizabeth Bennet in the drawing
room, he had taken leave of his senses.

You and I, diddle, diddle, must lie together

Dear Lord! He prayed no one else had heard the indecorous lyric. It was bad enough she had. Then he had fumbled
an apology—and lied through his teeth—saying he had not
meant she and he must lie together. *I thought the ensuing
mighty thunderclap was God Himself about to strike me dead for
uttering that falsehood.* He was a fool, but she was meant to be
his wife. Ergo, he was meant to beget Pemberley's heir by
her. Singing bawdy lyrics and speaking to her so familiarly
certainly were not the proper way to convince her of that, let
alone encourage her to see him as a worthy suitor.

Elizabeth. He had the opportunity—nay, damned good
fortune—to prove himself to her now. Rather than going to

Hertfordshire, he would woo the dickens out of her at Wishinghill. And he had a whole day and a half to do so, in a household celebrating love and marriage. *Splendid.*

But a balance had to be struck between the strait-laced boy he had been and the crooning, lecherous rake he had just acted. Darcy lay in bed, devising a plan. *I shall kiss her hand.* Bingley, he remembered, had always promoted dancing as a sure step towards falling in love. *Oh, that is good. I shall request two sets at the ball.* Then, when the time came to renew his offer, he would go down on bended knee like a mawkish hero of some missish fairy-tale romance. *Excellent. As I once told Bingley, winning a wife requires blessed little effort.* He groaned. *So long as one does not insult the lady to whom he wishes to propose.*

Thunder rumbled in the distance. Lightning flashed, illuminating his room. But when he closed his eyes, all he saw behind the lids was Elizabeth Bennet in her dressing robe and hair in a plait. *How am I supposed to sleep after witnessing such a sight?*

Barely had he fallen asleep when he heard his valet. "Good morning, sir." Jonesby drew back the window curtains. "I trust you slept well despite the storm and the to-do up in the state rooms."

Darcy closed his eyes, snuggling deeper. "I shall linger here awhile."

"Very good, sir. I shall see to it that Miss Bennet and the others are informed you will *not* join them this morning."

Sitting up, Darcy gave Jonesby a glare that would have had weaker men quaking in their shoes. "Join her—them —where?"

"Someplace called the Fabrick, sir." The valet placed a laden tray in front of his employer. "And, as customary, I have anticipated your needs."

A maid arrived with a steaming pitcher while Jonesby set out towelling, soaps, brushes, a razor, and morning attire.

Arriving in the vestibule, Darcy found the entire party was gathered; Miss Taylor, Browne, and Elizabeth were pulling on hats, scarves, and warm gloves and about to step outside. After he asked to accompany them and agreement was cheerfully given, Darcy enquired whether anyone else would be joining them. Mrs Browne said she was not in the habit of walking. Glancing upwards, Mr Taylor indicated he could not spare the time, having to oversee repairs to the damaged state room. His wife explained she would be busy with preparations for that evening's ball. So the outing would be only the four young people...unchaperoned. Darcy's hopes soared. *Better and better!*

They took a shortcut lined with gorse, bilberry, and other low, heathland shrubs and made their way upwards to the gritstone ridge. "Ashover," said Miss Taylor, leading the way, "is situated near the Peak District's eastern edge. The valley has been mined for lead and quarried for minerals since Roman times, and our church has a magnificent lead font dating from the twelfth century. When we reach the top, you will see the area known as the Fabrick, the highest elevation for a considerable distance. Were it a clear day, we might see the Crooked Spire at Chesterfield, nearly eight miles distant. Later, I shall tell you the myths, most involving the devil, about that twisted steeple. Ten bells were installed in its belfry last year, and they can be heard for four miles around. A curfew peal summons four hundred paroled French army and navy officers, allowed freedom within two miles of Chesterfield, back to their barracks."

Hoping to take Elizabeth's mind off devilish spires and roaming prisoners-of-war, Darcy added, "In Ashbourne, some local girls married captured officers who have their own servants. One such French cook introduced a tasty gingerbread to the area. If we had more time," he added, looking at Elizabeth, "I would take you there and purchase some for you."

"I would have liked that, Mr Darcy." She smiled at him. "Gingerbread is a favourite of mine."

"You may have some in the morning," called Miss Taylor from ahead. "Gingerbread will be included in the bride's breakfast"—she gave a little squeal—"tomorrow!"

Darcy then overheard her telling Browne one of the Crooked Spire myths—the one in which the Chesterfield church was so surprised to see a virgin, male or female, being married that its spire turned round for a closer look and became locked in a twisted position. It would supposedly return to its true form should another virgin ever marry there.

Upon reaching the rock outcrop known as the Fabrick, Miss Taylor caught Darcy's eye and winked several times. Gesturing towards Elizabeth, she pulled on Browne's arm and moved away with him to point out distant landmarks unseen in the brume. *Does she suspect I want privacy?* They had been friends all their lives, and she could read him like a book. *Did she and Elizabeth talk about me? Does she know about my travesty of a proposal?* Darcy's ears burnt. *Why do women have to tell one another everything?* From the corner of his eye, he saw the engaged couple wandering off.

No matter how tightly Elizabeth held her bonnet, several dark locks escaped from its confines, whipping round her face. Darcy nearly reached out to still their assault.

"My word," said she, gazing at the scenery. "I had not realised the village was so charmingly situated. We arrived in Ashover at nightfall."

"While I am partial to Kympton and Lambton, Ashover is

pleasant." When the lady said her aunt Gardiner hailed from Lambton, he added, "That is but five miles from my estate. Is this your first time in Derbyshire?" Elizabeth told him the farthest she had travelled from Longbourn until the past week had been to Oxford.

Turning towards the huge rock outcrop, she asked whether he had been up there before. Darcy said he was fortunate to have come on a sunny day with the Taylors when Miss Taylor and he were adolescents. "Years later, I came with my Fitzwilliam cousins. Their father's seat, Torway Hall, is just outside Matlock, a little over four miles from here."

She nodded and asked why the place was called the Fabrick. He pointed at the gritstone formation. "Similar stone was taken from here and used to build All Saints. Property left in trust for church purposes is 'fabric land' because it provides material or revenue. Other local places have unusual names, too. Ravensnest, Cocking Tor, the Rattle." How he longed to show her his estate, his Derbyshire! "Pemberley, by the by, is in that direction," he said, pointing.

"Ah," was her only reply before she gazed up at the clouds. "Despite the grey blanket covering the green valley, 'tis beautiful up here but bitterly cold. Is the sky always so gloomy hereabouts?"

"Gloomy? It appears rather bright to me." *Because you are here.* To Darcy, she was all sunshine and sparkle, exuberance and joy. She loved not only the natural world around her but life itself. *Would that she loved me as well!* Drawing closer, the more detail he perceived in her hazel eyes, so clear and bright, so dark, so changeable. *Oh, to spend a lifetime studying them, being enthralled by them!*

She shivered, leading him to suggest she put her back against the outcrop to shelter from the raw wind's bite.

"Miss Bennet," he said at the exact moment she said, "Mr Darcy." He indicated she should speak first.

Blushing, she did so. "Very well, but to assuage my own feelings, I may wound yours by dredging up the night of Mr Bingley's ball. I cannot go on without apologising for abusing you so abominably then."

"What did you say of me that I did not deserve? Any ill-founded accusations were formed on mistaken premises and, I believe, on another man's lies. And yet," he said, wincing, "my behaviour to you that night and the mode of my ambiguous declaration merited the severest reproof. Believing you to be wishing for, expecting even, my addresses, I made a lamentable offer with no doubt of success. Thinking any woman would jump at the chance to be mine, I deserved to be humbled."

"Let us not argue over the greater share of blame for that night's acrimony," she replied, grinning at him, "though I insist on claiming the better part." Her flippancy soon dissolved into contriteness. "What I said cannot be remembered without shame, without regret. You, who are not devoid of every proper feeling, must have despised me afterwards." When Darcy protested he could never do so, she shook her head. "You are too kind, sir, and of late I have heard nothing but laudatory remarks about you. The scales have fallen from my eyes. I see what should have been evident all along—you are a good man, Mr Darcy."

He absorbed her praise and, lost in the tenderness of her gaze, nearly missed her next words.

"So, are we agreed all is to be forgiven and forgotten? Please say you accept both my apology and my philosophy, which is to think only of the past as its remembrance gives you pleasure."

Extraordinary creature! "One should learn from past

unpleasantries, madam, but whatever you wish me to do will be done. And please, I beg you to forgive last evening's conduct when I sang so indecorously." Staring at her earnestly, his hand then over heart, Darcy spoke in a rush. "You know how much I admire you, but if your feelings are still what they were last week, please tell me so now. My affections and wishes are unchanged. No, that is untrue. With every moment spent in your presence, my affection swells till my heart may burst." Glancing at the ground, he decided against the down-on-bended-knee scheme. "Might you reconsider and…marry me?"

On the receiving end of an open-mouthed stare, he kicked himself. *The deuce!* Long had he been suspicious of others. But could he, himself, not even be trusted? *Aargh! To act so rashly and officiously to the one person I most want to impress!*

"Clearly it is too soon, and I spoke in haste." He offered up a weak smile. "Rarely do I speak impulsively or make any sort of offer without careful, comprehensive consideration… except where you are concerned. My plan was to return to Hertfordshire and attempt to win your hand there. But when I saw you, red as a beetroot, in the Taylors' drawing room, I —" He sighed. "A plan to pay my addresses to you here was the work of a moment."

"Your surprise could not have been greater than mine, then and now. Although I receive your assurances and addresses with gratitude and pleasure, I cannot give you the answer you desire without a better understanding of your enigmatic character. To that end, let us take time to become better acquainted."

Heartened by Elizabeth's gentle smile, he quickly replied. "Of course, yes, and you may expect me in Hertfordshire within a se'nnight. I thank you for allowing this second chance."

"It is no such thing, sir. A second chance is granted by one to another after some sort of failure. It comes tarnished." Her hand lifted towards him, then lowered as she spoke in a soothing tone. "Instead, let us call ours a fresh start. A new beginning. A clean slate, if you will. Our past has been wiped clean, with neither indebted to the other. Events of the Netherfield ball are to be replaced by tonight's at Wishinghill. We are to learn from our past mistakes and unpleasantries and never again repeat them." Her eyes shone as she asked, "Are we in accord?"

"We are in perfect harmony, as I wish us always to be." A sparrow-hawk atop a leafless tree across the way took flight, and Darcy tracked its trajectory while struggling to recall a name. "Pray, how fares your youngest sister? I understand there was some trouble involving Wickham."

Her expression shifted, and she replied coolly, "I understand your concern. Our possible future together depends on *Lydia's* reputation."

"No! Indeed not," Darcy blurted. *Even after your pretty speech, must you still think the worst of me?* He touched her arm briefly to underline the import of his words. "I am concerned about Miss Lydia. Concerned because my sister…"

Darcy told her then of Wickham, of Ramsgate, and how Georgiana had subsequently suffered.

During his narrative, Elizabeth's expression shifted from doubt to horror to mortification. Visibly shaken, she turned away, sniffling and swiping at tears he suspected were wrought by compassion rather than by the wind's bite. He stepped up and handed her his handkerchief. She thanked him and enquired after his sister's welfare.

"Georgiana is recovering. She even smiles on occasion." *What can I do to make you smile again?*

"The dear girl! But she learnt, the hard way, a most valuable lesson—one I can only hope my sister learns as well." She took a breath and looked away from him. "As you have seen, Lydia is hardly the picture of decorum at the best of times, but she was beyond the pale that night at Netherfield. That vile man laced her punch and took a few liberties, but, thankfully, they were discovered before the misconduct went too far." Her voice took on a challenging tone as she turned to face him. "I already understood Mr Bingley could not be trusted with a lady's affections, but he promised my father the incident would not be mentioned. I must say, Mr Darcy, I wonder at the company you keep."

He winced. "In the past, Bingley could be a capricious suitor, but he and Miss Oliverson are to marry in about a se'nnight. As for the company I *kept*, the others in the Netherfield party—Miss Bingley, the Hursts, Caulifield—were endured only for Bingley's sake."

He tipped back his head, looking skywards. "With regard to Wickham, I tried to tell you about him the night of the ball, but I should not have waited until then to do so. Too late, too soon. My timing never seems apt." He glanced down at his watch. "Speaking of time, we should start making our way back." He crooked his arm in invitation, and they walked abreast whenever the path allowed.

There was, for both of them, much to be thought, felt, and said. In doing so, they paid scant attention to the remains of what had been the big house of the neighbourhood until it was destroyed in the seventeenth century by Royalist soldiers. But it was at those ivy-covered ruins of Eastwood Hall that they encountered an elderly couple with their young granddaughter.

Tired, cranky, and too heavy for her grandparents to carry long stretches, the girl was hoisted onto Darcy's shoulders as though the weight of a feather. The little girl spoke in a thick

Derbyshire dialect, as did her grandparents. Elizabeth apologised for not always understanding them, but Darcy chatted as if they were old friends until parting company at the family's tiny cottage.

He offered his arm again, and she took it without hesitation. For a while, they walked in comfortable silence.

"You have a way with children, Mr Darcy. I noticed as much when you helped our tenants' youngsters find puffballs and allowed Ben to sit upon your great white horse. You will be a wonderful father some day."

He gave her a compelling look.

Blushing, she glanced away, clearly discomfited. "Good heavens! What could have become of my cousin and Miss Taylor? We must make haste, or I never shall be ready on time for the ball. The three maids will have their hands full as it is. Ladies take hours to prepare for such an occasion, you know."

"You, Miss Bennet, could spend an entire day in preparation but look the same as always." *Why is she narrowing those beautiful eyes at me? Have I somehow misspoken?*

"Are you implying I could have my hair dressed, primp and preen for hours on end in front of a mirror, wear my best gown, and still appear as I do now, all wind-blown and blowsy?"

"No. I meant you always are lovely. Always." She seemed appeased by the compliment—perhaps even pleased—and they walked on.

After a maid accepted their coats and such and before parting in the vestibule, Darcy asked for the pleasure of Elizabeth's first and supper sets. He kissed her ungloved hand and cherished the little gasp she gave and the tender look in her eyes as she agreed to his request.

Later, with Jonesby's assistance, he dressed with more

than usual care and prepared in high spirits to claim all that remained unconquered of the lady's heart, trusting it was not more than he could win in the course of the evening.

Chapter 22

Due to the next morning's wedding, the ball commenced early, at seven, and was to end around one. Guests had arrived, instruments were tuned, and Mrs Taylor went about ensuring everyone was looked after and single ladies well-partnered for dancing.

During introductions and while mingling, Elizabeth kept Mr Darcy under furtive observation. His deep, jovial laughter seemed drawn forth from pure enjoyment, and she smiled, knowing how at ease, how happy he was in the company of his neighbours. Wanting to be near, she skirted round him, stole admiring glances, eavesdropped on his discourses, and was thankful her family was not there to witness such smitten behaviour.

The first set was announced, and he was immediately before her, smiling, bowing, and offering his gloved hand. Standing opposite him, she read in others' expressions their amazement at the rarity of it. *Even hereabouts, does he not ask young ladies to stand up?* He looked fixedly at her without uttering a word, speaking instead with his eyes. *What are you saying, Mr Darcy? What is it you are thinking? What are you telling me? Let me hear what it is.*

"You must be as pleased as I am," said he, "that your cousin and my friend have found happiness together."

"I am. How could one not be pleased when a man and woman willingly, seriously, joyously set forth into the bonds of matrimony?" Her gaze strayed to Miss Taylor, who called the dance from top position. "On the morrow, I shall be honoured to witness their promises of lasting love and constancy."

"Since I am likewise honoured, it seems you and I shall meet at the altar tomorrow morning." A thrill coursed through her at those words, that deep voice, and his captivating eyes. "Come now, Miss Bennet," he said as they circled one another, "it is your turn to say something. I talked about us signing the church register. You ought to enquire about Derbyshire traditions or superstitions."

"Such as?"

"One tradition, of course, is well dressing. Then there is the tale of the Derby Ram. There also is much lore about our standing stones. And there *might* be a superstition about a person from Derbyshire finding marital happiness only with someone related to the Bennets of Longbourn." He grinned at her, eyebrows lifted in mock surprise. "Have you never heard that legend? Has Miss Taylor not mentioned something similar?"

"Not that I recall, but perhaps I should look for such happiness hereabouts. Mr Walker has engaged me for the next set," she said in a teasing voice. "Do you know him?"

"Yes. Dreadfully taciturn fellow. You would not get on." When Elizabeth asked about Mr Ward, the young man who had requested her fourth, Mr Darcy gave a dramatic shudder. "He croons scandalous lyrics to otherwise respectable songs. Off-key singing, I know for a fact, offends your delicate ear. You must forget about him."

Passing through the set, Mr Taylor complimented their dancing. After that interruption, Mr Darcy asked Elizabeth to remind him of the topic they had been discussing so seriously.

"Nothing so serious at all," said she with a smile, "and what nonsense we are to talk of next I cannot imagine."

When it was their turn to go down the set, he took her hand in his, asking what she thought of books.

"Our reading preferences do align, you know." Elizabeth grinned at him. "For instance, *Love in Excess; or the Fatal Enquiry.*"

"Ah," he said, after a pause. "I cannot, after all, talk of books with you in a ballroom. That one in particular. To speak of Count D'Elmont's amorous escapades would reflect no credit on my character, I assure you."

"It would reflect well on your character were you to ask other young ladies to stand up with you tonight." Her advice prompted him to smile, and he again assured her whatever she wished him to do would be done.

There were not many couples participating, so the set ended sooner than Elizabeth wished. Until Mr Walker approached for his requested set, Mr Darcy lingered beside her. Then, catching her eye, he bowed over her hand. "Until the supper dances, Miss Bennet."

Throughout the set, wondering whether she would find his gaze upon her, Elizabeth surreptitiously sought Mr Darcy's location while trying to spare a portion of her attention for Mr Walker. Finding the esteemed master of Pemberley always surrounded by admirers—young, old, male, and female alike—inspired within her a feeling she could not like. Although he deserved high regard, and she would never be the clinging, jealous type, she craved his undivided attention. *How extraordinary!* A mere se'nnight ago, she had wished him at Jericho. Since then, he had earned her approbation and respect. *And my affection.* Yet reservations lingered about his opinion regarding her family, his officious-ness, and his true feelings. After all, the word 'love' had not been uttered during either of his proposals.

After the sets with Mr Walker and Mr Ward, she sat down awhile and admitted to herself Mr Darcy had been delight-fully attentive during their half an hour together. *Now, at my prodding, he has asked another young lady to stand up with him. I can hardly hold that against him. Can I?*

Watching him dance with two more ladies, although not without partners herself, Elizabeth admitted not to jealousy but envy. She assured herself there was a difference between the two feelings and wondered at the emotions Mr Darcy could inspire in ladies. *Must we all become simpering, tittering Caroline Bingleys?*

Just before the supper set, Mr Darcy strode towards her with catlike, powerful grace. Other women stared hungrily after him, but he seemed unaware. "Come, Miss Bennet." He held out his hand. "Dance with me again."

Two Scottish reels, allowing little in the way of mean-ingful conversation, were performed before they went through for a light supper.

The formal dining room provided flavoursome fare under impressive ceiling murals, and Mr Darcy served Elizabeth from dishes close at hand and ensured her wine glass was replenished. She drank more than she ought while a gentleman bent Mr Darcy's ear about the folly of hermitages and walled ditches.

She thrived in company, but there were far too many people claiming her, or mostly his, attention. Her head began to ache from the pins in her hair, a pain only worsened as she realised forty-five precious minutes of their limited time together had been spent chatting with strangers rather than becoming better acquainted with one another.

Once both had eaten their fill, Mr Darcy slid his arm across the back of her chair and leant in close, extremely close, not quite touching but sending shivers up and down her spine. Then, within a hair's breadth of her ear, he asked whether she might care to stroll round the ballroom with him. With cheeks aflame and stomach aflutter, she knew not whether the wine or his proximity was at fault as they excused themselves from the table and put on their gloves.

While strolling arm in arm, he asked about her family and apologised for not giving them due respect. "To please you, though, I shall endure the connexion."

Before Elizabeth could respond, they were stopped by a neighbour soliciting Mr Darcy's sage advice on purchasing one of the Merino rams imported by the Duke of Devonshire. Counsel was given and duly appreciated.

Once that gentleman moved on, Elizabeth's emotions spilt over. "*Endure* the connexion? Do you think such would please me? If you spoke courteously to my parents and sisters, *that* would please me. If you came to know, appreciate, or hold them in some affection, that would make me very, very happy."

If he was not fully regretful of his words, at least Mr Darcy appeared abashed as Elizabeth spoke frankly about her family, praising their good qualities and admitting their flaws. She asked him to look beyond Jane's serene smile and see not a vapid creature but a compassionate one, to look beyond Mary's questionable musicality and piousness and see a young lady crying for attention, to look beyond her two silliest sisters' indecorous behaviour and see immaturity and a need for firm guidance.

"I bow to your superior knowledge," he said. "It was wrong to judge your elder sister in such a manner without better knowing her. As for the younger ones, were I in a position to do so, I would hire a music master for Miss Mary and send the other two to a reputable seminary." His voice softened. "I would ease all your worries, Miss Bennet, and your family's, if you would allow me."

They promenaded in silence until Mr Darcy pointed out her failure to add her own flaws to those of her sisters. "Not that you have any, of course. I find you perfect."

Such a ridiculous compliment could not go unchallenged. Elizabeth gave him an amused look. "How provoking you are, sir. You are well-acquainted with my faults. However, since we are supposed to be learning about one another, I shall confess something dreadful about myself: selfishness. Although I have no objection to comfort afforded by wealth, I would never wed merely for financial gain or to appease my mother's nerves. That is how selfish I am, how concerned for nought but my own pleasure. I think too highly of myself and have too many wishes and demands that must be met before I marry."

"You are right to have expectations. I know what you expect in a gentleman but not what you expect in a husband."

Elizabeth had never thought of listing her marital hopes and expectations, but Mr Darcy listened respectfully as she replied with requirements including mutual respect, succour, fidelity, and abiding love. "I could not surrender my freedom, which helps form my happiness, to a marriage lacking these qualities."

"In marrying me," he said, "you would have all that without giving up your so-called independence. You would be neither housebound nor tied to my side. There are duties —many, truth be told—expected of Mrs Darcy. But you would have wealth and leisure to pursue your own interests, to travel, to broaden your knowledge of—"

"You would allow such liberty?" She could scarce believe him!

"Within reason. I would not have you gallivanting—"

"You would curtail my countryside rambles?"

Mr Darcy gazed around the ballroom, where music played, couples danced, and conviviality reigned. "I was *going* to say I would not have you gallivanting abroad at present. It is not safe. But when Wellington trounces the tyrant, I would show you the world." He turned back to Elizabeth, his expression earnest. "There are many experiences I want to share with you."

"Would I have freedom to always speak my mind?" Her eyes conveyed a challenge.

Rubbing his brow, Mr Darcy sighed. "Is this another of those fatal enquiries?"

She repressed a laugh. "Whether it proves fatal or not depends on your answer."

He took up her hand, placing it on his sleeve. "Tell me, will your parents object to my appearing on their doorstep?"

"Heaven forfend! Never would my mother turn away a potential suitor." Head still throbbing from her megrim, she frowned. "You may think poorly of her, but my mother fears for our future. We shall be in dire straits when my father dies and...Oh!" Her grip tightened on Mr Darcy's arm. "Were you intending to stay at Longbourn? The three Brownes and six Gardiners will spend the twelve days of Christmas with us there."

"Absolutely not, no."

He seemed affronted, making Elizabeth wonder whether their conversation of moments ago had been easily forgot. "Is my home below your standards, sir, or do you object to my relations in trade?"

"Neither. I simply would not think of imposing on your

family at such a time. I shall find lodgings in Meryton for myself and my valet." They walked in silence for a few moments before he continued. "You mentioned the twelve days of Christmas. Do you presume I shall be in Hertfordshire until the sixth of January because it will take me until then to win your hand?"

"Oh, yes!" Striving to show more seriousness than levity, she said, "Being the mercenary sort, I must hold out that long in expectation of receiving the appropriate number of swans a swimming, drummers drumming, pipers piping, et cetera."

Much to her delight, Mr Darcy played along. "'Tis rather short notice, madam. I had best get to work straight away. Providentially, I should be able to procure for you, this very night, a quantity of ladies dancing, although their partners might object to my absconding with them. Five gold rings will not be a problem, but I hope to become your true love and place one gold band upon your finger. And I might manage one, not twelve leaping lords. However, he would not take kindly to being presented to you as a gift. In fact, I daresay the Earl of Matlock—my uncle, by the by—would be hopping mad. Would that qualify, in your opinion, as a lord a leaping?"

Elizabeth beamed at him. "I suppose so. But, even were it presently sitting, I would not have you storming the House of Lords for me."

If she had kept a list of prerequisites for a husband, a sense of humour and a knack for banter would rank highly. If not for a plaguing headache, the evening had been as perfect as she ever had known. The regrettable events of the Netherfield ball were being replaced by new and joyous memories, and she believed she could love that night's Mr Darcy. In good spirits—from wine and merriment—she schooled her expression into one of seriousness. "Please, sir, promise me now that none of those increasingly numerous gifts will be sent to Longbourn."

His gloved hand patted hers. "If you insist. But I do intend to bring along a miniature that might interest your family. Your elder sister bears a striking resemblance to the young lady depicted ...someone I once knew."

"How odd. It seems Jane has yet another twin out there somewhere. Mr Wickham also mistook my sister for a lady of his acquaintance."

Elizabeth was astonished when his complexion darkened, and she asked if he was well.

"Perfectly so, I thank you. Just...a sudden desire to take the air. Would you care to join me for a turn in the garden? A maid could accompany us." When Elizabeth nodded and mentioned Minett, he beckoned a footman to fetch her.

Minutes later, bundled in their coats and walking arm-in-arm, Elizabeth asked whether the night air had revived him. "I thank you, yes." He stopped and faced her. "And you? You seem uncomfortable. Are you chilled without a hat? I shall call Minett to fetch your bonnet."

"I could not wear anything over this hair, which," she whispered, "is the source of a beastly headache." He asked whether there was anything he could do to relieve her suffering, and Elizabeth groaned. "Would that you could remove these implements of torture imbedded in my brain." At his dumbfounded look, she huffed and waved a hand round her *coiffure*. "Aunt Browne insisted on this elaborate style, and using the myriad pins and combs now painfully poking my scalp, Mrs Taylor's maid outdid herself. Ergo, I am stuck like a pincushion." Frowning and looking round, she asked the whereabouts of the merciless Minett.

"She is behind us somewhere. Miss Bennet, there is

nothing I would rather do than relieve your pain and take it upon myself."

"Nay!" She laughed, imagining his glorious, dark waves arranged with pins and combs. "Such an intricate style would look ridiculous on a gentleman, and I would not have you suffer on my account."

"If it is any consolation, your hair is beautiful tonight. And you," he whispered, advancing on her, "are always beautiful. Always." Toe to toe, he reached behind her to tug on the loose ringlet at her nape. "Fair though blonde hair may be, it pales in comparison to warm, brunette tresses. How I long to see yours down. But if I removed those nasty implements, I would suffer the agony of knowing I cannot touch you and hold you the way I want." Leaning in, he murmured, "Torture most exquisite."

His warm breath tickled her ear. Lowering her lashes, Elizabeth took a few ragged breaths. If there were other sounds, evidence of a ball in progress, she heard none but his deep voice.

"Tomorrow we part," said he. "An eternity until I may see you again. You are the handsomest, most desirable, intelligent, courageous, infuriating woman of my acquaintance. The only woman I dare trust with the Darcy name, with Georgiana, with my household servants and with my tenants, with my legacy, with my heart."

A gloved finger tipped up her chin, his other hand settled at her waist, drawing her close. He exhaled her name along with a warm whiff of wine. Her pulse raced, and his scent— male with an alluring trace of sweet spice—surrounded her. He smiled, and his dimple softened her heart. Pushing him away never entered her mind even though she knew, she *hoped*, he meant to kiss her. *If he does, how should I respond?* Her first kiss behind Longbourn's old dovecote with William

Goulding when they were sixteen had been awkward, innocent, and hardly helpful. *Just kiss me. I shall learn the answer.*

He aimed for her cheek. She turned her head. Their noses
bumped, and he stepped back. "Please forgive me. I should
not—" Having none of it, Elizabeth yanked him by the lapels
and stopped his apology with her lips. He pulled back, hesitant, searching her eyes before moving in again. Craving the
connexion, she met him halfway. Reaching behind his neck
and wishing she had removed her gloves, she caressed the
dark waves brushing his collar and coaxed his face forwards,
planting her mouth on his. He took over, cradling her jaw in
one large palm, kissing her slowly and tasting of Madeira. No
fumbling schoolboy, Mr Darcy knew what he was about.

"Miss Bennet," called Minett from nearby, "wherever you
are, the next set is about to begin. Your partner must be
looking for you."

"Let him look," growled Mr Darcy before releasing Elizabeth and backing away, only to catch her upper arms as she
swayed. "Oh my, you seem unsteady on your feet. For safety's sake, tell your next partner you cannot possibly dance."

She lurched away, overheated to the core. The night air
did little to cool a heart that had done more than soften. It
had melted. "Oh, I shall be quite safe with Mr Walker, sir,"
she called over her shoulder. *You, on the other hand, Mr Darcy,
are a menace to a woman's virtue.* How easy it would be to
surrender to such potent inducement.

He strode after her. "What? Mr Walker! You are to stand
up with him a second time?" Placing Elizabeth's hand on his
sleeve, he escorted her to the ballroom and glared at the
other man's approach. Upon being forced to relinquish her
for the penultimate set and before bowing and walking away,
he said he anticipated being in her company again later.

If he means to apologise for being overly familiar, he had best not, or he will be sorry. While she danced with Mr Walker, Elizabeth's body still tingled from Mr Darcy's every touch—his breath against her ear, his hand branding the small of her back, his gloved palm against her face, and an all too fleeting, thrilling meeting of his lips with hers. *The man is like a lodestone. A magnet. Once repelling, now attracting.*

She sat out the last set, fanning her face and wafting what was not her customary fragrance. Beside her, Mrs Browne leant in, sniffing. "You smell suspiciously of sandalwood, Niece. When I gave you leave to like Mr Darcy, I meant at a *distance.* Your father entrusted me with your care. Remain by my side until we retire."

Mortified but having no regrets, Elizabeth joined the others in a toast to the happy couple and watched as Mr Browne led Miss Taylor to the dance floor for a third time. Standing there, envying them, she realised the comfortable life she knew at Longbourn no longer was the be-all and end-all of her existence. Her hopes and felicity aligned more and more with Mr Darcy's. She wanted to be his helpmate. His happiness and well-being would be her own.

Around half past one, while other guests departed, Mr Darcy approached the two ladies and, with utmost civility, requested a moment alone with Elizabeth. Her aunt, with narrowed eye and frosty tone, said, "It is late, and we have an early start tomorrow." Bidding the gentleman a curt good night, she whisked her niece to their apartments.

Before Minett could begin doing so, Elizabeth had pulled half the pins from her hair. She thanked the maid for her assistance and for her timely intervention in the garden. *Ill-timed interruption, more like.*

Other than the occasional call of a fox, the night was still with not a sound from the state apartments. She was abed and fast asleep by two.

Chapter 23

In the rush to have everyone at Ashover by ten, there had been no chance for Darcy to speak to Elizabeth, let alone apologise for his previous night's conduct. Feeling in his pocket the ring that would soon grace Miss Taylor's hand, he wondered when, or if, his own wedding day might ever come to pass. But progress had been made. Proud of himself for letting his heart and his passion speak for themselves, he accepted hat, gloves, and an umbrella from Jonesby.

Leading the way, his carriage transported the men away from Wishinghill while the ladies followed in the Taylors' coach. Upon arrival at All Saints, footmen armed with waxed umbrellas rushed to shelter the ladies from a sudden, light shower. When Darcy hurried over with his, Elizabeth seemed surprised by such chivalry. "Rain or shine, I always would be by your side, madam, protecting you, if you allowed it."

"You are a true gentleman, sir. Forgive me for once thinking otherwise." Smiling up at him, she added, "Thank you for providing shelter." He offered his free arm, and she remarked on the romantic sound of raindrops pattering overhead and how cosy it seemed there beneath his green silk canopy.

Her words warmed him greatly. "I cannot help but feel

remorse for my overfamiliarity last night. But if you keep smiling so sweetly and speaking of cosy intimacy, I may do something warranting an apology and earning a retraction of your opinion of me as a gentleman." He hoped his smile conveyed a gentle tease.

"It is rather bold of you to presume to know my mind," she replied softly, "particularly since I have no regrets."

"Delighted to hear it." He cleared his throat unnecessarily. "I hope your aunt was not unduly upset." At her reassurance, Darcy let out the breath he had been holding and whispered, "I had longed to kiss you since mid-October." Elizabeth looked up at him in amazement. "'Tis true. Almost from the moment I entered Meryton's assembly hall, your vivacity intrigued me. Then I looked into those uniquely beautiful eyes of yours. My father told me a woman's character could be discerned there. Your eyes gleam with intelligence, mischief, and compassion. At Netherfield, your warmth and kindness clinched the capture of my heart. Last night, I—" They arrived at the church porch, and the rest had to be left unsaid. Inside, they went in separate directions, she left, he right.

Attempts to listen to the rector's words and the couple's vows were defeated as Darcy's mind, no matter how diligently he directed it to stay on course, strayed from the ceremony to thoughts of deserving and winning Elizabeth Bennet's love.

In due course, the register was signed by husband, wife, and witnesses. Darcy was satisfied, judging by the couple's joyful countenances, that Miss Taylor and Browne, at least, had obtained the helpmates their hearts had chosen.

Outside the church, under a clearing sky, bells rang, and villagers greeted Mr and Mrs Michael Browne with tossed herbs and heartfelt wishes. The air smelt fresh, primal, cleansed by the earlier shower. Beaming, the bridegroom tossed coins into the cheering crowd before assisting his wife into a gleaming new carriage, his gift to her.

Back at Wishinghill, a sumptuous celebratory feast awaited with a variety of breakfast fare and beverages. The addition of piping-hot chocolate at one end of the table and a large bride-cake in the middle marked the significance of the occasion. A musician from the previous night had been retained to perform a few tunes, and although the affair was intimate and quiet, everyone remained in good humour. Mr Taylor made a touching speech, and Browne spoke some pretty words about his bride.

When wine glasses again were charged, Darcy stood to address the happy couple. "It is an honour to be here, sharing with you this momentous day. Observing the two of you together has renewed my trust in love. A significant feat, that." Raising his glass, he indicated others do the same. "Because I am a man of few words, this will be succinct. May your life be long and happy, your cares and sorrows few, and the many friends round you prove faithful, fond, and true. To Mr and Mrs Michael Browne!"

Hearty agreement rang out with cries of "Hear, hear!"

"Thank you, Darcy," said Browne. "Men of few words are the best men, at least according to Shakespeare."

The bride's cake was served with dignity, not broken up over the couple's heads as might have been done farther north. A slice was preserved for their first anniversary and others were set aside for servants to later enjoy with wine; some would be packed for Elizabeth to take to Longbourn. The remainder would be delivered to a few elderly relations along Mr and Mrs Browne's route to Willersley Hall. There, at the Arkwright castle on the slopes of Wild Cat Tor, they would spend several nights before travelling to their new home, a leased house near the Gardiners on Gracechurch Street. After prolonged exchanges of affection between family and friends, the happy couple departed under a light rain.

His own departure nigh, Darcy awaited a private word with Elizabeth, but her wary aunt hovered protectively, never far from her niece's side. His chance came when their hostess engaged Mrs Browne in a small wager over when they might become grandmothers. The women's distraction was assured.

"Before I leave, Miss Bennet, I hope you might join me for a stroll. We could share my umbrella again or, if you prefer to stay inside, walk along the picture gallery." She reminded him the second storey was closed. "Closed? No. It is rarely used but never, to my knowledge, completely closed off. I have been up there many times throughout the years but had no reason to do so during this particular visit."

"Miss Taylor—rather Mrs Browne—indicated I would not be interested in the portraits or gilded furnishings, but I suspect she did not want us up there at all, which seems odd. When we arrived, I noticed a woman and child in a second-storey window. I also heard voices up there even before the roof leaked. I admit curiosity."

"Come, then. I shall show you." Darcy offered his arm. "The Taylors will not mind, and I have something to give you. Be not alarmed, madam. It is nothing so ominous as a kiss, or an offer, or circular bands of precious metal set with gemstones." Those, he hoped, would be bestowed in the near future.

Upon reaching the second storey and after viewing a few paintings, Darcy led Elizabeth to a window at the end of the long gallery. Standing behind her, he pointed out Pemberley's direction and expressed his wish to show her the estate. Then he withdrew from his pocket the linen-wrapped offering and asked her to turn round. Blushing, she hid her hands behind her back, saying she could not possibly accept a gift.

A kiss is acceptable but not this? With great theatricality, he unfolded the pristine serviette. "These were the last two. I thought you should have them." The pair of gingerbread biscuits, shaped into prettily decorated flowers, elicited from her a delightful, musical peal of laughter.

Thanking him, she said she would accept one biscuit, but he must have the other. Standing close, gazing into her smiling eyes, he saw streaks of topaz, amber, and warm honey melting into the browns and greens radiating from her pupils. Lost therein, Darcy envisioned his future...their future, together.

Munching the crisp, fragrant cakes, they walked, arm in arm, towards the staircase whereupon they espied a chambermaid backing out of a state-room in the west wing and speaking to someone within. "That," whispered Darcy, "is the apartment my parents were assigned whenever we visited as a family. Odd. I had no notion anyone else was here."

She must have felt his arm muscles tensing, for she looked up at him before following his wide-eyed gaze to a winsome, black-clad lady at the chamber's threshold. Giving a little gasp, Elizabeth darted ahead, crying, "Jane! Jane!"

Breaking into a cold sweat, Darcy strode forwards as the panic-stricken maid slipped into the servants' passage. "Miss Bennet, wait," he called as the other woman stepped back into the room. "She is not your sister."

Taking a hesitant step inside the chamber, Elizabeth whispered, "Jane?" The woman backed towards a shadowy corner. Leaving the door ajar, Elizabeth followed and discovered, on closer scrutiny, the woman was not Jane at all but a careworn, slightly older version. She begged the stranger's pardon and, shaken, turned to leave. As she neared the door, it was pushed from the other side with such force that it hit the inside wall, only to bounce back and strike whomever was behind it. Rubbing his nose, Mr Darcy entered. At the sight of his taut jaw and flinty eyes, Elizabeth's breath caught.

"Miss Bennet, please allow me to introduce to you Mrs Constance Maguire, formerly of Riverswood, near Darley Dale, less than eight miles from here. She and Miss Taylor attended school together. Mrs Maguire, please meet the inestimable Miss Elizabeth Bennet of Hertfordshire. Her cousin is now Miss Taylor's husband." Mr Darcy seemed uncertain what to say or do after his inelegant introductions.

The lady curtseyed, moved forwards with a swish of black bombazine, and spoke with a faint Irish lilt. "A *Bennet*! From Hertfordshire! 'Tis a genuine pleasure, Miss Bennet." Glancing his way, she added, "Mr Darcy. It has been a while."

The former Miss Amesbury...the one who broke his heart! But why would she be interested in Bennets from Hertfordshire? Bringing civility to bear, Elizabeth said, "It is a pleasure to meet you, Mrs Maguire." Suspecting the truth, she asked, "Have you just arrived here?"

The lady's reply, that they had been there since Friday, shocked her. *They? Oh, of course—the child!*

Mrs Maguire spoke then in a rush. "Pray tell, do you know a Mr Bennet of *Longbourn*?" Upon learning the man was Elizabeth's father, she fell upon the nearest Hepplewhite chair, hand over heart. "This encounter can scarcely be credited. Just recently I—"

Footsteps, more than one pair, tapped along the hardwood floor, stopping at the opulent apartment's threshold. Mrs Taylor stood there, staring in dismay, while Elizabeth's aunt cried, "Upon my word! Jane? Oh, no." Then she gave a bright, brittle laugh. "Please forgive me, madam. I mistook you for my eldest niece." Mrs Browne turned to their hostess and asked to be introduced.

Mrs Taylor complied, and, for Mrs Maguire's benefit, Elizabeth added, "Mrs Browne is my aunt, my father's sister."

The two bobbed curtseys, and Mrs Browne again apologised for her response. "I suppose every one of us has a double somewhere, but you could be the twin of my brother's eldest daughter."

"'Tis wonderful to make your acquaintance," Mrs Maguire exclaimed. "Just recently I learnt—"

From the sitting-room's side door, a very young voice whined, "Mama, cake?" A boy of three or so emerged, gaping at the assemblage.

Having forgotten Mr Darcy's presence, Elizabeth turned his way when she heard a gasp. The gentleman's lips silently formed a word she could not interpret. In the politest of terms but rather curtly, he thanked Mrs Taylor for her hospitality and said it was a privilege to have been invited. Then he looked at Elizabeth while addressing the room. "I beg your pardon. Reluctantly, I must leave you now and return to Pemberley. My sister is expecting me." He bowed before turning and walking away.

Torn between dashing after him or politely remaining, Elizabeth stood where she was, unable to understand what was happening except for two truths. He was leaving without a proper goodbye. And she loved him.

Chapter 24

From a window, Elizabeth watched Mr Darcy climb into his carriage—*without looking back!*—and take with him her heart. Behind her, Mrs Maguire spoke to the little boy she had affectionately introduced as her son, John.

When Mr Darcy's coach-and-four had driven out of sight, Elizabeth joined the others in an intimate seating arrangement. Tea was served, and Mrs Taylor apologised to her houseguests for all the secrecy, saying it had been determined, at the time, to be in everyone's best interests. "Mrs Maguire, as you see, is in mourning."

Looking towards Mrs Taylor, Mrs Maguire asked for a private word with the Bennet ladies; and their hostess excused herself from the room. After sending John to the far corner with a sliver of bride's cake, Mrs Maguire moved to a chair across from Elizabeth and spoke of a letter from her half-brother summoning her from Ireland to Riverswood, her childhood home. There, at her mother's deathbed, she had learnt Lord Darley had been her father only in name. "A cuckoo—me—had been let in his nest. Fortuitously a tiny babe, my premature arrival raised few eyebrows. Lord Darley died ignorant of the truth."

Elizabeth, somewhat bewildered by the lady's confession,

listened politely as, chin held high, Mrs Maguire continued speaking through tears. "I may have had a legal father to whom I was not truly related, but he loved me—which is more than I can say for either my mother or horrid Robert Amesbury, now Lord Darley. The instant Robert learnt John and I share no common blood with him, he evicted us from the estate. Both my maternal grandparents are dead, so, with no other place to go before arranging passage back to Ireland, we came here and found the Taylor household in the midst of plans for houseguests, a ball, and a wedding. Once I heard Mr Darcy would be in attendance, I requested our presence be kept secret." Bowing her head, Mrs Maguire added, "He courted me, but it was not meant to be. I married a stalwart soldier, my dear Captain Maguire of the Eighty-Ninth Regiment of Foot. May God rest his soul. Now, alas, I am once again in mourning." She dabbed her eyes with a lacy handkerchief.

The Amesburys and Maguires and their sordid secrets meant nothing to Elizabeth. The woman had mistreated Mr Darcy. And why would she relate intimate information to mere strangers? Anger and frustration battled with sympathy, but she spoke with sincerity. "How tragic to have suffered so many losses. You have my condolences, Mrs Maguire."

"I thank you. Saddened as I am by it, my mother's death resulted in the discovery of my birth father's identity." Tears gave way to what seemed a joyful gleam in Mrs Maguire's eyes, and she released a deep breath. "As she lay dying, Mother confessed my natural father is Mr Bennet of Longbourn. Mrs Browne, you are my aunt!" Dropping to her knees, she grasped Elizabeth's hands. "We are sisters! Well, half-sisters, which is why I am so thrilled to meet you. Is this not the most extraordinary coincidence?"

Elizabeth wrenched away her hands. Pressing back into the chair cushions, she stared at Jane's double and silently screamed, *No!*

"Your silence speaks of surprise and happiness too great for words. Yes, we are family! Is this not wonderful?"

"No!" cried Elizabeth, shock and anger sharpening her voice. "No, it can*not* be true. How dare you scheme to play my family false! What you insinuate about my father is impossible." Yet the evidence was kneeling right in front of her, staring back in dismay: *the same fair hair, blue eyes, and high cheekbones as Jane and Grandmama Bennet.*

"Lizzy, it is not impossible." Mrs Browne turned to Mrs Maguire. "You have given my niece quite astonishing news, and while your joy is understandable, let us confirm what you have said. What was your mother's name? Her maiden name."

"Henrietta Harris." She glanced between the two women. "Mother told me she met Mr Bennet in Oxford, where she lived, and he attended university. They fell in love there. But, concealing her condition from both men, my mother married Lord Darley."

Sighing, Mrs Browne moved closer to Elizabeth and took her hand. "Dear, you remember the story I told you about my brother," she said, her eyebrows raised and voice soft. "And you must have noticed Mrs Maguire's resemblance to my mother and Jane."

Elizabeth did remember, and she had noticed. And she recalled her father saying the happiest days of his life had been spent at Oxford. A gamut of emotions—scepticism, anger, mortification—settled round her like a scratchy, woollen blanket, and she itched to cast off the irritants.

"When will you return to Longbourn, Miss Bennet?" Mrs Maguire gave a little laugh. "May I call you Lizzy?" She leant forwards, eyes fixed on Elizabeth's face. "You must take John and me with you when you go. I shall write to the Maguires and inform them of our prolonged stay in England. Oh, I cannot wait to meet my real father! What a surprise he will have. Imagine his delight in learning he has a third daughter and a grandson. Do we have any brothers? Nieces? Nephews? I have so many questions!"

Struggling for the appearance of composure, Elizabeth remained silent until she believed herself to have attained it. At length and with a voice of self-righteousness and forced calmness, she said, "There are no nieces or nephews. I have no brother and only four sisters. None are married." Turning to her aunt, she silently begged for counsel and forgiveness. *Such uncharitableness!* But she did have only four sisters until her father told her otherwise.

Mrs Browne gave Elizabeth's hand a gentle squeeze while speaking to the other woman. "In such situations as this, it is proper to feel a sense of obligation. Mrs Maguire, you and your son are welcome to accompany us to Longbourn, where certain facts may be verified. We shall leave directly, but we cannot make much progress before nightfall."

Elizabeth's sense of unease—outrage, truly—with such a plan could scarcely be withheld, but she suppressed the protest she so desired to voice. *Oh, Papa, what upheaval will be brought to your door! 'Tis too much!* Long had Elizabeth realised her parents were not infallible. But she had held her father to a higher standard. Not knowing what to think or do, only with Minett's assistance did she change into travelling clothes and arrange the packing of her belongings. After thanking the maid, she went down the hall to the adjoining apartment with everything, within her and without, feeling peculiar.

In her aunt's rooms, she paced, holding her stomach.

"How can I bring this person to Longbourn? I cannot think... How can I possibly spring such a surprise on my father and—Oh, Lord!—on my poor mother?" Wringing, then shaking her trembling hands, she cried, "What is Mrs Maguire thinking? And how can you remain so composed and accepting in the face of all this?"

"Calm yourself, Lizzy. Being upset is understandable, but I have learnt that worry and anger over whatever is beyond one's control is not at all helpful. Besides, you will not face your family alone. I shall be there to help in any way I can. As for Mrs Maguire, I believe she thinks only of her own pleasure at finding family and not of the suffering she will inflict on your parents. For my part, if she *is* my niece, I will not disown her."

Mrs Browne took Elizabeth's hand and pulled her to sit beside her on the window seat. "Imagine losing the only father you ever knew. Imagine suffering the death of a husband. Imagine learning, on your mother's deathbed, that your true father is another man altogether. Imagine how dreadful it must have been to be ousted from the Amesbury family and her childhood home. Other than wearing widow's weeds, one might never guess that the poor woman is in mourning. Show some compassion, dear heart. The situation is not of her own doing. Mrs Maguire cannot be blamed for her mother's sin. She is innocent."

No, Aunt, she is not as innocent as you think. Like her mother, she was with child before marriage. "I am not unsympathetic, but—" *She betrayed poor Mr Darcy!* "In outward appearance, Mrs Maguire may resemble Jane, but she is, I fear, another Lydia."

"We shall see. In the meantime, hoping to spare my brother the surprise of Jane's likeness entering his home, I have jotted a short letter to him. Mr Taylor is arranging for it to be delivered by his courier, so it should reach Longbourn before we do."

Elizabeth was thankful her father would have hours, perhaps a day, to absorb the news. He often set aside his correspondence, but one delivered by a personal courier would quickly demand his attention, would it not?

"At present," her aunt continued, "the most difficult part of this unexpected connexion is the anticipation of how it will upend your family. Knowing your father, he will not want to face the imponderable complications of his past having caught up with him in this way. Whatever his response, you must promise to understand and forgive him for a past transgression that cannot be changed. Be forewarned, Lizzy. I suspect he will not break the news to your mother until our arrival. Heaven help us all."

For Elizabeth, the journey back to Longbourn seemed both endless and over too soon. For four days and five nights, there was no want of discourse because Mrs Maguire could not ask or answer questions fast enough. Even while John slept in the evenings, Mrs Maguire spoke of her mother with no sign of embarrassment, which led to subjects the other two ladies would not have alluded to for the world.

With more patience than Elizabeth could muster, Mrs Browne related the Bennet family history to its newcomer. Her goddaughter sat in abject misery, wondering whether she would ever see Mr Darcy again. He did not yet know that, should he decide he still wished to marry her, the woman who betrayed his trust would become his sister. Her power, she knew, was sinking. Everything must sink under such an oppressive weight. Turning to the passing scenery, she fought the onset of tears, heartache, and visions of spinsterhood. *Judging by his response to Mrs Maguire at Wishinghill, Mr Darcy would never accept such a connexion.* His image loomed before her, supplanting the view. Her love would be in vain. Never would she want another.

With the entire situation beyond her experience, she could have no lasting interval of ease, only anguish. Sorrow was displaced by an anger directed across the carriage to the creature she likely would have to claim as her eldest sister. But the truth was, after days and nights spent in close company, Mrs Maguire was not entirely loathsome, and John was a delight. He had neither notion of, nor care about, his mother's change of plans and was told they were to visit English relations previously unknown to them.

When he babbled some unintelligible words, Mrs Maguire explained her son was learning Irish from his Maguire grandparents. "I speak only a few words of it myself, but the Taylors think I have acquired a bit of an Irish intonation."

Mrs Browne said John spoke well and seemed intelligent for his age.

Mrs Maguire glowed with motherly pride as she said to him, "You are my brave soldier, *mo stoirín*, and, as your father did, you love me unconditionally."

Try as she might, Elizabeth's heart could not remain untouched by their loss and the affection between mother and son. But what would be her own mother's response when black sheep were brought into the fold?

In the carriage with Jonesby, Darcy had reached Lambton when he decided he must return quickly to Wishinghill Park. He feared he had been unpardonably abrupt there. Barely a 'by-your-leave' had been offered, and more than one apology was in order, even if it meant seeing Mrs Maguire again.

After speaking with several merchants as to whether Wickham had been spotted in the area, Darcy made alternate arrangements for Jonesby's conveyance to Pemberley. Left in his care were notes—for Georgiana, Mrs Reynolds, and his steward—explaining Darcy would go directly from Wishinghill to Hertfordshire. The valet had instructions about which belongings to pack—including Mrs Maguire's miniature from before her marriage, one satin slipper, and an heirloom ring. Then Jonesby was to take another of his employer's coaches and make haste to Meryton, where he was to secure lodgings, send the carriage to London, and do a bit of investigation. Another letter was dispatched to Darcy's London house, requesting Aether be ridden from the mews there to the stable behind Meryton's inn.

At Wishinghill, upon learning all of the Taylors guests already had departed, Darcy apologised to his good neighbours for his earlier discourtesy, took leave of them with utmost civility, boarded his carriage, and, in pursuit of Elizabeth's heart, embarked on his quest.

He had hoped to encounter her and Mrs Browne along the southerly route, but they must have stayed at different establishments.

Late on the first Saturday in December, he arrived at the Meryton inn, where his valet had secured lodgings. Jonesby ordered a meal and a hip bath for his employer and reported on Wickham's disappearance and the debts he had left behind. All Darcy cared about was that he would have to wait at least another day to call on Elizabeth.

On Sunday, he spotted Mrs Bennet and her four daughters on the main thoroughfare, entering what he assumed was their relation's house. It would be an excellent time to call on Mr Bennet and get his blessing.

The master of Longbourn did not exactly give him the cold shoulder, but it seemed he had little time or patience for his visitor, preoccupied as he was with an open letter on his desk. His attention repeatedly returned to the written words, and several times Darcy had to clear his throat to remind him he had company. When asked whether he was well, the ashen gentleman looked up. "Am I well? Yes, yes, well enough—although I ought to feel out of sorts."

It was none of Darcy's concern, but he had to know. "Is all well with your family, sir?" He could not bear it if some tragedy had befallen Elizabeth.

"Is all well with my family? Hah! It seems I *might* have dug a hole for myself. We shall see how deeply when Eliza and Lizzy return late tomorrow." No further information was volunteered. After half an hour of a mostly one-sided conversation on Darcy's part, Mr Bennet got up, patted the younger man's shoulder, and accompanied him out of the book-room. "Since you condescended to ask so civilly, your request will not be refused. But let me advise you to think better of it. Particularly now."

What the deuce? Darcy collected coat, hat, gloves, and riding whip from a young maid while listening to more abstruseness.

"You may have considerable wealth of one sort, but I wish you all the good fortune in the world if you attempt to acquire the treasure in my keeping. Dig deep, young man. More than financial resources will be required to secure the rare jewel you covet." Mr Bennet then spouted nonsense about mountains to climb, slippery slopes, and the difficulty

Darcy would have in gaining a foothold. The patriarch opened the front door himself, nearly pushing his visitor through it.

His attempts to shut the door were foiled by the toe of Darcy's expensive, highly-polished Hessian. "Then resourceful I shall be, sir," said he into the gap. "The reward will be well worth all expenditures of time and effort."

Aether was turned towards Meryton at the onset of a light shower. As a landowner and gentleman farmer, Darcy appreciated rainfall. It made growth possible. *Would that a good soaking might bring about my own growth into a better version of myself. Admit it, man. You thought every desirable quality a person possibly could possess already was yours.*

Near the market town, the sun broke through the clouds, and his face turned skywards. After his unchivalrous departure from Wishinghill, he wondered whether Elizabeth's warmth would shine his way again. *Dear God, please let her feelings germinate, sprout, and bloom into a love matching my own attachment.*

Chapter 25

The following Monday, just before sunset, in a golden glow casting long shadows across barren fields, her aunt's equipage—clopping, creaking, clanking—entered Longbourn's gravel sweep and came to a stop. The manor's front door opened, and her parents and sisters spilt out, gathering in a solemn group. Once the footman helped her aunt alight, Elizabeth accepted his assistance. Stepping down, she saw anxious faces and heard hushed tones rather than customary smiles and loud greetings. The pervading mood convinced her the news had been revealed before their arrival. Considering such advance intelligence in a favourable light, she closely watched everyone's expression as Mrs Maguire, carrying John and smiling Jane's serene smile, exited the carriage.

Mrs Bennet hit the cold ground in a dead faint. Hand over mouth, eyes wide, Jane seemed on the verge of following that fine example and passing out alongside her mother.

Servants were summoned, and as pandemonium ensued, they scurried about—hoisting up Mrs Bennet, carrying in the baggage, fetching smelling salts, taking coats, and getting in one another's way. Stupefied sisters asked questions no one answered while Mrs Maguire, still holding her son, stood in the hall, stared at and whispered about by all and sundry.

So much for advance intelligence, or any intelligence at all hereabouts. Elizabeth rushed to Jane's side while her aunt Browne and Mrs Hill took Mrs Maguire and John under their mother-hen wings. Through it all, her father stood aside, arms crossed, eyebrows raised at the commotion round him. The momentary disgust she felt, not for Mrs Maguire but for him, was pushed aside as Elizabeth embraced her favourite sister and lost no time in asking, "Did Papa not tell you about her?" Jane shook her head. "Then why was everyone so restrained when we drove up?"

Her father, Elizabeth learnt, had been in a bad temper since the previous day. Never having seen or heard the gentleman in such an irritable state, family and servants alike had given him a wide berth and asked few questions.

"Who is she, Lizzy?"

"Mrs Maguire is…a relation of sorts." Taking Jane's hand, Elizabeth forced a cheerfulness she did not feel. "You must have noticed her resemblance to Grandmama Bennet's side of the family, the Munsons."

"Well, yes. But it seemed akin to seeing my future self in some mystical mirror." Tremors in Jane's body echoed in her soft voice. "The surprise of it all quite robbed me of my faculties, and I know not what to think."

Already shattered by Mr Darcy's brusque behaviour, whatever was left of Elizabeth's heart went out to her sister. It was bad enough that she, herself, had become disillusioned. Must she also destroy Jane's respect for her father? *No. He must do the telling himself.*

After sending her two youngest, most unwilling sisters to sit with Mrs Bennet, Elizabeth told Mary to order tea for Jane and play her some soothing melodies. She peeked in on her mother and then went to the room assigned to the Maguires. Her aunt was with them, and while Mrs Maguire seemed bewildered by their reception, she assured Elizabeth of their comfort.

Then, although she had neither the desire nor strength for such a confrontation after travelling all day, Elizabeth went in search of the man responsible for all the turmoil. Her tap on his door went unanswered, so she turned the handle and peered inside. The sun was setting, and the book-room was cold and dim, with no fire, lamps, or candles burning. Motionless in a faded armchair, her father stared through the far window, an empty glass dangling from one hand, a single sheet of paper from the other. His countenance, already grave, gained in austerity as he bid her entry.

Her travels, his nephew's wedding, and Wishinghill Park were offhandedly enquired about, but he did not broach the all-important issue. *Heaven forfend it might make him uncomfortable!* The topic was skirted round until Elizabeth dared to initiate it herself. Seated in the matching wingback chair and recognising her godmother's handwriting, she gestured at the letter in his hand. "Aunt Browne hoped you might prepare my mother and sisters for the Maguires' arrival and the disruption to our family. You could have spared them such a shock, Papa."

"Yes, yes, I might have. But how could I speak of it to your mother?"

Elizabeth nearly shuddered. "So, is it the truth? Could Mrs Maguire truly be your daughter?"

"You have eyes. Of course she *could* be mine." With his bitter words hanging between them, Mr Bennet reached behind him for the brandy; his hand fell away and Elizabeth saw the bottle was empty.

"Her mother was intelligent and beautiful," Mr Bennet said in a tone Elizabeth heard as morose, "but you need not mention as much to your mother. I met Miss Harris at a *soirée* hosted by my uncle Munson and his wife. We courted an appropriate time and were engaged to marry, but Mr Harris withdrew his consent. I knew *nothing* of her being with child. Why did she not tell me of her condition?" He let out a breath and looked away from the scorn Elizabeth could not hide. "Being the jilted party, I might have sued for breach of promise. Instead, I came home to lick my wounds. Then I met your mother, who had the same sort of appearance as my beloved Miss Harris, and, well, what is done is done, and here we are. The past cannot be altered, only accepted. I do not intend to expend unnecessary time and energy railing against fate."

At a sound from the door, Elizabeth got up and let Rose in to light a few candles. When she returned, her father's eyes were averted, studying the portraits behind his desk, particularly, she noticed, the one of his blond-haired, blue-eyed uncle. No one spoke until the maid had completed her task, curtseyed, and left.

Shoulders slumped, seemingly weighed down by burden and responsibility, Mr Bennet heaved a sigh. "Having spent time with her, what is your impression of Mrs Maguire?"

She betrayed Mr Darcy! "In looks, she is, obviously, much like Jane. Even some of their mannerisms are similar. In other ways, she seems as spoilt as Lydia. Her character, I think, has been hardened by unfortunate circumstances. She certainly longs for an attachment, a connexion with us. She appears to be an excellent mother."

"And the boy?"

"There is something vaguely familiar about him, but your grandson must resemble the Maguires. At any rate, John's lively, cheerful nature will endear him to everyone."

"I now have a grandson, and he cannot inherit Longbourn. That news alone should endear him to your forbearing mother."

"Mama deserves to learn the truth directly, as do my sisters...though perhaps not Kitty and Lydia. Jane has already been told Mrs Maguire is a relation of sorts. The others only know there is a familiar-looking stranger in our midst." Elizabeth reached to pat his arm. "Do not hide away in here, Papa. Guide us, please, through this upheaval."

"Yes, yes. I shall rouse myself to meet and speak privately with Mrs Maguire before confessing to my imperturbable spouse." Shaking his head, he spoke more to himself than to Elizabeth. "Instead of spending my whole income, an annual sum should have been laid by for the better provision of a wife and brood of girls. Now I wish it more than ever."

"Surely you are not expected to support a widow. As I understand it, she and John live in a cottage with its own parkland on Maguire property somewhere in Ireland. They are considered a permanent part of that family. Your grandson is well provided for, and Mrs Maguire must have a substantial jointure from her late husband. It may not equal the dowry she—supposedly a baron's daughter—brought to the marriage, but certainly enough to afford the three servants she employs over there."

"Well, well, a bit of welcome news after yesterday's surprising discovery that I may have...that I *have* sired the sum of five and one daughters. A proper hexad of vexation. After I introduce your mother and my newest eldest daughter to one another, we shall have a family conclave in the drawing room and, I fear, some hysteria." He gave Elizabeth a weary look. "Excepting Kitty, Lydia, the boy, and our servants, please have everyone assembled before we dine. I shall meet you there and sit with you at dinner, but I have no appetite, nor can I stomach the disapproval evident in your eyes."

Leaving him to wallow in whatever emotion he was feeling, Elizabeth arranged the requested meeting and delegated to her two youngest sisters the care and amusement of John until dinner was on the table. Under strict orders not to set the place on fire, Kitty and Lydia, lanterns in one hand and John holding the other, set off for the kennel attached to the barn to decide upon names for the litter of gun dogs born some weeks prior.

Elizabeth then joined her aunt in the back parlour, where they speculated about the simmering pot about to boil over. The house—its exterior constructed from Hertfordshire puddingstone, its interior from oak timbers hewn from the estate's woodland—had stood solid and sound for generations before either of their births. There was nothing flimsy, nothing paper-thin about the Bennets' ancestral home. But, even within those thick walls, sounds carried. As expected, Mrs Bennet's shrieks and wails rained down upon their heads from upstairs. Elizabeth cringed.

"Well," said Mrs Browne, "sometimes when it rains, it pours. And the only thing you can do is to open an umbrella."

Oh, how I long to be under Mr Darcy's umbrella again! "I appreciate your agreeing to remain until midday tomorrow, Aunt, and for offering the Maguires our best guest chamber. While everything falls apart, your presence is a comfort to us all, and I am grateful for your sharing attendance on my poor mother. As expected, and as you hear, she is distraught." She paused and added softly, "I still cannot believe my father has a natural daughter."

"Let it be known I neither condone nor condemn what happened between my brother and Miss Harris, but it is not uncommon for engaged couples to anticipate their wedding vows."

Elizabeth shifted uncomfortably at her aunt's words, coming only days after Miss Taylor had become Mrs Browne. Clearly, Aunt Browne's thoughts tended elsewhere as she continued. "But consider this: What would have happened if Lord Darley had no heir when he married Henrietta Harris and, instead of giving birth to a Miss Amesbury, she had produced a male child? The baron's title and estate would have passed on to another man's son. You see, Lizzy," she continued in a lower voice, "there is justification for high-born and wealthy men to want chaste brides. Some wait for over a month to ensure she is not with child before marrying. I am no prude, but there are other valid reasons to wait for the ceremony. What would happen to the woman if her intended changed his mind or died? What if she then discovered she was with child? Although Mr Darcy is an honourable gentleman, do not allow your passions to over-rule your good judgment when he returns here."

Elizabeth opened her mouth to protest but was fore-stalled. "Remember, Niece, I know you already have been in his embrace."

"Mr Darcy will pay me no further addresses. I was told by your new daughter, under condition of trust, something that makes it impossible for him to do so."

Elizabeth could not doubt he would withdraw from such a connexion. His wish of procuring her regard, which she was assured of in Derbyshire, could not, in rational expecta-tion, survive such a blow. She was humbled. She was grieved. She repented, although she hardly knew of what. She certainly was most heartily sorry she ever went up to Wish-inghill's upper floor. But Mrs Maguire eventually would have found her way, by another means, to Longbourn.

Sensible of some pleasure upon hearing her aunt's steadfast belief that Mr Darcy's attachment would endure, Elizabeth offered up an unconvincing smile as they walked towards the drawing room.

At the threshold, Mrs Browne spoke to her three eldest, acknowledged nieces. "Now, girls, remember we, none of us, are angels. People make mistakes and deserve forgiveness." Jane and Mary exchanged anxious, bewildered looks, then went in to claim their seats.

Due to unfortunate timing, Elizabeth's mother and Mrs Maguire came out of their rooms at the same moment. The more strident voice continued making its displeasure known all the way down the stairs and to the drawing room. Mr Bennet hissed at his wife to keep her voice lowered, ushered everyone inside, and closed the door behind him.

"I will not be silent! Not with this misbegotten person of yours in my house!"

"Mrs Bennet," said Mrs Maguire, "about my being misbegotten...Lord Darley did not disown me before or at my birth. Having been born seven and a half months after the solemnisation of his and my mother's marriage, I was recognised as his daughter."

Elizabeth seated her querulous mother in a favoured armchair and whispered, "I beg you, Mama, do not aim bitterness and resentment at the two innocent souls who have entered our lives. Please, for your own sake, do not allow anger to imprison you in misery for the rest of your days."

"Oh, hush, Lizzy! Go and sit somewhere." Her mother waved a soggy handkerchief.

Taking a seat and feigning calmness by sipping from the steaming teacup her aunt forced into her hands, Elizabeth watched her father escort Mrs Maguire to the middle of the room, where he formally introduced her to Jane and Mary. Then he settled her on the sofa and caught, in turn, the eye of each person in the room. "I expect all of you to welcome the Maguires to our family. As some of you already are aware, Mrs Maguire is the daughter—and John the grandson —of whom I knew nothing until yesterday."

Wide-eyed and blooming red, Jane gasped but otherwise remained silent as the one person Elizabeth thought might show some sign of shamefacedness at making such an announcement in front of his family displayed none.

Mr Bennet clearly did not wish for a scolding from anyone. Mary, with a countenance of grave reflection and hands primly folded on her lap, tut-tutted. "This most unfortunate affair will be much talked of, and—"

Her father's narrow-eyed glare quelled moral remarks into pursed-lip silence. "No, Mary, it will not be 'much talked of'. Our servants and neighbours only need know the Maguires are Bennet relations. That should satisfy any curiosity about Mrs Maguire's resemblance to my mother and Jane. Being guarded at such a time may be difficult, particularly"—he looked at his wife—"for some of you. But I insist upon it."

Mrs Maguire was not at all more distressed than Elizabeth. Her manners were so pleasing that, had her parentage been exactly what it ought, her smiles and easy address would have delighted them all. When prompted by Mr Bennet, she charmingly described her childhood at Riverswood and growing up as the daughter of Lord Darley. Then she spoke of her marriage to Captain Maguire, of Ireland, the joys of motherhood, and her mother's passing.

Eyelids red and swollen, face blotchy, Mrs Bennet glared at her husband. "And do you expect me, at my age, to become Mrs Maguire's mother? I accepted you, Mr Bennet, when we married. I did not accept this daughter of yours by another woman."

"None of us can have a quarrel with either Mrs Maguire or John. They are innocent in all this."

"So am I!" Mrs Bennet flailed her sodden handkerchief, inadvertently extinguishing a candle. "And now my spirit has been greatly shaken by knowledge of your past conduct with some"—her next word was spat out—"trollop!"

Everyone gasped, and her husband demanded an apology. Sniffling into the wet linen, she mumbled some words of regret. Her subsequent complaining of suffering and ill-use earned a degree of silent sympathy from Elizabeth and more vocal concern from another quarter.

Jane grasped her mother's hand. "After losing the man who raised her, Mrs Maguire must not be cut off from her true father. How can any of us refuse to warmly receive her and her son?"

Mr Bennet patted Jane on the head and thanked her. To his wife, he said, "What good will it do to rail against fate, my dear? Life is not only unpredictable but far too short. I shall not spend the rest of my days reproaching myself. I have done enough of that already. You may criticise my past, Mrs Bennet. But if you do not like it, feel free to journey back and remedy it yourself in whatever manner you see fit. I refuse to exert myself to do anything other than accept the situation as it is. Upon my honour, I look forward to getting to know Mrs Maguire and John."

Crossing the room and taking his eldest's hand, he bowed over it before sitting beside her. "What I want all of you to understand is that—although it was very wrong of Miss Harris and me to have anticipated our wedding vows—Mrs Maguire was not the product of a regrettable dalliance. When I was a young man, still at Oxford, I was captivated by Miss

Harris's…good humour. To cut short a long story, I proposed marriage, she accepted, and Mr Harris consented. Soon afterwards, though, he forced her to marry a wealthier, titled man with an estate twice the size of Longbourn. I was not informed of Miss Harris's condition nor our daughter's existence until late yesterday."

"But, no," said Mrs Maguire. "That is not what Mother told me. She said it was at her insistence she married Lord Darley. She wanted those things—wealth, a title, and Riverswood. She wanted to be Lady Darley, and the baron desired her. I am sorry to say my mother was not of such good humour as you seem to remember, sir. Their marriage was not a felicitous one."

"Serves her right," muttered Mrs Bennet.

Elizabeth was thankful her father seemed too stunned by Mrs Maguire's revelation to have heard his wife's spitefulness. Jumping to his feet, he fled the room. Her breath caught. *Both Papa and Mr Darcy were betrayed by their first loves— one by the immoral mother and one by the comparable daughter. Well, the apple does not fall far from the tree!*

Leaning towards the candlelight, Mary flipped through her commonplace book of extracts and read aloud comforting words about pouring the balm of Christian consolation into one another's wounded feelings. Closing the book, she smiled warmly at Mrs Maguire. "Rather than resisting their inclusion, let us treat the Maguires with affection and welcome them within the bosom of our family. Love must include forgiveness. Resentment has no place in a family rich in affection."

Mrs Maguire went to Mrs Bennet, knelt at her feet, and apologised.

Smiling through her tears, Mrs Bennet said, "It is not your fault." She patted the woman's cheek. "My, my, you have such a sweet face and lovely, golden locks so like Jane's, mine, and your late grandmother's."

Not long thereafter, she heard her mother saying to Mrs Maguire, "I see your bombazine is of the finest quality silk and wool. And your cap! Such a lovely drape. Oh, and the lace! What a shame you had to dye it black. Brussels, is it? Pray tell, dear, where do you purchase such finery?"

"Customarily, I shop on Dame Street. It is the place for silk, furs, jewels, and all the latest fashions from Paris. You must visit us in Ireland, and we shall take a trip to Dublin for shopping and…"

And there we have it. Any lasting animosity on Mama's part will be saved for my father. Now, if only Mr Darcy would come and accept that the woman who betrayed him is my sister…and that pigs may fly.

Chapter 26

Hoping Elizabeth had enjoyed a happy reunion with family and had a good rest after her long journey, Darcy was eager to call at Longbourn on Tuesday. Jonesby had chosen for him a rifle-green coat, new waistcoat, knee breeches of finest nankeen, and a cravat knot so complex and restricting his neck might never again see the light of day. Then, clad in his greatcoat, he eschewed his carriage, collected Aether, and rode off in search of future happiness.

Once out of Meryton, alone in the countryside, he broke into a low-toned rendition of *Lavender's Blue*, stopping abruptly at 'therefore be kind, diddle diddle'. *Will she be kind?* He had been boorish and stupid, departing Wishinghill without a more affectionate leave-taking of his sweetheart. *It was nothing short of desertion! Am I no better than that coward Wickham?*

As instructed, Jonesby, upon arrival in Meryton, had investigated the lieutenant's whereabouts and, with Darcy's generous purse in hand, gone about the market town settling the weasel's mercantile debts and gaming vowels. The absconder had not been seen since the night of Bingley's ball; he had disappeared without a trace and was, apparently, nowhere near Meryton.

While Mrs Hill announced him at Longbourn, Darcy stood behind her, drumming fingers on his thigh until she moved away. With unrestrained eagerness, he entered the sitting room where the family was assembled. Straightening from a bow, he froze, forgetting to breathe. The scene before him made no sense. For two heartbeats, three heartbeats, an eternity, he stood staring. Closing his eyes made no difference. When he opened them, Mrs Maguire was still there. *And Wickham's son...with Mrs Browne and the entire Bennet family!*

With every thought failing him, Darcy's eyes flew to Elizabeth's in painful confusion. Hers had a dazed, incredulous look within them. At first, she seemed happy but surprised to see him. *Did she think I would not come?* Her lips parted as though she might speak, yet she remained silent, all colour driven from her face. *How I long to hold her, comfort her!* But the presence of others, particularly Mrs Maguire's, made such a move impossible. *Elizabeth, my love, what—*

"Mr Darcy! Good gracious," cried Mrs Bennet. "Come in! Come in and meet Mrs Maguire and her son, John." During the introductions, the matron explained the widow was a relation on Mr Bennet's maternal side of the family. "Is it not uncanny? You must have noticed how she resembles my Jane. And Lord Darley, Mrs Maguire's late father, was a *baron.*"

Blushing, Mrs Maguire caught his eye. "Mr Darcy and I already are acquainted."

"Indeed, we are." Darcy enquired after everyone's health, then said nothing for several awkward moments before looking from Mrs Maguire to Elizabeth to Mr Bennet. "Forgive me, sir, but I wonder whether Miss Elizabeth might be permitted to join me in the garden for a moment. We have a matter of import to discuss." Without awaiting an answer, he bowed and strode away, knowing he was being unpardonably rude again but unable to help it.

〰

So, he has come! But now he will go away and never return. Elizabeth's brief joy gave way to reality. She would be left to pine for him for the rest of her days. Forgoing a pelisse in her urgency, she found Mr Darcy pacing up and down the gravel walk in earnest meditation, brow contracted, air gloomy. He seemed scarcely to hear her when she spoke his name.

Then he cast a look upon her that mingled shock, disbelief, and suspicion. "Why is *she*…Why are *they* here?"

There was no easy way to divulge what would be, for both, an uncomfortable truth. Yet she must be honest, irrevocably tearing them apart forevermore. Disappointment in her father was nothing to the agony of losing the good opinion of the decent gentleman before her, losing his respect and affection, losing him.

"I do not quite know how to tell you, as I have only just learnt myself, but…" Wrapping her shawl tighter round herself, she said, "My own father has a natural child." There was a dreadful pause while she tried to swallow past the painful lump in her throat. "And that child is Mrs Maguire. She is my sister. Well, *half*-sister."

"No, she is Lord Darl—"

Elizabeth watched the gentleman's handsome countenance as her words and the irrefutable evidence of Mrs Maguire and Jane's resemblance, struck him. His angular eyebrows pinched together while he stared at her in disbelief. A fist, seemingly holding back vitriol, pressed against soft lips that had once kissed hers. Warm brown eyes grew distant before he looked away. Steps heavy, he paced, shaking his head and rolling his shoulders. She prayed he was attempting to regain composure and that they might still have a future together.

"And the boy..." said Mr Darcy, revulsion writ upon his features. "Can you not see? He is Wickham's son. I suspected as much upon first learning Miss Amesbury had married and been delivered of a child earlier than she ought. My suspicion increased upon seeing the boy at Wishinghill. Now, having had a second look, there is no doubt. John Maguire looks exactly as Wickham did at that age."

Wickham's son! Unsteady, Elizabeth reached out for support, but there was none to be had. "Whether or not he is Mr Wickham's son, John Maguire is my nephew, and he is innocent in all this. As for his mother—" She paused, despising the entire conversation. "We are telling people Mrs Maguire is a distant relation on my grandmama Bennet's side of the family...hence the widow's resemblance to her and Jane. Of course, Mrs Maguire is far from being a distant relation, so it is only half true. But, please, in this, I beg your secrecy." Letting out a shaky breath when there was no hesitation in his voicing an agreement, Elizabeth thanked him.

"But you cannot expect me to rejoice at such a connexion." His voice was as grave as his eyes.

"No, sir. I cannot." The tremble of her lips and the catch in her voice were unbearable. She tightened the fingers clutching her shawl and found her backbone. "With two such additions to a family you already found wanting, I doubted you still would desire my company."

"I-I..." Mr Darcy sighed deeply and gave her a look that spoke more of anguish than anger. "The thought of becoming brother to her—the woman who played me false with Wickham—and of becoming uncle to their son...Every kind of pride must revolt against the very notion." He bowed and turned away.

Biting her lip and with tears stinging her eyes, Elizabeth watched him stride towards the barn and heard him ask for his horse. *Yes, go! Turn your back on me. I am glad to see that side of you!* Stumbling and stifling a sob, she returned to the house, struggling to contain overwhelming sorrow and rage. Unable to bear the company of others—particularly Mrs Maguire's—she evaded notice, fled to her chamber, and shut the door. Her silent wail accompanied the sound of Aether's pounding hoofs fading in the distance.

Flinging herself upon the bed, she allowed a few fat teardrops to fall. *No. No more!* She swiped the wretched wetness from her cheeks. *No more crying over that heartless man.* She knew how it would be. So why was she disappointed? Although she had lost a great deal of respect for her father, she acknowledged he was only human, which was more than she could say for Mr Darcy. *Cruel beast! He lacks the human qualities of compassion and mercy.*

She had no fear of her family's disgrace becoming known through his means. There were few people on whose secrecy she would have more confidently depended. At the same time, there was no one whose knowledge of Mrs Maguire's true parentage could have mortified her so, not after the hypocritical things she had accused him of at Netherfield. *Is this, then, retribution?*

Jane silently entered and sat beside her on the bed. "What troubles you, dearest? Why has Mr Darcy returned? Are the Bingleys at Netherfield?"

"No. I learnt, at Wishinghill, that Mr Bingley and Miss Oliverson are to marry soon in Brighton. I doubt they will return to Netherfield." Her voice broke. "Oh, Jane! Before I left for Derbyshire, you said I would wear my beautiful gown again and dance with handsome strangers—one of whom might be ideally suited to me, and you were right. While there, I fell in love. But it is a complicated, ill-fated, futile connexion."

A light tap on the door preceded Mrs Browne's gentle voice. "Lizzy, Jane, I am bound for London while the weather is fit. It appears there might be rain later. May I come in and take my leave of you?" With dry eyes and false cheer, Elizabeth bid her aunt entrance and expressed a wish she might stay longer.

"The situation here has settled considerably, and my many engagements in town beckon. But I shall return for Christmastide. As much as I enjoy visiting my ancestral home, country living is not for me. Even as a youth, I was wild to be away from here, to broaden my acquaintances, and see the world. And my dear husband fulfilled that wish." Mrs Browne gave her goddaughter a knowing look and a little nudge with an elbow. "Perhaps *you* will travel abroad sometime soon, Lizzy."

Ever the optimist, Aunt, but you have no notion of what just passed between Mr Darcy and me. Elizabeth thanked her for consoling with the family during hours of confusion and conflict and for taking her to Derbyshire. *How I wish I never went there at all!* "We look forward to your return. Kindly let Mr and Mrs Browne know Mrs Maguire, our *distant* relation, is here."

Their aunt took her leave of them after embraces and fond farewells. Then Jane sat down, and Elizabeth told her of Wishinghill Park and Mr Darcy.

Having been forsaken by him, Elizabeth felt keenly how fragile were her sensibilities. Like eggshells under pressure, her finer feelings had cracked a bit the previous evening after dinner when her father had summoned his two eldest daughters to his book-room. Mrs Maguire and Jane had remained with him for well over an hour while in the bedchamber she shared with Jane, Elizabeth had waited and waited until she heard Mrs Maguire enter the guest room down the hall. Her dearest sister, however, stayed away another half an hour.

Later, Jane had assured her all was well. "After Mrs Maguire—whose wish is that we should call her Constance—after she had retired, Papa and I had a long, lovely chat, one such as we never before shared. When he bid me good night, he kissed my forehead and told me he loved me. Never before had he said such a thing. I believe our bond actually may strengthen because of all this."

Such ready acceptance of the situation was admirable, but it still set Elizabeth's teeth on edge. Had she lost not only Mr Darcy? Was she also to be replaced by her two elder sisters in her father's affection? Dire thoughts gave way to such unhappy reflections as she had never experienced, and Elizabeth found herself beset by a niggling headache. It was nothing a brisk, solitary walk would not cure, so her afternoon was spent roaming country lanes where her only companions were flocks of starlings, a couple of squirrels, her troubled thoughts, and a few tears. But she was not formed for ill humour and was nothing if not irrepressible. Upon return to the house, she dressed for dinner, ate little, and retired far earlier than her wont.

The eggshell cracked again on Wednesday morning upon entering the breakfast room. Jane, as was customary, sat at her father's right hand, but her own usual position at his immediate left already was occupied. Patting the empty chair beside her, Mrs Maguire—*Constance*—indicated Elizabeth should take that seat. Directly across the table, Mary gave her a sympathetic smile. Wanting no one's pity, Elizabeth returned it with a false one of her own. Then, with feigned cheerfulness but genuine curiosity, she turned to Constance and enquired about the flora and fauna round Brierly Cottage.

With everyone determined to make Constance and John feel welcome, the awkwardness of having two relative strangers in their midst gradually eased. That tension was replaced by the awkwardness of having a mother who gave her husband the cold shoulder, childishly refusing even to speak to him unless absolutely necessary.

Constance, however, as she confided to Elizabeth, was almost sickeningly fond of Mr Bennet. He was her dear papa, and she was sure he would love her better than anybody else in the world, even Lord Darley, ever had.

Elizabeth thought her father enjoyed getting to know the Maguires, though their true kinship was still painstakingly kept from Kitty and Lydia. It was considered a mixed blessing that her two youngest sisters were rather indifferent to Mrs Maguire's presence and much more interested in that of the militia.

There was no escape for Elizabeth that day, no solitary place, such as Oakham Mount, to go and cry in peace. Rain kept everyone confined to the house. In company, she took deep breaths, put on a brave face, and dug fingernails into her palms. Needing occupation, she spent hours in the still-room. The maids there went about their tasks, casting puzzled looks her way as Elizabeth angrily brushed aside the dried lavender stalks that she, in frustration, had mutilated to flinders.

A sense of displacement had overtaken her. Food was tasteless, and her humour was as grey as the sky. The day dragged on. She wanted everything to go back to how it was before Constance entered her life, back when Mr Darcy loved her. *Except*—she realised, with deepening melancholy—*he never directly said he did love me.* But what did it signify? He was gone. What an escape! What a triumph for him! How he must congratulate himself. She knew, to be fair, neither smugness nor malignant pleasure was in his nature. Such a man would never gloat over his own success at another's misfortune.

Cooped up in his room at the inn after visiting Longbourn, Darcy stewed. He knew he had not been kind to Elizabeth—undoubtedly, he had been awful—but he had been incapable of discussing the situation with her at that moment. He had to consider it from every conceivable angle, and being alone gave him time to do so. He frowned, he fretted, and he paced. Even at a crossroads, he knew which way he wanted to proceed. Turning back and walking away was not an option. A lifetime of regret and loneliness lay in that direction. But, in going forwards, a bumpy road led to the Bennets and their relations. Was he willing to walk a course rife with obstacles, a route burdened by encumbrances? Was he willing to avoid that path entirely and leave?

No. But how can I...

If he could not accept Mrs Maguire and John, he and Elizabeth would never marry. He would either remain a bachelor or enter a loveless marriage if he could not marry her, for he doubted he could love another. *Not as I love Elizabeth.* Ergo, if he wanted her in his life—and he did!—he would be compelled to accept her entire family. It was a simple enough quandary to solve but difficult to put into action. Accepting a connexion with the Bennets had been troublesome enough before the Maguires became part and parcel of the problem.

As I told Mr Bennet, the reward—happiness—will be well worth any expenditure of time and effort.

It was more than his happiness that mattered. The sadness in Elizabeth's eyes—eyes made for joy and laughter —wrenched at his heart. If the arrival in her life of an unwanted, unknown half-sister had shocked and shamed her, how had his own response affected her? He had treated Elizabeth abominably, twice running away from her in fraught moments. She too was suffering, and from far more than a heart bruised by another's indiscretion. *She was in tears, and I left her.*

Have I broken her heart?

The following morning, in a stinging rain, valet and restless employer, under umbrellas, ventured out on missions: one to procure the best brandy to be found in Meryton, the other to the nearby circulating library. There, the gentleman asked for titles by Thomas Fuller. The proprietress, claiming not to know Darcy from Adam, demanded he deposit the full value of the books before she handed them over. He must not have made a lasting impression the last time he had given her his custom, for he had visited there twice before while staying at Netherfield and lamenting its pitiable library. Thinking it might please Elizabeth were he to ingratiate himself with her family and her neighbours, he engaged Mrs Clarke in small talk, the bane of his existence. From her, he learnt all the tittle-tattle of the neighbourhood—the juiciest piece being that the relation visiting the Bennets was the daughter of a baron. Darcy made an effort to show interest but made no mention of knowing the visitor or of his own connexion to the peerage.

Back at the inn, soaked to the skin, Jonesby reported there was no brandy to be found in Meryton, but he had procured a couple of bottles of Rhenish wine. Darcy put paid to those over the course of the day and evening while struggling to tolerate a difficult situation. Acceptance did not come easily, but he would do anything for Elizabeth. *She is faultless in these events, innocent and doing her best to accept the results of her beloved father's failings. If she can endure the connexion, so must I. I must do right by her.*

Leafing through the library books, he came across something befitting his predicament. 'What cannot be altered must be borne, not blamed.' *Yes, yes, but easier said than done.* He could not change what had occurred in the past, so he would have to learn to tolerate Mrs Maguire in the present.

Chapter 27

Before sunrise on Thursday, sitting by a dark window no longer attacked by pelting rain, Darcy tucked into a repast more befitting a ploughman, finishing with tea and preserved fruit while watching the grey dawn break mild and misty. Breakfast and thoughts sat heavily, and he craved an outlet for physical activity.

Wishing he could wield a rapier at Angelo's, he walked towards the militia encampment where Colonel Forster was conducting a training exercise. To his delight, the commanding officer, unlike the librarian, remembered him well, and arrangements were made for a private match then and there between the gentleman and the regiment's finest swordsman. Feeling much lighter after having bested the best but knowing it was far too early to call at Longbourn, Darcy bided his time by taking Aether for a galloping ride through the idyllic countryside. Overhead, a glimpse of blue sky appeared amongst scudding clouds.

Serenity allowed time for additional reflection about the incident at Riverswood some four years earlier. He had been but twenty-three at that time, still gaining experience and understanding through his mistakes. He certainly had learnt a valuable lesson: to never act like Wickham and never to betray someone's trust. But just when he had finally learnt to pin his hopes on a lady, had he betrayed her trust? Two days had passed since he had left Elizabeth standing forlorn outside Longbourn. *Is it too late?* He desperately needed to talk to her—if she would ever again speak to him.

Approaching Longbourn, he glanced at his pocket watch. It was still too early for a morning call. As Aether was turned towards the chalk ridge in the distance, Darcy had an epiphany. He could have prevented Miss Amesbury—Mrs Maguire—from succumbing to a rake's seduction. After all, he was well aware of Wickham's tendencies from his behaviour at university. Why did he not warn her? *Was I too enraptured by the teasing words she directed at me? Perhaps.* But if he had cautioned her, and if his warning had prevented that young lady's fall from grace, he would have married her, been bound to her for life, and not been free to love another. However painful for him, the betrayal at Riverswood had been a godsend.

He could face Mrs Maguire, set aside bitter indignation, and be grateful things had transpired as they did. He need not dwell on what had happened in the past. If Elizabeth would allow it, he could hope and plan for a future with her and embrace her philosophy—to think only of the past as its remembrance gave him pleasure. A weight had been lifted from his shoulders, and he sat a little taller in the saddle while raindrops pattered upon his hat. Glimpses of blue sky had been obliterated by ominous, gravel-grey clouds.

Attracted by a peek of blue sky amongst wind-driven clouds, Elizabeth had left her five sisters with their work-baskets and directed her steps towards Oakham Mount. Ascending with energy accumulated after the confining rain, she rejoiced in the stiff westerly wind and the occasional ray of sunshine upon her face.

Underfoot squelching caused momentary guilt over the state of her half-boots and hems, as well as a fleeting concern for her mother's resulting nerves and additional toil for the maids. But she refused to become overwrought by sloppy hems. Besides, a good length of trim sat at home in the bottom of her work-basket, waiting to be stitched over such a stain should it resist coaxing out with soap or lye. *As a family, we have covered a different sort of stain with another kind of lie. Well, a half-truth. Still, it rankles.*

In retrospect, her attention might have been better aimed at the heavens above rather than earthly matters. By the time she had reached the chalk ridge's summit, blue sky had disappeared, and a cloudburst sent driving rain full in her face. With a little determination, she might have reconciled herself to the torrent had not an unexpected clap of thunder scared her witless. Obliged to turn back, for no shelter was nearer than the house, Elizabeth hitched muddy hems and ran down the hilltop's homeward side.

A false step on the slippery slope brought her crashing to the ground. Flat on her back, the wind knocked out of her, she remained where she had awkwardly fallen, wincing in pain and staring at an angry sky until the dullness above was rent by a tremendous lightning flash. Scrambling to stand, a stab of pain in her left ankle confirmed it had been wrenched. Crying out, she sank to the wet ground, clutching her foot and cursing her recklessness.

Through the fury of elemental forces, either her yelp of pain or unladylike oath had been heard by a mounted gentleman rounding the bottom of the ridge. In a trice, he was out of the saddle and racing to her side. His voice rose above the downpour. "Miss Elizabeth!"

Under the sodden brim of her bonnet, she looked up, a few tears mingling with the raindrops running down her cheeks. Wet, bedraggled, and helpless, her mortification was complete upon identifying her rescuer. "Mr Darcy!" Having thought he had long gone, never to return, her surprise at seeing him there was as great as it had been at Wishinghill.

Effortlessly, he took her up in his arms with neither hesitation on his part nor permission on hers. Without a word, Mr Darcy carried her to his horse and sat her sideways upon the saddle with him astride behind. They took off at a gallop across puddled fields and through the garden gate. "We must talk," he said, "but not now. Now we must get you warm and dry and tended."

Once in the house, Elizabeth was besieged by sisterly concern, and she answered their questions while she and her rescuer dripped upon the carpet. Mrs Bennet and Mrs Hill rushed in, asking about the nature of her injury and adding to the commotion and fuss. Assuring her mother, Elizabeth replied, "Having several times twisted an ankle during my rambles, I know this is but a slight sprain."

In due time, she was settled in her chambers. Mrs Hill examined the slightly swollen ankle and oversaw the peeling of wet clothing from Elizabeth's shivering body. The housekeeper then called for hot water, a herbal compress, and ice.

Made comfortable in her bed, Elizabeth watched through her rain-streaked window as Mr Darcy reclaimed his horse and rode away. From Rose, she learnt he had been invited to have tea with the family but had declined due to his wet and dirty state. *More likely due to his seeing Constance still here amongst us.* "Did you say my father issued the invitation?"

"Yes, but Mr Darcy went in the direction of Meryton." Rose fussed with the pile of pillows beneath Elizabeth's injured foot. "Simon says the gentleman has been staying at the inn there."

"How odd." Shifting her leg, causing pain to shoot through the afflicted joint, Elizabeth wondered why he had not fled when he had the chance, and she asked whether anyone had determined the purpose of his lingering.

"Simon says Mr Darcy has been taking care of business hereabouts."

"Business? What business has he riding about in the rain, rescuing a fallen woman?"

"You might care to rephrase that," said Lydia as she breezed into the room, "lest Rose and I assume you lost more than just your footing today." Cackling with laughter and sitting heavily upon the mattress, she jostled her sister's ankle. Elizabeth hissed in pain and embarrassment.

"What is the matter?" Crossing her arms, Lydia huffed. "I have come to keep you company, but if you are going to be ungrateful, I shall not bother. Are you not curious about Mr Darcy's presence?" At Elizabeth's nod, her sister explained she had heard, through a trustworthy source of hearsay— being, it was assumed, Simon, the young manservant in their employ—that the gentleman had been gossiping with Mrs Clarke and clashing with the militia. "And I heard from Harriet, who heard it from Colonel Forster, that Mr Wick-ham's outstanding debts have been paid by persons unknown."

"I cannot imagine who would do such a thing."

"Nor I." Lydia heaved a mighty sigh. "Of late, so much has happened—Mr Wickham's disappearance, Netherfield's rushed evacuation, your going away and coming back with strange relations, Mr Darcy's mysterious presence. The entire neighbourhood has gone wild with conjecture about the vaunted Netherfield party. I am surprised Mr Darcy dares to show his face hereabouts." Springing from the bed, she again jostled Elizabeth's ankle.

Restless that night, Elizabeth carefully slipped out of bed and quietly, so as to not awaken Jane, lit a candle, pulled on a dressing gown and mules, and hobbled into the passage and down the stairs to her favourite indoor place.

In the still-room, she stood at the wide bank of windows, frowning at her reflection and breathing in the soothing scents of herbs and flower petals. With a start, she noticed another face in the glass and quickly turned. Wincing in pain, she cried out.

Candlestick in hand, her father rushed to her side. "I apologise for startling you, Lizzy. I heard the stairs creak and feared we had been invaded by an ill-advised thief come to purloin your mother's paste jewels. How fares the ankle?"

"Much improved. See?" Forcing a smile, she limped to the trestle table and sat on the bench. "Swelling has gone down while restlessness and irritability increase proportionally. Tomorrow I must be allowed outside or shall run mad—once I am able to run, that is."

"Tell me what, other than an entire day of immobility, has you so dispirited?" Settling beside her, he listened while Elizabeth spoke at great length of her mistaken first impressions of two very different men.

"And when I looked at my reflection just now," said she, glad for her father's undivided attention, "I saw not the mature, clever creature I thought myself to be. I saw a stupid, credulous, green girl. Weeks ago, Mr Wickham warned me about Mr Darcy. Or so I thought, but all the while, he was playing a glib game, telling me about himself. Contemptible man! And to think I once complained about slugs leaving behind slimy trails. Mr Darcy, on the other hand—"

"Are you aware he paid me a visit even before your return? It seems I have gained one daughter just as I am about to lose another."

Elizabeth startled. "I-I…What?"

"Oh, you deny it, do you?" Mr Bennet chuckled. "At any rate, Mr Darcy is a likeable fellow—once he takes the trouble to make himself so. Coincidentally, I might have mentioned slippery slopes to him. It seems he came to your rescue twice. In addition to saving you from a chill and a painful hobble home today, he earlier saved you from a far worse fate —Mr Wickham's clutches. Similarly, decades ago, another country gentleman saved your mother from a redcoat of unsavoury character. He married her."

Heroes, Elizabeth realised, did not wear shining armour. They wore dripping coats that smelt of wet, superfine wool, horse, leather, and sandalwood soap.

"You may believe otherwise, but your young man is intent on winning your hand. He said you agreed to his pursuit." Candlelight caught the twinkle in Mr Bennet's eye. "Are you going to be missish now?" He chucked her beneath the chin. "Do you remember, long ago, we sat in this very spot, and I predicted you would be discovered some day by a gentleman worthy of your regard?"

"I remember asking whether he would be a sensible man. I have not much to offer."

"And I said only an intelligent man would see your true worth." When the long-case clock struck two, and Elizabeth yawned inelegantly, Mr Bennet ordered her back to bed.

He helped her up the stairs, then kissed her forehead. "Although Mr Darcy never looks at any woman but to see a blemish, that fine gentleman of yours is quite an intelligent fellow. And he deserves you." Chuckling, he walked away, leaving her gaping after him but knowing she had not been replaced in her father's affections.

Chapter 28

A t a loose end the next day and suffering from a sleepless night warding off the inn's army of fleas and bedbugs, Darcy wandered to the apothecary shop and asked Mr Jones about treatment for a sprained ankle.

"My stock of comfrey is depleted. However, should you happen to visit Longbourn, you might ask Mrs Hill, the housekeeper, for assistance. One of the Bennet girls, Miss Elizabeth, grows comfrey by the stream. The family's still-room should have all the ingredients for a herbal compress. As we speak, one is probably being used on the young lady to ease such discomfort."

When Darcy enquired about a balm to soothe skin and something to repel blood-sucking insects, the apothecary suggested lavender water for the former and lavender stalks in mattresses for the latter.

Splendid. Just what he needed. Elizabeth Bennet's fragrance surrounding him in bed.

Less than an hour later, Darcy was ensconced in Longbourn's sitting room. Unsettled by Mrs Maguire's presence across from him—and unable to keep his gaze from Elizabeth —he engaged in a stilted conversation consisting of many fits and starts. He managed to make enquiries about her discomfort, and he wished her well. How soon his own pain might be eased, he could not tell.

When Mrs Maguire was called away to attend to her son, he breathed a sigh of relief. Miss Bennet and Miss Mary exchanged sly glances and busied themselves with tea preparations while, behind their hands, Mrs Bennet and her two youngest daughters whispered. *About me, I suspect.* Darcy moved closer to Elizabeth, speaking softly. "We must talk soon and in private. But first, I must beg your pardon for walking away when you told me about Mrs Maguire." Her mother seemed to be listening, so he leant back and spoke in a lighter tone. "And now, I have something that should be returned to its rightful owner." From a pocket, he retrieved the dainty, satin slipper. "Might this be yours, madam? Shall we determine its fit?"

"My treacherous and aptly-named slipper! You may have noticed it is not a straight shoe but made specifically for the left foot." She pointed at her bandaged ankle where it rested upon a footstool. "Presently, my left is not right, so the wretched thing might fit now."

Smiling, Darcy handed her the shoe and gestured to an open book on her lap. "I cannot help but notice that scrap marking your place." He would purchase for her something decidedly better than a streaked, torn piece of coarse brown paper. *An elegant satin ribbon, perhaps, embellished with lace and—*

"Is it not the most precious treasure?"

He peered more closely at it. *No.*

"A tenant's daughter, Miranda, expressed an interest in drawing, so I gave her some paper and a few of my pencils." Turning the picture in his direction, she asked his opinion.

"An admirable effort, I suppose. Tolerable, for one so young and untrained. But tell me, is it octopus or centipede?"

"Did your sister never proudly present you with a rudimentary drawing for your admiration?"

"Of course. But, from an early age, Georgiana has had an art master, and she became proficient at charcoal sketches and watercolours. Why do you ask?" Seeing some vexation in her expression, he said, "Good heavens, you cannot compare these immature squiggles to an accomplished young lady's artwork."

"No, I cannot. Nor should you. Miranda's efforts have nothing at all to do with your sister's drawings. My little friend worked diligently at this. Satisfied with her achievement, she presented it to me with pleasure and affection. Thus, I cherish the gift. And, for your information, it is—" Elizabeth turned the paper, contemplating it. "A cow, I think."

Ah! And here, I considered myself a connoisseur of fine art. What do I know?

Darcy drummed his fingers on the armrest. The acceptable time for his call was coming to a close. Why were they discussing a child's drawing rather than more important things? In addition to being impatient, he was deeply uncomfortable. He tried not to squirm, but the itching from the insects' bites was driving him to distraction. After six nights at the inn, even though the bed had been stripped and remade with his own superior linens, he had awakened covered in welts.

Mrs Maguire's presence was an itch under his skin, so perhaps that was the irritant rather than parasitic bites. Or the itchy rash might have resulted from nerves related to Elizabeth, but he was taking no chances. As soon as Mr Morris's office had opened that morning, he had made arrangements for Netherfield Park and the hiring of a few local servants.

He went there after taking leave of the Bennets but was again at a loose end. There was nothing to do but wait for Elizabeth's ankle to mend so he could speak to her privately.

That afternoon saw the arrival of the confections he had sent for from London shops. Off he hied again to Longbourn where Mrs Bennet—with unaccountable suspicion—reluctantly accepted the gifts of marchpane and sugared almonds. It was his hope she would, at least, share them with their intended recipient. As a single man, he could not give the sweetmeats to Elizabeth. But when they became husband and wife, he would give her everything her precious heart desired.

He requested titles of books she might fancy during convalescence and fetched them for her from the circulating library, where Mrs Clarke greeted him with a smile and addressed him by name. The books, delivered on his speedy return to Longbourn, engendered a discussion about one another's reading preferences. He asked Elizabeth's opinion of Fanny Burney, Maria Edgeworth, and their ilk. Her verdict was those authoresses, having written intelligent novels, were as relevant as Fielding and Goethe.

Darcy chastised himself for having disparaged one of Bingley's ladies for being a bluestocking. Why was it considered beyond the pale for a woman to have a literary bent or an intelligent mind? Elizabeth certainly was a rational creature with enough common sense to have rejected two of his inauspicious proposals. God willing, she eventually would see reason and accept his third.

When he returned to Netherfield, he learnt the items ordered from a London fruiterer had arrived. *I cannot call at Longbourn a fourth time in one day!* He picked through the crate himself and removed a few bruised apples for Aether. Noticing no mould on the grapes, oranges, or apricots, he ordered a footman to transfer them to a beribboned basket and make the delivery.

The following day, Darcy accepted the ladies' thanks for the fruit and took the seat nearest Elizabeth, who was propped on a sofa, injured foot on cushions, legs covered by a blanket. Across the room, Mrs Bennet's shrewd stare narrowed as she noted his preference. *Yes, indeed, madam. I should like to crawl beneath that blanket with your second eldest and make you a grandmother.* But first, he had to make the young lady amenable to the thought of him as her loving husband and father of that child. "Have you tried the apricots, Miss Elizabeth?"

"They were sent to the kitchen. The Brownes and Gardiners, including my four little cousins, will spend Christmas here, so Cook is making apricot cakes and sugarplums for the youngsters. I hope you will have a chance to meet the Gardiners, but I suppose you will leave for Pemberley anon."

Did she not remember their banter at Wishinghill about the twelve days of Christmas? "Quite the contrary, madam. Christmastide will be spent in Hertfordshire this year. As you know, I am residing at Netherfield and hope my sister will join me there." It would be a happy Yuletide to have his two most beloved ladies meet and become friends and, ulti- mately, sisters. "Will you allow me, or do I ask too much, to introduce Georgiana to your acquaintance when she comes?"

Elizabeth indicated it would be her delight. "And you may be pleased to know I might even walk the three miles to meet Miss Darcy. My ankle is perfectly sound. It was a very mild sprain, and I merely humour my mother by resting it."

The next day, her mother called from the other side of the door, "Lizzy! I would speak to you." Without awaiting an answer, Mrs Bennet stepped in and plunked herself at the foot of the bed.

Setting aside her unread book and reveries of a joyful Christmastide that included the Darcys, Elizabeth asked after her mother's visit at Lucas Lodge.

"That is not what I want to speak of, child. While Jane and Constance remain there with Charlotte, I wish to talk to you about men."

In the middle of the monologue, Elizabeth asked herself, *Why me? Why is Mama telling me all this?*

"And even though a dear girl, Constance is a reminder of my husband's life prior to our marriage and of his involvement with that woman. 'Tis difficult to accept he had a lover before me and that a child resulted from their dalliance." Heartbreakingly genuine tears slid down her mother's cheeks.

Where is her handkerchief? Botheration! For once, she truly needs one and is without. "Here, Mama." Elizabeth sat beside her and wiped away the wetness with her own handkerchief.

"How can your father expect me to accept all this with a smile? I have accepted Constance, but I cannot love her the same way I love my own daughters."

Elizabeth embraced her mother and wondered when was the last time she had done such a thing.

Composing herself, Mrs Bennet patted her daughter's knee and took a huge, shuddering breath. "To that end, I must warn you about Mr Darcy. His purpose is plain. He wants you, and I shall not allow it."

"Not allow it? But, Mama—"

Mrs Bennet shook her head. "I shall not allow it, although it might mean our salvation. I will not have one of my daughters suffer through an unhappy marriage, crying herself to sleep while her husband is off somewhere committing adultery."

Palms cool against red-hot cheeks, Elizabeth cried, "Mama! My father has been faithful. You know he has. Mr Darcy would never be disloyal and never betray someone's trust. He may have flaws, but being inconstant is not in his nature."

"Good heavens, Lizzy, of course it is. All gentlemen of that station are proud, unfaithful creatures. He probably has a mistress already. Just recently, I heard from Hill, who heard it from Mrs Nicholls, who heard it from a footman, that Mr Darcy importuned you the night of the Netherfield ball and made you an indecent proposition." Elizabeth muffled a gasp as her mother continued. "He is not worthy of you, even with all his wealth and connexions. What kind of mother would I be if I allowed you to marry a man with whom you have nothing in common, a man who might hurt you, if not physically then emotionally? You and I will not be bribed with marchpane confectionery, sugared almonds, and assorted fruits."

"It was not a bribe but a gift, Mama, and you are completely wrong about him. Mr Darcy is the very best man I have ever known."

While despondent over her mother's misgivings, Elizabeth was persuaded the next day into a game of blindman's buff on Longbourn's lawn with the Lucas brood, a handful of militia officers, her own four sisters, an unacknowledged half-sister, and John. To the latter, she laughingly cried, "Enough! Stop spinning me!" Her eyes covered, she reeled to the left. Righting herself, she staggered a few steps in the other direction, her ankle tender and weak. Other players, laughing and taunting, moved round her. Sensing someone behind, she turned to tag them but batted air.

Off to her left, Maria Lucas shouted, "Buff me if you can, Eliza."

All movement, all noise diminished into stillness. Turning in a circle, Elizabeth cried out, "What is happening?" She reached to remove the blindfold, but the chatter began anew. Air rushed past and players darted near. She recognised Captain Carter's harsh perfume as he tapped her shoulder, but he dodged away before she could buff him.

Concentrating, she sensed someone else close by. A hint of leather, of horse, and...tobacco? No, but distinctly masculine. A rich, creamy, woodsy scent. She reached out. Cedar? No. Sweet and spicy. Sandalwood. His fragrance was unmistakable. After all, he and she had kissed at Wishinghill, and the gentleman recently had carried her in his arms. But she also detected lavender.

"Mr Darcy." She waited, but he made no evasive move, even when she touched his chest.

"You have caught me, madam." Removing her blindfold, he whispered, "But we both already knew *that*. And, as pleasurable as your touch is, we, unfortunately, are not alone."

My touch? What touch? His heart pounded beneath her palm. She snatched away her gloved hand just as Kitty called out that everyone was going inside for warming cups of tea to chase away the chill. *Chill? What chill?* As an active sort of person, exertion was nothing new to Elizabeth, but the gentleman's proximity had increased her body's internal heat to a melting point.

With others out of earshot, Mr Darcy asked whether she had ever played the more indecorous version of blindman's buff. "No? Well, were we playing *that* wicked game, you would have identified me by touch...while seated on my lap."

"Scandalous!" There, again, was that bit of devilry inside him. And Elizabeth rather liked it. "I could identify you, sir, without sitting upon your lap. Without touch, even." She gave him a teasing smile. "But I shall say nothing more of it."

"I know how." Constance startled them with her presence. "You have a telltale scent, Mr Darcy." Sidling up, she took his arm. "Even while courting me years ago, you smelt deliciously of sandalwood soap. Remember, sir, down by the river when we—"

"At that time, I knew not what I was about." Disengaging her hand from his sleeve, Mr Darcy replaced it with Elizabeth's. "And I would rather not dredge up unpleasant memories on such a fine day as this. Now, Miss Elizabeth, were you not going to show me the prettyish little wilderness over there? You will excuse us, Mrs Maguire."

Elizabeth wondered what might have happened years ago down by the river. *Did they kiss or...?* Knowing Constance had lain with Mr Wickham, she fretted over her half-sister's intimacy with Mr Darcy. *They have some sort of amorous history. He even kept her miniature. At Wishinghill, he told me so himself, albeit inadvertently.* But had she given him more than a token of love? Had she granted him her favours as well? Elizabeth was about to remove her hand from Mr Darcy's sleeve, but Constance did it for her.

"No, I will not excuse you, Mr Darcy. You and my sister

require a chaperon." Eyes wide, Constance clamped a hand over her mouth and looked, with evident desperation, at her half-sister. "Silly me! I meant, of course, to say my *cousin*, my distant cousin, not sister."

Elizabeth shot a disapproving look towards her. "This is the sort of thing Walter Scott meant when he wrote, 'Oh, what a tangled web we weave, when first we practise to deceive.' But it matters not. Mr Darcy already knows the truth."

"Indeed." The gentleman replied to her sister with all politeness, but Elizabeth could hear the cool disdain underneath his words. "Do you not remember, madam, your disregard for the woman who held the chaperon position at Riverswood? If you please, you and I will speak in a moment." He bowed, turned his back on her, then moved away to speak softly to Elizabeth.

"The woman is your sister, so I shall tolerate her and her son's place in your life. But I wish I had never known her." He gave Elizabeth's gloved fingers a gentle squeeze. "We need to have a talk, you and I. But let me assure you there is nought to fear regarding Mrs Maguire and me. Nothing and no one will turn me away from you. You alone have the power to do that."

Mr Darcy's deep gaze nearly undid her, but his next words awoke her curiosity.

"Now I must have a few words with that sister of yours. Will you wait? What I have to say to her will not take long."

Chapter 29

"Lead the way, Mrs Maguire."

It being too cold to sit upon stone benches, they strolled round the withered garden. Darcy walked with hands clasped behind his back, keeping his distance while Mrs Maguire tried to close it.

"Here we are." She tittered. "A bachelor and a widow and no chaperon in sight. I wonder at your intentions."

Darcy gritted his teeth. He had to admit she still was a beautiful woman, but he was repulsed by her simpering tone and coy, inviting smiles. "Allow me to be direct. My intentions are to make Miss Elizabeth my wife."

Facing him, Mrs Maguire gave a throaty laugh. "Surely not! Even in Ireland, I had access to old copies of *The Morning Chronicle* with its fashionable intelligence and reports of the 'illustrious Mr FD of Derbyshire'. Each year I wondered which young heiress or peeress would win the prize. You must be aware my half-sisters have no dowries worth mentioning and no connexions, other than me." She gave him a significant look. "Remember, sir, you once hinted at marriage to a baron's daughter."

"Yes, I did, when we were younger and foolish. Back when you held my tender heart in your hands." Darcy's tone grew sharper, its edge tainted by years of anger and hurt.

"Then your fingernails dug into that tender heart and squeezed out every last drop of hope and trust inside it. Despite not seeing you for four years, you continued to wound me in a way I can never forget. You injured my pride, you see. Afterwards, I found it almost impossible to trust. Now my pride is under good regulation, and I have learnt to entrust my heart to another. And that honourable young lady is the most worthy of women despite having neither dowry nor connexions. I may have no choice but to accept you as a sister, but there never will be anything more between us."

"As I remember it, Mr Darcy, your forgiveness was sought and granted before you left Riverswood. I assumed that was the end of it. That I left *such* a mark upon your heart! Goodness, I had no idea." Mrs Maguire's fingers started walking up his sleeve. "But I could vanquish painful memories and regain your good opinion. You know what they say about widows, do you not?"

He removed the intrusive fingers from his arm. "Yes, I do. Widows are expected to remain loyal to their late husbands, and remarriages are thought to result from base motives. I am sorry for the many losses you have suffered, Mrs Maguire. But when you betrayed me, you forfeited any chance of regaining my affection." Her treachery offended him. "I have just stated my intention to marry your half-sister, and still you would pursue me? Have you no feeling for Miss Elizabeth, who has shown you nothing but kindness?"

She pouted and sniffed, but her eyes remained dry. "Well, yes, of course. You are free to pursue her." She patted her hair and sighed. "That is that, then. Tell me, whatever happened to that scoundrel, George Wickham?"

Darcy gave a brief summary of all he knew about the man's exploits spanning from Cambridge to the militia.

"Over a fortnight ago, your son's father disappeared without a trace." Her eyes, showing hints of vulnerability and fear, flew to his. "Do not fret, madam. Miss Elizabeth knows, but I expect few, other than our mutual friend, Mrs Helen Browne, have made the connexion. However, John is the very image of Wickham when he was a boy." *And I wager there are other children bearing a similar resemblance.*

Mrs Maguire seemed about to swoon, so Darcy removed his greatcoat, placed it on the cold bench, and helped her sit. "Forgive me for distressing you, madam, and please accept my apologies for not warning your younger self about Wickham's wicked ways."

Mrs Maguire sighed and looked away. "I once was a selfish creature, thinking only of myself. That changed when I became a mother. Strange," she said, speaking more to herself than to him. "My birth affected no similar alteration in my mother. On her deathbed, she admitted to having been more concerned about her own well-being and pleasure than anyone else's." Her eyes welled up. "At eighteen, I did not understand love because I had not been the recipient of it. Lord Darley showered me with everything my heart desired, but that is not love, is it?"

Darcy tried to be patient, although he yearned to be with Elizabeth. "It never should be the means of earning someone's love or trying to regain it. But, yes, I like to think of gift-giving as an affectionate gesture. Lord Darley obviously thought of you while he was in London and wanted to see your face light up with joy when he brought you presents."

"John brings me rocks and stubs of wildflowers, and I treasure them dearly." Smiling, she placed a hand over her heart. "My precious boy thinks the greatest gift of all is the time we spend together doing simple things like rambling round the park or driving in our jaunting car."

"You are fortunate to have one another. But, speaking of time, I must return to Miss Elizabeth."

They politely took leave of one another, not as friends but as the sort of relations one has to endure. While Mrs Maguire went to see her son, Darcy returned to Elizabeth in the little wilderness and apologised for keeping her waiting in the cold.

"It is not nearly as bitter as that day at the Fabrick," said she. "While walking about, I thought back on my Derbyshire sojourn—moments of mortification, hours of insight and delight. Then...anguish. You left with hardly a word. After our accord at the Fabrick and the perfection of the Taylors' ball, I expected more of a fond farewell than a cursory bow."

When her voice dropped, Darcy's heart followed suit.

"Do you often just walk away, sir? You did so again here, days ago when you confronted me about the Maguires. In both instances, it seemed you did not care a jot about me."

"I *do* care, so very much! But I was...discomposed."

"So was I," she cried. "You should have spoken to me about your distress instead of turning away and storming off on your high horse."

He wanted to pace but dared not turn his back on her, not when her expression so clearly showed the hurt he had caused. "Forgive me. It was never my intention to dismiss your concerns. Rather, I had hoped to spare you my ill temper. As well, I-I am not comfortable discussing feelings. Taking action and controlling my emotions, without expressing or worrying about them, was inculcated in me at my father's knee."

Elizabeth, arms crossed, studied him closely. "If we are to consider marriage, sir, we first must agree to communicate unreservedly. It is the only way to resolve conflicts. And, believe me, you and I will have conflicts."

Darcy dragged a palm down his face. "When—*if*—we disagree, I give my word I shall try to remember this conversation. But if I feel it best to distance myself from an argument, I shall suggest the matter be deferred. We might even agree on a time limit."

She appeared to approve of his suggestion; when she thanked him, Darcy managed a rueful smile. "You know, Miss Elizabeth, I was thinking...Do you remember storming off in the middle of our set at the Netherfield ball?"

"You have an annoyingly prodigious memory, sir. And that particular past remembrance—of my 'storming off', as you call it—gives me no pleasure at all. But, if you remember, we are discussing *not* walking away." Elizabeth's gaze drifted from him to a point in the distance before she continued in a softer voice. "If I ask you to tell me about Constance, will you comply or flee? I know there was some sort of betrayal. But,then—" Gripping her upper arms, she hugged herself tightly as though bothered, after all, by the chill in the air.

Darcy longed to enfold her in his arms to comfort and warm her. Then she asked the burning question he had been dreading.

"Did you love her? My—" Elizabeth's cheeks pinked as she hesitated. "My half-sister?"

Damnation! Her downcast expression wreaked havoc on Darcy's heart. Ashamed of feelings he once had harboured for a less worthy woman, he would speak nothing but the truth to the deserving one in front of him. "I *thought* I loved her. I almost asked for her hand." With remorse, he caught the wince Elizabeth, by turning away, tried to hide. "You seem taken aback, and rightly so. She was eighteen, and I but twenty-three. I was daft to think myself in love with her. What happened four years ago with Mrs Maguire—Miss

Amesbury—was nought but a foolish infatuation. I assure you there was no true affection, on either side."

When Elizabeth turned her beautiful eyes back to his, he was saddened to read doubt in them. She studied him, long and hard, searching for truth, it seemed, within his very soul. Finally, some understanding dawned within those intelligent hazel depths, and Darcy felt a glimmer of hope.

"If not for the strong bond between mother and son," she said, "I might think Constance was incapable of love. But she does seem starved of it from others. Within my family, she tries to ingratiate herself in a bid for affection and attention."

"As I understand it, after Lord Darley died, she had no one to shower her with affection, so she"—Darcy cleared his throat—"sought love in other ways."

"That sounds so sad."

Darcy agreed. "My own youth was somewhat solitary, too. Cosseted at Pemberley, I was spoilt and sheltered from unpleasant realities. Mother praised me and thought me quite perfect, and her rare but gentle caresses gave me great comfort." *But your touch, Elizabeth, gives me so much more than simple comfort. The mere touch of your hand floods me with joy, love, and desire.*

Recollecting himself, he said, "Perhaps, in Miss Amesbury, I stupidly thought I had found a kindred spirit. But, please, believe me...Had I known *you* were in the world, I would not have given her, or any other woman, the time of day. I pray that, despite my lonely past, I shall know a happy ending with you."

With a sympathetic smile, Elizabeth enquired about his father.

"He was an excellent man, benevolent and affable, but I strived for even a crumb of his approbation. While demanding outstanding performance from those who served him—and particularly from me, his heir—he was neither strict nor protective when it came to his perfidious godson. Growing up, everyone, except my father and Wickham, told me what a special boy I was."

"Now, you are a very special man."

Her praise was sincere, warming him and giving him ease to continue. "I thank you. But when I was younger, I had an appalling lack of judgment and experience and an appalling abundance of conceit and pride." He contemplated her for a moment. "I wonder what sorts of blunders the young, irrepressible Miss Elizabeth Bennet might have made. Were you impertinent to your mother?"

"Me?" She laughed. "Impertinent? Never! I prefer to call it 'educated insolence'. No, my sole mistake—believe it or not, and I recommend the latter—was letting a neighbourhood boy kiss me. Or I kissed him. I have forgotten quite how it transpired."

Darcy yearned to enfold her in his arms and kiss her until any memory of her youthful folly was annihilated from both their minds.

A pretty blush graced her cheeks as she continued. "The next time I was kissed, or perhaps I kissed the gentleman, was during the Taylors' ball. *That* was no mistake, and I pray you not think otherwise. Although I do not regret our closeness that night, I do regret my forward behaviour. At times I am too bold for my own good."

He reached for her gloved hand and pressed it. "I rather enjoyed your forwardness. Such intimacy was nothing short of bliss. Truth be told," he said, leaning in, "I long to repeat it. But we should not." *Because if we start kissing, I might never stop.* "We are not yet engaged. Besides, we are within plain sight of the house." Darcy glanced at the windows and retreated a few steps, clasping his hands behind his back. "It remains my hope that we may reach a deeper attachment, one rich in respect and devotion. But I realise your trust in me must be earned. Never again shall I repeat such ungentlemanly behaviour as to walk away from you."

"I appreciate your assurances. And speaking of walking away, shall we?" Elizabeth had a bit of a twinkle in her eyes as she accepted his proffered arm and indicated which way they should go. "As Charlotte once told me, men are like tea. Real strength and goodness are not properly drawn out of them till they have been for some time in hot water." She gave his arm a little squeeze that delighted him no end. "Now, back to Constance...If it was nought but an infatuation and there was no true affection on either side, why did her betrayal affect you so? I understand the blow to your pride, but—"

How he hated the enduring repercussions of such a brief and misguided fascination. "I was foolish to have allowed it to haunt me for such a duration. Wickham had already lost my good opinion, but the former Miss Amesbury knew my intentions, and—" Darcy's shoulders slumped. "While my heart was untouched, my feelings were wounded. And the blow to my pride was severe. I despised being proved naïve in front of Wickham. After their betrayal, I had great difficulty trusting people. Now I know it all happened for the best. I was never meant to marry her. *You* are my destiny, Elizabeth. For you I will happily accept your family. All of them."

"Ah, but what if my family does not accept you, sir? My mother has refused to give us her blessing and has spoken to me of her suspicions about your—"

"Lizzy!" Mrs Maguire ran up to them. "Mrs Bennet has sent me to fetch you. Pardon us, Mr Darcy." She linked an arm with her half-sister and tugged her towards the house.

Over a shoulder, Elizabeth looked back at him. Annoyed at Mrs Maguire's timing, he was left confused and anxious. *What did Elizabeth mean? Why would her family not accept me? How can her mother refuse?* His eyes narrowed. *Suspicions about my what?*

Chapter 30

T he air was filled with cheers and laughter the next afternoon as Darcy rode towards Longbourn's greensward. *She is there,* he noted happily, *surrounded by the children.* He dismounted and tethered Aether so he might graze but not wander afar. He tut-tutted as Elizabeth—bonnet nowhere in sight—hitched up her hems and joined the youngsters, John Maguire included, in their shouting, laughing, and dashing about the lea.

It was an altogether enchanting scene. She was, to him, a masterpiece, an original, a manifestation of the marvel of nature, energy, and life itself. As staid as he was, he could not help but be drawn to her vivacity.

She was so natural, so at ease with herself, uninhibited, unconstrained, yet ladylike and gracious. A lily amongst brambles, an ember amongst ashes. Unlike other women, Elizabeth never tried to impress him. *But I must try to impress her!* Heart thumping, he approached the merry troop with determined strides.

Ben, the first to spot him, pointed. "Look, Miss Lizzy. There's that mister from afore." She lowered the boy's hand, admonishing him for pointing.

Darcy removed his hat and bowed. "Good day, Miss Elizabeth and children."

She greeted him, curtseyed, and instructed her charges to pay obeisance to the gentleman. Then, reaching behind her skirts, she brought forwards a sturdy-looking club.

Bemused, he took a step back, eyebrows raised. What had Mrs Bennet said to her? "Be not alarmed, madam. You have nothing to fear from me."

Rolling a fallen acorn beneath her boot, Elizabeth lowered her lashes. "I know, sir. I was never in danger from you, of all people. You have come to my rescue more than once. I am grateful for that and for your assurances yesterday about my family...all of them." Looking up, she smiled and held out the bat. "Would you care to join our game?"

Returning her smile, he could do nought but see the piece of wood transform from a weapon to a peace offering. He reached out his hand to grip the bat, the sturdy oak a bridge connecting him to Elizabeth.

"And, Mr Darcy, I hope you paid no attention to what I said about my mother. She will change her mind about you. She must. But we may speak of those concerns later. Now," she grinned, her eyes shining. "It is time for play!"

He had lost sleep over Mrs Bennet's suspicions and refusal, so Elizabeth's faith lessened his worries. And, although sorely tempted, he fretted about engaging in such sportive abandon with unknown children and the woman he loved. He had not run round a field since university days. Dare he let her witness him at play? Dare he let her see that side of him? Consternation gave way to an overwhelming impulse. He took the bat firmly in hand. "I thank you. It would be my pleasure to play rounders with you."

He removed his cumbersome greatcoat and tossed aside his hat, but in deference to propriety, he remained in his frustratingly restrictive coat. The players divided into two teams, and when his turn came, he delivered the ball with a gentle, underarm toss. While at bat, however, he either forgot his own strength or unconsciously tried to impress Elizabeth with his prowess. The ball soared across the field. He ran to base, crunching leaves underfoot, while she and the children shaded their eyes against the lowering sun, watching the ball clear the trees and become forever lost in dense woods beyond.

Apologising profusely to what seemed to him a sea of unhappy faces, Darcy suggested improvisation. Fallen acorns were gathered, and the few remaining wild apples, clinging tenaciously to bare branches, were plucked away.

Along with Elizabeth and her charges, he laughed when acorns mainly proved impossible to hit, and the apples, to everyone's delight, splattered into pulpy pieces when struck. No one cared their game was in ruins; they were untroubled and merry. Particularly pleased when Elizabeth spent a few moments brushing away apple fragments lodged in his hair, Darcy closed his eyes, glorying in her touch while his heart raced in such close proximity to its desire.

To his dismay, after a moment, she turned away and began gathering her belongings. "We shall leave now, sir. I must escort the children to their homes before nightfall." He had not noticed the gathering darkness; Elizabeth was warmth and sunshine, and he had basked in her glow. "Thank you for joining our game, Mr Darcy, and for your fruitful solution to the problem of our lost ball."

"Which, if you recall, was my fault to begin with." He begged permission to accompany them, and she agreed. After donning his greatcoat and hat, he fetched his horse and asked Ben, the older boy, to lead Aether while the younger children took turns in the saddle. "And stay well behind Miss Bennet and me, understand? Good lad!"

Darcy walked then beside the woman he wanted forever

by his side. "Do you know that I met with your father before you returned from Wishinghill?"

"So I heard. What was the nature of that meeting?"

Glancing back, he ensured the children were out of earshot. He offered his arm; she accepted. "My intentions always have been honourable. I made them known to your father, who gave his consent." Perchance it was the fresh breeze blowing in their faces, but he liked to think he had put the bloom in her cheeks.

Withdrawing her hand from his sleeve, she fidgeted with her glove's cuff.

"Do not tell me this is unexpected," he said with some urgency. "You know my wishes, and I intend to prove myself worthy of your, and your mother's, regard. And to woo you *properly* this time." Hearing a giggle, he turned and glowered at the children. They looked back at him with angelic expressions. *Imps.*

Miranda, in the seat of honour atop Aether, called out, "Mith Lithy, what doeth woo mean?"

Heaving a sigh, Darcy turned his eyes heavenward, then glanced at Elizabeth, gratified to see he was not alone in flying colours. "Tell me, do you take care of these delightful charges every day?"

"No, not at all. In fact," she said, frowning fiercely in the children's direction, "they deserve an early Christmas holiday, a respite from my so-called instruction."

"Excellent idea." Reaching for her hand, Darcy replaced it on his arm. "They seem good students. Of course, they have had an excellent teacher." They stopped walking so he could lift Miranda off and hoist another little girl upon the saddle. When the child was secured safely, he ordered the others to stay well back. *At least far enough not to overhear my so-called wooing.*

Placing Elizabeth's hand upon his sleeve, he stepped up their pace. "Despite my impatience, I plan to be persuasive and tenacious while remaining honourable—always honourable. Gladly I would propose again this minute, but I understand your need to know me better. I am in this until the end, the last man standing and all that, even if there is only a slight chance you might, some day, stand beside me at the altar and thereafter beside me as my wife and Pemberley's mistress."

Elizabeth looked down, then away. When she finally smiled at him, it seemed tentative. "While unashamed of my more humble upbringing and education, I am doubtful of my fitness for either task. Your connexions, I understand, are noble and your estate grand. After Mr Collins spoke to his patroness about my family's behaviour, my father received a letter of chastisement from your aunt. Lady Catherine wrote of our unworthiness and said my sisters and I would never marry well. Now I have not only connexions to trade but a connexion to—" She leant her head closer and whispered so John would not hear her words. "To the Maguires and, consequently, Mr Wickham."

"Let us dismiss that connexion for a moment and speak of your upbringing." Stopping to pick up an acorn, Darcy bounced it on his palm. "You know what they say about this little nut, fruit of the oak. Something small, from humble beginnings, like the kernel inside this shell, can become impressive over time. I see your potential, Miss Elizabeth Bennet." Passing her the acorn, he whispered, "And you, madam, will be a magnificent Mrs Fitzwilliam Darcy."

Cheeks alive with colour, she grinned at him. "Should I rejoice in being favourably compared to a nut?"

"Yes, you should. Dormant within that nut is a mighty tree. Within you is the ability to become a powerful woman.

Much will be expected of my wife, and—no matter what my aunt thinks—I have faith you will fill the position admirably."

"For such confidence in my capabilities, I thank you." She waited until he walked beside her again after effortlessly hoisting another child upon Aether's back. "You seem quite determined about my role in your life. But neither of us, at this juncture, knows enough about the other to consider my putting such an important mantle round my shoulders. I always believed myself clever and a good judge of character, but where you were concerned, I was nought but a stupid green girl."

"I have been wondering," he said, glancing her way. "Why did you have such an ill opinion of me? How did it begin? What set you off in the first place? Was it Wickham?"

"No." She stared at her boots. "Earlier than that. It was here, in the lea, with the children. You and others in the Netherfield party were riding by but stopped to watch us. I did not recognise the voice at the time, but I overheard unkind comments. About me."

The deuce! Miss Bingley, no doubt. Darcy observed Elizabeth with concern. "I do not recall. What was said and by whom?"

She looked up at him, consternation writ upon her features. "The Bennets have been landed gentry for centuries, and I am proud of my heritage. Still, it hurt when you called me, and I quote, 'an unkempt, country maid not worth your bother', and...um...riffraff."

"You think *I* said those words? About you?" Thrust forwards by a godawful shove, Darcy stumbled, bracing himself for divine retribution. Elizabeth held fast to his arm as together they glared over their shoulders at Aether. "If I did say those words, please allow me to retract them and beg your pardon. You are the most worthy of all women and deserving of admiration from any gentleman with sense and good taste...and eyesight."

They walked on awhile in companionable silence. Then Darcy said, "Some of my behaviour needs correction, I admit. Yet I shall never be a humble man. I could, I suppose, aim to be less critical, less solemn, less pompous."

"I cannot think of a grander goal."

Her light laughter washed over him, goading him to reply as sternly as a happily bewitched man could. "You may make sport of me all you like, madam. But be forewarned. I may be forced to take action. As a matter of fact—" His mock severity only made her gaiety grow in volume. "By all means, do continue twitting. I have a plan for stopping your mouth."

Her laughter ceased, and behind them, Ben made ghastly kissing sounds. Darcy wondered what sort of dunderhead wooed a woman amongst a flock of disrespectful moppets. The mother of his future children turned to the boy and bestowed upon him a gentle admonishment. *Bless her heart.* He would not have to be the sole disciplinarian in the family. How could he ever chastise a daughter should she resemble her adorable mother?

Once the last two tenant children were delivered to their home, Darcy asked whether he might escort Elizabeth and John to Longbourn. She agreed he could accompany them as far as the garden gate.

His world glimmered with hope as the gloaming settled upon them. As it had been upon leaving the Fabrick, walking and talking with Elizabeth gave him unprecedented lightness of heart. "I intend on changing for the better, and if that is what it takes for you to pledge me your troth, it shall be done. While I presume you no longer loathe me, I wish I could be as sanguine now as when I first came to you without a doubt of my reception."

"I never loathed you," she protested.

With a small smile, he asked, "May I resume my addresses?"

Elizabeth's reply was quick and, while full of warmth, did not provide him all he sought. "You may. For the nonce, let us see how we get on."

He would withstand her stubbornness. *In time, I shall offer marriage again. As an oak growing from an acorn, slow and steady, her love may take time, but I am determined it will flourish.*

"May I ask how long you plan to remain, sir?"

"As long as it takes. We spoke at Wishinghill about the sixth of January, but the duration is entirely in your delicate hands. I am here until you tell me to go away." When she asked about his duties elsewhere, Darcy assured her. "I am fortunate to have excellent people in my employ—particularly two trustworthy housekeepers and butlers and an outstanding steward. At present, unless something urgent occurs, my affairs can be conducted from here. Other duties can wait until you decide to share them with me."

"You have vowed to be less pompous, but you are insufferably sure of yourself."

"I am sure of *us*, Elizabeth. That we belong together, shoulder to shoulder, tackling life's problems. Giving one another succour. Raising a family. Laughing and loving and growing old together. You make me want to be a better person, and I want…I need you in my life. And I think you need me in yours."

Her eyes widened. Just as Darcy wondered whether his speech had overwhelmed her, Elizabeth smiled at him with something greater than mere fondness. At the garden gate, while Aether snorted and John ran ahead, Darcy bussed her gloved knuckles and promised to call on the morrow.

Chapter 31

On the eighteenth, with Kitty and John chattering behind her, Elizabeth led the way to the dell near the chalk winterbourne. On a mission to inspect the ivy growing on hornbeams in the hollow, they hoped to find it fit for later use as festive greenery.

Moving about in the crisp December air demanded physical exertion—a much-needed distraction from the thoughts and reflections which had kept her up late into the night. The previous day's encounter with Mr Darcy, and his declarations of her worth and his admiration for her, had been more than welcome. His assurances were like a treasured possession kept within her heart. Despite her doubts and his flaws, Elizabeth knew she had fallen in love with Mr Darcy. His alluring words about possibilities had spoken to her of a future far removed from her everyday life, a life by his side. He respected her and cared about her, which was of the utmost importance. But he had not expressed one essential sentiment. *Does he love me? If so, why does he not say it? If not, how can he speak such beautiful words to me?*

As Jane slept quietly beside her the previous night, Elizabeth had lain awake and thought about the man who had won her heart. He was not a perfect person—*nor am I*—but he was a good, honourable one. She was sure he fulfilled all his duties responsibly and knew he filled his clothing admirably. His way with children had her imagining events that would make him a father, a loving one. She could not like his reservations about her own family. Still, she understood—and could share—some of his opinions and was at least glad they could talk openly about fraught subjects, including his past with her half-sister, known then to him as Miss Amesbury.

From the treetops, rooks cawed harshly, disturbed at their party's approach to the hollow—or perhaps the presence of something or someone already there. Ahead, Elizabeth discerned the figure of her half-sister leaning against a birch, head bowed. When John and Kitty's chatter grew louder, Constance turned, swiping at her eyes with a handkerchief. "Please, Lizzy, do not let my son see me like this."

Elizabeth turned and swiftly walked back to the pair. She asked Kitty to continue to the dell with John and tasked them with marking the most vibrant ivy to be culled closer to Christmas. She handed her nephew a few bright red ribbons for that purpose and told him to keep his gloves on and watch for wildlife amongst the greenery. Once they were out of sight, she returned to Constance and rubbed her back. "What troubles you so? Grief over your mother's death?"

"No, 'tis not so much that." Constance wiped her nose, took a deep breath, and stood taller. "My dear father loves me. I know that is true, and the rest of you have accepted me and treated me well. But your lives have been disrupted, and my being here necessitates lies and half-truths to our two youngest sisters, your friends, and your neighbours. I cannot even tell my son he has another grandfather!" Composing herself, she reached for Elizabeth's hand. "I wish to go home to Ireland and the Maguires. We have made a life there at Brierly Cottage."

At such unexpected but welcome news, Elizabeth

inwardly heaved a sigh of relief, then felt a degree of guilt for it.

"Lizzy!" Kitty's voice could be heard behind them. "We have found some splendid woody vines, all glossy green and—"

"Please mark the vines, and take John back to the house. I am speaking to Mrs Maguire. We shall be along directly." Kitty obeyed but turned to look over her shoulder a few times as she walked back to the little boy.

Linking arms, the half-sisters began walking. Elizabeth assured Constance that she and John would always be welcome at Longbourn, but the lady was adamant in her desire to return to her home across the Irish Sea.

"Lizzy, there is one more matter I would discuss with you," she added. "Mr Darcy." Elizabeth baulked, feeling all the awkwardness of such a conversation, but Constance insisted. "I shall not provide details, but I treated him ill, indeed. Only yesterday, after he and I spoke, have I admitted it to myself. He was smitten, and I was stupid. You may have wondered at the extent of our intimacy, but fear not. We were young, and it was nought but a chaste kiss."

Elizabeth hoped her relief was not evident. The speed with which Constance continued speaking assured her it was not.

"Mr Darcy is an honourable gentleman. Any woman would be fortunate to have even a speck of his regard. I know he admires you and means to make you his wife." She grasped Elizabeth's hand. "He is rather benevolent of heart, knowing and accepting our true connexion. I do hope you hold him in some affection."

I do. I love him. Elizabeth had admitted as much to Jane, but she hesitated to be as open with a sister she had known for mere weeks. "Yes, I do hold him in affection. He is quite dear to me." It was all the declaration she could offer the lady. Mr Darcy was the one who first needed to hear of her love. *And how I long to tell him—if it was proper, and if he first would speak such sweet words to me.*

She glanced at the blonde woman walking beside her. *And it is too bad for you, Sister, to have just now realised the man's worthiness.* Elizabeth's blood still boiled at the thought of Constance's betrayal, and she was surprised the lady could even recognise Mr Darcy's benevolence or care about his future. She looked forward to time alone with him without her half-sister lurking about.

Later that morning, Constance made known to the Bennets her intention to return to Ireland and invited them to visit Brierly Cottage one day. Mr Bennet insisted she and John remain, but she was determined to be home before Twelfth Night.

Mr Darcy arrived at Longbourn soon afterwards and, upon learning of Constance's plan, spoke to Elizabeth, then asked for a private word with Mr Bennet.

The instant the gentlemen left the room, Mrs Bennet was on her feet. "Lizzy, what private business has that man with your father?"

"Mr Darcy wishes to offer his assistance in the Maguires' journey," explained Elizabeth, relieved that Constance and John were in their chambers and unable to join in the conversation. "He intends to arrange their conveyance to Liverpool and pay their passage across the Irish Sea to Dublin, where Constance has friends who will help them get home. The voyage will depend on tides and weather, and the ship may face fierce headwinds or become becalmed. God willing, she and John may reach their destination by Christmas, but it is doubtful."

Mrs Bennet seemed appeased and not entirely sorry they would soon be gone from Longbourn.

Arrangements for the Maguires' journey necessitated a trip to London, though Darcy was loath to part from Elizabeth. Upon his return late the next afternoon, he stayed away from Longbourn. While difficult to do so, he wished to give the Bennets and Maguires their privacy during the last full day of their visit. He called there the next morning and found the household in the midst of preparing for their guests' departure.

Half an hour later, he stepped up, bowed over Mrs Maguire's hand and wished her Godspeed; then he ruffled her son's hair. Standing aside, he observed as the Bennets and Maguires hugged and shed tears. Fond wishes for health, happiness, and Christmas joy were exchanged, and promises were made to correspond faithfully.

Joining the others waving farewell and calling 'Safe journey!', Darcy stood beside Elizabeth as she watched the coach disappear round the bend. He felt her take a deep breath before sighing.

"Now that they are leaving, I am sad to see them go," she said before looking up at him. "It was generous of you to do so much to assist them in their journey."

"I had the means and ability to ease their way." He shrugged, unable to voice his true reason for any generosity towards Mrs Maguire. *I did it for you.*

"Well, I must be off now myself. I wish to make some purchases in Meryton for the Gardiner children. Would you care to join me and—speaking of easing one's way—carry my packages?"

With alacrity, he agreed. As they walked towards the market town, Darcy greeted locals he had met during his stay there. Elizabeth's smile spoke of how well-pleased she was with such small, effortless civilities. He suspected his announcement would disappoint her as much as it had him. "While eager to meet you, and despite my assurances, my sister has decided to spend Christmas at Park Lane with our relations. Her other guardian, our cousin Colonel Fitzwilliam, was recently injured in battle but is now ambulant. Georgiana and her companion are currently travelling from Derbyshire to London. In her letter, she expressed hope that your Christmas may abound in the season's gaieties and says she envies the cheer and good-will I anticipate sharing with you and your loved ones."

Elizabeth's warm smile assured him that Georgiana's envy was justified, and he ventured onto a trickier topic. "In a postscript, she enquired why I have not yet asked you to be my wife. Shall I tell her I have done so twice?"

"Please, no. I will not have your sister think me a simpleton." They walked in companionable silence awhile, but Elizabeth glanced at him several times before speaking. "We have already discussed what I expect in a gentleman and in a husband. Tell me, please, what you expect from a wife."

"The same things you expect in a husband: mutual respect, succour, fidelity, and abiding love. I would expect you—my wife—to continue the traditions of my Darcy ancestors, such as charity and fairness. But I would not have us cling to outmoded customs and conventions in the manner of Lady Catherine," he said as they passed the milliner's shop. "I believe we Darcys must prepare for the inevitable changes being brought about by industry. I have stakes in steam power and iron smelting and am interested in improved transportation, new agricultural practices, and scientific experimentation."

"I posit you, sir, are a liberal man."

"I see the inequity of my position compared to that of my scullery maids...and the gap betwixt the Prince Regent and those poaching to feed their families, which, by the by, rarely happens at Pemberley. Change may not come in our lifetimes, but, God willing, our descendants will know a more just society." He felt her nod and added quickly, "Do not misunderstand me, however. While charitable, I owe it to my antecedents and descendants to pass along the Darcy legacy intact, if not in better condition."

"All of this is admirable, sir, as is your skill at avoiding my question."

Assured by the amusement in her voice, Darcy grasped Elizabeth's hand. "Indeed, how have we strayed so far from what I expect or want in a wife? All I truly want is for her to be you, for you to be my wife and partner in all of this."

A moment later, he released her hand, and the couple entered the sundries shop in companionable silence. Once she had acquired a few chapbooks and toys, Darcy carried the parcels in one hand and again offered his arm to Elizabeth. Upon their return to Longbourn, while she put away her purchases, he waited outside for her to show him a litter of gun dogs named by Miss Catherine, Miss Lydia, and John Maguire eleven days prior.

In the kennel attached to the barn, Mr Darcy seemed only mildly interested in the antics of the chubby puppies. Unable to resist the furry bundles of joy, Elizabeth stripped off her gloves and plucked one from the straw-lined box. While cuddling and petting the little dog, she became unsettled by the gentleman's intense stare. "Should your intent be to unnerve me with that disparaging look, I shall give you no satisfaction." She rubbed her face against the soft fur. "I take delight where I find it, and presently I find it in this simple pleasure." Her words did nothing to diminish the ardent look in his eyes. "I suppose you, a man of the world, consider me quite the rustic."

"Rustic is not necessarily an uncomplimentary description." He leant against the wall, arms crossed, smiling. "Your guilelessness is refreshing, captivating. You cannot believe I am, in any way, disparaging of you."

"You are a rather strange man of the world," she teased, "choosing to spend time here amongst the lower gentry instead of the sphere where you belong. While I am pleased you will join us for Yuletide, beware our country manners do not rub off on you."

"Spending time with you is where I belong, madam. You know why I stubbornly remain here when I should be at Pemberley." The intensity of his fixed look became too much, and Elizabeth glanced away. "Besides," he said in a gentler tone, "I always have been a country gentleman at heart. Now, more and more each day, I have come to appreciate the simplicity and charm found here in your company, in your neighbourhood."

"I am pleased you find our society charming and that we have become friends."

The intensity vanished from his gaze, replaced by incredulity and, perhaps—thought Elizabeth—some injury. "*Friends?* Our friendship is cherished, but you know I desire a more intimate association. You know why I am here and what I want. Shall I ask you again? Are you ready for that question now?"

"I...Not quite." *Because you have not said you love me. Dare I ask whether you do?* Scuffing straw with the tip of her boot, Elizabeth rested her cheek on the sleeping puppy's head, avoiding her suitor's eyes. Mr Darcy turned his back to her. The puppy awoke and squirmed in her arms. She held fast, its warmth giving her comfort. *Either he loves me, or he does not. I should not have to pull the words from him.* Caught between guilt and frustration, she murmured, "Are you going to walk away now?"

His expression had been unreadable when he turned towards her, but a fervent light entered Mr Darcy's eyes while the puppy licked Elizabeth's face. He took the little dog from her and placed it amongst its brothers and sisters. Tipping her chin upwards, he murmured, "Dog slobber and all, may I kiss you?"

Palm over heart, she looked round the kennel. "Here?"

Glancing at the spot where Elizabeth's hand rested, he smirked. "No, not there. As pleasurable as that might be, I had planned on kissing your tempting mouth."

Face afire, heartbeat frantic beneath her palm, she closed her eyes.

He kissed one corner of her mouth. "Forgive me." He kissed the other side. "For unsettling you."

Opening her eyes, she discovered her palm resting not on her own chest but his. They gazed into one another's eyes. His head lowered, foreheads touched, breaths mingled. Ripples became waves, waves a maelstrom as heated pleasure surged through her.

Pulling away, Mr Darcy murmured, "Someone approaches." Picking up two puppies, he handed one to Elizabeth as Mr Bennet's voice reached their ears.

"Ah! Lizzy. Well, well, and Mr Darcy, too. Fancy meeting both of you here, alone together." Her father did not seem at all surprised to find them. "May I assume you like dogs, young man?" Mr Darcy indicated he had a variety of them at Pemberley. "Wonderful creatures, dogs, are they not?"

Mr Bennet looked fondly at the puppies capering round his legs. "Caring nothing about a person's station or intelligence. Not judging people by connexions or wealth or lack thereof. Open your home, your larder, your heart to them, and, in return, they give unconditional loyalty."

Eyes fixed on her father, Elizabeth spoke indirectly to the younger, taller gentleman. "Devotion is an admirable quality, one we humans would do well to emulate. A recipient of such constancy would be blessed, indeed."

She was pleased to see Mr Darcy's eyes soften.

"Speaking of opening one's home and larder," said Mr Bennet to Mr Darcy, "would you care to dine with us this evening?"

"I would be delighted, sir. Thank you."

As the three walked towards the house, Elizabeth pondered the invitation. The Bennets were genteel, but for Mr Darcy to join her family at dinner and see all their deficiencies—Simon's haphazard serving at the table, Lydia and Kitty's unrestrained behaviour, pulling dishes about as they chose—would be dreadful. It would be a true test of the gentleman's avowal to accept them.

To Elizabeth's surprise, after a dinner with fewer awkward moments than expected, Mr Darcy complimented Mrs Bennet on the meal and requested a private word.

With Mama? What on earth?

While awaiting his return, Elizabeth stared at her embroidery and sighed. When her suitor failed to appear after a quarter of an hour, she flung aside her mangled stitchery. "What can they be doing in there?"

"If I had to make a wild guess, I would say they are discussing you," said her father. "Hark, I recognise your young man's determined footfall as we speak."

Mr Darcy approached, looking a little weary but smiling earnestly. He pretended to admire Elizabeth's work as he whispered, "I shall go to Netherfield now, but you must attend your mother in the back parlour."

As soon as he had exited, Elizabeth moved quickly to find Mrs Bennet walking about the small blue parlour, looking exhilarated and not a little teary-eyed.

"Oh, Lizzy! Come. Sit and bide with me awhile." Settled together upon the sofa, Mrs Bennet patted Elizabeth's knee. "I was terribly wrong about your Mr Darcy. What an honourable gentleman! And, having promised to always be faithful, you will have an excellent husband. The dear man told me some heartless young lady betrayed him. Thereafter, he made a vow to himself to never inflict that sort of pain on another person, let alone a woman he loves."

Ah, but does he love me?

"I suspect such a man is accustomed to getting whatever he wants. And he not only wants you, but he must also truly love you," the lady said while fanning flushed cheeks. "Regardless of whether or not you will accept him, he has purchased Netherfield Park for—should he be so blessed—a second son. Of course, it is also a good investment, but here is the best part! Should I be left a widow, he promised that I —and any unmarried daughters—shall have a place there to live."

Stunned, Elizabeth's mind was awhirl—*he bought Nether-field? Regardless of my becoming his wife?*

Her mother was still talking. "Oh, do not make him wait, child! Mrs Nicholls told Hill that he gets very little sleep. He stays awake all hours, writing letters of business, personal correspondence, and instructions for his steward and his housekeepers in Derbyshire and London. You must accept the dear man and make him as happy as he has made me tonight."

As Elizabeth left her bedchamber just before sunrise the following day, Mrs Hill pressed into her hand a nosegay containing dried lavender spikes, rosemary sprigs, and basil leaves, all bound together by a slip of paper and tied with a white ribbon.

In answer to Elizabeth's puzzled expression, the house-keeper said, "A Netherfield footman delivered it, but I wager those herbs are from our own still-room. Your mother and your admirer were in there last evening."

Elizabeth ducked back into her room, untied the ribbon, unfurled and unfolded the creased paper.

Dearest Elizabeth,

Only after confessing my irrepressible feelings for you to another did I realise how terribly remiss I have been. Forgive me for not speaking three very significant words to the person most deserving of hearing them. Expressing emotion never comes easily to me, but such profound admiration and affection cannot be repressed. I love you, Elizabeth Bennet. Never have I loved another so ardently, so deeply, for you—a rarity amongst women—have no equal. Just as you hold this, my first attempt at a billet-doux, you hold my heart and my future in your delicate hands. To become your husband is my fondest wish. I love you in a way that cannot be undone. Will you accept this enduring love? Will you accept my hand? Will you marry me? In the hope you soon may need them, I send these fragrant herbs, which once were considered love charms and are still used in wedding cere-monies. I hope you will meet me this morning and give me your answer.

Your humble servant,

Fitzwilliam Darcy

Chapter 32

Dawn had broken hours earlier, but the winter morn's weak light had not the strength to banish a gentle, low-lying mist hanging over the countryside. All was silvery-blue and eerily quiet as Elizabeth stood waiting at the garden gate, wrapped in her ruby-red shawl over a warm pelisse.

Through the blanket of brume, Mr Darcy appeared far earlier than expected; her heart lurched. *If each dawn is a new beginning, I pray this morning might prove the same for him and me.*

They greeted one another quietly and strolled arm in arm through Longbourn's park. With deep regret and guilt, Elizabeth noticed the dark circles beneath his eyes. He seemed morose, and she feared it was due to her not yet mentioning his *billet-doux*, the love letter that had vanquished her last doubt and all resistance.

"I hear rumours of your remaining awake, working until all hours over there at Netherfield."

"'Tis nothing," said he. "I have been busy with correspondence."

"Because you remain here rather than journeying to Pemberley. Because of *me*. You are losing sleep because of me."

He smiled, giving her fingers a gentle squeeze. "I have not slept well since the night we met."

"But it is detrimental to your health. It is time, Mr Darcy, and you must go to Pemberley."

He turned to her with such hurt in his eyes that she rued the unintended cruelty of her scheme. "Are you telling me to leave?" He backed away as she handed him the posy of herbs. "You are returning it? Did you not even read—?"

He ripped off his gloves and fumbled to untie the ribbon. "There is a note, you see, just here." Unfurling the paper wrapped round a single lavender spike, a rosemary sprig, and leaves of basil and ivy, he sucked in a breath, eyes wide. "This is not my tussie-mussie...nor is this my penmanship." Silently, he read the words she had written.

Aloud, she recited them. "It is time, Mr Darcy. You must go to Pemberley...with me as your wife. This little nosegay would look handsome upon your lapel the morning we meet at the altar. In, say, three weeks? In the meantime, I am, now and evermore, yours. Elizabeth."

Her words had struck him speechless. Thrusting the herbs into a pocket, he looked upon her with such fervour that she shivered. Silently closing the distance separating them, he backed her against the derelict dovecote and untied the ribbons beneath her chin. Casting aside her bonnet, he, with both hands, brushed back unruly curls the damp air had sent rioting round her eyes. Cupping her face in his hands, he whispered words of love and devotion before feathering kisses across her brow.

How could I ever have thought this man unfeeling?

Leaning in, he angled his head and brought his lips to hers. It began in tenderness but escalated into something deep, wet, and wild. Her arms slid round Mr Darcy's neck, and she clung to him for dear life. Their sweet but short-lived kiss at Wishinghill paled in comparison, and no one intruded until the need for more oxygen did.

Swept up in love and ardour, Elizabeth lost herself in the intensity of his impassioned eyes, in his whispered endearments, the nearness of him, his scent, his rapid, ragged breaths. "Mr Darcy, how I love you, you dearest, most wonderful man!" Kissed again, long and hard, she floated away, drowning in the heady deliciousness that was Fitzwilliam Darcy.

Pulling back, chest heaving, he murmured, "I love you, my darling. I am sorry to have taken so long to make that clear to you." He kissed her temple and whispered, still panting a little, "Like flame and fuel, we are incendiary together. We must stop, lest we ignite an unstoppable fire."

He unwound her arms from his neck, picked up her bonnet, took her by the hand, and they started walking. "Many years ago, my favourite cousin accompanied me to the Pneumatic Institution in Bristol where we attended one of Humphry Davy's nitrous oxide trials. We not only attended but participated in the chemist's experiment. The instant I removed the bag, I unconsciously laughed. The sensation was pleasurable, thrilling even. Afterwards, though, I was mortified by how giddy I had been. Fitzwilliam, of course, thought it a great laugh."

He stopped to embrace her tightly. "You may wonder why I am telling you this. Well, as pleasurable as that sensation was, it was nothing to how elated I feel now, knowing you love me and that I shall be your husband, the one to provide for you, protect you, love you." He placed the bonnet upon her head and lingered while fidgeting with the ribbons. "I should go to your father with the marriage settlement, then visit your vicar to arrange the reading of the banns." He heaved an exaggerated sigh. "What a *pity* our wedding cannot take place while all your dearest relations will be here for the twelve days of Christmas."

Elizabeth smiled into his eyes. Enjoying his actorly flair and bantering tone, she matched it. "Oh, yes. And what a pity you cannot afford a common licence. Alas, we shall have to wait a full three weeks for those silly banns to be read."

Darcy tied her bonnet, then took both her gloved hands in his. "And if only my family friend in London was a bishop." As an aside, he added, "Which, by the by, he is. And 'tis fortunate I already have your father's consent."

They grinned at one another.

First, Mr Darcy sent to Netherfield for his valet and carriage. Next, they informed Elizabeth's father. Then Mr Bennet had everyone summoned to the sitting room where he made the happy announcement to his wife and daughters. They all rejoiced and congratulated the betrothed couple, but only Mrs Bennet kissed Mr Darcy's cheek and asked after his favourite dishes.

Without awaiting his answer, she cried, "We shall have soup and sherry, then fish and Rhenish." With nary a breath, she itemised three more elaborate courses and accompanying wines. "I shall invite the Philipses, Lucases, and Gouldings to share in our joy. The dishes will be fifty times better than anything we had at Lucas Lodge!"

"Mama, we prefer to wait until the Brownes and Gardiners arrive, so we all may celebrate together. Mr Darcy is going to London now to procure a licence. We wish to not only celebrate our engagement during the twelve days of Christmas, we plan on marrying before Twelfth Night."

"Good heavens, Lizzy, you cannot mean to marry so soon! 'Tis too much! How am I to plan a dinner party, Christmas celebrations, and a bride's breakfast?"

Mr Darcy stepped forwards, gently grasping and bowing

over the woman's hand. "Mrs Bennet, forgive us for causing distress. But, please, do not make yourself uneasy. If you will compose a list of requirements, I shall hie to town and return promptly with enough cooks, maids, footmen, supplies, and such an unlimited assortment of viands that you might host ten such occasions. And, should you wish to hold festivities there, Netherfield will be at your disposal. Together you, your daughter, and our combined household servants will plan feasts the envy of all your neighbours."

At such largesse, Mrs Bennet could merely nod before tottering off to do as requested. To Elizabeth—who thought her mother might utter some embarrassing remark about the gentleman's deep pockets being as good as a lord's—such quietude was astounding.

Once Mrs Bennet handed him her extensive list, Mr Darcy tucked it away inside his coat, kissed his intended's hand, and boarded his carriage. With a last, longing look, he signalled his coachman to drive on. Elizabeth was left to wonder how she would endure without him while he was gone.

Her only consolation came late the next morning upon receipt of a letter from him. Mr Darcy sent his love, confirmed the licence had been procured, and said he had called at Park Lane to inform his relations and Miss Darcy of his betrothal. He also hinted about bringing a surprise with him.

⁶⌇⚬

Darcy returned two days before Christmas and sent word to Longbourn immediately.

Upon being informed when Mrs Bennet and all her

daughters arrived at Netherfield, he—anticipating happy reunions and introductions—greeted them in the vestibule, bowing over each hand and keeping Elizabeth's in his while escorting the ladies into the drawing room.

Cries of delight rang out as the six Bennet ladies and the three Brownes spotted one another. Darcy was gratified to see that part of his surprise—their relations' early arrival—had brought smiles to their faces until one of his guests nearly knocked him over as she rushed forwards.

Once Elizabeth detached herself from the lady's embrace and greeted her aunt and cousin, she introduced the ebullient Mrs Michael Browne to her mother and sisters. Upon first beholding Miss Jane Bennet, the younger Mrs Browne stared until nudged on one side by Darcy and the other by her husband. "Oh, I do beg your pardon, Miss Bennet. My husband's mother told me of the resemblance. The similarity is striking."

With a sly grin, Darcy then presented Georgiana to the Longbourn ladies.

"I am delighted to meet you, Miss Darcy." Smiling, Elizabeth returned the girl's curtsey, then shot Darcy a puzzled look. "Your brother said you were to spend Christmas with your cousin."

"Oh, but I *shall* spend it with him," said Georgiana, "here at Netherfield. Please allow me to introduce to you my dear cousin and co-guardian, Colonel Fitzwilliam."

Darcy stepped in, made all the necessary introductions, and nearly groaned as he glanced at his cousin. It was clear Fitzwilliam would remember none of the ladies' names—nor his own—after being presented to Miss Jane Bennet. *Yes, yes, gaze upon her fine form, but whatever you do, do not look into her eyes!* He listened while the colonel, with customary ease, engaged the Bennets in conversation.

"What a pleasure to make your acquaintance, ladies. Miss Elizabeth, having heard so much praise from my besotted cousin, long have I wished to know you." When Fitzwilliam's eyes again strayed to her elder sister, Darcy vowed to himself to remind his cousin of his family's opinion about his own future bride.

A few days earlier, when Darcy had visited Park Lane with his happy news, his relations—Lord and Lady Matlock, the Viscount Winster, and Lady Catherine, there with her daughter Anne for Christmas—had voiced severe disapprobation of his betrothal to an unknown country girl with neither wealth nor connexions. Demands had been made for him to end the engagement. He had left in a fury but uncaring of such foolish opinions; he knew they would come round once they met Elizabeth.

Still, the earl would never accept Miss Jane Bennet as a worthy bride for his second son. 'Tis no matter. Fitzwilliam knows he must marry an heiress.

While others sipped from glasses of sherry or ratafia and chatted merrily, Elizabeth and her mother absented themselves to meet with Darcy's London housekeeper. A childless widow with no family with whom to share Christmas, Mrs Stanhope had brought a few maids and footmen who, likewise, had no family in town. Mrs Hill had arrived an hour prior, and, together with Mrs Nicholls, the women were to discuss the division of the festive goods between Netherfield and Longbourn and plan the proceedings.

Wishing for some private intercourse with his intended upon their return, Darcy was approached not by Elizabeth but by her mother. *We had much more time alone together before being betrothed.*

"Mr Darcy, I hope you, the colonel, and Miss Darcy will dine with us at Longbourn tomorrow." Mrs Bennet smiled happily. "The Gardiners should arrive anon, and Lizzy is eager for you to meet them. Please, come."

After consulting with Georgiana and Fitzwilliam, Darcy accepted with gratitude. More and more, he began to appreciate Elizabeth's mother. It was strange what being in love did to a person and what being offered a home in case of widowhood had done for Mrs Bennet and her infamous nerves.

The air on Christmas Eve was damp and cool as Darcy, Georgiana, and Colonel Fitzwilliam stepped down from their carriage. When Simon opened Longbourn's front door to greet them, music and laughter escaped from inside the house.

"My goodness," said Georgiana. "How very lively it sounds."

"That, Miss Darcy, is the happy noise of the Bennets, Brownes, Gardiners, Philipses, and a few neighbours." As she met them at the entrance, Mrs Bennet's agreeable words brought smiles to the newcomers' faces.

Darcy had been in Longbourn's drawing room before, but it had been rearranged and smelt deliciously of greenery, spices, and beeswax candles. Lintels, picture frames, and the mantel were bedecked with sprigs of holly, ivy, and boughs of fir and pine. Behind him, in the hall, an elaborate kissing bough was suspended from the ceiling. A Yule log burnt in the roaring fire, competing with and adding to the happy noise, of which there was an abundance. The room was crowded with the Bennets and their relations and a family whose surname Darcy could not recall, another couple he had never seen before, as well as the Lucases and quite a quantity of children.

Elizabeth linked her arm with his. "Finally, I may claim a moment with you. I hope you do not mind, but these people are my friends, neighbours, and loved ones. After our marriage, I may see them infrequently." Lowering her voice, she added, "It is true what they say about absent lovers, for I do believe I fall more deeply in love with you whenever we are apart."

Darcy looked behind him at the kissing bough, then upon her with fervour. "I am barely resisting the urge to pick you up, set you down beneath that mistletoe, and kiss—"

"Ahem!"

Standing at his other shoulder, a fine gentleman of fashion sent Darcy such a glare that a pistol pointed between his eyes might have felt less threatening. "Um, Miss Elizabeth, please do me the honour of introducing your…friend."

The introduction was made, and he started when she named the gentleman as her uncle Gardiner. Upon being presented to the man's elegant wife, Darcy entered into an engaging conversation with the couple about Lambton and its environs. Elizabeth listened attentively, glorying, it seemed, in her relations' every expression and every sentence. By all appearances, they were intelligent people of good taste and excellent manners. Who would think poorly of them?

Mrs Gardiner pointed out two girls sitting at a table chattering with Elizabeth's youngest sisters. "They are our daughters, Jenny and Anna."

Darcy smiled as the four fashioned pretty ribbons into flowers. Two riotous younger boys, in high revel, grabbed something from the table and, giggling, tottered about the room waving ribbons behind them. Elizabeth hastened after her cousins and gently scolded them to take care round lit candles, then she gave the moppets loving hugs and little sweetmeats.

How I love my future children's mother! His thoughts became too intense as she returned to his side; all he could do was beam at her, then kiss her fingers, all the while wanting so much more and far less company.

Twenty minutes later, standing beside Mr Bennet, he surveyed the room for Georgiana's and Elizabeth's whereabouts, wanting to ensure their safety and comfort. He longed to be by his intended's side and to share in her conversation but was content because she looked happy. *In fact, she is laughing at something that fair-haired man is whispering...in...her...ear! Who the devil is that?*

Mr Bennet patted Darcy's shoulder. "There, there. He poses no threat, and I shall not have you crushing the poor fellow. Your jealousy is unfounded." Darcy insisted he was not the jealous sort. "Good. According to the *Song of Solomon*, jealousy can be as cruel as the grave."

"I am curious, though. Who is the gentleman? He seems awfully close to my intended, in both affection and proximity."

"William Goulding and Lizzy have been friends since both were in leading strings. He taught her to climb, fish, run like the dickens, throw...and, I suspect, to throw a punch." Mr Bennet grinned. "And here is some additional, unsolicited advice. Should your jealousy and excessive protectiveness be set loose, you will smother our dear girl. Without control or oppression, teach her all she needs and wants to know. That daughter of mine is no angel, but she was born with wings, with potential." Her father's face shone with pride. "Teach her, allow her, to use those wings and soar. Leave those glorious wings unclipped, and let her fly on her own a bit. She may plummet, but my Lizzy will rise again."

"I have heard Miss Elizabeth say her courage always rises at every attempt to intimidate her."

Chuckling, Mr Bennet patted Darcy's back. "Have you? Well, good, good. She is an impressive girl, my Lizzy. So for pity's sake, do not forbid those few friendships she has cultivated over the years, William Goulding included. There are not many people she loves and even fewer she respects."

"I, for one, am honoured to have Miss Elizabeth's love and respect, sir."

"As you should be." While his future father sized him up, Darcy fought an urge to fidget. "Like you, Lizzy has a bit of pride about her. She is a clever woman, and she knows it."

"Miss Elizabeth's intelligence and indomitable spirit are part of her vast appeal."

"If I discover you, in any way, have stifled her spirit, you shall know my wrath." Mr Bennet sauntered away and whispered something in Elizabeth's ear.

Left alone then, Darcy noticed her glancing in his direction and heard her say, "Pray, excuse me." Only then did she hasten his way and ask whether he was well.

Taking her hand in his, he caressed her fingers. "I must confess something dreadful."

"Nothing can be so dire that we cannot overcome it together, Mr Darcy. Tell me this dreadful confession."

"I was—or perhaps I *am*—jealous of your closeness with that Goulding person."

She laughed in his face, and Darcy could not disguise the hurt thereon. Lifting his hand to her lips, Elizabeth kissed his knuckles, then gave his fingers a gentle squeeze. "Never, ever, doubt my affection, sir. It is steadfast. Eternal. I may converse and laugh with other men, but you are the only one in the world whom I could ever be prevailed upon to marry." Still holding his fingers in a crushing grip, she, with passionate fierceness, whispered, "I love you, Fitzwilliam Darcy. You! And until the day I hold our son in my arms, there never will be another male I cherish so dearly."

Raising their joined hands to his heart, he was appalled to find his eyes welling. Either the fireplace was smoking terribly, or someone had become a sentimental noddy.

With a happy glance round the room, he spotted Georgiana smiling widely at something Mr Bennet was saying to her. Fitzwilliam was laughing heartily with Browne and Mr Gardiner. There came, then, a great revelation. *This really is the most agreeable family and the most pleasant, most comfortable house I have ever been in.* Although it was one of the year's darkest days, Longbourn abounded with light, warmth, and lightness of heart. *This is much more than a house. It is a home.*

Chapter 33

The weather on Christmas Day morn was favourably mild but damp. It was the type of weather Elizabeth often enjoyed on her morning rambles, but that day's walk was directed to church with her family.

The usual sort of sermon was delivered, a few hymns sung, and—although the Netherfield party sat farther back—Elizabeth keenly felt Mr Darcy's presence tickling her nape. His voice, raised in song, made her shiver pleasantly.

With hearts full of joy, everyone filed out of St Mary's to exchange words of peace and goodwill with the vicar and their neighbours. Mr Darcy smiled and bowed over Elizabeth's hand, but, to her frustration, he excused himself to speak to the Gardiners and enquire whether their children might be prevailed upon to sing some festive songs at Netherfield. *To think that a mere month ago, I might have laughed had someone suggested Mr Darcy would be eager to speak to my relations. How can I possibly begrudge his doing so now?* However, Elizabeth could only scold herself a little; with so many people about the day before, there had been precious little opportunity for her to be alone with her betrothed. *Particularly thanks to my aunts! Aunt Browne and Aunt Gardiner were vexingly strict chaperons; Aunt Philips, somewhat less so.*

Arm in arm, Miss Darcy and the younger Mrs Browne

approached and were happily voluble in telling her they had never seen Mr Darcy in such robust health and high spirits. Elizabeth smiled at them while watching the gentleman chat with her father, the two of them looking her way.

Having bid a 'Merry Christmas' to all and sundry, the Bennets and Brownes piled into their carriages. With Mr Darcy's coach leading the way, they set off towards Netherfield while the Gardiners made for Longbourn to fetch their sons, both considered too young to sit through services.

Upon their arrival, Mr Darcy stood in Netherfield's vestibule—a kissing bough suspended from the ceiling and greenery draped over the grand staircase's hand-rail and above lintels—and greeted his guests. Mr and Mrs Philips were the last to arrive. In a kind gesture, Mr Darcy had dispatched a carriage to fetch them from their house in Meryton. Elizabeth prayed she could count on her aunt and uncle to behave properly; unlike her other relations, the couple could incite both hilarity and mortification.

Once every guest was settled, Mr Darcy invited them to join him in the servants' hall, where the Gardiner children were to sing a few songs. The offer was taken up by the children's parents and Elizabeth, Jane, and Miss Darcy. The others were left behind to merrily partake of negus, ratafia, or arrack punch—a particular favourite of her aunt Philips, Elizabeth knew.

Once the children had sung and gone off with their nursemaid to Netherfield's nursery to enjoy new games, books, and small toys, the adults joined the rest of the party in the drawing room for parlour games. Although Mr Darcy was too dignified for snapdragon, hot cockles, and bob apple, Elizabeth was pleased when he agreed to participate in charades and rhymes.

She was further impressed when they filed into the dining

room, and Mr Darcy asked them to remain standing. Mrs Nicholls gestured for the cook and all the hard-working maids to enter and stand about the room with the butler and footmen. Glasses of wine in hand, each person listened and cheered as Netherfield's new master proposed a toast to Christmastide. At such consideration for his servants, as well as the earlier kindnesses shown to her aunts, uncles, and cousins, Elizabeth could not have been prouder or more in love with him. *I am so blessed to be the one he chose to stand by his side.*

A well-pleased Mrs Bennet presided over the festive table with its abundance of rich dishes, mincemeat pies, wine, comfits, sugarplums, and, finally, a brandy-soaked plum pudding, set alight when brought in. While others exclaimed about the flaming dish, Elizabeth reached beneath the table-cloth and grasped Mr Darcy's fingers. Unabashedly and in plain sight, he lifted their joined hands and kissed her knuckles.

Her mother eventually stood, indicating it was time for the ladies to withdraw and leave the gentlemen to their port and whatnots. The women all got on well, and Miss Darcy—as reserved in company as her brother—seemed to enjoy the cordiality of her five future sisters. However, her eyes did grow wide several times at Lydia's audaciousness and Mary's pedantic conversation. In a private, heartwarming moment with Elizabeth, she reiterated her delight at the news of the engagement and how she looked forward to better knowing her in the coming days. Already envisioning the joys of her future life with Mr Darcy, Elizabeth assured her future sister how pleased she would be having her reside with them at Pemberley.

Once the sexes were together again, the evening continued happily, with laughter, lightness of heart, and some off-key singing—led by a merrily inebriated Aunt Philips—filling the hours. When stifled yawning began and gaieties drew to a close, Mr Darcy requested a private moment with Elizabeth's father and asked her to accompany them to the library. Once there, he lit lamps and removed a linen-wrapped object from his breast pocket.

"Mr Bennet, four years ago, I attended a house party celebrating the come-out of Miss Constance Amesbury. There were miniatures of her available, and one ended up in my possession, though I had not intended to keep it. Now I would like you to have it."

Elizabeth watched with some trepidation as her father folded back the cloth and took up Constance's tiny portrait. Gazing upon the miniature, he traced a finger round the oval frame. "She looks just like her mother did at that age. I thank you, son." Mr Bennet shook Mr Darcy's hand, nodded at him, then turned on his heel and strode out of the door, shutting it behind him.

Is he leaving us alone? He is leaving us alone! A flood of emotion—surprise, gratitude, anticipation—overtook Elizabeth as she looked up at the man beside her. "That was very thoughtful of you. I believe you and Papa may become great friends, for you share a common history of being unlucky in first love." She danced fingers up his waistcoat. "Speaking of which, have I told you tonight how much I love you, my first and only love?"

Mr Darcy's gaze softened. "This morning, after church, I asked your father to permit us some private time together, and he agreed. But, darling, we—"

Elizabeth slid fingers through his hair; her lips neared his.

Wrapping her in his arms, Mr Darcy whispered words of love before covering her face with passionate kisses. With a hand at the small of her back, he pulled her closer, tighter, and moved against her. She found herself pinned between him and an empty bookcase without knowing how she got there. Long, strong fingers slowly slid along her jaw, caressing the sensitive skin beyond her ear while his mouth and hers did wondrous things. When his body pressed harder, more insistently against hers, Elizabeth whimpered not in pain but in desire.

He backed away, wide-eyed, breathing heavily. "Forgive me! I wanted this time together not to force myself on you but to bestow upon you a gift. On Friday morning, I shall place upon your finger a golden band, an heirloom that has been in the Darcy family for generations." He removed a tiny velvet pouch from his pocket and tipped it into her palm. "This keeper ring will go above your wedding band, guarding it, just as I promise always to protect you. Soon, you will possess all that has, for centuries, belonged to the presiding mistress of Pemberley—her jewellery, her personal apartments, her chatelaine, her gardens…and the master of Pemberley's heart. But you have owned *that* for months now."

She stared at the thin gold ring encrusted with gemstone chips. "Are those emeralds?" Mr Darcy nodded. "And the brown ones? Oh! Depending on the angle, they also glow green or amber." He explained they were Ceylonese brown tourmalines that reminded him of her eyes. Astonished, she looked up at him. "When did you…?"

He had gone to town, he said, in the rain, days before the Netherfield ball to have the settlement papers drawn up and to purchase the gift. Wincing, Elizabeth felt the pain he must have known when she refused him that night.

"Dearest man! I am honoured and shall wear this beautiful ring with pride. And I shall strive to be the best mistress Pemberley has known and the best keeper of its master's heart." She kissed his cheek, returned the ring to its pouch, and handed it back to him. "For now, please keep it for me. When we leave the church as husband and wife, you then may place it where it belongs, and never shall I remove it."

He kissed her brow, lingering and pulling her into a tender embrace before escorting her to the vestibule. There, they glanced at the closed drawing room doors, then upwards to the festive bundle of mistletoe. Grinning, Elizabeth quickly situated herself beneath it.

He followed and kissed her hand while gazing into her eyes. "Merry Christmas, my love. Thank you for bringing light, warmth, and joy to my life. Thank you for being the spark that sets my soul afire. Speaking of which," he glanced around the hall, ensuring no servants lurked about, "just *one* quick kiss now, or I shall run mad." After a brief, chaste kiss, he took a step back and sighed. "Most of all, thank you for loving me."

Chapter 34

Two days later, an heirloom band and a keeper ring newly snug on his wife's finger, Darcy sighed happily and gazed through the window at Longbourn's winter gardens. Filled with anticipation, he contemplated what he and Elizabeth might achieve together throughout the coming years.

All his thoughts and hopes were with his beloved bride who, at that moment, was in her bedchamber—her *former* bedchamber—preparing for travel to Grosvenor Square. As he awaited her in Mr Bennet's book-room, the fragrance from the sprig on his lapel reminded him of the day Elizabeth had agreed to marry him. *I thought that had been the happiest day of my life. I was wrong. This morning's moving ceremony far surpassed any memorable occasion during my twenty-seven years.*

Our union has been blessed, he thought, smiling as he recalled the number of kisses he and Elizabeth had shared between the church and Longbourn. When they had stepped down, Browne's teasing about swollen lips and mussed hair was testimony to all that the pairing was a joyous one. *I try to avoid weaknesses that might expose me to ridicule, but Elizabeth is both my weakness and my strength.*

Oh, hurrah! I hear her sweet voice on the stair.

In the carriage, Elizabeth traced a forefinger over the intricate, floral design on the rosewood and mahogany surface of her new writing slope. "The artistry is extraordinary."

"Open the cover."

The box opened to a leather writing surface, its facing inlaid with mother of pearl. Beneath it, the interior had lidded compartments with ink-pot, pens, sealing wax, tiny candles, elegant hot-pressed paper, and a personal seal with Elizabeth's new initials. "How lovely!"

"There is more." Darcy leant across and pointed at a lever. "Press there."

"Oh!" *Lavender's Blue* plucked away inside a hidden recess.

"It is a *carillons à musique*. Do you like it?"

"Very much so." She thanked him for the music box, but it was the Darcy crest on the topmost sheet of paper that, knowing its significance, had deeply moved her. "Pray tell, wherever did you find such a treasure?"

"I found her in an unremarkable assembly room in a market town called Meryton, but my first glimpse was while she—hems hitched above well-turned ankles—scampered about a lea, surrounded by an adoring little band of moppets." Darcy pressed his lips to Elizabeth's gloved hand. "And she is, without question, a treasure."

"You are a dear man to say so." She gave him an arch look. "But, as you are aware, I meant the *carillons à musique*."

"I have connexions who were instrumental—no pun intended—in its acquisition. I purchased it and your keeper ring on the same day. The mechanism, crafted by a master watchmaker in Switzerland, was incorporated into the bespoke writing slope."

How this man could overwhelm her! "You went to so much bother and expense. Thank you. It is both beautiful and practical. You give me so much, and I give you nothing."

"Nothing?" Darcy shook his head in disbelief. "Elizabeth, you give me everything I want and need and did not know I wanted or needed. You give me joy and love. Do you know the last time I felt such happiness? No? Well, nor do I."

Having secured the writing slope in a receptacle beneath her seat, Elizabeth rummaged in her reticule. "I do have something for you."

"For me?" He sat back. "You bought me a gift?"

She hesitated, unsure whether she should tease him. "No. I have had something of yours for some time, and it should be returned to its rightful owner."

His brow furrowed. "Elizabeth, this morning I vowed to bestow upon you all my worldly goods. Whatever the item is, you may keep it."

While he sat motionless, appearing wary, she pulled a packet from her reticule. "I have no use for this. Never had, really." Leaning forwards, she held out a stack of papers. "Nor do you...any longer."

"What the—? My list!" Accepting the creased bundle, Darcy looked guiltily at his bride. "How long, may I ask, has this been in your possession?"

"I found it behind a cushion in Netherfield's library the morning we were alone there for half an hour. You remember that day, do you not?" Casting her gaze downward, Elizabeth shook her head. "Perhaps not. You adhered most conscientiously to your book, not even bothering to look at me."

"I can scarcely look at you now, knowing you have seen some of the ghastly entries on this list." Darcy handed the pages back to her and begged her to burn them. "You may be assured I *was* looking that day and loving everything about you, although I was resolved to remain steady to my purpose."

"Which was?"

"To believe in and follow, most dutifully, that worthless compilation of exacting specifications. It was a futile endeavour in the end." He clasped Elizabeth's hand and slowly peeled away her glove. "May I continue, or does this make you uncomfortable?"

"I am not uneasy."

Darcy blew out a breath. "Good. One criterion I insist upon is honesty, which, I believe, was an entry—one of the list's more useful recommendations—from my late uncle, Judge Darcy. There always must be openness between us, my dear. So, you will tell me if ever my attentions discomfit you. Agreed?"

She nodded as he slipped off her other glove and made love to her fingers one by one. Clearly pleased by her dazed expression, he moved across to sit beside her. Leaning in, he set his mouth upon hers. Enveloped in an ardent embrace and kissed in a delightful manner, Elizabeth gave a low moan of pleasure, a direct contrast to the unsettling sounds uttered by her husband of mere hours—sounds more of annoyance than enjoyment. She pulled away, realising that her bonnet's stiff brim was poking into his forehead. He fumbled with the ribbons beneath her chin and growled, "Off!"

"Wait, please. Should you continue, you will throttle me." She untied the knot and flung away the hat. "We should stop until we are at home, in the privacy of our own apartments." Colour high, Elizabeth lowered her lashes.

Darcy sat back. "Forgive me. You are wise and correct, of

course. Further shows of affection must be postponed until we are settled in town. Quite right."

"You have misunderstood my reluctance." She gathered the stack of papers. "I am abiding by one of your exacting standards."

"At present, my mind is incapable of clear thinking, and I do not at all catch your meaning. What exacting standard?"

She glanced through the papers. "Here." She handed over a page, pointing to the pertinent section. "Read."

"'Mrs Darcy will act with restraint and be habitually elegant, fashionable, and decorous in both dress and deportment.'"

"Those, sir, are your own words regarding an acceptable wife. Behaviour such as I have just encouraged is certainly not restrained."

"I doubt you are so fastidious about showing affection to a wedded husband who ardently loves you." He kissed her cheek.

"Not at all!" She fidgeted with her rings, then spoke with quiet determination. "Should you refer to almost any item on that list, I shall be found wanting. Yet there is one requirement I have already fulfilled and promise to continue doing so for all the days of my life."

"I hope you mean my final entry. The only one that matters." Darcy plucked the bottommost sheet from the stack. Clasping Elizabeth's hand, he held it over his heart. "I have no need to see the words upon the page." With reverence, he whispered the prerequisite. "She will love me."

"She does. You know she does."

That night, shown to great advantage in a burgundy silk banyan over a pristine nightshirt, her husband's tall form exuded power, confidence, and masculinity. *You, Fitzwilliam Darcy, are more handsome than any man has a right to be.* An urge to caress his neck's tantalising, exposed skin was overtaken by a stronger, immodest desire to taste it. She supposed that initiating such intimacy would be terribly unladylike, so Elizabeth stood rooted to the spot, trembling in greedy anticipation.

"You are shivering." Darcy grasped her hand in his. In doing so, a button on his cuff caught on her delicate lace trim. His lips quirked as he struggled to extricate it. "It seems we have been joined together, madam."

"The attachment is strong, sir." Elizabeth smiled while deftly freeing the button.

"Come." He led her to the sofa. "Sit with me awhile by the fire. Warm yourself." Angled towards him, legs tucked beneath her, Elizabeth insisted she was not cold. He kissed her hand. "But you were shivering." Wispy fabric slid off one shoulder as she shrugged. Darcy seemed transfixed until she dragged the edge back into place. He raised his eyes to hers before she could mask her anxiety. "You are not afraid of me, are you?" Cupping her face, he kissed her brow, then leant back. "Darling, look at me."

Obeying his husky tone, Elizabeth surrendered herself to sensation as his thumb stroked the corner of her mouth. Closing her eyes, she let his deep voice and familiar scent soothe her.

"I promise to be as gentle as possible. But, if ever I am too forceful, too overpowering, all you need do is tell me to stop."

Encouraged by his concern, Elizabeth whispered, "That will not be necessary." With her left hand clutching his banyan's lapel, she touched her right palm to his neck, stroking the pad of her thumb across his throat. His Adam's apple bobbed as he swallowed. "After being a bad judge of character, I am determined to be a very, very good wife."

Just after midnight, Darcy drew back the curtain on his side of the bed. He knew Elizabeth was there beside him, and he knew he had not been dreaming because he had not yet fallen asleep. His senses were alive to her every breath, her slightest movement, her sweet fragrance. Needing to see her, to confirm her presence, he turned his head. Bathed in a bright shaft of moonlight, his bride slept facing him. *My precious wife is exhausted from today's doings*—he smiled to himself—*and tonight's.*

With Elizabeth lying so near, it occurred to him that he might never again care for slumber. Staying awake, cherishing every moment of her closeness, was a far more agreeable occupation. Never, in his entire life, had he slept in the same bed as another person. While ecstatic to have her there, and knowing he soon would become accustomed to sharing his mattress, her proximity was unsettling. *This lovely creature is now mine to have and hold, but it is my responsibility to protect her —even from myself and my selfish desires.*

"I love you, Mrs Darcy." The sentiment had been whispered, but her eyelashes fluttered.

"Mmm. Fitzwilliam." Her murmured response aroused his hopes. Snuggling closer, she whispered, "I love you." She slipped again into sleep as he was about to wrap her in an embrace.

There was an almost painful ache in his chest as he rolled

to one side, propped himself on an elbow, and gazed upon her. *My heart may burst from her beauty, the joy of having her here, and knowing she loves me.*

He eventually drifted off and slept undisturbed until the sun made itself known through the open bed curtain. Then, face to face, the connoisseur in him examined his wife, noting a few precious flaws. One lock of unrestrained hair, straighter than the rest, had an auburn tinge. The sprinkling of freckles across her nose was more prominent in the morning light. Counting them, he tut-tutted at the uneven number—*eleven tiny, golden kisses from the sun.* Then there was that horrendous lack of symmetry. *How dare one eyebrow be a fraction of an inch higher than the other?* His forefinger traced the arch without touching it. *Adorable how it climbs higher when she is sceptical, challenges me, or is about to argue a point.* He espied a faint scar above it. *How did that happen, my darling little dare-devil?* He startled as her dark eyes gazed into his.

"My father was correct, after all." She brushed back a wavy forelock dangling over his brow.

"Your first thought this morning—our first morning together as husband and wife—is of your *father?*" Sliding an arm round her waist, he drew Elizabeth closer, cherishing the feel of her warm body against his. "Although curiosity runs a distant third to desire and jealousy, I am compelled to ask. About what was your father correct?"

Her smile was sleepy, her words warm and teasing. "You never look at any woman but to see a blemish. As a child, when I suffered that cut above my eyebrow—and, believe me, there were many such injuries, for your wife was quite the tomboy back in the day—someone kissed it and made it better."

"I shall endeavour to keep you safe from harm, my

beloved Mrs Darcy." He kissed the scar. "But if you suffer as much as a paper cut, I promise to kiss away the pain."

And thus began the first full day of their—sometimes blissful, sometimes tumultuous, sometimes grief-stricken—married life.

Epilogue

Journal Entry: December 27, 1812

It has been a twelve-month to the day. Yet there are times I enter a room only to be arrested by the sight of her there, precisely as imagined in my reveries of over a year past. Her warmth colours my days. My wife, my life, is both friend and lover, a compassionate, passionate woman. The feel of her hand in mine or her hands in my hair never grows old, and I treasure each time her body clings to mine. She makes me smile and laugh. I delight in our debates, her wit, her teasing, her playful manner, her intelligence, her curiosity, and her thirst for knowledge. Held dear are our talks long into the night, snuggled together, limbs entwined. Elizabeth comprehends what Pemberley means to me, listens to my problems, and offers opinions, arguments, and suggestions. She loves, understands, respects, and appreciates me for who, not what, I am. She brings commitment to our marriage and to the prosperity of the estate. She touches everyone with her kindness, and everyone benefits from it. Her honesty, openness, dedication, and fierce loyalty have restored my trust in humanity. Elizabeth Darcy stands by my side, and I am happy and complete with her here.

Journal Entry: September 17, 1813

Today, Elizabeth accomplished the most extraordinary thing. Well, two things, truly. Although I thought my affection already too immense to be calculated, my remarkable wife has made me fall more deeply in love with her by bringing boundless joy into this home and a bundle of joy into my gladdened heart. The birth of a Darcy heir will cause much rejoicing across the estate. Even now, as I write, church bells ring out at Lambton and Kympton to celebrate the news. A feast, to be hosted here at Pemberley for the tenantry, is being planned and—

D arcy threw down his pen. He absolutely needed to see his son again that very moment to marvel at the miracle that was Benedict Fitzwilliam Darcy.

By leaps and bounds, Darcy's joy grew with every addition to his family—but that was only after countless hours of prayer and frantic worry as his wife laboured to deliver each son or daughter.

Following the birth of their fifth child, Elizabeth shared with him a congratulatory letter from her half-sister in which Mrs Maguire recommended the simple regimen of separate bedchambers.

They both laughed uproariously.

The End

ACKNOWLEDGMENTS

For being so welcoming, helpful, friendly, and professional, Jan Ashton and Amy D'Orazio of Quills & Quartos Publishing have my heartfelt gratitude—though that sounds trite and totally inadequate. Amy deserves a medal for her patience and insistence during the developmental stage of *Enduring Connexions*, and Jan gets my undying thanks for not only making the story better but for making the entire copy/line editing process such great fun.

I'm thrilled that Q&Q provided the services of multi-talented Susan Adriani of CloudCat Design for the novel's beautiful and perfectly themed cover. And I was fortunate to have another popular and prolific author in the Q&Q family, Lucy Marin, read the first draft of my manuscript and provide invaluable feedback. The four ladies mentioned above deserve praise and my thanks for their time, wisdom, and generosity. Next, there's Christina Boyd—another wonderful editor I've worked with in the past and, now, a gifted author—whose support, advice, and encouragement I've very much appreciated over the years.

Ultimately, for putting up with me and my sense of humour, I thank my husband—although he's never read a blooming thing I've written other than weekly grocery lists. When I'm preoccupied with a story, he provides sustenance, both the support and nourishment kind, keeping me from despairing and/or starving to death. Ergo, he is as much responsible for this novel as I am. So, if you didn't like it, please feel free to throw the book at him.

ABOUT THE AUTHOR

J Marie Croft (Joanne) is a lifelong resident of Nova Scotia, Canada, but spends a lot of time in Regency England with Jane Austen's beloved characters. She has written ten Austenesque stories and is working on more. Joanne shares with her husband a love of their adult twin daughters, the great outdoors, geocaching, and a spoiled calico cat.

You can learn more about J Marie Croft on her website: https://jmariecroft.wixsite.com/j-marie-croft

f facebook.com/jmarie.croft

BB bookbub.com/authors/j-marie-croft

a amazon.com/stores/J.-Marie-Croft/author/B004HZD22W

ALSO BY J MARIE CROFT

NOVELS BY J MARIE CROFT

A Little Whimsical in His Civilities

Love at First Slight

Mr Darcy Takes the Plunge

Play with Fire

MULTI-AUTHOR ANTHOLOGIES

Dangerous to Know: Jane Austen's Rakes & Gentlemen Rogues (The Quill Collective)

The Darcy Monologues: A romance anthology of "Pride and Prejudice" short stories in Mr. Darcy's own words (The Quill Collective)

Elizabeth: Obstinate Headstrong Girl (The Quill Collective)

Rational Creatures: Stirrings of Feminism in the Hearts of Jane Austen's Fine Ladies (The Quill Collective)

Sun-Kissed: Effusions of Summer

Yuletide: A Jane Austen Inspired Collection of Stories (The Quill Collective)

Made in United States
North Haven, CT
16 July 2023

39136932R00200